HIPPIE HOLLOW

Murder on a Nude Beach

By Denniger Bolton

a B. B. Rivers Mystery

Javelina Books

Copyright © 2007 by Javelina Books.

Javelina Books
P.O. Box 93152
Austin, Texas 78709
SAN 850-8046
Visit our web site at www.javelinabooks.com

First Edition: September 2006
Second Edition: April 2008

Bolton, Denniger
Hippie Hollow, murder on a nude beach/Denniger Bolton – 1st Ed.

ISBN 0-9785221-0-9
Library of Congress Control Number: 2006903601

Printed in the United States of America on acid-free recycled paper

Epistle to the Non-Austinites

Hippie Hollow is an actual place. It really is a nudist reserve where real people of many different genders, political persuasions and ages go, with nothing on but their birthday suits.

There, they bake like potatoes on a hot Texas rock, until they can stand it no longer and jump in the lake. The politically correct term for this phenomenon is "bathing suit optional," but in Austin it's called dipping one's skinny.

Denniger Bolton

For orders other than by individual consumers, Javelina Books grants a discount on the purchase of 10 or more copies single titles for special markets or premium use. For further details, please write or e-mail Javelina Books, attn: premiums, P.O. Box 93152, Austin, Texas 78709 premiums@javelinabooks.com

For orders by individual consumers, write or e-mail Javelina Books, attn: sales, P.O. Box 93152, Austin, Texas 78709 sales@javelinabooks.com

Hippie Hollow is dedicated to Sid and Sara.

Can't thank enough of my readers: Kathleen Casey, Elizabeth Hanson, Richard Stark, Julie Farias, Judy Haralson, Jonathan Taylor, Gitana and Amelia Sweethardt, Ben Guyton, Barry, Claire, Hope, Ron and Cherie Bolton, Pat and Melissa Fogarty, Annette Towns, Elisa Keeley, Gretchen Stolfo, Jefferson Woodruff, Jimmy Joe Natoli, Michael Paparella, Ryan Kimbro, Gail Lord, Steve Cox, literary agent Jane Chelius, Brian and Annette Towns and Claire Bolton for the cover idea, Sam Wall for cover illustration, Peri Poloni for cover design, Jamye Peel for type design and my first readers, Cari Trevino, Shelley Seeley and Alison Sweetser.

Many thanks to my dad, Sid Bolton, whose career in law enforcement helped round out the cop characters and make them human.

Many thanks to my companion, Sara Bolton, who allowed me space and time to lay this Hippie Hollow mystery novel out for all to see and who helped round me out and make me human.

p.39 vs 194
p271 whitman

Prologue

"When you come to a fork in the road, take it."

Yogi Berra

"Hey, Travis, you're in no condition to drive, my man," said Moses Harper. "Why don't you get in back and leave the drivin' to your ol' pal Mo. You've exceeded your limit on the pink stuff and since I'm not drinking..."

"Fine!" Travis climbed through the sliding glass partition to the back of the limo. "But you gotta wear the hat."

"I'll wear the damn thing but you keep the cloak. The pink would clash with my burnt orange shirt." Moses reached through and took the chauffeur's cap. It was a couple of sizes too small and perched on the top of his curly black hair. He looked at himself in the rearview mirror, shook his head, and smiled.

"Are you all going to be alright?" Asked Lucinda sticking her head through the open passenger window.

"We are going to be just *fine,* Auntie Loooooo." Travis took pains to enunciate his words but got stuck on the Loooooo. "Now that Reverend A's not coming, we're going to stop off at Hippie Hollow after all. Goin' to dip our skinnies, Auntie Loooooo."

"Take care of your sister, Travis. Remember she's only fifteen."

"We'll be alright, Auntie Loo," said Merrylee, "Mo is our designated hitter, I mean driver. Whoops, guess I've had a few too many pink lemonades myself."

"Bye, Auntie Loooooo." Travis hung out the back window and waved.

The old Mercedes pulled out of the driveway and down the hill.

Poodie Slack had been trying to free his Geo from the parking lot. He was the first guest in line for the party and had pulled in, parked too close to a boulder and some asshole had pulled in tight behind him leaving but an inch of maneuverability. Poodie was disappointed he had failed for the tenth straight year to win the coveted Prince of Pink award even though he decked himself out in a very stylish hot pink suit with white suede shoes. He had worked up a sweat and was taking off a suit coat when the limo went by.

The gate opened as Reverend Arvin Tanner's limo approached. The guard looked up from his *Penthouse* Magazine as they passed the guard shack.

"Take a left, driver," said Travis.

"What's up there?" Asked Moses. "Hippie Hollow is down the hill."

"Windy Point is up there a couple of miles," said Merrylee. "but it's closed this time of night. We need to go right."

"No!" Said Travis, sinking into the soft leather seat. He had his hands over his face. Moses pulled the selector down to activate the blinker for a right turn onto Comanche Trail.

"Why don't you scoot over closer to me?" Moses offered his hand to Kristie who was leaning against the window, pouting. Her evening had not gone well.

"I believe I will," she addressed the backseat and the slumping Travis Tanner and scooted across.

"Methinks young Master Tanner imbibeth too much. Does anyone want a hit off this?" Merrylee held up a joint. Travis looked at it, groaned, turned green and buried his head deeper into the seat. Kristie looked back through the window.

"Yeah, pass that sucker through." Merrylee took a long drag and squat walked to the front as Moses took a hard right followed by a hard left navigating the curvy Comanche Trail.

"Whoa there, big fella." Merrylee lurched from one side of the limo to the other.

Kristie took a huge hit. Holding. Holding. Coughing it out. Offering it to Moses.

"No thanks. When I'm training, I don't drink, I don't smoke. And until I sign with the NFL I'm *always* in training."

"You're no fun." Kristie hit Moses on his huge biceps and took another drag and coughed again.

"Wait a minute!" Moses grabbed the burning joint from her and snuffed it out between his thumb and index finger. Kristie gave him that *hey, dude, that's the last straw* look. He cranked down the window and flipped the joint out into the juniper trees beside the road.

"Hey Mo," said Merrylee, "what the fuck...?"

"Cops," said Moses. "Bet they're writing up some late night D.W.I. business off your Auntie's party. You guys forget to make your payoff this month?" He cranked the a/c up to full blast. "Merrylee, why don't you roll your window down and let some of this smoke out."

"Good thinking," said Merrylee.

"Fortunately, I have not been drinking. Let me handle it." The others were more than willing for Mo to do that. Kristi was scared. Merrylee was cranking the ancient car window and mourning the loss of the joint. Travis was dealing with an overabundance of food and spirits. Mo drove slowly.

A uniformed police officer stood in front of his cruiser with a flashlight and motioned them over into the Hippie Hollow parking lot. Moses turned the classic '54 Mercedes 300 Limo with excruciating slowness, scrunching on the gravel of the parking lot, pulling all the way through to the trail head, allowing the limo's inside airing-out time.

Moses opened his door, figuring he'd step out and close the door before the cop could say yea or nay. Give the others a chance to pull it together. He was not going to allow the cop to check out the limo.

The cruiser spun around making a tight circle, coming up even with the limo, driver side door adjacent. Moses was half out when the policeman shone the high-powered flashlight in his eyes.

"Please remain in the vehicle," said a commanding voice. Moses left the door open, easing back down, hands on the steering wheel. The light blinded him and he didn't see the weapon. "What the fuck," said the cop looking in the back seat, the weapon an inch from Moses' head. He fired.

Thunk!

Moses slumped over the steering wheel. The horn honked. The chauffeur's cap stayed on what was left of the young man's head. Kristie screamed and attempted to crawl under the slumped body of Moses.

Thunk! "This is all wrong," said Travis. "This is not supposed to be happening. I'm going to upchuck." Travis opened his door to rid his system of pink fluid, bits of salmon, salsa and tortilla chips. At that moment the policeman fired at Travis, the bullet catching him in the side, nicking his right lowest rib and exiting out his back.

To Merrylee, the scene played out in slo-mo. All traces of bogus lemonade were overrun by adrenaline. She saw it all. The cop flashing the light in Moses' eyes as he approached, gun beside his leg. She agreed with her bro. It was all wrong. God, girl, think! Think!

First *thunk!*—Moses. Second *thunk!*—Kristie. Third, fourth and fifth *thunk! thunk! thunk!* Travis flew out the door, blood splattering on her pretty cocktail dress. The horn honking all the while.

She smashed the overhead light with the heel of her shoe and pressed the button on her camera and opened her door. The flash lit up the inside of the limo.

Merrylee never heard *thunk* number six entering her temple.

Chapter One

"Cowboys—No shirt, no service.
Cowgirls—No shirt, free Lone Star"

Sign at the front door of Kickers bar

Last night, a fully loaded patron took it upon himself to dismantle the watering hole where I work. Kickers is uncommon for a bar, not because it opens onto Sixth Street, Austin's prime party scene, not because the restrooms are marked Dudes and Dudettes, but there's a rodeo arena out back where I barrel race, calf rope and wrestle steers for tips, which gain stature the more dirt I eat. Unlike sanctioned rodeo, it pays to be imperfect on the saloon cowboy circuit. My boss, Jimmy Don, who owns Kickers, fills in as our rodeo clown, and passes the Folgers can after my ride.

In addition to cowboying, Jimmy Don hired me to keep the eclectic clientele—yuppies, bikers, rednecks, tourists and collegians—from destroying the place. And if tact and patience fail (which happens a lot), I'm paid to bounce their rowdy asses out. I grabbed my latest ejectee by the back of the neck like a rattlesnake, and we headed for the exit. He kicked over a table, a couple of barstools and a washtub of Mexican beer swimming in ice; cerveza and finger-food were flying, but I held on. As we danced through the swinging front doors, he called me an "overweight mesomorph." I pegged him for a college student. Bikers lack the vocabulary.

"What the fuck's *that* supposed to mean?" Cowboys are not all that wordy either.

"Look it up, asshole!" I was tempted to pop his nose. But on those all too frequent occasions, words Jimmy Don hammers into us bouncer personnel, splinter free:

"We want 'em to come on back, but not with their lawyers."

The throng coursing Sixth Street two-stepped around as if we were an island in their stream of humanity, a blip on the radar, scarcely worth noticing and definitely not something to get involved in.

I shoved our ex-patron gently downstream away from the front of the bar. I'm a big guy and *gently* is relative at six four (in sock feet), 250 pounds and moderately agitated. I looked at him sprawled amongst the beer cans, half eaten turkey legs, pizza crusts, Copenhagen spit and nightly litter of The Street. My curiosity got the better of me.

"Okay, at least spell it." I pulled a Sharpie from my boot.

"O-v-e-r-w-e..."

"Fuck you," I turned for the swinging doors. The guy was not funny.

"Hey, Cowboy?" Folks call me Cowboy because of the Stetson, bright white western shirt, creased jeans breaking half inch above the pavement, pointy-toed reptilian-hide boots, hard-earned but admittedly ostentatious, or as we say around here, *Austin*-tatious, rodeo belt buckle *(Texas Steer Wrestling Champion)* affixed to a hand-tooled Mexican leather belt.

He lobbed me the bird. Pathetic.

"IQ or blood alcohol level?" Love to use that one.

"Overweight, well I don't need to look up that." As I nestled my frame into my overstuffed couch, I leafed through the dictionary. "Let's see, *mesomorph, an athletic body type.*" Sounds like me, alright. Twas a good thing I hadn't redecorated his nose. I grabbed a handful of Boulder Malt potato chips, a Dos Equis and did a finger workout with the remote control. That was last night.

In the light of this June, Austin, Texas, afternoon, standing in front of Captain Hollers' door, I found myself grappling with a handful of undeniable truths:

I didn't want to be here.

I didn't want to submit myself to another pointless job interview.

I didn't even want a job.

Unlike most folks, this cowboy knew exactly what he wanted and where he wanted to be.

A simple ambition really — to be semi-prone on my couch, drinking mass quantities of cold, dark cerveza, taking my chances with sports programming until the old movies kicked in. Exactly where I would be if not for this job interview.

During my formative years at the family ranch in Blanco, in the Texas Hill Country an hour west of Austin, we didn't have cable TV. No satellite dish in the yard. No HBO, no ESPN, no CNN. What we had was Channel 7. For me, the *perk* of being a townie was cable.

What possible reason then could there be for standing at the door instead of hunkering down with the International Pygmy Bowling Invitational?

Patricia Pearsall.

Patricia's the reason I bailed the ranch for Austin.

She and ESPN.

And she's the reason for the threads, the starched white shirt, the western-cut, khaki colored wool sport coat with leather elbow patches, the silver and turquoise string tie.

Captain R.A. Hollers
Vice President — Investigations

Deep breath. Knock. Wait.

I've been a big guy for awhile. As a kid, my mother dragged me to the "Husky" rack at Monkey Wards but this past year with the lifestyle change and all, I've noticed extra padding on the gut. Had to relocate that little metal thingy to the next notch on my belt.

But here's the point: While gaining non-musculature weight is uncool, so too is hauling my butt out of bed at five to jog around the block. Lots of things I'd rather be doing at that ungodly hour. Sleeping comes to mind.

Early this morning, after my long ass shift at Kickers, after escorting seventeen drunken dudes through the swinging doors and wrestling the same goddammed steer a dozen times to the point where he'd see me coming and roll on his own, after I ate a bucket of dirt mostly for looks, I slathered myself with Ben-Gay and slept in, missing my five A.M. jog again.

Damn.

I knocked on the Captain's door a second time and heard a booming voice.

"Quit the damn racket and open the damn door!"

"Captain Hollers?" I yanked off my Stetson. A mop of red hair jumped free.

Jabba the Hutt loomed behind a huge oak desk. Sleeves rolled to the elbows. Shirt soaking wet. Telephone cradled between shoulder and ear. He was the fattest man I'd ever seen. The guy in the *National Enquirer* story trapped in his bed. Too obese to hoof it to Subway. I smiled, feeling better about my piddling extra inch or so, wishing I could share this wonderful moment with someone. Not with Patricia. Richard A. Hollers, Vice President of Bergstrom Investigations, was her uncle.

Uncle Rick told Patricia about his latest investigation, that he'd be hiring an additional investigator. She told Uncle Rick about me, about my experience in law enforcement. It was my first and only referral interview in the year since I left APD

"Set!" Hollers aimed a fat finger at the straight backed wooden chair in front of his desk and returned his attention to the phone.

Like a real detective, I did a quadrant scan. Antique gun cabinet with glass front, shotgun, 30-06 with scope, pistols and knives, hat rack in the corner, Astros cap, Round Rock Express cap, two cowboy hats, summer straw, winter felt, size 80 sports coat. Photos on the wall. Governor of Texas, President of the United States, and a couple of unfamiliar men in suits on either side of a plate glass window overlooking I.H. 35, Austin's very own interstate highway. Filing cabinets. Stacks of Office Depot file boxes covered one wall. Water cooler. He has his own water cooler. Large oak desk with neat stacks of folders. The man was maybe fifty and pushing 400 pounds. What the hell, made me feel slim.

I wondered if the beautiful, slim, Patricia shared any DNA with the man. Maybe a fat gene showing up at some unsuspecting day to haunt.

I sat in the hard-backed chair, sweating. It was June and getting, as we say around here, warm, very, very warm. A mere preview of July and August, when it's hot, very, very hot. And yet, Captain Hollers' office was beyond warm, beyond hot. It was stifling. Sauna-esque. Amazonian. Amazonian in the steamy river sense rather than the tall women with large breasts and spears sense (although that can be hot, too). I watched a fat bead of perspiration well up on his balding head and flow like a Lone Star Beer commercial, down his nose. I could see the sweat and the irritation in his eyes. It was pitiful.

By this date, deep in the *Corazon de Tejas*, summer is here to stay for the rest of our goddamned lives. Like ancient pagans who felt the December sun was going, going, gone, Austinites facing two or three more months of this shit, feel it will never, ever, be cool again.

There are but two choices for those who would dare live here:

A. Vacation to Colorado for the season, or,

B. Stay home, float a loan to cover utilities, situate oneself in front of the cranked up a/c consuming mass quantities of iced tea or cerveza until about October.

As a Plan B-er, I knew the futility of flapping my jaws about how hot it was. Complaining will not make it any cooler. One must carry on, visualizing snowcapped mountains, dashing from air-conditioned home to air conditioned vehicle, taking air-conditioned trips to the local swimming hole, movie theater or mall.

Since Hollers was busy with his phone call, I took off my coat, hanging it over the back of the chair. Sweat tickled as it dripped down my sides. I looked out the window, watched the traffic. I didn't bring anything to read and there was nothing around. I popped my spine straightening my back to my full six foot four. I was erect, no thanks to the idiotic bullriding episode in high school. It was one of those occasions you know from the get-go to be a foolish choice. It was a dumb idea to mount the beast. His name was the Sterilizer for Christ's sake. The Buckle Bunnies cried as they looked at the bloody heap that was once my body. All were concerned I'd never have kids or ride horses again. The memory of getting stomped shakes me so much I avoid Jimmy Don's mechanical bull.

I've cut back on horse riding since I live in town now. My rodeoing these days is of the urban cowboy genus at Kickers. I turn a few barrels, throw myself onto a fleeing baby steer and wrestle him to the ground, rope a calf or two, lasso a couple of human fillies every night (they love it).

As for the issue of progeny, it's a sore subject around the townhouse and bull riding doesn't have a thing to do with it.

For the first year after my downward departure from the Austin Police Department, I'd squander the A.M. drinking lattes. By P.M. I had segued into cerveza. During the lucid time after caffeine but before alcohol, I'd do interviews with police departments, security companies and detective agencies.

One night six months ago, with no full-time employment prospects in sight, and rodeoing for tips, I was washing down the evening's dirt with *seis equis de cerveza* (third bottle of *Dos Equis*) when called upon to do something, in retrospect seemingly foolish. I grabbed an antique lasso off the wall, alleged to have belonged to Charlie Goodnight, and I roped and hogtied a couple of belligerent bikers who'd been hitting on Jenny, one of the waitresses. I don't mean they were winking at her and telling her how cute she was. They were actually slapping her around. She was awful with change, but was it enough reason for fisticuffs? I stepped in and did the Tom Mix thing. Jimmy Don watched the scene and when I came through in one piece, offered me a job as a bouncer.

"You're a natural."

I figured what the hell, I'm in here most every night drinking beer, might as well make some walking around money, and it was good being a natural at something.

The work was easy enough since those needing an escort to the street more often than not, underestimated my cute little (okay, cute big) Opie Taylor looks. Bright red hair. Matching freckles. Precious country accent. The typical ejectee seemed not to notice the nose broken half a dozen times, until presented directly in his face. He might get in a lucky punch or kick but he *would* be on his way somewhere else, off-the-wall comments about mesomorphedness notwithstanding.

As I waited for Captain Hollers, random thoughts dripped like Chinese water torture upon my head. I thought about how, like it or not, I was attracted to pain. Or maybe pain was attracted to me.

There was job pain from bouncing drunks who didn't care to be bounced. Ear. Lip. Gut. Shins. Nose.

Football pain still gnawing ten years later. Knees. Hamstrings. Back. Shoulders. Ribs.

Patrolman pain from sitting on my ass eight hours a day. Lungs. Knuckles. Asshole. Brain.

Rodeo pain. Stupid ass Brahma bull kicking me in the groin, pain.

Ranch pain. Grabbing hold of barbed wire cutting through the glove, pain. Cow stepping on the foot, pain. And the ever popular, horse-kick-in-the-chest, pain.

And lately, a new, subtler nuance, the painful sound of escape routes, one by one slamming shut, leaving only the holy matrimonial aisle left to walk.

Hidden deep within me, under the forever adolescent, cowboy gene was an entrepreneurial gene fighting to manifest. I thought about the marketing program for the private detective agency I intended to open. Implementing the plan took a mere investment of $11 for an ad in the *Greensheet*. To my surprise, I was getting work from it, although not enough for me to say, "Hey, look at me, I'm a real detective!"

Missing cats. Stolen trucks which, with some digging, proved to be repossessions. Following the errant husband or wife. Surveys. And I didn't have a P.I. License or a permit to carry a handgun.

Shortly after I got run from the Austin Police Department, I interviewed Bergstrom, the largest agency in the state and the one most likely to employ me, but they turned me down. Not hiring. Cutting back actually. That was a year ago.

Hollers was now looking for an experienced investigator. As a patrol cop for three years, one does not do a lot of detective work. Knock on some doors. Ask a few questions. Mostly, I drove the streets of Austin. I watched. I reacted. I told folks to move along. I tried to avoid hitting my head on the cruiser when I got in and out of the thing. And I figured Hollers was seeing me to be polite.

Dang it all, I looked pretty good on paper though. Degree from Southwest Texas State University in San Marcos in Criminal Justice – Law Enforcement, enrolled at Austin Police Academy, graduating in the top ten percent. Plan was to stay with the Austin Police Department, retire from APD like my dad, Harry Rivers.

I patrolled Quail Hollow, a seedy, gang and drug-infested neighborhood in East Austin. And me, who didn't even like drugs (except for an occasional left-handed cigarette and ibuprofen for the pain habit). There were disagreements, complaints, a few citations and a few more reprimands.

My career at APD and my invitation to the Texas Patrolman's Hall of Fame, came to a screeching halt the day a gang of dealers set up a street pharmacy across from an elementary school.

Pissed me off.

I asked them to move along. They didn't and we commenced to duking it out. I won the battle but was in the wrong place and of the wrong complexion to win that war.

"Department's damned lucky you didn't cause a race riot."
Lt. Ashby, my supervisor had his hand out. "Badge and gun,
please." He didn't like me much and I wasn't sure why. Maybe it
was the nickname I laid on him. *Lt. Ass Wipe.*

"You are a disgrace to the uniform. I personally cannot wait
to hear what your father, the great policeman, has to say about
this." My dad before he retired was Ass Wipe's boss. Ashby and
Dad worked Homicide and for some reason Ashby was trans-
ferred to Traffic. After Dad retired, Ashby brownnosed his way
back to Homicide.

"You're just jealous, since Dad actually made some arrests."

"I'm going to call him right now."

"You might get him on the phone but I doubt if he'll know
what you're talking about. It's the Alzheimer's. Every time I see
him we have to be reintroduced."

"Harry Rivers was an asshole. He was always pretty fucked
in the head and..."

Lt. Ass Wipe never developed that particular line of thought
because I decked him. Lying on the floor out cold, I knew I had
crossed the goddamned line again and tossed my police issue
Smith & Wesson and police issue badge on his police issue stomach. I resisted the urge to kick him in the ribs and walked.

See? I *can* control my temper.

Chapter Two

"Welcome to Austin, Texas –
Loud Music Capital of the World!"

Johnny Gimble

Didn't show for my hearing at APD, which pretty much relegated me to the pavement. After six months on the latte/cerveza circuit, I took the bouncer job at the pseudo-country and western honky-tonk frequented by more yuppies and college kids than real shit kicking cowboys. Pretty sure I was the only fence mendin', cattle truck loadin', horse ridin', chaps wearing cowpoke who ever pushed through the swinging doors. Cowboys avoid Sixth Street, finding it impossible to find a parking place for the horse trailer.

I frequented the place not because of a fondness for yuppies but for the opportunity to ride a horse in the city, (I let my Appaloosa steed, Too Tall, out to pasture at the ranch. He was about twenty and was my rodeo horse all through high school and on the circuit). And I liked throwing down the extra cold Shiner Bock and Dos Equis. And Jimmy Don let me park the Bubbamobile, my F-350 dually with oversized tires and King Ranch motif, on the sidewalk.

The ranch in Blanco is a good fifty miles ride (by pickup) to Austin. I *flat* wore out Dad's old '57 Apache commuting and went shopping for some new wheels. Soon after I bought Bubba, Patricia and I reconnected. She dropped into Kickers one night with her roommates, and we closed the place dancing to "Together Again," and rekindled something we had fired up in college. At Southwest Texas State I was more interested in the quantity of women than the quality. Patricia carried the distinct honor of being the highest caliber woman who would still carry on a conversation with me without crying or pelting hard objects at my head.

She sensed I had matured some since college and with a little sweet talking I found myself in a townhouse lease in South Austin where we set up housekeeping. The time was ripe for me to exit the ranch and she needed to get shut of those roommates who were driving her crazy.

Hard to believe at thirty I had never lived with a woman (with the exception of my mother) and was learning many wonderful and scary things.

Moving in with Patricia was a balancing act. She was morning; I was night. She hated the toob; it was my best friend. She was salad; me steak. She was neat... Since we reconnected, she was the moderating influence. If not for her, I'd not be looking as good as I did for my interview. If not for her, I would not be on this interview.

She worked me hard but never put me up wet. Tried like hell to get me in church on Sunday but I warned her, "I'd just embarrass you. Trust me." She knew me, not just the façade I showed to the world, but saw something deep down I was not so sure was there.

On another level, there is a rep I carry around this corner of Texas, due in no small part to sending the gang of punks to the hospital, that I'm a hard-hitting, head-banging (not in the rock & roll sense but actual knocking of one guy's head against another's), ass kicking, go it alone, cowboy. The perfect bouncer but not the profile of someone modern day law enforcement was looking for.

I booked dozens of interviews and could talk the talk, but any checking of references uncovered the salient fact: I was fired from APD (for further details contact Lt. Ashby). The hiring process stopped right there. Who knew what Lt. Ass Wipe was saying to those prospective employers. The only blessing? He never mentions I cold-cocked him, although everyone in the department and surrounding P.D.s knew about it. Probably a male thing.

I work three to four nights a week at Kickers and nail up my P.I. shingle in the daylight hours. Not a shingle really. More like a piece of cardboard left on the dashboard of the Bubbamobile, so it won't get towed.

Coming from an ad in the *Greensheet*, my latest bit of work was conducting product surveys door to door, discovering which shampoos, toothpastes, soaps a household uses and then handing out samples of our brand.

"Ma'am, would you like to try an exciting new bath soap? Here's a free sample for you." There are boxes and boxes of samples in the garage at the townhouse.

Hollers slammed down the phone and shuffled the dozen or so folders on his desk into an order he seemed happy with.

"Maintenance can't get the fuckin' a/c workin'! Even when it was working it's still hotter than a fresh pile of cow shit in here." Hollers messed with the folders, trying to line up the edges, tough since the paper kept sticking to his fingers.

"You know, Rivers, three things goin' to happen here." He showed me three fat fingers and bent them over as he made his points. "Either those assholes fix this a/c, or I'm going to retire, or I'll become a field agent again. Air-conditioned cruiser blowing cold air in my face seems pretty invitin' 'bout now. Maybe spend the afternoon in a titty bar where they keep it at 68. Makes the gals' nipples all hard."

I smiled and shrugged. Didn't sound half bad. Maybe I'd stop by the Yellow Rose after the interview. 'Til the traffic died down. *My* nipples were getting hard thinking about it.

"First off, I want to thank you for comin' in on Friday afternoon on such short notice."

I nodded, like sure, man, it took me three lattes to get here and all.

"Let me get right to the point. We need you."

"Really?" I inched forward in my chair. It felt good to be needed. All those interviews. All those turndowns. The City of Bulverde turned me down for Christ's sake.

"We have a special assignment that's been dropped in my lap."

And a pretty substantial lap, too, I thought. I was feeling better now. And then it hit me. He doesn't know about APD But surely he must. He's the number one investigator in the fucking state. But what if he hadn't heard?

"Wanted to see if it's somethin' you might be interested in. Been hearin' some good things about you."

"I'll take it!" Get the job. Sort it out later.

"You don't even know what it is."

"Whatever it is, got to be better than handing out toothpaste door to door. Or rousting drunks."

"I see what you mean." He laughed. "Done both those things. Surveys are good for a stray piece now and then. The bar scene, too." He got a little dreamy eyed. "Now, don't you be telling Patricia I said that."

"Oh, no, sir." Patricia would dig it out of me for sure.

For some wild ass reason I think Hollers just offered me a job.

"Says here in your file," Hollers slid the top file folder off the stack, "you got three APD commendations." Hollers ran a finger across his brow and flicked half a cup of sweat across the room. I've seen Hill Country thunderstorms with less water. I tracked its progress through the air until it hit the carpet.

"You worked Quail Hollow? Tough neighborhood. Don't envy you that one, son. But APD let you go because you used, what was the exact wording, *excessive and undo force in the apprehension of suspects.*" A line of sweat rolled down his nose and jumped off, splashing on the papers in the open folder.

Well, I guess he heard about it.

"Damn. I'm sweatin' like a pig on a spit."

"It was six suspects, I said. "Excessive and undo force while apprehending six suspects."

"Yeah, I see that. Sent 'em all to the hospital. What happened, they gang up on you?"

"I guess that's why they call 'em a gang." It was one of those—I thought it funny he didn't—moments. I sent the grin to where unappreciated grins go and got serious.

"Something bothers me, though," said Hollers. Oh shit, here it comes. I get to this same fucking spot in every interview and they all want me to start 'splainin'.

"Probably bothered other potential employers, too," Hollers shifted in his chair, "although don't get me wrong, it bothers me a lot less than some folks. Well, just between you and me," he whispered, "I've done a bit of head knockin' myself."

I bet you have.

"It says here, after you got 'em down you continued to hit them with your nightstick and kick them 'til they were unconscious. A little Rodney King action? I'm not saying I wouldn't do the same under the same circumstances but is there anythin' here you care to tell me about that?"

"Well, sir, problem was, they kept trying to get up. I thought they'd run off once I gave them the chance. But they didn't. Every time I let one up, he'd come at me. It was crazy. They were cracked up or on dust or something. One guy'd get to his feet and try to hit me so I'd knock him down. Then another would get up and I'd bop him."

I knew it wasn't funny, but I couldn't help smiling. It wasn't I enjoyed busting heads. *Como no.* Sure, at the moment there was the adrenaline rush of hand-to-hand combat. But it wasn't that. It's this quirky little glitch in my makeup causes me to laugh at inappropriate times like funerals, weddings, church service and in the middle of fist fights.

Our pre-marriage counselor, Patricia and mine's, thought it a sign of insecurity.

Can't do church. Can't do funerals. Meemaw's funeral was a tragic example, because at the most solemn moment I was possessed with this overpowering urge to laugh. I choked it down, my face in my hat, I bolted for the door. "Poor little guy couldn't handle it." I smile just thinking about funerals.

Hollers, busy flipping through a folder, missed my shit-eating grin. Just as well. It was so easy to misinterpret. Lt. Ass Wipe tried real hard to wipe it from my face. It just got bigger. I smiled at the Brahma bull back in high school. Pissed him off good. The Sterilizer knows when one is too cocky. A big ass bull is nothing to show your teeth to, not if you're attached to them.

Hollers read aloud the all too familiar APD file of my transgressions and I zoned, my eyes defocusing, Chinese water torture, daydreaming about my second favorite fantasy—being a *successful* private investigator. My favorite fantasy involved Julia Roberts and large quantities of aloe vera gel. But that's another story.

As a kid, I loved *Rockford, Magnum P.I., Mannix* and *Mike Hammer.* Dad and I watched them all, and we made intricate plans to open up a family detective agency. *Harry & Son.*

Later, after I thought I forgot the boyhood dream, on the day I filled out my college registration forms as a freshman raw out of Blanco High, I checked off Criminal Justice—Law Enforcement instead of Phys Ed as my major. I figured up until the check 'em off point I'd be a high school coach.

But no.

I've wondered since then, what in the hell was that all about?

As Hollers droned on, thoughts of Patricia oozed across the swampland of my mind. If she got her way, which she did the vast majority of the time, okay *all* the time, we'd get married, I'd make a Rivers out of her and we'd produce a little creek or two (family humor). I love her like crazy, but dang it all, I wasn't sure I was ready for THE BIG STEP. (I laugh at weddings too). Of course weddings contain more humorous moments than funerals.

Patricia was not ready for my dream to open my own P.I. shop. It's a "pipe dream without the pipe," she says. What she didn't want was for me to open an office and sit behind my desk all day watching ESPN and drinking lattes or cerveza (I could do that at home for free) and flirt with the receptionist I hired from the Yellow Rose, who couldn't type worth a shit but sure looked good. She's got me figured.

If I could score this job at Bergstrom, we're talking about acceptable. A real company paying a real salary. This could be good for both her and me. The old proverbial win/win. She'd get a regular paycheck coming in, contributing to her happiness. I'd be working as an investigator, which ought to make me happy too. I say ought to, because I'd never done it before. And I hadn't brought in a regular-sized paycheck for over a year.

I knew I *could* do it though. Be a private eye. I longed for it. I wanted to hear myself say, "I think somebody wants me off this case!" I wanted to call for backup. I wanted to be sitting at my desk, drinking a latte and smoking a cigar when the good looking blond with the blue eyes comes in and sits on my..."

"So, what do you think?" The question shattered my reverie.

"What? I'm sorry, what did you ask me? This heat is making me a little woozy."

"Understandable. I said, this is a temporary assignment and even though your time with APD was, let's say, overexuberant, a trait might not be all bad with this assignment."

I let that sink in.

"Here's the deal," said Captain Hollers, "between you and me and the various bugs and listening devices in this office, we acquired an angel. Angel in the underwritin' sense. Our angel retained Bergstrom to run an audit on the Austin Police Department's and the FBI's handling of a past investigation." He slid the next folder off the pile toward me.

"It's a temporary assignment. However, if the person who took this did a decent job I can pretty much guarantee a permanent spot for that person, or..." Hollers let it hang for a long moment.

"Or?" I asked. This was getting interesting.

"Or, if that person wanted to work it as an independent agent, a contractor, it would be okay as well. It might be a better way to go." Hollers opened the folder, taking out a sheet of paper.

"I know my niece. We've talked about you, you know. I know what's goin' on. She wants a family. She wants you with a steady job. Who's to blame a woman for that? But here's the down and dirty, Rivers," he whispered, "I know you want to go solo. Every dick worth his salt wants to open his own shop."

I smiled, trying to imagine a dick worth its salt.

"Either way's okay with me. Probably best for both of us if you hire on as a contractor." He slid the paper across to me.

"Wow. That's a nice little number. Is the decimal point in the right place?"

Hollers gave a half nod; a smile forming at the edges of what I presumed was his mouth. "Maybe," Hollers took a folded white handkerchief from his pants pocket and sopped sweat from his brow, "you ought to take a look at this." He slid the next file over. Nobody was going anywhere until he slid the whole stack. He wasn't even halfway through. Damn, it was hot.

Chapter Three

"There are two tragedies in life. One is to lose your heart's desire, the other is to gain it."

George Bernard Shaw

"Read it over. I'm in the middle of something here." Hollers yanked up the phone and pounded four numbers with a fat index finger. "Yeah, it's me. Again. Where in the hell are those a/c guys?"

While Hollers expressed his disappointment with the maintenance department, I flipped through the folder.

"Oh my God, it's the fucking Hippie Hollow murders. I didn't know we were talking about that."

"Still interested?" Hollers had a paw over the mouthpiece, looked to me and then back to the telephone in disgust. "I'm on hold. I know you know about APD policy never closing a murder case. Goes double for this, bein' so high profile and all. But it has been five years."

I leafed through the file.

"I'll get you up to speed." He opened yet another folder. "In April of this year, a review board includin' the police commissioner, the chief and the mayor, took a pretty thorough look at the accumulated evidence. Determination was, the APD took that dog out but it refused to hunt." (People in Texas, bless them, are always taking their proverbial dogs out to hunt and the vast majority of the time the damn dogs do not hunt. It's a real shame because Texans love both hunting and dogs).

"They made Hippie Hollow inactive, not closed, but nobody'll be workin' it. Leaves the option of going back active should somethin' develop." Hollers continued. "Our angel got wind of them tossin' it on the bone pile. So now we're gettin' to take a crack at it."

"Okay."

"You know Captain William Warlick?"

"APD captain. My dad worked for him. Dad was working on Hippie Hollow when he retired."

"That's right. I knew Harry Rivers, did I tell you that? He's a good man. One of the best. Ever talk to you about the case?"

"Nope."

"Your father still ah...?"

"Yeah." Dad was out where the buses don't run. He lives with my mom in Blanco, Texas, where there literally is no bus service except the school bus.

"That's too bad. How well you know Captain Warlick?"

"Never met the man but I crashed his retirement party at the Driskill Hotel." I was looking for Lt. Ass Wipe—just as well I didn't find him. Too many witnesses. The good lieutenant suspended me without pay and filed to send me to a review board. "Captain Warlick and I left APD at the same time. They gave him a party, a paycheck for life and a watch. I got a pink slip and a kick in the butt."

Hollers smiled.

"Warlick ran the Hippie Hollow Task Force for three years. He co-coordinated the efforts of APD, Travis County Sheriff's Department, Park Police, Texas Rangers, Department of Public Safety. The Task Force made no arrests. After Warlick retired, a couple others fucked around with it for a couple years or so, but they didn't come up with jack shit.

"Feds didn't stay on. Hauled ass after a couple of weeks. They'll take over a kidnappin' or when there's a terrorist group involved or a perceived threat to national security. I think their motivation at the time was to take a quick look and get out. You might remember all those federal buildings being bombed about then."

I squinted my eyes, trying not to visualize that one. Think baseball. Try to remember the World Series. The Yankees. No, not the Yankees.

"FBI crime lab was up shit creek. Too much on the ol' plate. On the other hand, for Warlick, Hippie Hollow was priority numero fuckin' uno, the biggest thing ever to happen in this one horse town. Ten detectives bustin' their nuts, plus the support staff. But you know Rivers, whoever did those kids was as clean an operator as we've seen around here. It was a professional hit if you ask me.

"So anyway, there's this person," his tone secretive, "a politically influential person and one with some pretty deep pockets who would appreciate our havin' a look-see." While Hollers talked, his telephone disappeared back into a fold of neck fat. Only the black spiral cord hung out. I smiled and somehow through sheer will power, controlled myself.

"What's the goddamn problem?" He bellowed. I jumped. He was looking at me but I realized his wrath was directed at the telephone. A bead of sweat popped from my forehead, careening into my open mouth. Salty.

"I'll tell you what your problem is...! I don't believe this shit. The sonofabitch hung-up on me!" The captain's hard-nosed, get it done creds didn't appear to impress the boys down at the physical plant.

"You know what the real predicament is around here?" He said to me. "This fuckin' buildin' is fallin' apart around us." I re-scanned and noticed cracks in the walls and ceiling. Were they there when I walked in?

While Hollers punched and re-punched the phone, ranted and re-ranted about the a/c, I read the first sheet of the folder. It was a summary report of the crime which had taken place five years previously.

Numerous witnesses reported seeing Moses Harper Junior, Kristie Bentley, Travis Tanner and Merrylee Tanner leave a party at 3:30 A.M. July 10th. The party was hosted by Lucinda Tanner at her residence on Lake Travis, twenty miles west of Austin, Texas. The four teenagers had traveled approximately two miles in a '54 Mercedes 300 Limo belonging to the well-known minister, Reverend Arvin Tanner, where they parked the vehicle at the Hippie Hollow trailhead leading to a swimming area of Lake Travis.

Witnesses reported the teenagers mentioned they would be stopping at Hippie Hollow Park on the way home to Austin after the party for the purpose of midnight skinny-dipping. The park is notorious as a hangout for gays and drug users and is patrolled by Austin Park Police and Bee Caves Police.

According to the Coroner's Report, time of death for Moses Harper and Kristie Bentley was placed at 3:45 A.M., plus or minus 15 minutes, Saturday morning, July 10th. The body of Harper, aged 18, was found slumped over the steering wheel in the front seat of the Mercedes Benz Limo. One projectile entered his left temple, close enough to cause powder burns, consistent with the theory a weapon was fired at extremely close range, a distance of one to two inches. He died instantly. Harper was an all-state football player for Rollingwood High School, had graduated and was to attend the University of Texas in September.

The body of Kristie Bentley, aged 17, was also found in the front seat a projectile having entered her left temple, also causing powder burns, although not as close as Harper's, but at close range, possibly twelve to eighteen inches. She died instantly as well. Both front doors of the limo were found open when the first law enforcement officers arrived on the scene, which was estimated to be approximately thirty minutes after the incident. She was a cheerleader for Rollingwood and to be a senior at that high school.

Merrylee Tanner, age 15, was found lying on the ground outside the back passenger side door. A projectile from an estimated distance of six to eight feet, struck her in the head but did not enter, resulting in a comatose condition. (See attached medical report). Star Flight Helicopter Service transported her to St. David's Hospital in Austin. Doctors who treated her did not expect her to survive for longer than a few hours. Even though she is still alive as of the date of this report, doctors hold little hope of her coming out of the coma. Merrylee was to begin 10th grade at Rollingwood.

The body of Travis Tanner, age 20, was not recovered; however, significant amounts of Type A blood, the same type as Travis', was found on the back driver's side seat of the limo. A large pink cloak-like fabric was found next to the limo splattered with the same blood type. More of the identical blood type was found on the ground beside the vehicle, as well as on the trail to the lake. Even though the body was not recovered, assumption is he died at the scene. No determination of the reason for the removal of the body was given. Travis Tanner was to be a sophomore at Texas Christian University in Fort Worth, Texas. Travis and

Merrylee Tanner were brother and sister and the children of televangelist, Reverend Arvin Tanner of Austin, Texas, and Lily Tanner of Aspen, Colorado.

Robbery was ruled out as a motive since both the murder victims possessed cash and credit cards on their person and Travis Tanner's wallet was found on the backseat of the vehicle. The wallet contained several credit cards and five, one-hundred dollar bills.

In addition to the APD investigation, the FBI investigated the crime for two weeks but made the determination it did not warrant further involvement by that agency.

The crime appears to be a murder for hire. An additional indication that the murders were committed by a professional, suffering from psychosis. To wit, on all three bodies, the right "pinky" finger had been removed. FBI profiling failed to connect the "modus operandi" to a person or persons in their files and no motive was ascertained for this action.

Reverend Tanner was thoroughly investigated, but was not charged.

Because of the popularity of the park during summertime, there were many tire markings and footprints. The job of isolating those of the killer or killers was not possible. No shell casings were found. The projectiles that were recovered from the bodies and in the vehicle were made from a soft leaden material (See attached ballistics test) that collapses on impact.

After five years of investigation, following up on hundreds of leads, no arrests have been made.

Therefore, it is the determination of this body to dissolve the Task Force and to place the investigation on inactive status.

"Wow. This is some heavy shit." I remembered reading about the murders but the papers hadn't written about the missing fingers. My father had worked on the Task Force but since I was living at a dorm in college we never talked about it.

"As you might imagine, there was a shitpot full of paperwork on this. A friend of mine at APD got us this stuff." Hollers indicated the file boxes. "Read everythin' here and everythin' you can dig up on it. If somethin' don't smell right..."

Hollers lifted his leg and used the leverage to heave himself out of the chair with a grunt, leaned over and picked up one of the file boxes and placed it on his desk. On top of the box was a #10 manila envelope. Hollers grabbed it.

"This is Lucinda Tanner's gate control number and keys to her lake house. She's the aunt of the two Tanner kids and Reverend Arvin Tanner's sister, and the kids had just left her party up the hill from Hippie Hollow. I understand she's been working at her art studio down in Mexico. We handle security for both her homes and I'd like you to go on out to her lake house and check it out. I'll put this inside the box."

As he stepped around the desk with file box in hand, Donna, the Investigations Department receptionist/secretary, opened the door, almost knocking the box from Hollers' grasp.

"Whoops! Sorry," said Donna, hand on her heart.

"Donna! Would you please be more careful? And what about knockin' first? I'm in a meetin'!"

"I brought you some donuts," she said, almost singing the word, *donuts*. Like duh, this is important.

"What? Oh, okay. That'll work." Hollers put the box of files down by the door and grabbed a donut from the white paper bag. "Sorry, Donna, didn't mean to snap at you. This a/c thing's got me in a foul mood. This is Rivers."

"We met downstairs." Donna shook my hand. Good grip. She was a big girl. "Would you like a donut, Mr. Rivers?" She stood beside her boss holding out the bag.

"B. B. Rivers." I smiled at the cute couple, my smile vanishing as Hollers turned toward me. He grabbed the bag and without another word, she left.

"Don't get me wrong. I don't believe there's a chance in hell you can make headway on this. Some pretty good detectives worked on it, including Warlick who was APD's best. Also includin' your dad, who was just as good. I can tell you're a smart kid but I want more than smarts. I want your gut. If it turns out APD did an upstandin' job, that's fine. That's what I expect. But, if you do come up with somethin', we'll need to turn it over to APD Everythin' goes through me though. Got that?"

"Got it."

"Good. Some housekeepin'. You'll need to check in with me every Friday afternoon. I'm putting down three o'clock." Hollers penciled in the appointment on his calendar. "Jus' bring your written report to the office. Here's a sample of how to fill it out. If I'm not in, report goes in one of these." He held up a large manila envelope. "I keep them here. Report in the envelope. Envelope in the in box. Also, on Monday at 8 A.M. is our Investigations Department meetin'. Like you to be there. That way if there are questions about your report, we can talk after."

I nodded.

"I already called the local FBI office and asked them to send us a copy of their set of files."

"That's good."

"Course they won't send it. We'll need to go to their office to look at them."

"I can do that."

"Well, that's the good news. The bad news, for some reason only they know, the files were moved to Dallas."

We both shook our heads as if to say *the Feds are fucked.*

"We'll reimburse expenses. Moderately priced hotel, okay? Turn in receipts for all your expenses in a separate envelope." Hollers showed me where he kept the envelopes.

"Okay. Let me ask something? Why me? Why not one of your other detectives?"

"Good question, Rivers." Hollers put a whole donut in his mouth and said something like *"Goonk kerstone Ribbess."*

"What's that?"

He swallowed. "One, I got everybody assigned. And two, we're talkin' temporary. We're only going to pursue it for as long as our angel keeps financing it." He popped another donut.

"Like the competition, we're movin' away from investigations and towards guard service and alarm systems, more lucrative arenas. Even though old man Bergstrom started the agency thirty years ago as a P.I., now days we're suckin' hind tit in that venue. To make any money in investigations you gotta move into electronic surveillance. Computer geeks fresh outta shitty diapers gettin' the business now. When I retire, which the way I feel today, goin' to be real soon like, they'll sell this department."

I nodded.

"Good, alright. Here, add this to your paperwork. This file," he sat on the edge of his desk, an enormous cheek holding him on, and reached over for a thin blue folder, "is on a fellow who lives here in Austin."

Turning the folder sideways, I read the two words that were printed on the tab. Words that would alter my sheltered, little life as I had known it.

"Maximus Culpepper." Saying those two words sounded so innocent that first time. Like a goodnight kiss so harmless and sweet that morphs into marriage, mortgage and grandkids.

"Maximus Culpepper." Hollers glassy eyed me. "Old Max. Cranky old fart twenty years ago. Who knows what he's like now. Probably worse. Now, you may or may not believe in psychics..."

"Psychics?"

"Yeah. Not that I believe in your new age crapola, but Max is either very intuitive or very smart. Probably both."

Hollers popped a powdered sugar donut into his mouth. I was getting hungry myself, so I gave a look I'd seen from my dog Hank back at the ranch whenever I walked by with a hamburger. Funny how I was so much more of an interesting character to Hank when I was holding a hamburger. Hollers offered me the sack. I pulled out a chocolate covered and dreamed of a Starbuck's latte to wash it down.

"Captain Warlick is one of my oldest friends and we single guys, he's divorced and I'm a widower, would stay up with a bottle of scotch 'til the paperboy rattled the screen door. The subject always ended up on Hippie Hollow.

"When you miss the quick bust on a high profile murder case and it begins to drag on, someone says, *Call in the psychic! What you got to lose?*

"But our local headline hound, Rodriquez would've had a field day. 'Local Police Haven't Got a Clue—Call In Psychic.' He's the one who wrote the crap about how the police weren't up to the job. What an asshole."

"I remember wondering myself," I blurted, "why APD never came up with anything." As soon as I said it, I wished I'd kept my big mouth shut. Fortunately Captain Hollers was busy choking on a donut. His face turned a bright shade of crimson and his eyes bulged. He spun around to the water cooler, poured a drink in a cone shaped paper cup, downed it and spun back around.

"Those were hard times for APD and Warlick was sensitive about it. I remember one evening. We were a third of the way down our second Johnny Walker Black when I mentioned I'd worked with a psychic once. Told him I'd be happy to bring the guy in on Hippie Hollow. He threatened to kick my ass outta the house. Fortunately we were in my house.

"I met Max twenty years ago. My mother passed. That's when …did I mention he was a florist?"

"A florist? Oh yeah, I see that." I had been flipping through the sheets in the blue folder. "He was 'Florist of the Year' last year."

"Max does weddings and funerals and so forth. Still does. Here's this old dude with an English accent, workin' out of a dilapidated mansion off Enfield. Somebody recommended Max for the flowers for Mother.

"I hired him to do the funeral. Did a wonderful job. Used the same kind of flowers she grew in her yard—sweet peas, larkspur, bluebells, snapdragons. She sure was proud of her garden. She grew the most aromatic sweet peas you ever laid a nose to."

I smiled. My mother had sweet pea vines winding up the cedar posts on our porch at the ranch. I hadn't seen my mother or dad for an embarrassingly long time. Would have to make the trip out soon.

"The aroma of the flowers brought her back." said Hollers. "One whiff and I was ten again, smashing croquet balls through her white picket fence.

"Workin' my first murder case for Bergstrom. Told Max about it. Old man Bergstrom's reputation was for crackin' impossible cases. It was the Old Man and me and a secretary back then. His son, who runs the agency now, was still in high school. The police were gettin' nowhere, just like Hippie Hollow." Hollers spun his chair poured another cup of water and looked out the window at the upper level of Interstate 35.

"Week after the funeral he calls me. Says he can help with my case if I have access to a database of criminals. I didn't know what the fuck a *database* was. Gotta remember this was twenty years ago."

For a long moment Hollers stared out the widow at the cars grinding to a Friday afternoon halt.

"This is between me and you."

And the various bugs and listening devices in the room, I thought. Hollers turned back and looked me in the eye and lowered his voice to a whisper.

"Friends of mine at APD left some doors unlocked. I snuck Max in to look at mug shots. Max looked. I slept in a corner. At 5 A.M., he woke me up.

"*Voilá,* said Max. I almost dropped my cookies right there. The guy he tagged, name of Russell Dewitt? I talked to the asshole. Had a sheet. Nothin' violent. Petty theft. Possession. Not considered a suspect. No motive, had an alibi. I remember thinkin' as I interviewed him, this is a fuckin' waste of time. But when Max told me Dewitt *was* the guy, it changed the reality for me. You know what I'm sayin', Rivers?"

I nodded.

"I didn't believe he was the killer so I didn't do the necessary things I needed to do to nail him. Next day, I ran the guy through the sifter to see what shit fell out and turns out his alibi didn't hold any more water than a Hill Country stock tank in August. To make a long story shorter, we got him."

"Wow," I said, meaning it.

"Yeah, wow. Mr. Bergstrom was proud of me. The wife, she was still alive then, was proud of me. Max too. He wasn't interested in any of the credit. Said I shouldn't let on to *anybody* what actually happened. Then again it wasn't hard, because, I've never known for sure what did happen. I haven't told anybody. Except Captain Warlick and now you."

"I feel honored."

Hollers gave me the one-eye. Was B. B. Rivers being a wise ass? I'd been on the receiving end of that look many a time, due to among other things my tendency to bust out laughing at inappropriate occasions. Hollers either couldn't get a read on me or gave me the benefit of the doubt. He continued.

"The more I thought about it, the more I figured in my gut, Max must be involved in the murder somehow. As an investigator you tend to rely on your gut. But you know Rivers, gut feelings only *seem* right."

I nodded.

"I flat confronted the man with it. How could he know about DeWitt without being in on it somehow? I demanded an explanation but he said there wasn't one. Told me to go home, think through our experiences, the funeral, the chats, the late night visit to APD Then, I was to begin the process of opening my mind and heart to alternate possibilities. My brain refused to believe the man, any man, was psychic." Hollers shook his head. Sweat flew. "I remember telling Max it was dumb luck we met and just lucky he picked out the killer. You know what he said? Said it wasn't luck. Everything was connected to everything else. A little hard to swallow, right?"

I nodded.

"So, even though I couldn't, or wouldn't, let myself believe, I knew something unexplainable happened, so years later I made the suggestion to Warlick he bring in Max. He wouldn't hear of it. Christ, you think I'm conservative? Warlick makes me look like Jesse fuckin' Jackson. You understand what I'm saying here, Rivers?"

"I believe so, sir."

"One day, Warlick just got fed up with it all. He retired and moved off."

I nodded and we looked at each other for a long uncomfortable moment.

"I haven't given Max Culpepper much thought until the other day. I saw his photo in the newspaper. What's interesting, later the same day I get the call from our benefactor, the person who is financing the reinvestigation of Hippie Hollow. Coincidence? You tell me."

"I don't know."

"Max told me *watch for coincidences*. All these years I've been doing that. Like telling my niece about the job opening and she tells me about you."

In the article was a photo of a tall, slim, white-haired man standing next to a huge floral arrangement. "Says here he's in his seventies and swims every morning at Barton Springs, even in winter. Bet he's one of those old philosophers who swim laps at the crack of dawn."

"So, Rivers, before we're so deep in shit we can't paddle our way out, you'll take the assignment?"

"Yes sir."

"Money alright?"

"Money's just fine, sir." Seemed a good time to negotiate but I knew this job would work for Patricia just fine the way it was. That's all I needed to know. If it would make her happy, then dang it all, her happiness (within reason) was the most important consideration.

"You'll need to sign this." After a quick once over, I signed it and slid it back.

"I took the liberty of cuttin' a retainer check for your first two weeks."

I nodded. Somehow Hollers knew I'd take the job, knew I would take the retainer check. Maybe he was psychic.

"So, here's the down and dirty on Maximus Culpepper. First thing every morning, regular as an Ex-Lax commercial, Max takes a swim at Barton Springs Pool. And I mean dawn. He lives in an Airstream travel trailer across the street from the pool. Then he goes back to the trailer, eats breakfast and peddles his bike to his flower shop off Enfield on Niles Road, and gets to the shop at ten, which I think is pretty civilized."

I nodded in agreement, even though my routine was to sleep until noon (Would Hollers think this behavior was civilized?), and start knocking on doors giving away toothpaste at two and get out of the neighborhood before the husbands got home from work. Except for my Kickers nights, I'd get up with Patricia, drink a cup or two of java with her, tune into ESPN and then take a nap on the couch.

"The crime's five years old, so the interest level has waned, sort of like a sleepin' dog. Let's step over it lightly, and maybe it won't bite us on the ass." Captain Hollers rose. "And, take this psychic shit with a grain of salt. I don't want it to assume a relevancy it doesn't deserve. What I'm askin' for is old fashioned leg work. Put in your time. Make us look good. And, if you can't do it, at least don't make us look bad." Hollers smiled. "Max might help here, might not. He may not feel inclined to help. No reason why he should."

With a grunt, Hollers picked up two more boxes and stacked them in my arms. Even at 6'4", I had so much stuff I couldn't see over it.

"One more thing, I'm asking you not to question the detectives who worked on the case, which was just about everyone in the department. Least for now. I'm afraid it might be too disruptive and like I said, this needs to be low profile. No use rubbin' APD's nose in it. Start on Monday, get a hold of Max, interview the families of the victims, the various witnesses, get yourself up to Dallas, check those FBI files. Ought to keep you busy for 'bout a week."

"Aye, aye, sir." I saluted, I don't know why, almost dropping the file boxes. It just seemed the thing to do after saying aye, aye, sir.

"And tell Max hey, will you?"

"Will do, sir."

"You know, Rivers, your dad was a fine man. Sorry he's..."

"Thank you sir. I appreciate it," I peeked around the stack to make eye contact.

"And how's your mother?"

"She's fine, sir."

"Good. So, Rivers, you're welcome to work here, make your phone calls, whatever."

"Thank you, sir."

"While you're here, work on Hippie Hollow. No personal shit. No side jobs." He waited until I nodded. "Now, I set you up with an office. Well, not an office. It has a desk and a phone. You'll be in room B-28. Ask Donna how to get there. And if you see any a/c guys out there loafin' in the hallways, you have my permission to kick 'em in the ass. God, it's only June."

Chapter Four

"The day after tomorrow is the third day
of the rest of your life."

George Carlin

"Will you change the station *pleeze?*" pleaded Merrylee from the back seat of her father's limo. "You know I can't stand shit-kickin' cowboy music. Something else, *por favor.*" She popped her bubble gum.

"Come on, Sis." Travis was driving. Their chauffeur was in D.C. with Reverend Arvin Tanner. "But I really like George Straight," said Travis, picking up speed on F.M. 2222, the curvy four-lane connecting Austin to the Lake Travis area, thirty minutes west.

Travis longed to be at the wheel of his silver Z-3 Beamer. *Two Twenty-Two Two* was perfect for a Z-3. The highway was not wonderful in the family station wagon, the two-ton hunk of metal.

Reverend A was weird. And scary. 'Reverend A' was Travis' pet name for his father. Winslow Christian, Travis' roommate at Texas Christian University, said televangelists were the pro wrestlers of religion. Got that right, Mr. Christian.

The BMW roadster was a high school graduation gift from his mother. He was not living with his mother though and his dad, the world famous preacher of the Holy Word, placed unreasonable restrictions on its use.

In order to drive it: 1.) Travis would pay for his own insurance. That was reasonable, but quite a nut to cover since he was barely twenty and insurance on a sports car was astronomical for his age group. 2.) Reverend A required Travis to work his summer vacations for the Church of the Ark. The Ark, last refuge of the saved.

He didn't like it, but he could handle it. The money wasn't good but he could work as many hours as he could stand and he did need a job to pay the insurance.

But the restriction that got to young Mr. Tanner, Reverend A forbade him to keep the Beamer at TCU during his freshman year.

"You must tend to your studies and the car would be a distraction," said the diminutive Reverend A in his nasally voice. So, the beautiful Beamer sat collecting dust in the garage at the Westlake mansion with Reverend A's auto collection. It was parked next to his dad's '57 turquoise and white Thunderbird. They looked cute together, but sadly, his wheels remained there throughout the school year except for Thanksgiving, Christmas and semester breaks.

She was such a fine machine. Travis figured she was a female and named her Winona after his favorite actress. He couldn't get enough of her. There were two women in his life. Winona and Angel. He daydreamed of driving Angel in the Beamer along the chain of Highland Lakes up to the headwaters of the Colorado River.

Travis admitted though, the more practical choice for this evening was the big, ancient, clunky hunk of junk, which he named Clyde. Reverend A was scheduled to make a rare family appearance at Auntie Loo's party, announcing there was something he needed to discuss with Lucinda and Travis. He cringed at the very thought of Reverend A's tiny little butt in Winona's passenger seat where Angel's perfectly proportioned body should be sitting.

"Well, I got a surprise for you, Dad!" He slapped the steering wheel with the palm of his hand.

"What is it?" Asked Kristie Bentley, his date for the evening. She sat next to him on the chauffeur's bench seat. Kristie was beautiful but dumb, he thought, nothing like the exotic Angel Chai, with her upswept Asian eyes and her skin the color of milk and tea.

"Nothing. Just thinking out loud." His little sister Merrylee and their mutual friend Moses Harper sat in back. The sliding window separating the working class from the elite was open.

Moses Harper Junior, All-State defensive end for the Rolling-wood Armadillos, at 6' 9", 280 pounds and still growing, would have been too much for Winona anyway. To further complicate the logistics, Reverend A wanted to be "carried" back home to Westlake after the party. The evening was not turning out as expected but it would get better. He was sure of that.

"Okay brat. Here, how about this?" Travis poked a button on the dash and the CD player engaged. *"And now the time has come,"* Frank Sinatra's smooth and mellow tones wafted from the state of the art system.

"Uhhggg!!" all four riders groaned together.

"Now *that's* some wrist-slashing music," said Moses. Everybody laughed.

"... I did it my way."

"Quick change it," said Kristie.

Kristie and Travis's hands bumped as they groped for the button that would eject the CD and get the radio back. The radio initiated scan mode.

"How many more miles?" asked Merrylee, popping her gum. It was their oldest family joke. As soon as a vacation began, when the station wagon, back when it really was a station wagon, backed out the driveway, Merrylee or Travis would ask, *"How many more miles?"*

Travis brought Clyde up to 80 as they cruised past the Austin 3M plant. He muscled the limo left onto FM 620, the north/south four-lane skirting Lake Travis' eastern shore. The traffic light was well into yellow as he gunned it, tires squealing. The radio continued to scan while Kristie read the operations manual.

"Just a couple more," said Travis smiling. Those were the good old days, he thought. And if tonight works out as planned, it'll be like playing a country and western song backwards. I'll get my car back, my girl back, and a much better life.

"How many years we been coming to the lake for Auntie Loo's flamingo parties?", he asked getting in the right lane for his turn onto Comanche Trail.

"Couple hundred," said Merrylee. She blew a huge pink bubble that deflated, covering her face. "Hey Mo, look," she gave Moses a wide eyed look. He laughed big, barrel-chested. A big laugh for a high school kid.

Kristie looked up from the manual and pushed a button. The radio made the rounds of the preset FM channels. About half were set to easy listening stations, half to country. The Mercedes was made available as a courtesy of the Church of the Ark for the use of dignitaries, both religious and political, who were visiting Austin. The radio settings catered to a conservative taste in music.

Travis did not share his father's political or religious beliefs. But they agreed on one thing, a love of country music. Before Reverend Arvin Tanner was born again, turning his life over to Jesus, he cut a dozen gold records. His last album was a compilation of gospel favorites, sung in his unique nasally style.

Travis needed to assume command of the radio. He tried the old computer reboot trick. Pulling off the road onto the shoulder, he turned off the radio, turned off the key, waited a moment, whistled the first few bars of a Garth Brooks song and restarted Clyde. He turned the radio back on. He picked up a rock station.

"Madonna! Now *that's* more like it, driver," shouted Merrylee as she reached her hand with camera attached through the sliding window. She snapped a shot of her brother."

"Whoa, Merrylee. Enough already." Travis could see big blotches of white and blinked repeatedly until they went away. Merrylee sat back down in the back, lacing her fingers behind her head, her bare feet in Moses' lap.

"Y'all are going to like Auntie Loo," said Merrylee. "She's a hoot. She travels a lot. Art shows and openings. Has a precious little art studio on a hill overlooking this quaint little town in Mexico. Christmastime and Easter we all get together. And every year she puts on this party. Like St. Patrick's but instead of wearing green to avoid being pinched, slight variation, everyone wears pink to avoid getting thrown in the swimming pool."

"I don't have anything pink on," said Moses in a voice matching his XXX size.

"I have a sneaking suspicion Auntie Loo will take care of that little detail. She doesn't miss much and I doubt anybody'll want the job of throwing you in." She wrapped both hands around his huge biceps. "Look at the size of this thing!" Moses blushed through his dark skin.

Travis wheeled the heavy Mercedes onto Comanche Trail and began the two-mile climb up the hill, past Hippie Hollow, towards Lucinda Tanner's lake house.

"Hey, there's the Hippie Hollow turn off," said Moses. "You all ever go there?"

"Quite a lot when I was a kid," said Travis. "They named this lake after me." Silence. Travis was named after the hero of the Alamo. "Maybe we can go skinny dipping after the party. They close it at ten but I don't think the cops will bother us. And it's a full moon tonight."

"Great idea," said Moses.

"Can't wait." Kristie rolled her eyes.

"Oh, fuck," said Travis.

"What?", sked Moses, Kristie and Merrylee together.

"I forgot, we're going to have to 'carry' Reverend A back to Westlake after the party."

"Whatever." Kristie checked her lipstick in the rearview mirror.

"Auntie Loo, and I'm not exaggerating am I, Merrylee," said Travis, "has a couple of thousand pink plastic flamingos in her yard for this party. Who knows where she stashes 'em from August to June. But come July they're fucking everywhere, under the cedar trees, in the flower beds, on the roof."

Along Comanche Trail one legged pink flamingos pointed their beaks in the direction of Auntie Loo's lake house.

"And the highlight every year is when some lucky girl and some lucky guy are named the Princess and the Prince of Pink."

"Our dad was Prince the first year. That was ten years ago, I think. Yeah, that's right. I was five, and now I'm fifteen, almost sixteen. The most fun I've had in my short life is at Auntie Loo's flamingo parties. I mean it's an incredible honor just to get invited to the thing.

"For the first few years before Dad weirded out, we'd pile the whole fam into the station wagon and Dad would drive. Then somewhere along the line, I guess when Papaw Tex and Meemaw died, we must have gotten rich or something, 'cause then we'd take a limo out here with a "real chauffeur." She said "real chauffeur" with quite a bit more volume than necessary.

"Hey, I'd rather be taking these curves in my ultimate driving machine," said Travis. Smiling, he thought about his recent conversation with the family accountant. He couldn't wait to tell Merrylee how rich they were.

"Okay, Tra-*vis*. But anyway, for several years now, Dad's been avoiding alcohol and Auntie Loo, who has been known to toss down a few."

"Where is your father?" Asked Moses.

"He has a condo in D.C. Lately he's been meeting with the president," said Merrylee proudly. "But he did say he would be at the party sometime tonight."

"Merrylee! That's supposed to be a secret."

"Whoops," said Merrylee. "Hey, there it is." She pointed to a large two-story pink granite house perched on a cliff overlooking the lake. Travis turned the Mercedes into the drive, cranked down the window and punched in 7465 on the gate phone.

The gate swung open. A line of cars, several hours early for the party, were parked on the shoulder waiting for the okay to enter.

"PINK. P on the phone dial is 7, I is 4, get it?" Travis maneuvered the limo up the driveway that wound along the edge of the cliff.

"I won't tell anybody," said Moses.

"Oh, Auntie Loo will change the code tomorrow morning."

"No, not that," said Moses, "I mean I won't tell anyone about your father and the President. *But,* let me ask you this, what's the poster boy for the religious right doing commingling with our left wing president anyway?"

"Whoa!" Moses interrupting himself. "Look at the size of that house! It's a mansion." Moses Harper's home was modest, one side of a duplex on East 11th Street in Austin. His goal was to win a NFL first round draft pick. Quarterbacks may win the Heisman but what the NFL needs are linemen. So, in his junior year at UT., he'd throw his name into the NFL draft. Then, he'd buy a new home for his mom and dad who were getting up in years, and move them on up to the west side.

"Actually," said Merrylee, "this is Auntie Loo's lake house. It's like a summer cabin compared to her real home in Westlake on Lake Austin. She lives next door to us. Our grandparents bought a bunch of land on Lake Austin and Dad and Auntie Loo ended up with it.

"This one here is her little house facing south over the big lake and Westlake is the big one facing north over the little lake. It all depends on what mood she's in."

"Must be nice," said Kristie. "We only have the one house, and it's quite a bit smaller than this *little* one."

"To answer your question, Mo," Travis wound the limo up the curvy driveway and into the compound; pink flamingos were everywhere, "it's all politics. My dad is not as moral as he appears. You have no idea what he's been up..."

"Parrrttteee!!!" Merrylee stood up through the skylight and waved at some scruffy looking roadies. They waved back. One mean looking dude with a huge beard and red bandana wrapped around his head, did not wave.

"Try to be good, Merrylee." Merrylee got back down. "We're early," said Travis, "and I told Auntie Loo we'd help her set up. You all up for it?"

The others were up for it. The roadies were called back to unloading equipment by the foreman. A touring bus with an airbrushed scene of cowboys riding herd on longhorns was parked on the lawn. In an hour, security guards would go down to man the gate. In another hour they would open the gate, allowing only those guests with coded invitations access. Guests would be directed to the parking lot on the lower level and would walk up the steps to the lake house.

Travis parked the limo in the circular driveway. Since they were early, there was room close to the house. Orange traffic cones were ready, as per Reverend A's instructions, to guarantee a rapid departure if need be. Fig ivy climbed the walls and huge palm trees attempted to shade the home from the intense Texas sun.

The four got out and walked across the lawn to the huge Colorado River flagstone patio as the catering crew unfurled white tablecloths with a snap. Purple wisteria blossoms and pink bougainvillea hung from latticework overhead. Misting machines were placed between the hanging plants, lending a cloudlike aura and cooling off the scene. The patio offered a magnificent view of Lake Travis below, bright blue in the late afternoon sun.

Travis wore jeans, loafers with no socks and a white shirt with Ralph Lauren in pink lettering. Moses wore jeans and a burnt orange UT jersey. Merrylee and Kristi wore the same pink cocktail dress.

"Dillards?" Asked Merrylee, slipping on her black, spiked heels.

"Foley's," said Kristie.

"Wow, look at this view!" Said Moses. "I wish Mom and Dad could see this."

"Hey, we ought to bring them out sometime," said Merrylee.

Sailboats slashed deep white streaks across the surface of the lake. In the distance the top of Mansfield Dam was visible, a speedboat with a water skier swept by close to the rocks 100 feet below.

"How's about pink Alaskan salmon flown in fresh today?" Came a voice behind them.

"Auntie Loo!" said Travis and Merrylee together, happy to see their aunt. They gave her a group hug. Lucinda Tanner was Reverend Arvin Tanner's older sister. Tall, slim, long jet-black hair tied straight back in the style of the Euro-rich. Green eyes. A handsome woman. One knew she must have some years on her but one was also aware of her striking good looks.

She wore a white silk kimono with matching pink obi and bandana tied across her forehead with matching finger and toe-nails. She was barefoot. In one hand was a pink margarita. In the other a long thin panatela cigar.

Lucinda never married. "Too independent." She would say of herself. "Too ornery." Her brother Arvin would claim.

Three months out of the year she lived at her mansion on Lake Austin in Westlake, another few months here at the lake house. Throughout a typical year, she attended gallery openings in New York, Santa Fe, Taos and the Bay Area of San Francisco. The time remaining she worked at her studio on a hill above the artist's colony of San Miguel de Allende, Mexico.

Lucinda was an artist. But not a starving one, never having to sell her work or worry about production. Never having to cross the line from creative to commercial, a line that bothers so many artists. Her work was good and it sold. Monies made she donated to charity.

"This is going to be the best flamingo party ever," said Lucinda. "The salmon she's a-coming in on the 6:10 flight from Juneau. Your father called me, first time in at least three years, maybe more. He is going to pick up the salmon at the airport. I don't know what's gotten into the boy. He's being nice to me. There's a-gonna be flamenco dancers..."

"Flamencos and flamingos?" Asked Moses.

"You got my little joke!" She winked at Moses. "And for the kids, and I'm defining kids as anyone under the age of forty, I have a special treat. Old Blue Eyes himself."

"Not Frank Sinatra," said a disappointed Travis. "We've already had one crooning incident today."

"No, no, no, I would not inflict that blue-eyed gentleman on you all. Come on now." She handed her margarita to Moses and grabbed her niece and nephew by their chins, her cigar clenched between her teeth. "The other one. You know, Willie."

"Willie Nelson! *Alright!*" Willie was Travis Tanner's all time favorite. Merrylee frowned. Willie was not her favorite. The thought of a 60 year-old man in grey-haired pigtails wearing a red bandana on his forehead was ludicrous.

"Now, Merrylee," Auntie Loo knew the exaggerated frown of her niece's. "I know there's no room in your heart for cowboy music. I know that, soooo," she gathered the group together and walked them up the steps from the patio to the lake house, "I've got something that is going to blow everybody's and especially your, socks off. You are my favorite niece after all."

"I'm your only niece, Auntie Loo." She snapped off a picture.

"That makes you all the more special." Lucinda gave her a double pinch on the cheeks.

"So, who is this mysterious sock blower?" asked Merrylee and seeing the confused look in her aunt's eyes, "you know, the one who's going to blow my socks off?"

"Now you know me better than that. How's about we keep it under our hats a little bit longer? I know you're going to totally dig him. Trust your Auntie Loo. Now, who are these fine looking people?" Lucinda took her margarita back from Moses and put her free hand on Kristie's shoulder.

Introductions were made. Small talk about football, cheerleading, Rollingwood's chances for another state championship this coming season (not good since Moses had graduated).

"Here you are," said Lucinda to Moses. You might want this." She slipped a pink garter over his hand and up over his biceps. She raised an eyebrow in Merrylee's direction and got a smile out of her. Then she assigned jobs to each. Travis and Moses to help the roadies unload equipment and set up the stage. Merrylee and Kristie would go with Lucinda to handle all the little details that would make it the most perfect pink flamingo party ever.

As the sun descended into the blue waters of Lake Travis, guests emerged from the stairway that came up from the parking lot. All wore at least touches of pink. The first to arrive was an obese fellow in a hot pink suit with a wide white belt and Pat Boone style white suede shoes, complete with the white talcum powder to keep them just so. As he pranced around the grounds, little puffs of talcum dust arose to meet the dry July Texas evening.

Lightening bugs clicked silently on and off in time to the racket of the cicadas. Within minutes, girls in pink polka dot bikinis frolicked in the swimming pool. The pool contained round tables, each with a beach umbrella and barstools underwater Acapulco style.

The official drink for this festive occasion was, of course, pink. Pink margaritas for those after a serious change of consciousness. Pink lemonade for those who could handle reality without enhancement.

Sailboats, jet skis and cabin cruisers anchored off shore, in anticipation of the annual free concert. Most would be pleasantly surprised to hear Willie and totally blown away by the surprise guest. Lucinda was adept at keeping the identity of the entertainment under wraps until the last possible moment. None of the guests and not even her closest friends had the foggiest idea who was on tap each year.

Willie and his band were on stage in an alcove carved out of the limestone hillside. They set up in the dark. The first few lines were delivered in the dark.

"Pink mar-gar-ri-tas take my mind," sang Willie. All who had ever been to a Willie Nelson concert knew Willie always opens with "Whiskey River Take My Mind." This was his inside joke, he got a roaring laugh and the party was officially underway. The scorching sun was down and the lights were on and the crowd buzzed with excitement. Air horns blasted from the boats anchored offshore.

"Waaaahhhh!!!"

Alright Willie! Came out of the crowd. *I love you, Willie!* Screamed a topless teenage girl on one of the speedboats, her voice carrying over the dark water of the lake and up the cliff. Everybody laughed. Everybody was very happy now.

This was Lucinda Tanner's Tenth Annual Pink Flamingo Party. Every year the party was better than the year before. The entertainment was always top shelf. One year she brought in the fiddle player Charlie Daniels, another time Delbert McClinton, yet another ZZ Top. Last year, Joe Ely. The year before, Marsha Ball. Riders in the Sky before that.

But if there was a musical hero who summed up all that was Austin, Texas, it had to be Willie Nelson. Rumor has it, if you die in Austin, your soul goes to Willie's house. Willie played the first flamingo party. So, it had come full circle. And after the tragic events that would occur later that evening, would this be the last pink flamingo party ever?

Chapter Five

"There are two ways to live your life.
One is as though nothing is a miracle.
The other is as though everything is a miracle."

Albert Einstein

The flower shop occupied the front rooms of one of the mansions on Niles Road, in the Enfield-Windsor district of West Austin. A former governor lived next door. The mansions were built by what was left of the upper crust after the American Civil War. The bottom crust, servants, ex-slaves of those rich folks, threw up shanties in neighboring Clarksville. Maximus Culpepper invested his Army mustering out money and bought a fixer-upper.

"That's Max there, sir," said the young lady at the front desk of Culpepper Florist. I didn't like hearing the sir part. I sucked in the gut and smiled, attempting to appear friendlier. She was cute. Early twenties. I caught the scent of herbal shampoo from her long blond ponytail swinging past my nose as she turned to point out Max.

The owner of the upscale flower shop was sweeping discarded petals and stems into a pile. His latest creation sat beautifully on the workbench. He was talking to himself.

Maximus Culpepper had been in business so long there wasn't a florist in town who remembered when he started. Max was *the* Old *Pro* and half of Austin's florists studied under him. His customers included the governor's mother, the mayor's great aunt, Lady Bird herself and other museum quality democrats.

"Mr. Culpepper?" I looked down on Max's white curly hair as he stood up gracefully, dumping a dust pan into a large plastic trash can. Max had a nice tan. Bright blue eyes.

"Hel-loo," said Max, a trace of British there after fifty years in Texas. "I would appreciate it immensely if you would deem to referring to me as Max, please." Max looked over the top of his glasses, which he wore on the tip of his nose, and took me in as he talked, pausing a long moment on my Stetson, which I wore low on my forehead. His eyes shifted to my rodeo belt buckle and then back up to my turquoise and silver string tie.

"Are you a law enforcement officer?"

"Private detective." Damn, I was not expecting to get busted so quickly. "Name's B. B. Rivers. I'm working a case with Bergstrom Investigations. Got a minute to talk? Somewhere private? It's important."

Six floral designers, three men and three women, cocked a collective ear as Max walked me back through their workbenches. As we passed through, he told me about the arrangements they were working on that day. He stopped at a designer's table. I almost ran into him. He looked at the designer's project for a long moment and pulled a flower stem from the arrangement, replacing it with a different one. I watched the process and couldn't see any difference. Tommy, the designer, looked frustrated.

"You hate me, don't you?"

"I don't hate you, Max," said Tommy. "It's just..."

"Just what?" Over the glasses look.

"I don't get it. I don't see what you're seeing." Tommy, Max, the other designers and I stared at the arrangement. Max nodded and with no more conversation, led me across the hall to an office at the rear of the shop. As we left the front, the motif changed from borderline elegant to funky. Max left the office door ajar.

"The *zinnia elegans* is a marvelous flower. The matronly zinnia evokes apple pie, grandmother, Chevy to the levy, etcetera. They are the little old ladies of flowers. Conversely, Tommy's arrangement, commissioned as it were for a leading Austin businessman, was to be strong, masculine, a veritable Rolls Royce. There is no earthly reason to feminize it with a zinnia. That zinnia was screaming to be removed from there."

"You talk to flowers?"

He smiled. "Let us say, we converse. But, what might I do for you?"

I lifted the brim of my Stetson off my forehead, repositioning it to the back of my head, releasing a mop of red hair and considered how I should begin.

"Bergstrom you say? How's Ricky Hollers doing?" He began it for me.

"Ricky?" I smiled. Someone weighing 400 pounds did not seem like he should be called Ricky.

"He's fine, sir. I met him for the first time Friday. Said to tell you 'hey.' Suggested I talk to you about this case we've got."

"Ricky still a lard ass?"

"He's a little on the chunky side, yes sir." I smiled, sat down on an overstuffed leather couch and took off my Stetson. I looked for a place to put it. Finding nowhere to put it in the cluttered office, I held it in my lap.

"I have been following Ricky Holler's career for some years now." Max moved a stack of papers and sat down next to me. He sat so close. I hoped he wouldn't do the hand on the knee bit. In my college days, I invaded the space of many a young dudette at the local bootscootin' establishment. I hoped this wasn't some sort of karmic retribution for my past wicked ways. Max didn't go for my knee but popped off the couch and dashed out of the office.

"Just be a sec." Max was back at Tommy's workbench taking yet another stem from the arrangement and replacing it. I'd hate to work for that guy, I thought. While Max did a replay of the Chevy to the levy talk with Tommy, I quadrant scanned.

Hollers' office with the guns and cowboy hats was more my speed. This place was odd. Tribal masks and burlap coffee bags were tacked to the walls. Mayan stone carvings and Mexican pottery competed for space with the books on shelves. I got up and looked out an open window onto a tree-shaded alley.

Alleys are a tradition in the older neighborhoods of Austin. Houses in front on paved streets. Garages and carports on dirt alleys in back. I noticed a bike path of decomposed granite a couple of houses down the alley.

Moving my eyes past the window, up against one wall was a desk piled high with books. Flower books. Plant books. History. Geography. Woodworking. Japanese gardening books in Japanese. The Bible. The Koran. A book of astrological tables. A book by Hazrat Inayat Khan sat on the arm of the couch. I sat back down and leafed through it, reading a passage at random.

Do not go directly into the temple; first walk fifty times around it!

What the hell does it mean? I liked it, but didn't know why. Maybe because the closer I got to walking down the aisle with Patricia, the more I wished I was somewhere, anywhere, else. I wrote the quote on my pad and put the book back on the couch. Stacks of books and magazines were everywhere, covering every available place. Crossword puzzles filled out in ink were strewn about the room, on the floor, on the desk, stuffed between books on the shelves. The overhead ceiling fan—the office was not air- conditioned, was animating some of the papers. Two brand new Pentium IV computers sat on the desk and a couple of older models were stacked one on top of the other in the corner, more books perched on them. Ancient cobwebs formed in the corners of the high ceiling.

When Max came back, I moved a pile of floral sketches onto a pile of magazines giving us elbow room on the couch. The man did look ageless. Thick crop of bright white curly hair. Granny glasses worn on the tip of his nose, looking over them with intelligent, blue eyes. He wore khaki pants with bicycle clamps wrapped around his ankles. As he sat, I scrutinized him. Slim, six feet tall, weighing 170 to 180 pounds.

"I weigh 176 pounds, I'm 6' 1," and my age is my business."

"How'd you know what I was...?"

"Perception, dear boy," he said in an exaggerated English accent. "When you attain my advanced age, you realize there are nevertheless few thoughts a person may employ. Individuals such as yourself, in the field of law enforcement, are predisposed to the categorization of others as suspects, filling in the height, weight, age, color of hair template you file away in your head."

I shrugged. He about nailed that one.

"Now, my first thought," Max, took off his glasses and placed them over his knee. He massaged his eyes with his knuckles, "to show you how predictable we humans are, when someone tells me their name is B. B. Rivers, curiosity gets the better of me and I most certainly must ask, what does the B. B. stand for?"

It was a common and predictable question and yet one for which I did not have a standard answer. I'd tried everything from, "None of your fucking business." Doesn't go over well with most folks. To, "Gawrsh, it's kinda personal." My Goofy impression. When asked, I'm just as surprised as anyone what issues forth from my mouth.

"It's not something I share." Yet, I thought, felt, the grand-fatherly old man could be trusted with it. "Okay, I'll tell you. But there is a story that goes with it."

"Jolly well then," Max rubbed his hands together. "I love a good story. Is it an action/adventure?"

"More like a romance."

He nodded.

"Some time in the '60s, my father was a young police officer here in Austin. My mother grew up on the family ranch in Blanco and went to UT She was younger by several years than my dad and was experimenting with being a flower child."

"I like flower children."

"Somehow I figured you would. She and Dad met downtown. He arrested her on Congress Avenue for dancing."

"Dancing? There is a law against dancing?"

"Dancing on the roof of her V.W. Bug, joint in one hand, a bottle of Boone's Farm in the other. At least it's the way they tell it. There must have been an attraction. Even though he arrested her, he put up her bail."

"I think I like your father."

"Mom had him wrapped around her little finger. He adored her. He still would adore her if he knew who she was. Whenever they'd have words, he'd belt out in his booming voice, *"I'll make all the major decisions around here, like which Democrat to vote for and you can make all the rest."* I figured naming the kids fell under the all the rest category. B. B. stands for one of Mom's literary heroes."

"Brendan Behan?" He clapped his hands in glee.

"Bilbo Baggins." I replied.

"Bilbo Baggins?" An uproar of laughter from the old guy. "I believe I like your mother too, Bilbo. This *is* wonderful. May I call you Bilbo?"

"I'd just as soon you wouldn't. Most people either call me B. B. or Rivers. My girlfriend calls me Billy."

"I think Bilbo Baggins is an admirable name but it is not right for you?" I shook my head. "Okay then. B. B. seems a trifle diminutive for a strapping chap like you," he slapped me on the shoulder, "and I shall not impose on your girl-friend's pet name. All said and done, I believe I shall call you Rivers."

"Good, now that that is settled, Mr. Culpepper..."

"And you shall call me Max. Everyone from the Governor of Texas on up, calls me Max."

"Max, I'm here about the Hippie Hollow murders."

"I know. I know. What a tragedy it was." Max shook his head and looked out the window into the alley for several moments. How did he know why I was here?

"Max, since we're coming clean here, I've figured out how you knew I was a detective. The broken nose, sports jacket, right? I mean I look like a cop, right?" Max nodded, his eyes twinkling blue over the top of his granny glasses. "But how in the world did you know I was working on the Hippie Hollow murder case?"

"Well, now Bilbo. Whoops, I've already done it, haven't I?"

"That's okay."

"Rivers, I've known for some time now I would have an involvement in this particular murder case. Call it a prediction. Call it a premonition. I am surprised it has taken this long for you to come by."

"I don't understand. You're telling me you knew I was coming to see you? I didn't even know until yesterday I'd be working on it."

"I would venture to say there may have been clues you missed.

"Maybe so, but how did you know you'd have an involvement in it?"

"I am very good at two things, and I am good at them because they occupy a natural interest for me."

"What sort of things? Like florist stuff?"

"Of course, florist *stuff*," he smiled at my adorable use of the English language. "The love of my life is flowers. I cannot get enough of them. Here I am, a florist for 50 years and the stamen, the blossom corolla and calyx still fascinate me. I will bet you did not know flowers have ovaries?"

"I did not *know* that!" I said doing what I thought was a pretty good Johnny Carson impression. Patricia always laughed. Max didn't. Bet the old fart didn't even own a TV.

"I appreciate the way the blooms relate to each other in an arrangement. How it is possible to create something greater than the sum of its parts. And then, there are the colors. The forms, the shapes. Each flower stem has a life, an individuality of its own. It excites me to no end."

I nodded.

"I dare say in addition to skill acquired in over half a century in floral design, I know the Latin names and the culture of several thousand species of flowers. I have yet to miss a floral convention both in Texas and nationally. I teach a class at the community college on floral arranging. I have written three books on the subject." He pointed to three large books on his book shelf. "I even visit local flower farms and work with the farmers in their fields."

"That's interesting, Max." All I wanted to know was how he might help with the murder case. Patience has never been a strong suit for me.

"And yet people will not allow themselves the liberty to get carried away by something that cultivates their happiness, as I have with flowers."

"I'm with you. Nobody I know is happy in their job, except you and my girlfriend."

"How about you, is there something you love so much it consumes you?"

"I don't know. Maybe detective work. Don't know yet. I've had the fantasy since I was a kid of running a detective agency but this is my first real case. I've been a private investigator for how long has it been? I would estimate, let's see, for about a day."

Max chuckled.

"There, I admit it, I'm wet behind the ears. But, I've seen every *Rockford* and *Magnum P.I.* at least a dozen times."

"Are you taking pleasure in it thus far?"

"Yeah. It's like a puzzle. I'm just trying to fit the pieces together."

"Good analogy. I love puzzles as well, which segues into the other obsession in which I hold an abiding interest."

"Crosswords?" I asked, picking up a *New York Times* Sunday Crossword filled out neatly and completely in pen.

"No. It's spirituality, the occult, prediction, fortune telling, the lifelong quest if you will, to comprehend why we are here and where, if anywhere, we are off to subsequent to this life."

"Really?" Every so often, I wondered what the fuck it's all about, Alfie. I didn't lose sleep over it. I make it a point not to lose sleep over anything. Call me shallow but I figured I'd deal with the next life whenever I got to it. I admit I am more concerned about how the Dallas Cowboys will do next season.

"I read between the lines of our day-to-day existence, behind mere physical events and slip into the gap allowing one access to the inner sanctuary. I listen. I watch. I observe. I intuit. And yes, I even guess, but the vast majority of my conjectures I feel are on the mark.

"You know Yogi Berra used to say, *'you can observe a lot just by watching'*." I smiled. I liked Yogi and had not heard that one. Max continued, "People and situations can be predictable if we ardently observe. Scientists tell us we operate in nine different dimensions. Most people are fortunate to be aware of two or three. Time and space for instance."

"Nine. Wow." We were still not talking about Hippie Hollow. I wondered if Captain Hollers was playing a twisted joke on me.

"When someone enters the shop, let us say a male customer, he's here because of an obligatory holiday, Mother's Day, Valentines, a birthday or he wants to make amends with his girlfriend, boyfriend or wife."

Ponytail came swinging into the office wafting Herbal Essence and asked if we wanted refreshments.

"Coffee? Tea? Juice?"

Coffee for me. Cream and sugar. Tea with soymilk and maple syrup for Max. She left.

"See the fellow there?" Max pointed to a man who had entered the shop.

"I see him."

"It's late June now. July is rapidly approaching. July is the absolute worst time of year for flower sales. Independence Day? Not a big flower day. People are more interested in bottle rockets and M-80s than roses and sunflowers. They are not coming in demanding red, white and blue bouquets, you see. The offspring have graduated. Mothers Day has come and gone. Sometimes there is a wedding but ninety nine times out of a hundred, the female of the species will buy for that one. What is left, you ask?" He looked at me until I answered.

"Okay, what's left?"

"Excellent question, dear boy. Process of elimination, our fellow has either someone who has recently died, perhaps has been hospitalized, there is guilt about something or a secretary's birthday perhaps? After 50 years of this, that's all there is. However, I don't feel this fellow employs a secretary. See the dirt under the fingernails?"

You got to be kidding, I thought. I could barely see the man.

"The face? Not nearly morose enough for the dead or dying event. See the embarrassed smile?"

I nodded even though he looked like an ordinary Joe with an ordinary face.

"It is not sorrow, misery or angst. My educated guess? Trouble with the S.O."

"The S.O.?"

"Significant Other."

"Oh."

Ponytail was back with the coffee and tea. I took a sip.

"Now this is some good coffee!"

"Thanks, Kelly. Organic Peruvian espresso. A friend of mine air freights beans from a little organic coffee plantation in the Andes. Roasts the beans in his garage. He took me down there a few years back. Actually 'down there' is a misnomer. 'Up there' is more accurate since the plantation is at a much higher altitude. Coffee beans are green when they are harvested. Did you know of this?" This guy has a wealth of information about things about which I did not give a shit. I smiled.

"I did not *know* that! I just assumed they were brown."

"Green. I don't drink much coffee, I save it for special occasions."

"I drink a lot of coffee. And this is good."

As we sipped our beverages, Max told me of his studies with the Lamas in Tibet and with a Kahuna on the big island of Hawaii. We watched Kelly as she talked with the customer. She held up a finger as if to say *just a minute* and came bouncing back to the office.

"Sorry to bother you again, Max. There's Mr. Sullivan." She turned toward the man and waved a little wave. He waved back. "He had a fight with his wife and now he's regretting it. Said some things he wished he hadn't. Wants to make up big time. Asked if we could make her a real nice arrangement?"

"Okay. Tell Mr. Sullivan I'll be right there." Kelly bounced out. "Rivers, I have a pretty busy schedule today. There's Mr. Sullivan, and some members of the local chapter of the Procrastination Association are overdue. With my help they are going to create their own floral arrangements for their banquet tonight. I just hope they show up." Max flashed a smile but I didn't think it was funny, especially since he didn't laugh at my humor.

"It's nice of you to teach them."

"Altruistic? Not by a long shot. I receive a phone call a day from one organization or another for donations of flowers to their various and sundry causes. Instead I offer them fresh, organically grown flowers at a fair market price, and then offer a free mini-design course. It allows them to create their own arrangements. I get to work with my flowers and they learn to appreciate them as well."

I nodded.

"Anyway, Rivers, I would love to help with your project. As the Sufi master, Hazrat Inayat Khan once said, 'Destiny is not what is already made; destiny is what we are making.'"

"Ah, Hazrat," I said, looking at the quote I wrote. Do *not* go directly into the temple; first walk fifty times around it!"

"Excellent form, dear boy. Wonderful you know Hazrat Khan. And it is *so* true, is it not? Let us do this—meet me at Barton Springs Pool tomorrow morning at six A.M. We will have an opportunity to talk at length then."

I gave him my Hank the dog look and Max picked up on my angst.

"You *do* want my help?"

"Well, yeah. Sure, I'll meet you there. Should I bring my swimming trunks?"

"Only if you want to go swimming."

That'll work, I thought.

Chapter Six

*"All are lunatics, but he who can analyze his delusion
is called a philosopher."*

Ambrose Bierce

I maneuvered my new white F-350 Ford diesel dually pickup with the oversized tires through early morning traffic. I know, the truck's overkill for Austin. A ranch truck in a Lexus town, and I didn't need for folks to show me their I.Q. score to know that. Dad's '57 Chevy Apache had served me well. He for sure wasn't using it, but like Dad and Too Tall, the old Chevy was put to pasture. Mom was using it as a planter. It's a country thing.

Fuel for the Bubbamobile required large jack, even though diesel was a few cents cheaper than regular. When I bought it, the salesman told me going diesel would save me on fuel. I told him, "It don't matter." I liked the truck, I needed the elbow room and dang it all, I was going to buy the damn thing. When I bought it I did have a good job as a patrolman with the APD.

Buy a pickup in the Hill Country (the proverbial *sticks*) and it comes with a gun rack in the back window as standard equipment. But my 30-06 was at the townhouse in the closet next to my shotgun. In the rack instead, I carried my South West Texas State University maroon and gold Bobcat umbrella. The chances of rain in June, July and August were pretty damn slim in Central Texas, but a cowboy needs something in the rack.

Out in the hinterland it's perfectly okay to tote a shotgun, deer rifle, a weapon that could bring down a grizzly or a terrorist attack, whatever. But in Austin, San Antonio, Dallas or Houston, 'tis not politically correct. It's an etiquette thing. Maybe even a city ordinance thing. Best a cowboy can do to show he's a country boy just in town for a spell, is "When guns are outlawed, only outlaws will have guns" bumper sticker or the slightly subtler "Charlton Heston Is My President," next to the *NRA* emblem.

I caught the MoPac Expressway from the townhouse Patricia and I shared in South Austin. Exiting Bee Caves Road, I zipped through Zilker Park, past the Botanical Gardens, past the boulder island in the middle of the soccer fields, (vigilantly on the lookout for the park cops who would ticket you for a mile over the limit while all the while smiling and saying, "have a nice day"), on to Barton Springs Pool.

My mother brought me to the pool as a baby. Little red headed Bilbo, already the size of a full grown Hobbit, in my husky swim trunks, learned to swim here. Learned to dive here. Took my first date here. Saw my first set of topless feminine breasts here. (Not counting Mom's). Smoked my first joint here. I practiced hatha yoga on the hill with the Austin yogis. The Springs was as much home as the ranch in Blanco.

Austin grew up along with me, from a sleepy little cow town whose biggest employers were the state government and the University of Texas, into a city striving to replicate California's Silicon Valley. Positioned on the edge of the Balcones Escarpment, to the east the land falls away to black land prairie. To the west, it climbs into the Texas Hill Country. Cutting across from west to east is the Colorado River which winds down through the Highland Lakes of LBJ, Buchanan, Travis, Austin and Town Lake—the Colorado tamed and widened by the Longhorn Dam in East Austin.

Barton Springs is a natural pool and believed by Austinites to be the heart and soul of the city. Yellow Dog Democrats and Dyed in the Wool Republicans, liberals and conservatives, socialists and libertarians, populists and feminazis, protect the Springs as if it were their own heart and soul. Which, of course, it is.

In ancient times, the seven springs existing today were seven fountains, spewing cool crystal clear water high into the pre-Texas air. That was before the Spaniards *discovered* the place back in the 1500s. The Comanche and Tonkawa who lived in the area *must* have noticed the fountains. Even in these times with all its upstream use for golf courses, malls and development, each day millions of gallons of fresh water course through the middle of the pool and flow into Town Lake and ultimately dumps into the Gulf of Mexico.

No matter whether I visited the pool once a year or once a day, the first dive into the 68-degree water was an eyeball popper not to mention a gonad shriveler. The hotter the day, the colder it feels. Looking at the sparkling dark blue water, I realized I had been too many years away from the heart and soul. At college in San Marcos I still allowed myself time to drive thirty miles to Austin to swim at the Springs at least once a month. The Police Academy kept me captive and tampered with the connection. APD finished it off. My trips to this magical spot had become less and less frequent and then stopped altogether.

I walked briskly through the gate.

"5:57, good." The pool didn't collect money until eight o'clock. This is the time to get here. It was light but not bright and a dozen swimmers were already knifing through the water. I looked around for Max and when I didn't see him, entered the men's changing room, an open air patio with benches, sinks, showers and toilets around the edges. In the middle was a grassy patch for nude sun bathing.

"Hi, Rivers," said Max emerging from a shower stall. He put on his swimsuit and slung a towel around his neck. He wasn't wearing his glasses and squinted as he looked at me.

"Morning, Max." I glanced at my watch. Six A.M. on the dot. "I understand you're a regular at the Springs. How long you been coming here?" I asked taking off my clothes and pulling on my swimsuit.

"Yes I am a daily visitor. When the war concluded, World War II that is, I visited Austin. Barton Springs was out of town in those days. Not many autos, so the preferred method of access was by train."

"Really?"

"It has been spiffed up over the years. There were no sidewalks as we have now and the trees were at the water's edge." Max turned and exited, leaving me still getting changed. I hopped along behind the older man trying to get my boot off.

"I was with the British Commandos, attached to an American outfit. One of my best friends was a Texan. He told me about Barton Springs, which sounded too good to be true. But it was not." I had to agree with the man, Barton Springs was magical.

"I had an astrological reading done by a lady fair in France. I was concerned with where to settle after the war. She enlightened me on some possible locales such as Tibet, the Big Island of

Hawaii and Paris, which I love, and interestingly enough Austin, Texas. She said Austin would be a spiritual place for me. And you know what?"

"What's that Max?" I got my boot off. Since the pool was not officially open, we carried our street clothes with us.

"She was correct. After bumming around Europe after the war, I went to India and eventually I trekked to the Himalayas and Tibet. And then when the Reds came, I thought I would try the next place and came to this lovely town and I have been here ever since. I love to travel, love the occasional adventure like to the mountains and the Left Bank but there comes a moment on every ramble when I cannot wait to get back to Austin."

"I know that one. You were in World War II?"

"I lied about my age and they believed me or had such a dire need for manpower, my youth mattered not. I joined the British Commandos in time for the Normandy Invasion in '44. *Omaha was a beach* the Yanks used to say. I will never forget..."

Max didn't finish the sentence and was down the limestone steps and walking along the wide sidewalk that runs around the pool.

"Are you ready?"

"Sure. Been a couple of years since I hit the water but I used to come here a lot when I was a kid."

"I remember you. You were a cute little tyke. Do you remember me?"

"Well, you do look sort of familiar but come on now. This is a little *too* weird. You're telling me you remember me?"

"On the hill." Max pointed to the slope of green grass and pecan trees behind the diving board on the other side of the pool. "A couple of dozen chaps practiced hatha yoga on the hill, while co-eds in skimpy bikinis romped past. The objective of the yogis was to attain peace through meditation. The objective of the co-eds was to attain entertainment as the boys lost concentration. More than one young yogi took a nose dive in the grass."

"You did yoga on the hill?"

"Of course. There were the twins, the quiet chap with the curly black hair and beard, you with the red hair, wore it longer then. Skinny as a string bean. I was there. You didn't have much interest in *me* though. Too many pretty birds."

"Girls. There were always good looking girls, weren't there?"

"I have come to the pool every day for fifty years now. Rain, snow, no matter."

"You swim in winter. Why?"

"Actually Rivers, when the air temperature is 35, the 68 degree water temperature seems quite warm." Max took a three-step run by the lifeguard tower and dove in. He skimmed just below the surface of the frigid darkness for half the width of the pool, for what seemed a minute or more and reappeared down stream.

I tossed my things on the grass and dove in after him. Max neglected to mention when the temperature is 100, 65 degrees seems pretty damn freezing.

"Whoa!" I regressed to the dog paddle, trying to catch my breath. After a few moments, the coolness opened me to a clearer, brighter reality. The colors were sharper. I counted 256 of them. The huge pecan trees overhanging the pool were now greener. The light danced and sparkled on the water. A sliver of sunlight from the east peered over the tallest bank building in downtown Austin.

My usual witty repartee had been reduced to a monosyllable, namely, "Whoa."

Max swam a lap and then another and another. A full hour of laps. I did five, which I thought was pretty damn good but got bored long before Max got tired. I climbed out and lay on my towel under a pecan tree, soaking up the early morning sun. The air temperature at 8 A.M. was 80 degrees. By ten A.M. it would be pushing 90.

Sprinting barefoot across the black top parking lot to my rig, the Bubbamobile, I grabbed my briefcase and brought it to my open air office under the tree. Ah yes, life in Austin could be mighty fine. I grabbed a fistful of paperwork. Items I had found interesting from my reading the night before, I post-it noted.

As I lay there on my stomach, I compiled a *to do* list on a lined yellow pad. I swear by *the list*. It helped me graduate from college (it took seven years, but who knows how long it would have taken if I hadn't prioritized). I loved the feeling of accomplishment crossing off items gave me. I liked to include tasks which had been already accomplished, so I could have something to cross off. Immediate gratification.

- Max @ flower shop
- Max @ Barton Springs Pool

- FBI Dallas, call first
- Reverend Arvin Tanner – father of Travis & Merrylee
- Where is Lucinda Tanner? – aunt of Travis & Merrylee
- Go to Hippie Hollow, the scene of the crime
- Go to lakehouse
- Merrylee @ sanitarium
- Travis and Merrylee's mother, still in Colorado?
- Moses's parents
- Kristie's parents
- Reporter, T. Rex from newspaper
- Compile a list of APD detectives who worked on case

"That's a jolly good list." Max was wearing his glasses again, standing behind me. Water dripped from his body onto the grass. I closed the yellow legal pad and tossed it on the briefcase.

"Too late, I already saw it."

I could feel my face turning a couple of shades closer to my hair color. Like being caught with a hand in Mama's cookie jar.

"What I'm working on is confidential. It's a natural reaction to want to protect your information. It's not like I have something to hide from you, it's just at this point I don't know what you could do to help or even if you want to."

"I wouldn't have invited you here if I did not want to be of assistance to you. There is a concern with your list. It appears you have omitted some essential items."

"Like what?"

"Not the appropriate question."

"What?" I was getting a little pissed now and could feel the heat rising in my face.

"We can talk about it later. The process of investigation has more to do with continuing on than it does in being concerned about outcomes. The journey is the important component, not the destination. And so, I have faith any additional items you may need to add to your list will be revealed to you as you proceed. With faith, all will be brought into the light of recognition. That is the way it works. It is like climbing a mountain. You ever climb a mountain?"

"Sure."

"On foot?" He was looking at my pile of clothes—pointy toed cowboy boots, blue jeans, western shirt, big ass belt buckle, jacket and cowboy hat.

"No, I had a horse under me."

Max thought about it for a moment.

"It's the same. On a horse or on foot, you cannot see around the bend until you get there. You may have but thirteen items on your list at this moment but you cannot know the ultimate number with which you will end up."

I hadn't counted the items. Could have been ten, could have been twenty. I counted them. Thirteen. Okay, the guy was an *Evelyn Wood Reading Dynamics* magna cum laude.

"So, I suppose you know what's in store for me on this case?"

"Actually, no. What I do know is there will be bends and turns in your path and there will be oodles of fascinating adventures waiting for you."

"Oodles?"

"A large assemblage. May I have a sheet of paper?"

"Sure." I ripped a sheet off my pad and handed it over. He sat on the grass next to my towel. Even as a kid up on Yogi Hill, I could not get into the position he was in, soles of his feet pointing skyward, resting on his hip bones.

"And so, young man, you should now recognize I am willing to help you and," he paused, "if you want my help and I am assuming you do, because if you did not, you would not have entered my world twice, then you will have to bear with me."

"I want your help." I craned my neck to look at an early morning co-ed as she pranceu by. She stopped in front of us and squeezed her long blond hair, bending over so the water flowed into the pool. We both looked. He's not so above it all as he makes out, I thought. I also thought about how much I loved Austin.

She walked on. "This is what I require. Max handed the sheet of paper back to me. He recovered from the co-ed far quicker than I did. Ah, the benefits of age. I watched her walk down the sidewalk and up the steps. "You may add this to your list if you like." There were ten numbered items.

I stared at the paper. "I don't understand, Max. What is this?"

"My request may seem unconventional." He paused. "But you should know something about me."

"What's that?"

"I have folded myself into the fabric of the universe, into a layer of reality if you will, I can only surmise you are not familiar."

"Say what?" Up until then, I assumed I was a reasonably intelligent individual, a college graduate even. Although it took me seven years to get that piece of paper suitable for framing, I rationalized the excessive time was due more to excessive partying than to excessive stupidity. And yet, there were concepts my mind refused to grab a hold of, like trig. I figured I wasn't programmed to work like that.

"It's simply this, I bring to *this* physical reality," Max grabbed a tuft of St. Augustine grass and tossed it, a light southerly breeze took it out across the pool, "a depth of understanding, some believe is supernatural."

"You've *got* to be kidding."

"On the contrary, I am not. Kidding that is. Supernatural is a trifling beyond natural, sort of extra-natural. It's not like man and superman. More like regular unleaded and super unleaded. Are you familiar with the *Tibetan Book of the Dead?*"

"The what?" losing me big time. "How about the shamanistic practices of our own Native Americans? The Aborigines of Australia? Shambhala? The path of the warrior? That is *our* path, you and I, whether you realize it or not."

"I don't know, Max. I don't see myself as being a *path* type person." But, I thought, if I *were* on some sort of path or mission, it would be the path of the warrior. I could dig it. Maybe that's why I kept walking around the temple so many times.

"All human beings are on a path, Rivers. Whether it's the path of the Buddha toward enlightenment or the path of Christ consciousness or the aimless path through the drive-through at McDonalds..."

"Maybe you know things I don't," I said. "All I am sure of is Captain Hollers told me you helped him in ways he couldn't comprehend either and I'm here because *he's* got faith in you, period. So *super*-natural, or *extra*-natural, or just *plain* natural if you can help me out, I'll take it."

"I shall endeavor to reside with it on that basis," Max chuckled. "I suppose the upshot of my list is this, are you able to furnish me with the information? And are you willing to let me worry about what to do with it?"

"Well sure, I don't see why not. It's pretty straightforward. Yeah, all this should be available but I still don't get it."

"And the next question is how long will it take you? It is rather important, you see."

"Not long. I'm going out of town today. When I get back."

"Number three on your list. *FBI Dallas.* Don't forget to call first."

"Ah, right. Whatever. Anyway, I'll be up there for a day, maybe two and when I get back I'll get it for you."

"Alrighty then. Max got up. "Let us take it one step at a time. You obtain the data at your earliest convenience and I will refrain from tossing too much mumbo jumbo into the mix."

"Deal," I shook his hand.

"A quick piece of advice though. I may not be a professional sleuth but I discern enough about the process to be on the look-out for coincidences. It is in the incidence of coincidence," he looked up at the clouds passing overhead, seeming to admire the sound of what he just said, "you shall uncover the secret to solving this case. And I do have faith you will uncover some hidden secrets very rapidly now. The moment is ripe for the solving. Keep your eyes open when you are up there."

"Yeah, what did Yogi Berra say, "You can observe, what was it?"

"You can observe a lot just by watching." We both laughed.

"When is *your* birthday Rivers? And do you know what time of day you were born?"

I told him and he said, "Ah ha!" And started to walk away. "I'm overdue for my domino game. We play *Texas 42* on the hill now instead of standing on our heads. Seems we grey heads are not as fetching to the coeds as you younger studs, you know."

I smiled. It was nice to be thought of as a stud, even if it was a seventy year old man giving the compliment.

"Max?"

"Yes?" He turned around at the edge of the pool.

"You said *ah ha* when I told you my birthday, what was that all about?"

"You are a Sagittarius, dear boy. Of course you are aware of that. It is your Sun Sign. It reveals to me you are an adventurer. You will, as the *Fabulous Thunderbirds* used to sing, *be in the mood to tear it up.*"

I liked the T-birds who were from Austin and I often sang Kim Wilson's lyrics in the shower.

"You have fire in you, my boy. But, your rising sign, the sign you *appear* to be, is Cancer."

"What does it all *mean?*" I asked, doing my Austin Powers impression.

"It means," he didn't laugh at my impression, "you *appear* to others to be a homebody. You play the Hobbit like Mr. Baggins. But if you remember the story, Bilbo was at heart an adventurer such as yourself."

I shrugged. Sorry I asked.

"If you will resist the false instinct to remain in your hobbit hole, you will live some wonderful adventures and..."

Max took off his specs and slipped them in his swimsuit pocket and dove in the water. I missed the end of his sentence. He had his towel and clothes held up over his head to keep them dry. I watched him swim one-armed and get out on the other side, above the spot where the largest of the seven springs bubbles into the pool. That's where the Barton Springs Salamander, Austin's very own endangered species lives.

I read through Max's list again, shook my head as I paper clipped his list under mine on the yellow pad. I stuffed the papers back into my hand tooled leather briefcase and got up, sprinting up the grassy hill to the men's changing room, emerging a few minutes later in street clothes. I crossed the parking lot to the pickup. It was nine o'clock and warming rapidly. Time to crank up the a/c, shove a *Johnny Cash* in the CD player and take Barton Springs Road across town to the Interstate.

"I killed a man, just to watch him die," sang Johnny.

And what was the bullshit about tearing it up on some adventure? There is nothing I'd rather do than kick my boots off, pop the cap off a Shiner Bock and fall asleep on the couch watching ... zzzzz.

Chapter Seven

"There is no trick to being a humorist when you have the whole government working for you."

Will Rogers

Leaving the townhouse before breakfast to meet Max, combined with five laps at Barton Springs and two hours of fighting traffic on I.H. 35, all contributed to my ordering the *Hardy Breakfast* at the Elite Café in Waco. Four strips of bacon, three eggs, four pieces of toast, butter, jam, a stack of pancakes, maple syrup, a pile of grits, hot sauce, massive quantities of coffee with cream and sugar and orange juice.

In addition to the Elite Café, Waco, Texas is known for massive quantities of Baptists, dwindling Branch Davidians and the Texas Rangers (not the ball club but the law enforcement types) Hall of Fame. Franchise capital of the world and home of the Dr. Pepper Museum, Waco is halfway between Austin and Dallas and like Fort Stockton in West Texas, an oasis where you stop to fill up your tank and your stomach (every fast food franchise in America) and then get back on the road.

There was no better place to eat (in Waco) than the Elite, and my standards were low enough to eat just about anywhere.

A couple three times a year, in transit to a Cowboy, Rangers, Mavs, or Stars game or maybe a gun show, I'd swerve off the freeway, maneuver three quarters way around the only traffic circle this side of Paris—and that's not Paris, Texas, that's Paris, Oklahoma...and pull into the world famous Elite Café. It's a white washed wooden structure, a bit art deco and a notch above funky. Elvis, and that's not Costello, ate there. Folks at the café are damned proud of that. Not only had the King grabbed a burger there, he had caught some z's in a corner booth.

My waitress, who looked like a character from *Greater Tuna,* wore coke bottle thick, gaudy red glasses swept up to a point. It made her blue eyes seem extra large, like she was perpetually surprised. Her hair was as platinum as my visa card. *LURLEEN* was stitched across the right breast of her lime green uniform. She was chewing gum. Juicy Fruit.

"You got a good appetite." She noticed how I was tossing down the food. "You one of the Boys?"

"What boys?"

"You know, the Dallas *Cow* Boys."

"No." I laughed. I was re-reading the page and a half of data the FBI furnished to the APD Task Force. I looked up at Lurleen. "No, ma'am I'm nobody."

"Where you headed?"

"Dallas."

"Big *D,* huh? You know, I've never been to Dallas."

"Really?"

"Never been very far outta Waco." She cocked one hip higher than the other with the coffee urn resting on it. Fascinating. It was good for me to get out of Austin, to get on the road again, meet some new people. I was feeling good. Frisky. Maybe I was an adventurer after all, even though I could hardly wait 'til the day was over and I could kick off the Ropers, chug a cerveza or two, put my feet up and scan through the hundred or so channels on the tube until I found an old movie worth watching.

"How come an attractive girl like you never made it to the big city? Dallas is not far away. Two hours and you're in a whole different reality."

"Mine is a long, sad story. First I tended to my Meemaw and now it's my maw I'm watching after, but you don't want to hear all that." She sloshed coffee into a cup already just the way I wanted it, a perfect balance of java, cream and sugar.

"Tell you what, take off the apron, put down the coffee pot and come up to Big D with me. Right now. What do you say?"

"You're a bold one." Lurleen pinched her chin and looked off into space, considering the offer. I knew she wouldn't come, I mean, I hoped she wouldn't.

"Can't get away but tell you what, you see J.R., you tell him "hey" from me. They all came in here back when they were making the show. You know, *Dallas?* Larry Hagman and a bunch of writers and producers and whatnot, came in. He invited me up there too and I guess if I didn't take J. R. Ewing up on *his* offer, I'm going to turn you down too."

I stuck out my lower lip pretending to be hurt.

"Lots of celebs come in here."

"Like Elvis." I pointed to the plaque where the King once sat.

"Well yeah, of course. The Elite is famous for celebs. I never needed to go to Hollywood, 'cuz sooner or later they'd all show up here. But none more famous than Elvis Aaron Presley. I know this is going to date me but I was waitin' tables here at the Elite Cafe the night he came in. I was just a teenybopper. He sat right where you're asittiin'."

"Sure enough?"

"Oh, I wouldn't kid 'bout that. He asked me to come on up to Dallas and I turned him down too."

"Well, shoot. I don't feel so bad now."

"You want more coffee?" I put my hand over the cup. I drank about half of it so I could add more cream and sugar. And it was hot.

"Naw. I'm floating. Gotta get back on the road."

I figured I'd better ask for the check while she was there, which I did. I worked on a plan for the rest of the day, which is good since planning never has been a strong suit for me. The plan was, get up to Dallas, spend the remains of the workday with the Feds, make copies of anything new or interesting, and for the evening, take in a Texas Rangers baseball game. After which I'd find a *modestly priced* motel somewhere around the ballpark and stay up half the night watching crappy cable movies, eating potato chips, drinking dark beer and for dessert, Ben & Jerry's Ice Cream and peanut M&Ms.

Dropping a ten on the $8 breakfast check, I collected my papers and walked out into the bright sunlight. An Arvin Tanner tune was wailing away on the jukebox. "*I Left My Heart in Waco.*" Had to be a hit in these here parts. I think I heard it last time I was in Waco.

It took another two hours to get to Big D, find the FBI office, park the pickup and enter. There wasn't a sign identifying the building as the Federal Bureau of Investigation. After a series of Federal Building bombings where the FBI was targeted, other federal agencies asked them to get the fuck out of the building. Without so much as a press release, they moved in behind a Social Security Administration office.

I cooled my heels in the waiting room reading ancient copies of *Federal Employee* magazine, waiting for the clerk I'd talked with on the phone the day before. I asked him to get all the files the FBI amassed on Hippie Hollow ready for me. I figured, dang it all, it was my government, they ought to be working for me. Naïve, I know.

Photos of the President, the Attorney General, the Director of the FBI and the Dallas Agent-in-Charge, decorated the wall. An American flag hung in the corner.

After an hour, my man, a tall skinny dude of about fifteen showed up without explanation, apology or repentance for his tardiness and walked me back to a small room, a half dozen doors into the bowels of the FBI. Chair, desk, computer, telephone in a small windowless office. On the desk were a stack of files and floppy disks.

As I looked through the files, he said, "If you need any assistance, dial 7474 and I'll help you if I am able." I put up a finger to ask a question but when I looked up he was already gone.

I looked through the paper stack first. Not much. I identified the agents who investigated the case. This was a new piece of information. Agent in Charge Mark Davidson led the investigation. I was pretty sure this info was in the APD files but I had but scratched the surface on the multitude of boxes.

After a call to 7474, I found after holding for several minutes, none of the agents were still in Texas. One was in L.A., one in Chicago; one passed away, one retired. Davidson was now stationed at FBI HQ in Washington, D.C.

Of the floppy disks, eleven were labeled *Reverend Arvin Tanner* and one labeled *Hippie Hollow*. I loaded the *Hippie Hollow* disk into the slot on the p.c. I followed directions to open the thing and got a message in large threatening letters —

UNAVAILABLE FOR VIEWING
WITHOUT FBI CLEARANCE

It was the same nebulous guilty feeling you get with the — *this program has performed an illegal operation and will be shut down,* message.

I slipped in the first Arvin Tanner disk. Same message. The next ten all showed the same message. I added another item to my ever growing *to do* list.

Call my brother, John Rivers, a lawyer in Houston. John had legally changed his name to John. Only Mom persisted in calling him Gandalf. Like Bilbo Baggins, he felt Gandalf was not a serious lawyer name worthy of respect—such as Racehorse. I hoped John could fill me in on the *Freedom of Information Act* and could tell me if there was some way I could get access to those files.

First things first though. I dialed Bergstrom Investigation's 800 number. The phone on the desk wouldn't connect.

There was one more disk titled *Reverend Arvin Tanner*. I went through the drill and this one opened.

Only son of cattle rancher and oilman Tex and Rita Tanner, of Marathon, Texas, who died in 1960 and 1971 respectively. They left their two children Arvin and Lucinda each 1/4th of their estate, the remaining half to be divided between any children Arvin and/or Lucinda might have. While Lucinda has remained childless, Arvin had two children, Travis and Merrylee. The two children are entitled to receive 1/4th of the estate.

Arvin attended Texas Christian University, dropping out his junior year to join a country and western band named The Mavericks. The band's success was due in no small part to the popular singing voice of Arvin. After twenty years and a dozen gold records, he quit the music business when he was called into the Christian ministry.

In 1980, Reverend Arvin Tanner founded his own church, The Church of the Ark. It is located in Austin, Texas and church services are broadcasted every Sunday over the National Christian Network. His congregation is one of the largest in the U.S., at 2000 per televised service. The Church of the Ark runs a number of outreach programs and is best known for its stance against rap and hip hop music and sees the emergence of hip hop as a sign the end of world has begun and we have entered into the end times.

His closest friends are conservative politicians and other religious leaders. He owns a home in Austin, Texas, a townhouse in Chevy Chase, Maryland, a suburb of Washington, D.C. and a home in Aspen, Colorado. He is divorced from Lily Morganthal, the mother of his children, who lives at the Aspen home. His two children, Travis and Merrylee live at the Austin home.

The report droned on and on without revealing anything interesting except the position Reverend Arvin Tanner and the Church of the Ark held on the subject of rap music. They were against it. It was like saying they didn't like Blacks without coming right out and saying *I hate niggers*. Written before Hippie Hollow, I thought. Enough already, I dialed 7474.

"Yes sir. Can I help you?" The clerk sounded agitated.

"This is Rivers."

"Yes, I figured as much. Nobody else calls me. What do you want sir?"

"I've been looking through the files and computer disks and I'm not coming up with the information I want. For instance, I can't find anything about the investigation of the murders we talked about on the phone yesterday. Is there any way you can help me with this?"

"Exactly what *sort* of information are you looking for?"

"Well, as I mentioned yesterday before I drove *all* the way up here, I'm investigating the Hippie Hollow homicides hoping to find FBI data, interviews, conclusions, speculation, anything. We've provided you all with the case number and I understand my office in Austin obtained clearance from your office in Austin to go though this stuff."

"Okay, what's the problem?"

"All but one of these disks are marked "UNAVAILABLE FOR VIEWING OUTSIDE THE FBI" on them."

"Now, I *can* tell you why that is."

"Okay, I'll bite, why is that?"

"Because it's classified information and a matter of National Security."

"National Security?"

"Yes sir, this information is not available unless you are with the Bureau. And even then only on *a need to know basis*. Sorry. Will there be anything else?"

I felt the beginnings of a slow burn. I had experienced it before. The time the gang opened a pharmacy across from the school. Again when Lt. Ass Wipe bad-mouthed my dad. I figured I had better learn how to calm down, took a deep breath and continued.

"I tried to make a call to my office in Austin but for some reason the call didn't go through."

"I can tell you *why* that is."

"*Why* is that?"

"There is a policy here at the bureau. No long distance calls unless you first enter the code number."

"Oh, I see. What's the code number?" I was trying to sound cheerful. "I'd like to call my boss at Bergstrom Investigations in Austin, see if we can straighten this whole thing out."

"Sorry, I don't have the code numbers."

"Really?"

"No, sir."

"What good are you then?"

"Pardon me, sir?"

"Okay, where do I get these mysterious code numbers?"

"That I *can't* tell you but I can *try* to find out. No one has ever asked me that question." He reminded me of the little receptionist dipshit on *Saturday Night Live* who wouldn't let Jesus in to see his boss. *And you are the Son of Whom?*

I stared into the phone for one awful moment and took another breath.

"In the meantime you can use the pay phone over at the H.E.B. Grocery across the street."

"It's an 800 number I'm calling."

"Sorry. Can't make any calls from the FBI phones, without..."

"Without the code number?"

"Security reasons."

"National Security?"

"Just plain FBI security."

"Even if," I searched for an acceptable word, "okay I'll go across the street but first, is there *anyone* in this office who worked on Hippie Hollow or has had *anything* to do with the Hippie Hollow case? A clerk, a secretary, an agent, anybody?"

"I'll have to find out and get back to you. On second thought, can you come back tomorrow, we're getting ready to close and the Bureau has a strict *no overtime* policy?"

I left the papers and disks on the desk, walked out of the office, up to the front and out the door without signing out. Damn I'm a rebel. I then walked past the Social Security office and across the street to the H.E.B. Grocery. I called Bergstrom from the pay phone. I wasn't surprised Captain Hollers had already left for the day. Why the hell not? Goddamned fuckin' perfect end to a perfect fuckin' day.

"This sucks," I threw my briefcase across the front seat of the Bubbamobile. It bounced off the seat, hitting the dashboard, it put a little scratch in the paint job and hit the floor scattering paper everywhere. "Okay." I banged my head on the steering wheel a couple of times until I realized it was a stupid thing to do. And it hurt like shit.

I pulled my hat further down on my forehead so the red mark wouldn't show and drove through the nearest golden arches, ordering a Big Mac, large fries and a Coke. I thought of what Max told me about aimless paths through McDonalds but who gives a shit, I was hungry. The eggs and grits of Waco had to my good fortune digested hours earlier.

I was already feeling better. The warm familiarity of the nameless clone who took my order cheered me up. The fact my dinner cost me $5.72, the same as it cost in Austin, was somehow comforting.

After dinner, I took I.H. 20 to Arlington hoping to score a ticket for the game. The Rangers were my team and they were playing the Dodgers in an inter-league game. The Dodgers were my favorite team in the National League. I liked them because my dad liked them. I needed to be at the game and if I couldn't score a ticket it would just about put me over the edge.

Games between the American and National Leagues were a new thing and even though baseball has been around for a hundred years it takes some time to come up with new ideas. I was afraid since this was the first time the Dodgers ever came to town it would be sold out. But I got a ticket! On the third base side, up in the nosebleed section. Felt like Bob Uecker sitting up there all alone, up where the beer vendors fear to tread.

I was a little early, with an hour and a half before the first pitch.

"Fuck this!" I got up and jogged down hundreds of steps to field level. *This is more like it!* Leaning over the railing, I watched the Dodgers and then the Rangers loosen up. When the landscape crew came out to roll and rake, I climbed back to my seat and opened my briefcase.

As the first pitch neared, the seats below me and around me, filled. There wasn't anyone above me since I was on the last fucking row. Disgusted looks came from fathers and sons who couldn't believe some asshole would bring *work* to the Ballpark. Sacrilege. What the hell *was* I doing bringing my briefcase to a baseball game anyway? Was I losing it? Had I become a worka-holic my first week of work?

Naw. I closed it and put it under my seat.

The game was a classic. First L.A. took the lead, then Texas. A nice kid with a Rangers hat in the next seat offered me a peak through his binoculars. It was 6 to 6 at the bottom of the ninth, two outs, two men on for the Dodgers and the Ranger hurler struck out the batter.

Extra Innings! A total of sixteen innings and three hours later, our shortstop connected with a hanging slider, floating it over the fence onto the grassy patch in center field. A dozen little leaguers up past their bedtimes scrambled for the ball.

Rangers win 10 to 9.

I stopped to buy a Dodger's cap to add to my collection which started with games in my childhood and walked with the crowd to the parking lot. It's great when the home team wins but an hour to exit the ballpark and another getting on the freeway dif-fuses the magic. I put in a *Flatlanders* CD and waited it out.

And stopped at the first motel.

"Good evening sir, did you have a reservation?"

"Well, no. Do you have any rooms? Non-smoking?"

"Afraid not sir. What with the Rangers in town, Water World and Six Flags, I doubt if there is a room in Arlington. Would you like me to check around, see if something's available?"

"Thanks, I'd appreciate it." I became one with an overstuffed velvet chair in the lobby. It had been a long day. I left home at 5:30 A.M. getting up before Patricia for once. Swimming laps at Barton Springs seemed like a week ago, then the drive in heavy traffic up I.H. 35, the afternoon with the Feds, the evening at the Ballpark and a couple of hours in traffic.

Just as I was dozing off, the clerk called me over. "There's nothing doing here in Arlington or Dallas but I was able to find something in Fort Worth, 30 minutes on Interstate 20."

"Great. I appreciate it." The clerk handed me the phone to confirm the reservation.

Forty five minutes later I was showering off the dust of the day. Wrapped with a white motel towel around my waist and dry-ing my hair with another, I picked up the phone and dialed home. Ah, this is living. Use two towels and drop them to the floor.

It was very late and Patricia would be long ago in bed. I got the machine and left her a short message about my day, then flipped on the tube. An old Julia Roberts movie, the one where she and Denzel Washington are chased across the swamp by bad guys. During a commercial I trekked across the expanse of my room to my fifth floor window and pulled the cord opening the drapes. I stood there naked as the day I was born, looking out over the Fort Worth skyline. Directly across the street was Texas Christian University.

"Wow, this is weird!" I had not consciously planned to visit TCU. This must be at one of those bends in the road, I thought. Max told me to watch for coincidences. "But this is a bit much!" Both Travis Tanner and his father Reverend Arvin Tanner were ex-Texas Christian students.

Chapter Eight

*"You can lead a boy to college but you
cannot make him think."*

Elbert Hubbard

I sat bolt upright in bed, a ringing sound bouncing through the canyons of my head. I was dreaming of swimming at Barton Springs. As I made the turn at the bottom end of the pool, the dam broke and the water gushed out, tossing me head over heels downstream. I careened into downtown Austin, down Sixth Street on a wall of water, past Kickers Saloon. My ex-boss, Jimmy Don, dressed in his rodeo clown outfit handed me a Shiner Bock as I rushed by.

"You can't just up and quit on me!" I floated past APD Headquarters. Lt. Ass Wipe had his hand out, asking for my badge and gun. I looked down and realized I was naked. No badge. No gun. I did have a humongous hard on. I laughed. Figured the joke was on him.

Captain Hollers shot past me in a giant truck tire innertube. I did a double take. Looking again, he had morphed into Elvis. The older, chunkier Elvis. He tossed me a scarf which I caught and put around my neck. It turned into an anaconda. I opened my eyes gasping for air. The sheet was wrapped so tight around my neck it cut off my air supply. Unraveling it, I saw the green neon letters of the hotel's digital clock radio.

6 A.M.

I picked up the ringing phone. I had been asleep a couple of hours.

"What took you so long to answer?"

"I was fighting a snake."

"Billy!"

"No, really. I was attacked by a giant anaconda."

"You wish."

"Who is this?" There was but one person who'd mess with me at such an ungodly hour. Quite a number of people would mess with me at just about any hour, but one I wouldn't hang up on.

"Billy. It's me Patricia." Mock hurt tones. "I spent the night all alone in this big empty townhouse with nothing to keep me warm except grandmother's quilt and Jay Leno." Fake sobs. God I loved that girl.

"Not the Italian guy again."

"How come you didn't call me before I went to bed? And who did you sleep with? Gotta a girl in the room with you?"

"No such luck. I did invite the waitress from breakfast to come to Dallas with me but she turned me down. She also turned down J. R. Ewing and Elvis, so I went to the Rangers game and they won." I have always felt honesty was best because it always sounds like so much bullshit.

"Uncle Rick put you on a pretty good expense account to let you stay at the *Four Seasons*. Tell me we're not paying for this."

"We're not paying for this. Bergstrom's picking up my expenses." They would pay for it. When I talked to the registration person on the phone I hadn't asked the cost and they didn't volunteer it. I suppose if one is staying at the Four Seasons, one should not care about such a trifling.

"Good. It's been twenty four and one half hours since I saw your big freckled butt get out of bed and I miss you terribly. Tell me you won't be doing too much traveling on this case."

"I won't be doing too much traveling on this case." I repeated her intonation. Women love it when you do that.

"Good. I'm off to the salt mines." Patricia worked in the accounting department at *Texas Highways* magazine.

"Okay Pat."

"Billy?"

"You don't like it when I call you Pat, right?" All during college, Patricia was Pat or Pattie. Now she was Patricia. This type of thing is hard on a man.

"I do prefer Patricia, but we need to talk."

"I know. But this job may be just what we need to get the financial stability we're looking for." I can talk the talk. "It's temporary but your uncle said if I did a good job there is an excellent possibility I can stay on with Bergstrom. I won't know for awhile but I *need* to do a good job with this." I can walk the walk.

"I know you will Billy. Let's set a time so we can talk about our future, okay? We've been putting it off for so long now."

"Sure. When?"

"How about Monday night? No Monday Night Football this time of year, right?"

"Right, it's a date. Say Pat, Patricia, before you run off, will you do me a favor? On the shelf above the headboard is my address book."

"Who you want me to look up, *Girls of the Metroplex?*"

"Now, *that's* funny. No, I haven't got time for that sort of thing on this trip." I was so above group sex with multiple good looking women. "I need my brother John's telephone number in Houston."

She gave me the number and we talked for a few more minutes and went our separate ways. Patricia to the accounting department. Me to the bathroom. I showered, shaved, dressed, re-packed and checked out of the hotel. My night there put a serious dent in my visa card. I was glad the god of plastic had let it fly. I jammed the receipt into the manila envelope to keep company with the receipt for breakfast at the Elite, dinner at McDonalds and gas. The Bubbamobile was not fuel efficient and I figured Hollers would shit when he saw I used two tanks getting from Austin to Ft. Worth, if he didn't shit over the Four Seasons bill first. Either way it would not look pretty. I threw my overnight bag in the pickup and walked across the street to observe some reptiles in their natural habitat.

I love a college campus and Miss Southwest Texas State University in particular. San Marcos, Texas—party town U.S.A. Three to four dudettes for every dude. A ratio to which I was able to relate for seven years. I hoped to feast my eyes on something decent while at TCU, albeit Christian. Some of the cutest women I have ever witnessed were Christians, such as Patricia. But in late June, TCU was as dead as a hornytoad crossing I.H. 20.

As I strolled along a tree lined sidewalk, I thought about Patricia. I was closing in on asking the woman I adored to walk the aisle with me. Unfortunately, she would say yes. We'd settle down and produce some kids. It's what we *both* wanted, wasn't it?

And yet, I'm a meat and potatoes, bacon and eggs, pepperoni on the pizza, red blooded American ex-jock, who dang it all, missed looking at and being looked at by, the red blooded American female. Maybe I'd outgrow it. Didn't seem like it would happen anytime soon. I still looked at myself as I passed by mirrors. I'm vain. Have to admit it. Reminds me of the lyric, *I bet you think this song is about you, don't you?*

The Office of Administration was running a skeleton crew. With no classes, students, faculty and administrators had no reason to be there. The only person working was a pert young thing behind the counter. Mousy hair in a bun with unattractive black rimmed glasses. I fantasized taking them off and letting her hair down. She found Travis' student file for me.

Travis was a decent student. Dean's List (a list that escaped me during my seven years at Southwest). He earned 34 credits his freshman year and pre-registered as a sophomore but failing to attend orientation, was dropped. Because of the tragedy, money for tuition, room and board was refunded in full to Reverend Arvin Tanner of Austin, Texas.

Accounting Major. Lived in a dorm. Must have had a roommate.

"Say Miss, sorry to keep bugging you, but could you tell me who occupied room 306, the Tanner Dorm Building?" Reverend Arvin Tanner donated a few mil. to the University and was blessed with an Honorary Doctorate and his name on a building.

"This coming semester? Last semester? What?"

"Oh, sorry. This would be five, no six years ago. One of the students in the room would have been this same Travis Tanner, the boy we just looked up. I need his roommate's name, if possible."

"Okay," she put down the file she was working on, got up and walked to the other side of the room to a bank of filing cabinets. Nice ass. "We keep these records for ten years."

"Yes, here we go. His roommate was Winslow Christian."

"I know this is a stretch but you wouldn't happen to know where Mr. Christian is these days, would you? Like a permanent address?"

"I don't have it in the file but..."

"Shit! I mean, darn it."

Got a smile out of her. "What I should have said was... he's still at the University."

"Really?"

She came over to the counter. "Winslow Christian is an associate professor at TCU. And I can tell you *exactly* where he is this very moment."

"Really? This very moment? Where's that?"

"He's in the main library. I saw him going up the library steps this morning." She picked up a University map. "Here we are and here's the library." She took a yellow highlighter pen and traced the route. "He's hard to miss."

"Why's that?"

"He's as big as you are." She gave me the look. Maybe she likes big. "His hair is so blond it's white. Played varsity football at TCU, you know. When you get to the library, go to the second floor, *Religious Studies*. Bet you'll find him researching his doctoral thesis."

"Winslow Christian? I knew I recognized the name. One of the top running backs to come out of TCU, maybe even the conference. The Cowboys drafted him but he didn't sign. Disappointed a lot of fans."

"I suppose he felt his education was more important than the NBA."

"NFL."

"Whatever."

"Here." I reached in my shirt pocket and pulled out the piece of chocolate the Four Seasons placed so tenderly on my pillow.

"Well, aren't you sweet."

"See ya, and thanks." I took a couple of steps, looked back and caught her watching me. She looked away. I smiled, pushed open the door and jogged down the steps. Ah, the ego-inspiring thrill of the stray look. God, I'm vain. And know this song is about me.

A four minute sprint and I was at the library. Three steps at a time to the second floor. Got the old blood moving. With the shortness of breath, I flashed back to running up and down the bleachers at Bobcat Stadium in football training camp.

Thought I'd be a high school football coach. Thought Coach B. B. would run up and down the bleachers with the guys, put on pads and hit the biggest guy. I would never lose the edge.

"Boy, Coach B. B. is one tough motherfucker. No wonder we always take the conference." I was losing the edge. I gasped for air at the top step.

Religious Studies took the entire second floor. Looking around the large room, my eyes locked on a tall, broad shouldered man with short blond hair pulling papers from a copy machine. I walked over to him.

"Winslow Christian?"

He looked me over, took in the boots, sports coat, jeans, rodeo belt buckle and bent back over his work.

"Let me do this and I'll be right with you."

I thought back to a TV press conference a couple of years back. The Dallas Cowboys traded their number one draft pick for the next two seasons, tossed millions on the table, coughed up a backup tight end to get local Metroplex hero, Winslow Christian. He was sewn up. He was theirs. The press conference was a formality to announce the signing. But old number 44 blew them all away.

As a Cowboy fan I was disappointed. They loved to disappoint me. I knew that. They would beat the 49ers one week and lose to the Saints the next. I got over it but doubted the Cowboy management would ever forgive Winslow Christian his transgression.

"Gentlemen I'm sorry, because of personal reasons I will not go into, I cannot in good conscience sign with your organization." He got up and walked out of the room. Never looked back, ruining any chance of ever playing professional football.

Christian lifted the lid on the copier and retrieved the original. He stacked his copies on a nearby table and picked up another original and placed it on the glass, pushing *start*. The ancient copier surged back into action.

"Cachink, cachink, cachink."

"This copier is old but it makes the best copies in Fort Worth. Okay, now what can I do for you?" He was my height and build and looked me right in the eye.

"Name's B. B. Rivers." I offered my hand to Winslow. "I'm working a case with Bergstrom Investigations in Austin. Doing a follow up on the Hippie Hollow murders."

"Don't tell me *that* is still out there?"

"Afraid so. I understand you roomed with Travis Tanner during his freshman year?"

Winslow nodded, glancing over to check the progress of his print job.

"You go to some of the same classes? Socialize?"

"I was a year ahead of Travis."

"You all party together?"

"No. At the time I was owned by the Athletic Department. Travis was in the Business Department, Accounting. The only time we spent together was lying in our bunks talking about our day."

"Did you know Travis before TCU?"

"My first year roommate joined the Marines, leaving an opening. Some strings were pulled and Travis was assigned to my room. His father's name was on our building."

"That would be Reverend Arvin Tanner?"

"Reverend A, Travis called him. I don't think they got along very well."

"How do you mean?"

"Travis thought Reverend A was a hypocrite and it very well may have been true. I don't know. I saw Reverend Tanner one time when he attended a father-son function. Little guy with a whiney Ross Perot voice. A tone that drives you up a wall. Turn on the TV any Sunday morning and there he is."

"I know what you mean."

"Travis came to TCU disillusioned with his father and, unfortunately, with Christianity as well. And I say unfortunately, because an anti-Christian attitude goes against the grain at a Christian university."

"I bet."

"He was sad. Unhappy. Angry. Unsure of himself. And then he met a girl."

"Really?"

"Oh, yes. Her name was Angel. But she wasn't. An angel that is. Not your typical twice on Sunday and Wednesday night church goer. She wasn't even Christian. From what I understand, in the beginning Travis did not know Angel was the daughter of the Black rap star Iced Chai."

"You got to be kidding?"

"No, I'm serious. And this is the interesting part, Reverend Tanner's life's work is the revelation—rap and hip hop music portend the end times."

"I hear that. What was the attraction?" I said it and knew right off what the attraction must have been.

"I don't know. Travis was rebelling from his father's influence and I remember thinking at the time Angel must have wanted to get away from some dangerous influences. You know her father was murdered, and TCU must have been the ticket. The fact they connected at all is, at the very least, interesting. She, of course, was black and Travis was white. That alone was an astonishing sight around here.

"Really."

"Iced Chai's music was very popular about ten years ago. His parents were African and East Indian. Iced Chai became more Anti-Christian and anti-white the older he got. To his credit, before he died, he started a foundation to help underprivileged children."

"So, Travis didn't know Angel's father was Iced Chai?"

"Not until the day she left."

"Wow."

As we talked, Winslow reloaded the copier and collated the copies on a big oak table.

"When was the last time you saw Travis?"

"The last day of his freshman year. He was on his way to Austin for the summer. I drove him to the airport. He traveled by bus or he'd bum rides. He hated that. After he met Angel, they would walk everywhere together. Not so bad for him then."

"So, he left about a month before his Aunt's party?" I made a note.

"I did talk to him on the phone a couple of times since."

"Really?"

"He called me the night he *disappeared*." Winslow did the quote thing with the first two fingers of his hands as he said *disappeared*.

"What?"

"He called me from his Aunt's house."

"Really?"

"Yes, really. You say *really* quite a lot. Did you know that?"

"So I've been told. I guess I don't *really* notice it myself." I did the quote thing.

Winslow managed a weak smile.

"You wouldn't remember what time he called you?"

"It was 3:05 A.M., according to the GTE long distance records. The FBI traced the call from his Aunt's house to the pay phone downstairs. Didn't take them long to figure out it was me he called. They showed up the next day. You didn't know this?"

"I'm, ah, sort of playing catch up. Like when a linebacker lets a half back like you through, hoping the secondary will pick you up and then they don't." I smiled.

"I hate football analogies."

"Sorry. So, what did you and Travis talk about that night on the phone?"

"He was high as a kite. Too many damned pink margaritas, he said. If he hadn't identified himself I wouldn't have recognized the boy. Did not sound like the Travis Tanner I had known."

"So he was drunk?"

"Most assuredly."

"Drugs?"

"Difficult to say." Winslow motioned for me to join him at a big oak library table. I sat across from him. "Travis was ranting about his father. *Reverend A is a hypocrite. Reverend A scared off Travis' mother.* He mentioned something about a deal his father was involved in. After a few minutes of incoherent ramblings, he began to laugh hysterically. Then he said, *You know I'm scared Winslow, real scared.* He and Reverend A had a big blowout. He also mentioned there was someone at the party threatening him."

"Well, we know somebody killed Travis. Did he say anything about who was threatening him? A description maybe?"

Winslow gave me a strange look I couldn't read.

"No description. I told him to lay off the juice, brew some black coffee and drink as much as he could get down. If he threw up that was good, get the stuff out and then call me in the morning. He said he would."

"I guess he didn't call you in the morning. According to the estimated time of death of the teenagers," I leafed through the file to the Coroner's report, "they were killed at 3:45 A.M., less than an hour after you all talked."

"You are correct, he didn't call back the next morning." Winslow gave me the same look, pushed the papers and books aside, glanced first to the right and then to the left, and looked at me for a long uncomfortable moment.

"What?"

"I'm going to tell you something, but ... and I'm very serious about this ... you must promise me you won't tell another soul."

"I don't know. Depends on what it is. I have an obligation if a crime has been committed to turn over..."

"Okay, I can live with that. But consider the possible consequences before you repeat what I tell you. It's a matter of life and death."

"Whose life and whose death?"

"Travis Tanner's for one. Maybe yours. Maybe mine."

"What are you talking about?"

"Well, quit asking so many damn questions and listen to what I'm saying." I opened my mouth but shut it again.

"Gotcha."

"I talked to Travis Tanner a couple of days after the party, and two other occasions since."

"What do you mean?"

"Just what I said, Travis Tanner is *not* dead."

Chapter Nine

*"When the gods wish to punish us
they answer our prayers."*

Oscar Wilde

Winslow repeated his revelation, this time slower and enunciating each word, as a teenager might talk to retarded parents.

"He is *not* dead. At least not two years ago, the last time we talked on the phone."

"What?"

"You say *what* a lot too."

"What did you just say? You talked to Travis?" The meaning of the man's words was slow to catch up to my brain.

"Here is the actual fact, Mr. Rivers," still talking slowly. "Travis Tanner was *not* killed as everyone has believed all these years. He phoned me three, maybe four, days after his alleged death. Until the phone call, I too believed he was dead."

"This is incredible. Who else knows about this?"

"Travis was adamant I not reveal his secret, not to the FBI, nor to the police and *especially* not to Reverend Tanner."

I let that digest, again looked out the window, trying not to interrupt, waiting for Winslow to continue.

"Travis called me again maybe a year later, asking a favor. He wanted me to try to contact her and to let her know he was alright."

"So did you do that?"

"I called a fellow I knew in the Iced Chai organization. Their office is in New Orleans." I wrote that down. I would need to talk to Angel. "My friend said he'd get word to her. So, I left a rather cryptic message for Angel saying something like, *Mr. T of Austin is still with us.* Or something I figured only she would understand. Neither my friend nor Angel called back. Travis called once more maybe a week later, to see if I located her. I told him about leaving her a message and that I wasn't able to talk to her. That was the last time he called." Winslow shuffled some papers.

"Okay. APD came to see you?"

"APD? Oh yes. The Austin Police Department. They were here. Captain, hmmm, I don't remember his name, an older gentleman."

"Probably Warlick."

"Yes, that's right. He came twice. First time was just after I had spoken with Travis and the boy said not to tell anyone he was alive. So I honored his wishes and didn't. The second time the policemen came was a couple of years later, said he was retouching the bases. Had I remembered anything? It was then I told him about the telephone conversations with Travis. I told him, because I felt Travis hadn't been forthcoming with me."

"How's that?"

"I couldn't go traipsing after some girl who cared less about him. I tried to level with the boy, but he refused to hear it. He hung up on me. And to be honest, I don't like being put in a position where the only choice open to me is to bare false witness. Three years had passed since the murders. And I felt Warlick was a decent enough fellow, genuinely interested in finding out who killed those kids. So I told Warlick everything. He told me if I wanted to keep Travis alive, I should never mention it again, to anybody. He said it could be very dangerous. There were some things at work that were complicated and there was a very bad man, a cold blooded killer who would not hesitate to kill me or Travis or anyone who posed a threat to him."

"I wonder what that is supposed to mean." I said.

"There's more." He looked around the room and whispered.

"About a month after Warlick's last trip up here, I was curious so I called the captain at the Austin Police Department. I wanted to know if what I told him had helped. What I found was that Warlick was no longer running the investigation. Another fellow had taken over and when he came on the line I asked him if Warlick had mentioned visiting me. He said he didn't know anything about our conversation and Warlick had retired a month earlier, which must have been very soon after we talked. I asked if I could get Warlick's home phone or address and he said it wasn't possible to do that."

"I was with APD when Captain Warlick retired and it seemed to be a hurry-up deal to me too. But one more question and I'll get out of your hair. And I want you to know I appreciate all this."

"Sure that's okay."

"During any of your conversations with Travis did he tell you what happened that night?"

"No. I did ask but he told me I would be better off *not* knowing about that night or where he was hiding out."

"Well now. This *is* interesting."

"What do you think?"

"This much we *do* know," I itemized the events on my fingers, "someone killed those two kids. He didn't kill Travis for some reason and doesn't seem to know where Travis is. The killer is presumably still out there somewhere. Waiting for something?" I shrugged. "Travis is alive but hiding. An APD captain covered up vital evidence and then *disappeared* himself." I did the quote thing.

"And a rather rich someone, wants this investigation set back on the *front* burner. Well Mr. Christian, you've given me quite a bit to think about. Appreciate it." I offered my hand as I stood up.

Winslow Christian stood and shook my outstretched hand and sat again.

"What are you working on there?" I asked as I put the yellow pad in my briefcase."

"It's my doctoral thesis on *The Rebellion of the Next Generation.*"

"Hmmm." I left the library feeling I asked some damn good questions and gotten some damn interesting answers. The questions I hadn't asked were more personal and not a part of this investigation. "Why Winslow Christian, best footballer to come out of TCU since Bob Lilly hadn't signed with the Boys? And if he had seen J. R.?

I found a payphone at the student union and called Bergstrom again. Hollers had stepped out. Donut break, I thought.

I called my brother John in Houston and asked him about the Freedom of Information laws. John said there were three ways for obtaining information from the Federal Government. To be an insider and steal it, buy it or sue their ass for it.

"Forget that shit, Bro! I need it today, not ten years from now."

I asked John if he heard from the folks. Our dad had incurred the double whammy of retiring from APD and before he could get a line in the water, was diagnosed with Alzheimer's type symptoms. We knew something was wrong with Dad but not what. He started investing in llamas, then boer goats and then emus. But always just after the craze hit its peak. He had brought in his first shipment of parrots when Mom put a stop to that shit. He went down hill fast after that and Mom ended up having to do all the chores at the ranch, raised and sold cattle, turkeys, chickens and llamas, goats, emus and all but one of the parrots – Paco, and worked an egg and raw cow's milk route.

Dad handled the TV watching and the singing of show tunes. He could sing the entire score from *Oklahoma!* and *West Side Story. When you're a Jet you're a Jet all the way from your first cigarette to your last dying day.*

Dad remembered every line from every song he ever heard, but couldn't talk or remember anybody he'd met and of course could not remember to do the chores. Seeing Dad like that was hard for me. I was away for college, stayed at the ranch only until I moved in with Patricia, which corresponded to Dad's breakdown. Mom's been mad about that. She and John talked on the phone once a week. Even though I lived an hour away, I hadn't seen or phoned her for months.

I ramped up on I. H. 20 east towards Dallas for FBI, *take two.* The sole piece of info I uncovered this time—was this—there wasn't anyone in the Dallas office who had worked on the Hippie Hollow investigation. I still could not access the files.

The traffic coming out of Big D at rush hour was a hell of a lot more intense than anything we get in the much smaller Austin. With three major interstates all colliding in Dallas, it took a solid hour of bumper to bumper to get to the outskirts. By eight P.M. I found myself back at the Elite Café in time for dinner, or supper, as they say in Waco.

"Hi handsome," said Lurleen, "You say *hey* to J. R. for me?"

"Naw, I asked around and kept my eyes peeled but I missed him this trip." I put my hand to my forehead like a salute and looked around squinting my eyes. "You must put in some hellacious hours." Lurleen showed me to the Elvis booth from the morning before.

"Actually Hon, this is my long day, six A.M. 'til ten P.M. and my dogs are barkin'. I've been at this way too long. You want some iced tea? I'll give ya a minute. Be right back with your tea."

I looked over the menu, made my choice and looked for Lurleen who went where waitresses go as soon as you make up your mind. I pulled out my yellow pad and rewrote my *to do* list.

- ~~Max @ flower shop~~
- ~~Max @ pool~~
- Visit Reverend A
- Where is Lucinda Tanner?
- Go to scene of the crime
- Go to Lucinda Tanner's lake house
- Visit Merrylee @ sanitarium
- Travis and Merrylee's mother, Lily Morganthal, still in Colorado?
- Moses Harper's parents
- Kristie Bentley's parents
- Interview reporter from newspaper
- List of APD detectives from Task Force
- Get a cell phone
- Contact FBI agent Mark Davidson in Washington, D.C.
- Max's list attached
- Warlick, retired, where?
- ~~Phone John in Houston~~
- Iced Chai's organization – in New Orleans
- Where's Angel?
- Ballistics man @ APD

I wrote John's name so I could cross it off and just finished adding Iced Chai's organization which Winslow had mentioned was in New Orleans, Angel's name and the ballistics man, someone I needed to see, and was thinking about how the killer shot those teenagers at pointblank range and I was picturing some faceless ogre cutting off the pinky fingers of his victims, when Lurleen showed up behind me.

"What'll it be?" I jumped.

"You alright?"

"I'm okay. Been a long day. Going to have the chicken fried steak, baked potato with the works, salad with bleu cheese and more tea."

By the time I took the South Austin exit and pulled into the townhouse, Patricia was in bed with the bedroom door shut. Whenever the door to our bedroom is shut, I see it as my opportunity to grab a Shiner Bock, turn on the TV, and watch the *Late, Late Movie,* the one where Cary Grant and Eva Marie Saint get chased through South Dakota by James Mason and a bunch of bad guys. I fell asleep before the unlucky dude fell off Washington's nose. Patricia must have seen me there in the morning and turned off the TV as she left for work without waking me up.

Chapter Ten

"There's a moment coming. It's not here yet. It's still in the future. It's on its way. It hasn't arrived. It's getting closer. Here it is. Aw shit, it's gone."

George Carlin

The next morning I awoke at ten, did the *three s* routine and drove downtown to Bergstrom and my sub-basement office. Between phone calls, I worked on the information Max asked for.

At noon, as the downtown offices emptied for lunch, with workers dashing for Manuel's or The Brick Oven, I drove the Bubbamobile to Max's flower shop. Max and I planned to drive to the scene of the crime at Hippie Hollow and visit Lucinda Tanner's lakehouse the scene of the infamous Last Pink Flamingo Party. I figured we'd stop for lunch along the way.

Max was hacking at a bamboo stalk with a machete when I pulled up. He looked over his granny glasses at my Ford F-350 Diesel with the oversized tires and light rack across the cab top (for varmint hunting). I left the engine running as one should with a diesel. It cachugged away, billowing up exhaust fumes. Max looked away and then looked back, shaking his head.

"I *am* glad you have a truck. Do you mind if I toss my bi-ped in the back? One never knows when one may need one's own wheels." Max sheathed the machete and placed it up against the building out of sight.

"No problemo on the bike-o."

"Isn't this a bit much?" Asked Max looking over the truck.

I shrugged. "What is it, Max? You don't like things slurping up mass quantities of petrochemicals?"

"There is a world of truth in what you say there, old boy." We talked through the window of the pickup as the engine continued to cachug. Max did seem a long way down there.

"I threw the *I Ching* this morning, and was blessed with a hexagram I haven't seen for years."

"You threw what?" Losing me big time again.

"The *I Ching*. The Oracle?"

"Don't know what you're talking about."

"Surely you have heard of the Book of Changes? It's an ancient Chinese strategy the purpose of which is the prediction of future events. Comes in handy at the crossroads and you are not sure which path to take."

"I know that one. I've been at a crossroads or two myself." Patricia and my future came to mind.

"It works on unrealized potential and thought, translating one's potential and thought into symbols. Confucius and Lao-tse both drew from the *I Ching*. I will show you how it works sometime."

"Sounds like fun." I rolled my eyes.

"The last time I received this hexagram, I was in France half a century ago. Some benefits of advanced age are the reruns of previous events. The war ended and I went to the freshly liberated Paris. There I met an intriguing woman at a sidewalk cafe on the Left Bank. We spent three wonderful days together."

"That's a long time to spend at a sidewalk café."

Max merely looked at me.

"That's interesting, Max. How can I get one of those hex, what was that again?"

"Hexagram, from hexad, as in six sided, a series or group of six or hexadic..."

"I think I've heard as much as I can ever hope to remember about those hex things, Max."

"Don't interrupt me, Bilbo."

"I'm sorry Max. One of my weaknesses—interrupting people. But, I'd appreciate it if you wouldn't call me Bilbo."

He nodded. "Ah, a negotiated settlement. But to answer your question, you cannot live another's prediction."

"I was afraid of that."

"How was your excursion to Dallas?"

"It was strange. I kept my eyes open like you suggested and noticed some weird events. I don't think I can share what I learned right now. Confidential, hush hush and all that sort of rot." My British impression. "You ready?" I was getting hungry, my stomach knew it was past noon.

"Just be a bit." Max went through the back door of the flower shop and returned with a bicycle, lifting it into the bed of my pickup. He got in and put a day pack between us on the seat.

"Here's the info you asked for." I handed him a couple of sheets of paper stapled together. "You wanted everybody's dates of birth, right?"

Max nodded, leafing through the papers.

"And the exact time of death of the two kids. We can't be exact exact but this is a pretty decent estimate from the County Coroner." I leaned over and pointed to the numbers. "Plus the physical location of everybody involved including me. Also an estimate. I was in summer classes at SouthWest Texas State University trying like hell to avoid a third senior year when I heard about the killings."

I invested two freshman, two sophomore, one junior year, and two senior years in my quest for a B.S. Degree. It seems there were so many more fun things to do in San Marcos than study.

"Why do you want to know where *I* was? Am I a suspect?"

"No, of course you aren't. However, that particular moment in time is a tapestry and everyone involved at a particular present moment plays a part of the fabric of that moment. There is more to our existence on the material plane than meets the eye. In actuality the past, present and future are not differentiated..."

I listened with half an ear as I backed out the driveway. Bamboo grew down to the street. When I saw no one coming, I backed out and shifted, squealing tires as I took off down Niles Road. All the other homes on the street had immaculately cut St. Augustine lawns with black men or Hispanics pruning the privets.

"Looking at our existence on Earth is like the wake of a speedboat through water. Earth, the material world, is not the water and it is not the boat. It is the trail the boat makes through the water. It is an event that has already taken place."

"I'm glad I got that straight." I turned on Windsor and then onto the MoPac loop. "You know Max, I'm a-catching about half of what you're a-tossing."

"Hmmm. Let me put it in terms to which you can relate." Max paused and collected his thoughts. "Ah, yes. A wealthy man bought a professional football team.

"*That's good!* Said his friends. But the team lost all its games.

"That's bad! They said. But next season because the team was *so* dreadful they found themselves eligible for the number one draft pick."

"That's good!" Now I was relating.

"They went after and signed the best player in college football."

"Well, that is good. Right?"

"On the surface one would think so. But no, it was bad."

"Why?"

"He wouldn't sign."

"That *is* bad!" I thought about Winslow Christian and how coincidental the conversation was getting.

"But there is a bottom line and it is this." I looked at the man while at the same time passing a car on the MoPac.

"Watch the road!"

"Ooops. Sorry." I swerved back into my lane.

He shook his head. "The investors were spared shelling out the big money that would have gone to a new franchise player. However, since the fans were confident their new star was locked up, the team pre-sold their season tickets making a profit for the first time in several years.

"That's good, isn't it?"

"That *is* good especially for the investors. The investors agreed with you. *Verily that is good!* So, here is the proverbial bottom line, Rivers. It is difficult to know from one moment to the next what is happening in the larger sense."

"I can sure relate to that." How was I going to handle Patricia and our *large* discussion?

"There is one place," said Max, as we headed North on MoPac and exited at FM 2222, "where one can gain perspective and that place is the present moment. You know Rivers, the present moment is the only reality. It's the only thing that exists. It is the boat. The past has gone; it is the wake left behind. The future is yet to be. It doesn't exist either. It is the empty lake lying ahead, waiting in a potential state for our passage. Our existence is but a string of present moments."

I wasn't so sure about that. I knew for instance, sooner or later I would need to deal with Patricia's concerns. Dang it all, I didn't want to get married but all my escape routes were one by one, slamming shut. The future *did* exist and it was lying in ambush for me. My problem was I was crazy for the girl. My only hope was she would eventually get so pissed with me she'd bootscoot me out the door. I wasn't counting on that.

"You know Max..." I looked at the man for a long moment and he pointed to the road ahead. I turned my attention back to 2222. "I understand the words and they sound good and all that but somewhere in the back of my brain a little voice is saying *something's not quite right about that*."

"That's what the Buddhists call your monkey mind. Don't misunderstand me. I am not trying to teach you religion; all I am noting is in the case of these murders, we can reconstruct a previous present moment, thus gaining insight into the dynamics of that particular instant. Instead of looking at it as the police do from inside a hole, we are free to climb out and take a generous look about. Open up to alternative realms."

I nodded, confused but interested. I had been a detective for what, a week? And I had learned so much it was scary.

"We can deal with space and time in the same manner. In *space*, we use a map. If we want to go to Hippie Hollow for instance, we look to the map which directs us north on MoPac, west on 2222, south on 620, and west on Comanche Trail. Simple enough. Conversely, in *time*, the map I use is an astrology chart or an I Ching hexagram or any of a number of prediction devices. Instead of highways we look at the astrological signs and houses and the way it all connects, whether it is a trine, a square or opposition or we look at the hexagrams and the changes. Capiche?"

"No, not really."

"You are just going to have to trust me then. Have you had lunch?"

"No I haven't." I was aware in this *now* moment I was hungry as hell. I searched old memory banks in the wake that was my past, trying to bring up from the depths of the lake of my being, where the hell that great barbeque place was. Somewhere around here. Max motioned I take the turnout below St. Luke's church, which offered a magnificent view of Lake Travis.

"I made us some sandwiches. Here's tofu and organic tomato, which I grew myself, the tomato that is. A wonderful ripe heirloom variety. It is topped with Patrick J. Timpone's salsa on a spelt flour baguette." Max took the sandwich from his green Whole Earth Provision Company daypack and held it out for me to see. Nothing at all outstanding about the tofu sandwich, as far as I could tell.

"Gosh, I don't know." My appetite was heading south fast.

"Or," said Max with a flourish, pulling out another sandwich, "how about hummus on a pita pocket, safflower mayo and homegrown cucumbers and bell peppers?"

"Isn't that some kind of fertilizer?"

"What?"

"Hummus."

"That's *humus,* Rivers."

"Good to know there is a distinction. But I'm a meat and potatoes guy. Wouldn't have a Big Mac and fries in there?" I stole a quick look at Max's pack. "No, don't suppose you would. Not on your path. Mom fed me tofu when I was a kid. Haven't had a nightmare about bean curd for several years now."

I took the tofu. Max the fertilizer on pita.

It was a beautiful spot for a picnic, high above the lake sparkling blue in the mid-day sun. Could have been romantic as hell except I was with an old English fart and not a beautiful ex-Bobcat cheerleader, who five years later could still make the squad. Down below, sailboats sliced the water. The islands were there. When the lake level is low there are islands. When the level is high they disappear from view. For boaters it's cool to remember they are there.

"See the sailboat down there?"

"I see it."

"See how it's making a wake through the water? That's the..."

"The past, right Max?"

"Right you are, old boy. You are catching on after all." We ate our sandwiches in silence. Max offered a bottled water which I took and downed in two huge gulps.

"Thanks to you and the data you supplied I will be able to configure an accurate astrological chart for the hour of the murders. I know it's not prudent to work while one is eating, however I'll make an exception and do an interim chart right now. This book will help me plot it." Max pulled a huge red book from his pack. "That way we will have immediate insight into that fateful night."

"But isn't it just a bunch of bunk? I mean, how could it work? I read my forecast in the Statesman. Like you told me, I'm a Sagittarius. I read it and it seems appropriate but then I'll read, say a Leo or a Virgo, and that seems to work too. It's so vague. *You will meet someone interesting or watch your finances for the next three days.* It's all hocus pukuss to me."

"Those forecasts are pretty general. I mapped a natal astrological chart on your time and date of birth and found some very interesting things."

"Like what?"

"Like the trouble you had with the police department was reflected by a grouping of very powerful planets conflicting in the house that governs your career."

"Bummer." How did he know about my trouble with APD?

I eased the pick up away from the overlook and back on 620 and turned up Comanche Trail. A couple of miles later I pulled into the parking lot at Hippie Hollow and paid the fee. Hippie Hollow had transitioned from a free hangout where boys and girls went to take off their clothes to a hangout with a fee where mostly boys went to take off their clothes. All around Austin all the free *in* places to swim had been taken over by various park services and now charged entry fees. The sign read:

Bathing suit optional
No camping
No parking
Between 10 P.M. and 6 A.M.

Max hopped from the pickup and bounded down the trail.

"See you at the lake." He was gone.

"What the hell?" I locked up and glanced in the bed at the bicycle. Italian job, expensive. "Hope nobody steals this thing." I looked around. Plenty of cars but no people in sight. I took the trail down to the lake, finding Max lying spread-eagled and butt naked on a huge boulder at the water's edge. For seventy or whatever, the man was in excellent shape.

"Max, what's going on?"

"Do not concern yourself, Rivers. I haven't been to Hippie Hollow in years. I used to frequent the place but it has become a gay meeting place."

"You're not gay?"

"Heavens no. I have many gay friends and co-workers though. Many florists are gay, you know." He flipped over and gave me the full Monty Python.

"Yeah, I did kind of suspect that." I looked away.

"A bit homophobic are we?"

"You could say I'm not known for my tolerance. Don't understand the attraction. I don't have any gay friends myself, but..."

"You'd be surprised at the number of gays in your line of work. Give me about ten to receive a tad of fixed father energy."

"Say what?"

"Soak up some sun. Then we shall check out the scene of the crime." He flipped back over on his stomach. "Why don't you lose the suit and tie? And the hat and those boots and become one with nature. It would do you a world of good."

I, Bilbo Baggins Rivers, was not about to shed my jeans and jockeys and lie naked on a rock. As I looked around, almost every boulder had a naked man, some had two. Not a pair of breasts in sight. At least not female breasts. A couple of the guys looked my way. Did one of them wink? Fuck this.

"I'll pass."

On the way up the trail I stopped, looked down and saw Max dive off the boulder into the lake.

By the time he returned, I had outlined the crime scene with orange surveyors tape.

"I'm pretty sure this is where the limo was parked. Here's the pin that marks the coordinates. I have the APD's dimensions and measurements and this is the murder scene diagram." I showed him the APD sheet.

"Well done old boy." Max did the little clapping thing with his fingers. He must do that when he's excited.

Max hopped the tape and sat on the dirt parking lot in the same impossible position I had seen at Barton Springs. He sat first where the driver Moses Harper had been sitting and then where the passengers Travis, Kristie and Merrylee had been.

"Yes, yes, yes. You have done well with your dimensions and measurements. Something tragic did happen here. I can feel the terror. After five years I can still feel the ectoplasmic presence of evil itself."

"Ectoplasmic?"

"Have you ever asked yourself what God sees?"

"I can't say I have but I'll bite, what does God see?"

"Well first of all, God is not this big guy in the sky who looks like Charlton Heston," Max grinned. He seemed to think it was funny. I managed a pathetic smile. "God is everything in existence. He couldn't be less. *No God but God,* as the Muslims avow. If you buy the premise God *is* everything, ergo, it would be impossible for God *not* to see all of existence at once. God would not see through limited human eyes. I mean cats can see a lot better than we. God's sight wouldn't and couldn't be limited. He's in the stars and in the atoms, the macro and the micro, beyond the atoms, beyond light and darkness. He would see and experience the dance of the atoms. He would see vibrations."

"You stayed up all night with that one, didn't you Max?"

"Actually Rivers, what I'm doing at this moment is seeing as the Creative sees, riding the six dragons that harness Nature. *When the dragons are flying in the sky, great people are working creatively.* I am now seeing the full vibrations of this place. I am not limited to space or time."

"Oh, I get it. You're playing God, is that it, Max?"

"Jolly good, Rivers! God is in me as me but even more appropriately, God is in *you* as you, as well."

"Well that explains it. But I notice you are saying God is a he. He's in the stars. That's pretty traditional isn't it? I expected more from you, Max."

"The Creative is God as Brahma. The same Creator Christians call Our Father. God as Shiva, the Created, would be Our Mother.

"Okie dokie then." I was never big on religion, a little bit of it goes a long way with me and I was losing interest in the conversation. I don't think I've ever met a man with whom I possess less in common than Maximus Culpepper.

"Speaking of tradition, at least in Christianity, God is the Creator, the Father, right?"

"That does sound familiar." I wondered if Max liked baseball. Was he a Democrat or a Republican? He had a cute receptionist. That was good. He wasn't gay.

"But you know, many non-Christian traditions look upon that which has *been created* and not just the Creator, as God. That madrone tree is as much God as the one who created it. I know that is difficult for some to take. There is no reason to differentiate. If God is in us as us, He's in the tree as the tree. I've done as much as I can here." He hopped over the tape and walked to my pickup.

"What's next?" He waited for me to unlock the door.

Chapter Eleven

*"Anyone who can see through women
is missing a lot."*

Groucho Marx

"What do you say we head on up to Lucinda Tanner's lake house, a couple of miles up Comanche Trail. Don't think there's anybody home. Maybe a caretaker. Ms. Tanner is traveling, I believe. Captain Hollers gave me the combination to the security gate."

"Ricky gave you the combination?"

"Yeah."

"Don't you see the significance?" Asked Max, as I downshifted into low. The needle on my gas gauge was dropping toward empty at an alarming rate. I loved my truck but my truck loved Texaco stations more.

"It seems a trifle easy if you ask me." We drove two miles of hairpin turns to the lake house. While I kept the Bubbamobile from going over the edge, Max did high speed calculations with pocket calculator and pen.

"Now that's a weekend cottage." The pink granite edifice came into view. I pulled into the driveway and stopped at the gate control box. The guard shack was empty. I punched in the code numbers.

"Bergstrom does the security here," I answered Max's question about the significance of me having the combination. The big iron-gate opened and we passed through. The lower level parking lot was as I imagined it from reading the reports. Limestone steps snaked up the hill following the natural contour of the limestone ledges to the upper level. Rounding a bend, the lake house came into view again. I parked along the circular driveway, got out and looked for signs of life. Even though the house and grounds were beautiful and the lake was fabulous, Max had not looked up from his calculations.

"Over there," I pointed out a man of indeterminate age, dressed in straw hat, khaki uniform, his face brown from many hours in the sun. He was hand-watering pots of bougainvillea which spilled over a low wall on the patio.

"Excuse me sir, I'm B. B. Rivers with Bergstrom Investigations." And this is my partner I thought to myself, he's a psychic. "Could we ask you a couple of questions?"

"Sí, señor."

"Do you speak English? Habla Ingles?"

"Sí, señor, I do."

"We are investigating the murders that took place down the road at Hippie Hollow."

"The señora told me Heepee Hollow was not a good place for me. No bueno for me. I don't go there and I don't know nothing about no murders." The man lost sight of the bougainvillea and began watering the stone patio. I stepped back. I was a good foot taller and a hundred pounds heavier. Probably intimidating him.

"This happened five years ago. How long you been working here?"

"I have been in Tejas one year, I am from Guanajato. I have papers, señor. I have a green card."

"Papers? Oh no. That's not what..." I shook my head trying to remember something appropriate in Spanish. The idioms coming to mind were either ways to order beer or insult someone's mother. Better stick to English. "I'm not here about your papers. What's your name?" I tried to befriend him, tilting the Stetson back on my head, smiling.

"I can assure you Felipe is perfectly legal, gentlemen."

Max and I turned toward the feminine voice. She was tall, at least six feet and stepped gracefully as a model might, down the stone steps as we three men watched. Wearing an elegant kelly green jumpsuit, her long jet-black hair was pulled back in a severe bun. In one hand she held a crystal tumbler, in the other a long slender cigar. As she talked, she exhaled cigar smoke. The smoke made her squint as it circled her face and wafted into her eyes.

"I'm Lucinda Tanner. Is there something I might help you with?" She brushed away the smoke and wiped a smoke induced tear with a red fingernail that complimented a glass bead necklace and matching bracelet.

"Miss Tanner?" I was face to face with the legendary Auntie Loo. "I'm ahh, B. B. Rivers of Bergstrom Investigations. I'm doing a follow up to the murders of those teenagers at..."

"What does the B. B. stand for?" Asked Lucinda.

"It stands for Bilbo Baggins." Max moved between me and the beautiful artist.

"Max!" A lot of people were all of a sudden calling me Bilbo. What was that all about? I watched Max take her hand in his and lay a kiss on it like Maurice Chevalier on Leslie Caron.

"And you are?" The cigar was in her mouth, Max holding her hand. Auntie Loo seemed captivated by the old fart.

"Maximus Culpepper, at your service, m'lady." He clicked the heels of his Dr. Martens and bowed smartly.

This guy is good. Maybe we did have one thing in common.

"Oooh. How charming. You all come in." Her voice which had a husky Lauren Bacall quality, now turned southern fried, belle of the ball, mint julepy, like Dolly Parton in *Steel Magnolias*.

She led us up the patio steps, through the huge glass French doors into a living room-atrium bordered on three sides by twenty-foot tinted windows overlooking the lake. It was a beautiful room, large and airy.

"Please make yourselves comfortable." She pointed to a couple of overstuffed white couches. "Elena, let's you and me rustle up some *te fria*." She and Elena went into the kitchen. Joe Ely's *Gallo del Cielo* played over the speaker system. The music seemed to be an integral part of the air.

Sitting on the couch, I could see into the open kitchen. Max did not sit but rather toured the room, looking over the top of his glasses at the objects d' art, his calculations rolled and tucked under his arm. On the walls were well known Lucindas (that never would be for sale), a Georgia O'Keefe, a Monet, an Amado Peña and a Gaugin down the hallway. Max wiggled a beckoning finger and I got up and went to where he was standing.

"There is an absolute fortune in art on these walls," whispered Max. I looked them over recognizing the New Mexico pueblo scene because I had been there. I loved New Mexico. I loved riding my appaloosa horse, up and down the mountain trails of the Carson National Forest around Taos. I shrugged and sat back down as Lucinda reentered.

"I figured you'd be off on some adventure," I said. Lucinda carried a lead crystal platter balancing a matching pitcher of iced sun tea, three matching crystal mugs, bowls of fresh cut limes and natural brown sugar. She put it down on a long coffee table in front of the couches.

"I was. A mild adventure. I've been in San Miguel de Allende, Mexico, for heaven knows how long, teaching an oils class at the *Instituto*. That's Mexico's premier art school. And I've been working on a portraiture of one of my childhood nannies. She's in her nineties now. I think I may have given her some of her many wrinkles personally. I spent a good deal of my formative years down there. The town is quaint. Up in the mountains. Do you know it?"

Max did. I didn't.

"But I've been too long gone. I thought it was high time to look into happenings in El Norte and I needed to visit my niece, Merrylee. As you know she's in a coma."

"Yes, I did know that." Merrylee had been comatose for five years. A regular Rip Van Winkle. She was still alive, if you call that living, at a sanitarium north of Austin.

"And your brother lives in town." It was more of a question than a statement.

"I don't have the slightest interest in seeing Arvin. He's not on my most favored people list." The tone of her voice took on a harder edge, just for a moment and then the moment was gone. According to my recent research, her brother, the Reverend Arvin Tanner was considered the prime suspect in the murders of her nephew Travis (who was not dead), Moses Harper and Kristie Bentley. Maybe she believed the right reverend had something to do with the murders.

"And Mr. Culpepper, in what capacity do you serve? You don't have that hard boiled investigator look about you."

And I *do?* I thought.

"I'm a florist by trade, m'lady. My shop is off Enfield Boulevard in West Austin." Max came back from his art tour and waited for our hostess to sit. I got back up to avoid looking impolite and uncouth.

"Why don't we all sit. And yes, I thought your name was familiar. I believe I've purchased flowers from your shop."

"Indeed you have. We have delivered floral arrangements to your home in Westlake Hills. Nevertheless, we have never met. I would have remembered that."

"You're sweet. You have the electric powered vans, don't you?"

"Yes we do. We decided when battery operated vehicles first came on the market. it would be our own modest drop in the bucket to save our endangered environment. Austin is such a sun rich town we have since converted to solar power."

"Admirable!" said Lucinda. "But what in heaven's name do you have to do with this investigation?"

"Well m'lady, Mr. Rivers, Elena," Lucinda's cook twirled in wearing a colorful Mexican peasant dress and frilly white blouse, carrying a platter of whole wheat blueberry muffins and feather light croissants. She looked to Max as he spoke her name but had no interest in the conversation. "Where some suspect, I know."

"Oh, my! That *is* quite a talent. What *do* you know? Gracias Elena." Lucinda selected a cigar from a cigar box beside the couch. Elena bowed, twirled and left.

"What do I know?" Asked Max. He looked to the ceiling, steepling his fingertips. I was glad he didn't do that Charlie Chaplin thing with his fingers. "I know for one, you Ms. Tanner, are funding the re-investigation of the so-called Hippie Hollow murders."

"Oh, my!"

"Really?" I sat up a little straighter, turning first toward Max and then Lucinda.

"I know other things, such as…your nephew Travis is alive and living under an assumed name in Mexico."

"Now, how could you know that, sir?" Lucinda asked, her hands shaking slightly as she clipped off the tip of a cigar with a gold cutter and flipped open a gold lighter and fired it up.

"That was an educated guess I'm afraid. However, by your response dear lady, I now know for certain."

"You rascal!" In one fluid motion, she put the cigar in an ashtray and playfully slapped his forearm. Her hand lingered a beat. "Now, I know why you brought Mr. Culpepper along, Bilbo."

"And I also know, by the surprise in your eyes, you are wondering *how* I know these things?"

She nodded, relaxing.

"And what you most want to know is it safe for your young man to return?"

She nodded again.

"Look at this," moving his tea glass aside and placing his pad with the numbers and graphs on the coffee table. Kneeling next to Lucinda, his elbow touched her calf. She didn't move away.

"It's an astrological chart, isn't it, Mr. Cul...Maximus?" She asked putting her hand on his shoulder. B. B. Rivers, ace P.I., observed Lucinda was no longer calling Max, Mr. Culpepper, but had begun to call him Maximus.

"Yes it is. A rather crude estimation of one moment in time, this one 3:43 A.M. central daylight time, July 10th, 5 years ago. As you can see, the two teenagers who died at Hippie Hollow exited the physical plane of existence at that time."

"Interesting."

"There's more. Your nephew, Travis? There was no exit for him. It was not his time nor will it be for years to come. That's why I was assured Travis is still alive. He has a destiny. And Lucinda, correct me if I'm in error here, I'll repeat your concern—should he come home to Austin at this time?"

"Yes, that's the question alright." Lucinda puffed on the cigar and sipped her tea and stared at the astrological chart.

"I don't know for certain." Max paused, removed his granny glasses and wiping them with a white napkin, he put them back on. "I need to identify this person." Max had drawn a skull and crossbones on the chart opposite the two victims. "This is the killer. I placed him somewhat arbitrarily, although I feel correctly, in opposition to the two murdered kids. This is your niece. Like Travis, she also was not in danger of leaving the planet. I'll do a more detailed chart on her. I want to know more about why she is in a coma."

"Gosh Max, you figured all that from people's birthdays?" I said, doing an outstanding Beaver Cleaver impression that would have been a hell of a lot funnier if these folks watched Nickelodeon reruns and were drinking beer instead of tea.

"Where's my brother?" Asked Lucinda.

"Here. He's not in opposition to the murdered kids, so I don't believe he's our killer." Lucinda nodded, took a drag and a sip.

"He is squared to them, which indicates a degree of tension however. There is a square or tension as well, between Arvin and Travis, between father and son."

"Tell me about it!" Said Lucinda.

"If I'm correct and the killer is here, Max tapped the skull and crossbones, "then your brother would be in a trine position with the killer."

'Which means?" I asked.

"Which means there is the possibility of a symbiotic relationship between Arvin Tanner and the killer. I say *possibility* because until I punch in all the data I cannot know for sure."

"Could he have hired someone to kill those kids?" I asked. The Austin Police Department and the FBI, although I had yet to see their files, took a hard look at Reverend A but came up with zilch. I remember reading the congregation at the Church of the Ark never lost faith in their leader and filed suit against the APD for harassment.

"Yummy tea," said Max. "One of my pastimes, is to map the most infamous murders in history and I found the killer is almost always in opposition to the victim. I feel pretty sure about these figures. Of course it would be beneficial if we had the killer's date of birth." Max smiled, put the chart down and took a sip of tea.

"Nice little hobby you got there, Max."

"Yes, very interesting. Where am I?" Asked Lucinda flipping her barely smoked cigar across the room. It hit the fireplace dead center. Sparks flew. Max and I looked at each other raising our eyebrows at the accuracy of the shot. Elena quickly brushed up some ash that fell along the way.

"This is you, here. It shows a pleasant relationship with your niece and nephew but a bit of a strain with your brother. Not a square but it's a little off center. And I'd rule you out as the killer."

"Well, I think you've nailed me," said Lucinda. "Fascinating. Speaking of nailing me, what are you doing this evening, Maximus?"

I almost expectorated tea and muffin crumbs but managed to keep them contained in my mouth and muffled a laugh through my teeth. I swallowed hard and coughed. No one seemed to notice except Elena had her brush at the ready position just in case.

And from Max sweetly. "What did you have in mind?"

Lucinda paused a moment, looked to the ceiling and smiled. "I envisioned a quiet evening. Swim. Maybe turn the air conditioning down to 50°. Fire in the fireplace. Old Hill Country tradition you know. I have this impetuous little bottle of wine I picked up last year in Tuscany. Who knows?"

Hey you guys, don't mind me.

"Sure beats doing the New York Times Crossword in my trailer. It will necessitate a call to the shop, to have them cover for me this afternoon. Would that be acceptable with you Mr. Rivers?"

"Hey, that sounds like an offer hard for anyone to refuse. Can I stay?" Lucinda and Max gave me the identical parental look, no this is a grownup affair, go rent a PG-13 DVD.

"Hey, just kidding." I held up my hands in capitulation. "Y'all have fun. Give me a call at Bergstrom tomorrow, Okay?" I was up and ready to go. I was free. I was thinking barbeque. I was thinking a sixer of Bock. I was thinking watching the sun set at the Oasis Bar just down the road, flirting with a waitress, while tossing mass quantities of Xs.

"Alrighty. Remove my bike from your truck, will you?"

I guess a guy never can tell when he'll be needing his wheels, I thought as I leaned his bike against Lucinda's garage.

Chapter Twelve

"Women deserve to have more than twelve years between the ages of twenty-eight and forty."

James Thurber

Max dove off the diving board of Lucinda's Olympic-sized pool and swam underwater to the shallow end. He popped out with age-defying ease, spun and flopped into a deck chair.

Lucinda glided across the flagstone patio in a white lace *Gideon Oberon* swimsuit and matching Tevas, a wispy purple shawl draped around her shoulders. Her thick black hair was worn loose around her shoulders. She carried a drink in each hand.

"I brought us some margaritas."

"Thank you. Max held a lead crystal glass by the stem, looking at the drink for a long moment.

"You don't drink alcohol?"

"It's the salt. Everything in moderation is my motto."

"I'm so sorry. I didn't know. Let me have Elena fix you another."

"No, that won't be necessary; I'll just wipe it off."

"Are you sure?"

"It will be fine." Max wiped the ridge of the glass with his thumb and finger. "Pink," he said looking at his fingers.

"Everything is pink around here."

"Everything, is it? Hmmm. Come sit here." Max reached out and grabbed an empty deck chair, positioning it in front of him. "I've waited as long as I intend to get my hands on you."

"Oh, Maximus." He guided her to the chair. She leaned forward against the back of the chair, her shawl falling from her shoulders. Max took her thick black hair and moved it to the side. He massaged her neck.

"You have the touch, mister. Yes, right there. Yes. Yes. Yes." Max worked her neck for several minutes. He was in no hurry. He moved to her shoulders. She shrugged blissfully as he squeezed the outsides of her upper arms. His hands worked seamlessly from her shoulders, down her spine to the small of her back.

Her body was a product of daily swimming, walking, tennis and health-giving food. His hands moved to her stomach. Holding her tightly, Max kissed her earlobes. First one, then the other. His lips followed the curve of her neck and slid across to her bare shoulder. Her back arched in delight and she reached her arms overhead, her fingers in Max's hair.

"That feels sooo good. You don't know how nice it feels to be touched. It's been awhile."

"Hmmm, I know the feeling, or I should say, *lack* thereof. Why don't you touch me so I might share in the fun?"

"I can do that." Lucinda let go of his hair and threw a long slender leg over the back of the chair and spun gracefully so she faced Max. She took off his glasses, putting them on the table and kissed him fully on the lips, her hand reaching between his legs.

"Something hard here, and whatever is that peeking over the top your swim suit?" She kissed him again and felt him move into her. Quick as a fox she was out of the chair. Max almost fell forward.

"Catch me if you can, you old coot!" She bounded across the patio, up the steps to the lake house wagging her finger and pouting her lips seductively. She turned and wiggled her butt in Max's direction and slipped through the door to the lakehouse.

"Who's an old coot?" He got up and tore off after her.

"Hey, Mr. Private Dick, up here," she shouted from the balcony.

"How did you get up there so quickly?" Max took the Tara-like steps two at a time to the second floor. He passed some remarkable artwork on the way up, glancing, cataloging but not stopping.

"Now, *where* could she be?" Playing hide and seek, the seeker trying to spook the hider, opening each door along the balcony.

"Not in here!" First, an empty guest bedroom, then a library, a sitting room, a storage room, a computer-game room, a bathroom.

The shower, which took up half the large bathroom, was running. The swimsuit and Tevas were in a pile on the colorful talavera tile floor. Steam poured over the shower door. Max could see the form of a woman, a very beautiful woman dancing to Asleep at the Wheel's "Get Your Kicks On Route 66" playing over the speakers. Max figured there must be stereo speakers in every room. He dropped his swimsuit on hers and opened the door to the shower.

"Hi, Maximus. What took you so long and what happened to Minimus?"

"What happened to whom?"

"Minimus, you know, Little Max," she stroked the little guy who began swelling from the attention. He understood without further discussion who Minimus was.

"Come here, big boy." Lucinda and Max lathered each other's bodies and danced in the roomy shower stall to the *Cotton-eyed Joe*. They both hollered *Bullshit!* at the appropriate moment. After their shower, they walked hand in hand to Lucinda's bedroom and hopped into bed and made love to *Under the Double Eagle*. Later Max and Lucinda fell asleep in each other's arms.

At his usual awakening time an hour before dawn, Max slipped out from under Lucinda's arm, tiptoed across the master bedroom so as not to awaken her, and opened the sliding glass patio door. He hoped there was not an alarm system in place and breathed out as the door opened silently. A sliver of a moon hung in the east. He spread his notes on a glass topped table. Willie Nelson's voice was ever-present in the background, something about a *bloody Mary morning that came on without warning, sometime in the night.* "How appropriate," whispered Max.

He remembered leaving his glasses down by the pool and squinted at his notes which he could just make out in the moonlight.

"Gee Max," said Kelly, "what happened to you? I don't think I ever remember your coming in late. Even Tommy was beginning to worry." Max passed through the shop, waving wearily at no one in particular, not even glancing at Tommy's latest arrangement. The screams of the zinnias for once went unheard. He went straight for the couch in the office and lay down. Kelly followed him in, ponytail swinging.

"I was up at least until two but still awoke at five," Max's arm was across his eyes and he did not look at Kelly, "and then this morning I rode my bike back from Lake Travis. It was a harrowing experience."

"Wow, Max. That's quite a ride, must be thirty miles. I've ridden out that way and the bike lanes are non-existent in places. Did you have a bad ride?"

"No, the ride was fine, it was the staying up all night that was harrowing. I guess I have my limits. My body is not as young as my brain believes it is. And you're too young to be thinking what you're thinking." He peeked out from under his arm at the smiling Kelly.

"Was her name Lucinda?"

Max got up on one arm. "She called?"

"Seven times. Must have been a pretty hot date." She gave Max an exaggerated wink and nudged him playfully in the ribs with her big toe. She stuffed seven pink *while you were out* slips into his hand. "If you keep dating Lucinda, we'll need to make a trip to Office Depot to stock up on message pads."

"Whew. I guess I had better call her." Max shooed Kelly from the office. The designers shared knowing looks as he closed the door.

"I've been working here two years and I've never known Max to close the door," said Leslie.

"Tell me 'bout it, man" said Alphonso in his rich Cuban accent. He jabbed a bright yellow marigold into a green chunk of oasis floral foam.

"Hi, Lucinda, this is Max."

"I was worried about you on 2222. It's such a dangerous road. We should have called a cab or waited for James to bring the limo out."

"It was *almost* uneventful. Thrust but once from the pavement by a solitary Suburban and yes, a jeep full of kids threw a Miller Lite bottle at me and yelled, *Hey Gramps get your fuckin' ass off the fuckin' road!* Fortunately the bottle was as empty as their craniums."

"You poor dear. You alright?"

"I'm fine. I'm going to take a nap now."

"I had fun last night."

"Me too. Got to go now."

"I love you, Max."

"Call you later." Max pushed books and crossword puzzles off the couch and was cutting zeds before his head hit the cushion.

The florist rose from the dead at noon-thirty, half a day off his usual routine. He missed his customary breakfast of dry toast, seasonal fruit and Morning Thunder tea. He missed his swim at the Springs. He missed his 42 game with the philosophers. To salvage what was left of the day, he checked in on his crew, answered a few phone calls and got to work on the astrology chart.

Everything was removed from the corkboard and stacked on the couch. With pushpins he put up the chart and accompanying mathematical equations.

He brewed a cup of chamomile tea and passed the afternoon looking at his creation. Looking for pattern. Looking for coincidence. He opened his *I Ching* book, a weather-beaten tome held together by rubber bands and removed three Tibetan coins he'd acquired in the Holy City of Llasa. The coins had been there lying in wait on the first page, *The Creative*.

After a twenty minute meditation, he formed a precise question. Holding the coins lightly, reverently, in his right hand, he passed them through the wispy white smoke of a burning *Blue Pearl* incense stick he brought back from Swami Muktananda's Ashram in India. The scent brought back fond memories. Max smiled at the recollection of the Swami's thick Indian accent and ever-present peacock feather he used to playfully swat his disciples.

"Maximus *Cul*pepper! What a wonderful name you have. Always remember Maximus, God is in *you* as *you*."

"I would like to know," said Max to the Oracle, "with regard to the Hippie Hollow murders, what happened and what pray tell is the essence of the present situation?" Max passed the coins through the smoke twice more and tossed them onto a royal blue velvet cloth. He threw them five more times to build a hexagram, a six-story building from the ground up.

Chapter Thirteen

"Don't torture yourself, Gomez. That's my job."

Gomez's wife

"Gosh, Billy, I haven't seen much of you lately." Patricia slathered peanut butter and then jelly on slices of whole wheat bread. She slipped the completed sandwich into a Ziploc which then went into her oversized purse. "You sure I can't make lunch for you?" She was a foot shorter than I and was what my coworkers at Kickers would call, stacked. Thick and curly black hair and a beautiful mole at the corner of her upper lip.

I was in my p.j.s depicting rodeo scenes she bought me for my last birthday and bathrobe, reading the sports page. Patricia left for work at seven A.M. Except for Kickers Nights when I got home at three or four A.M., I got up with her. She'd cook me breakfast while I tried not to be sucked into any important discussions. Reading the paper and ignoring her was a habit our pre-marriage counselor reckoned I inherited from my father, Harry Rivers. Now days Dad could no longer read the sports page but he could ignore a person as well as ever. Better read it when I have the chance, I thought.

"Huh?"

"I said, can I make lunch for you?"

"Oh. No thanks Pat, Patricia, I plan to meet someone for lunch. And if for some reason that doesn't materialize, I'll swing through McDonald's (the path of the Big Mac). Hey, the Rangers won again. All right. That's six in a row!"

"I'm happy for you. How much do you spend on those burgers? Five, six bucks?"

"I guess." $5.72 including tax. She was drawing me in, dammit.

"That's $25 to $30 a week, over $100 a month, and for what?" She waited for me to say something and when I didn't, continued. "The opportunity to clog your arteries? Jar of peanut butter and jelly cost about $5 a *month* and another $5 for bread." She looked up at, visualized her 10key adding machine, punched in the cost of a Big Mac and fries, not counting the Dr. Pepper. She drank water.

"Conservatively, at $4 per day times five days times four point three weeks in a month (there are not four weeks in a month, if that were true a year would have 48 weeks instead of 52), equals $107.50 per month. With a drink it's even more. I figure we can save $100 per month if you bring a p and j sandwich to work." To be sure, peanut butter and jelly was a notch above tofu in my mind. "If you do take someone out, will it be covered by your expense account?"

"Sure."

"If you don't go out, you can save, we can save, $4 to $5, even $6 a day! If we're ever going to afford a family," I knew she was talking about babies, Max would be proud of my emerging psychic abilities, "we're going to need to cut corners, Billy. I don't want to sound like a nag, I just want a family and I want you to live for a very long time. And eating a Big Mac is double trouble. It's expensive and red meat is not good for humans."

"I feel like I'm married already," I said into the box scores of last night's game.

"What's that?"

"You're right." Of course you're always right, I thought. "I'll cut down on the burgers."

"Red meat clogs arteries. Promise me you'll watch your diet? Eat a salad."

"Okay, I told you I would. It may not be a salad but I'll find something else, okay?"

"Here, take this sandwich in case." She pulled it out of her bag and made another. I watched her pack up her things and head for the door.

"See ya, Billy." Kiss, kiss, hug, hug. Out the door she went. Damn, why did she have to be so damn good lookin'? She was the perfect woman for me. Perfect in every way. Her skin was light but she tanned up and didn't freckle like I did. Her breasts were full and hard. Her butt was hard. Her lips full. Legs long. Hair thick and curly. Eyes blue green. She was kind and funny.

She and I fit in all the right places. And dang it all she was only trying to keep me alive.

In my sub-basement office at Bergstrom Investigations, which I had affectionately named *the cave,* I sat at my desk, which if you looked closely, resembled a door straddling two wooden produce boxes. I lugged an old IBM Selectric I found in a storeroom onto the desk and blew the dust off, pulled out the yellow pad with my notes, rolled in a piece of bond paper and hammered out the report for Captain Hollers. I enjoyed my first week as an investigator. Maybe Max's advice was sinking in and I was beginning to live in the moment, forgetting about the past and the future, which according to Max did not exist anyway.

At one time in my life, I did live, if not *in* the moment, but *for* the moment. That was back in college. It was be here now baby in those days. Hey, what a great title for a book, *Be Here Now – Baby.* I'd have to tell Patricia about that one.

My first week as a P.I. was history. It took me several trips but I managed to carry all of Captain Hollers' files down to the cave. The cave was Stephen Crachet-ish and even smaller with boxes lining the walls. About a third of the boxes I had opened and gone through. I saw Max three times and gave him the information he needed. Spent two days in Dallas with the FBI, visited with Winslow Christian at TCU. Found out about the connection with Iced Chai, uncovered that Travis had a girlfriend, Angel, discovered the APD cover up by Police Captain Warlick. Did Hollers know more about this than he was letting on? He was Warlick's best friend. I had met the famous and fabulous Auntie Loo and visited the scene of the crime at Hippie Hollow. I learned about how the APD had considered Reverend Arvin Tanner their primary suspect and young Travis Tanner, according to his roommate had something on Reverend A but what that was I did not know. Travis did not want his father, or the FBI, or the APD to know he was still alive.

I called Moses Harper's parents and talked with Mrs. Harper, setting an appointment for the next morning, Saturday. I talked with Kristie Bentley's mother earlier in the week. The murder of her only daughter was still bothering her five years later. She would never fully get over it. She had never met Travis or any of the Tanners and had never been to the lakehouse or a Pink Flamingo Party. Her husband, who had been her third, had left her. Kristie was a casual acquaintance of Travis in High School and it was their first, and last, date. Kristie had confided in Mrs. Bentley that she only went out with Travis because it was an opportunity to attend the hottest party of the year.

I left four messages for Mark Davidson, the FBI Agent-In-Charge of the Hippie Hollow investigation. He had not returned them.

I asked a friend of mine in Records at APD, to see if he could come up with an address on Captain Warlick. Of the two types of friends and acquaintances at APD, those who were my friends *because* I decked Lt. Ashby and those who were my friends *in spite* of it, this guy was a *because* friend. Lt. Asswipe did not generate a lot of love in the Department.

I found the ex-chief of the Task Force relocated to a ranch he owns near the West Texas town of Balmoreah. The file noted Warlick's request for immediate retirement. The reason given: Health Concerns. Did it seem logical Captain Warlick would retire two days after uncovering the biggest lead in the case? I don't think so.

Warlick had to be the key to the whole thing. Hollers didn't want me talking to APD detectives. Said it would be too disruptive, but Warlick was no longer with the Department. So, I called him, and dang it all he answered the phone and he agreed to see me.

"Sure, come on out," said Warlick. "I won't discuss the case on the phone but I will talk to you in person."

An expedition out Interstate 10 to the wilds of West Texas was in order. I set up an appointment with the ex-cop for Sunday afternoon. I could get on the road Saturday after my visit with the Harpers. Maybe Patricia would come along and make it a weekend on Bergstrom's nickel. We did need to talk. Patricia needed to talk. I needed to listen.

Patricia had wanted to visit Balmoreah, since reading about it in a past issue of *Texas Highways Magazine.* "It's a quaint little village with a state park and beautiful swimming pool spring fed from the Davis Mountains, the MacDonald Observatory, Fort Davis of Buffalo Soldier fame, Big Bend National Park, the Rio Grande or Rio Bravo (depending on if you were facing south or north when looking at it) and the mysterious Marfa Lights are all near by."

I made a date for lunch with the infamous muck raking maverick rogue reporter, T. Rex Rodriquez. Eating out was good, since the peanut butter and jelly sandwich would not hold me for long.

T. Rex had attended the Pink Flamingo party and accompanied Lucinda Tanner to Hippie Hollow when the bodies were discovered. From the beginning, his articles were a thorn in the side of the Task Force. Over his career, more than one irate citizen whose feathers he had ruffled had punched him out. I had no idea what I was in for. He had the reputation of being a loud mouth, arrogant, unpredictable and according to Hollers, a drug addict.

If that wasn't bad enough, two more distasteful items remained on my *to do* list.

One – Reverend Arvin Tanner. I didn't care for religion and ministers of the gospel even less. Their self-righteous attitude made me want to puke but I knew it was essential to suck it up and interview him. I called his office every day for a week and like the FBI agent, Reverend A did not return phone calls. At least not *my* phone calls.

Two – Merrylee Tanner, i.e., visiting Oak Meadow Sanitarium. I dreaded being in the same room with the girl's comatose body. My grandmother was in a coma for weeks before the family pulled the plug. As a kid I was freaked out by the thought of visiting Meemaw.

"Give Meemaw a kiss, Bilbo," said my mom.

"Do I hafta?"

My dad would give me *the look* and I'd lay a peck on her cold cheek. Twenty years later I could still feel that kiss on my lips. What was that all about?

Another item that wasn't on the list but nonetheless was distasteful, was visiting my dad at the ranch. He couldn't remember anybody. We all, including my mom, reintroduced ourselves to him every time we saw him.

"Hi Dad, its B. B. You know, your son?"

He could not, or would not, talk. But he could sing. Mom and I would be talking and something in our conversation would set him off.

"So, Mom, what are we doing for Saint Patrick's Day?"

"*When Irish eyes are smiling.*"

Strange.

The highlight of my week, was finding out Travis Tanner wasn't killed at Hippie Hollow but was alive in Mexico. That was good detective work. Dad would have been proud and I would tell him about it next time I saw him. He worked on Hippie Hollow and if anything could get through maybe this would.

Lucinda Tanner was just back from Mexico. Wonder how Max knew Travis was down there? Surely not that astrologic chart. Travis had been hiding (I supposed) from the killer. Why didn't Captain Warlick tell anyone about Travis being alive? Or had he? Too many questions. Not enough answers. Maybe after I talked with Warlick, things would clear up.

Another item was talking with Lily Morganthal, Travis' mother who lived in Aspen, Colorado.

Next week I'd work on Iced Chai. Could the Foundation have anything to do with this? Was Angel working at the Foundation? Or was she long gone? Maybe she was old and fat and living in Arizona.

I planned on making a stop in at APD after lunch. I agreed I wouldn't *bother* any of the detectives but I wanted to talk to Dad's old friend in Ballistics. I could do that after lunch since the station was also downtown and a few minutes walk from the restaurant where I would meet T. Rex.

All those questions and more I left hanging and closed the office, which amounted to pulling the cord on the overhead light. I walked from the Bergstrom Building, down Sixth Street, past bars and music venues, past Kickers (I peeked over the swinging doors—nothing happening this time of day). I felt bad about quitting on such short notice but Jimmy Don left the swinging doors open if Bergstrom didn't work out. I could always have my throwing out rowdies job back.

"B. B., I wanted to run an idea for a new club by you. How about this—a gay cowboy bar." It didn't seem like a good idea to me but Austin could handle it and everybody said putting a cowboy bar with its own rodeo arena ala *Billy Bob's* on Sixth Street, right in the heart of Austin's rock and roll district was a dumb idea. But the guy was raking it in.

"What do you think? How about *Sweet Tails* for a name?" Sweet tails are steers (castrated bulls) that are somehow attractive to fully balled bulls. Jimmy Don suggested with my rugged good looks I would add color to the place. Stand out front in my

Stetson, rodeo belt buckle and pointy toed reptilian boots and invite the boys in. Forget that.

"And get this, B. B., not only would it be the only gay cowboy bar in Texas, I'll save a fortune because I'll only need one restroom." It was hard to take the guy seriously with the big red clown nose and ever-present smile plastered on his face.

I wondered which he'd keep, Dudes or Dudettes.

As I walked down Congress Avenue to Las Manitas Café to meet T. Rex, I munched on the peanut butter and jelly sandwich.

One of those *Keep Austin Weird* V.W. vans was parked out front. This art car had a complete solar system on the roof, was painted every color under the rainbow plus a few, had telephones for door handles, various parts of the human anatomy sticking out here and there. Andy Warhol, eat your heart out.

Las Manitas, funky, authentic Mexican Café, the dining room is out back, through the kitchen. Smells like Mexico. Corn tortillas, frijoles, meat cooking on the rotisserie.

T. Rex said look for a six foot five, bone skinny black dude, wearing a colorful Guatemalan shirt, yellow yogi pants, flip-flops, frizzy salt and pepper hair, topped with a New York Yankee cap and a wide Tweety Bird tie. Garwsh, I wondered if I could pick him out?

Chapter Fourteen

*"A drug is a substance which, when injected into a rat,
will produce a scientific report."*

Anonymous

"Hi, Mr. Rodriquez, I'm B. B. Rivers." I went up to the first guy with a Tweety Bird tie. I lucked out, it was him.

"Hey Bro, call me T. Rex. Everybody does. Friends and Republicans alike. Have a seat." His voice was an octave maybe two lower than one might expect from his tall, skinny body, and rumbled ten decibels louder. Even with the café noise, everyone in the place could hear him easily. A sweet scent of sandalwood wafted from the man.

"Have you eaten here before?" James Earl Jones coming out of David Bowie's face.

"Never. Didn't know it was here. How 'bout you?"

"I eat here almost every day. Here and next door at the Greek place. I love their *spanakopita*. It's a two-minute drive in my V.W. van from the paper across the Congress Avenue bridge. I drive over twenty million bats every day."

"What's that?"

"The bridge is the summer home to the nation's largest colony of Mexican free tail bats." Patricia loved to come to Town Lake, sit on a blanket eating peanut butter and jelly sandwiches and watch the bats fly, millions of them, into the night sky to eat billions of mosquitoes. Once a bat swept down and knocked off my Stetson. That worried me. Too many late night Dracula movies, I suppose.

"I knew that." I looked through the menu. No hamburgers, no temptation. Just as well. "What's good?"

"Chiles relleno are to die for."

"I like the sound of that. Chiles *Re lay no. Re aye nose.* I've promised my girl I'd lay off the Big Macs, look at a new food group."

"I ought to tell you, I checked you out. High school and college football star, All-State Linebacker. Blanco County Champion Cowboy. Texas Champion Steer wrestler. After that your career kinda goes into the crapper. Ticked off the Austin Police Department after five years. Bouncer in a bar on Sixth Street. That seems logical. Maybe I should do a *what the fuck is he up to now* human interest piece on you."

I shrugged. At least he didn't call me an overweight mesomorph.

"You said on the phone you were looking into the Hippie Hollow murders? Easy Rawlins type, huh?"

"Who?"

"Easy Rawlins. Character in a mystery novel. You know, *Devil in the Blue Dress?*"

"Oh yeah, I saw the movie, it was good." Denzel Washington and this good looking babe get chased through L.A. by bad guys.

"So Rawlins, you don't mind if I call you Rawlins?" He didn't wait for a yea or nay. Better than Bilbo.

"So, I thought APD took Hippie Hollow off the market."

"Bergstrom Investigations has it now and they farmed it out to me, to do a follow up on it."

"Who hired *them?*"

"They never told me." I knew it was Lucinda Tanner but technically Captain Hollers hadn't told me. I figured *I'd* better do some questioning first. "From what I hear, as far as Hippie Hollow goes, you da expert."

T. Rex nodded. "Right place, wrong time or maybe wrong place at the right time. I got the scoop anyway. Up 'til then I worked the Austin music scene, freelancing for the *Statesman* and *Chronicle.*"

"You were at the party?"

"How long you been a P.I., Rawlins?"

"Not long, why?" Okay, what was I doing wrong?

"Just wondering, you've got a bit of a checkered past." He paused. "But who doesn't?"

"The party?"

"Yes, I was there. It was a hot night and you know how sound carries when it's hot. We all heard the police cars on 620 coming across the dam and turn toward us sounding like they were coming up Comanche Trail. The flamenco dancers stopped in mid-clack. Everyone there had the same collective thought. *Oh shit they're coming to bust the party.* It was the tequila talking. Lucinda is very straight when it comes to drugs."

"I met her yesterday."

"She's back?"

"Yep. A cigar in one hand and a highball in the other, but a beautiful lady."

"She's old enough to be your mother."

"I like older women. I like younger women, too."

T. Rex continued. "A few of us were at the ledge overlooking the lake, listening to the sirens. All of a sudden they stopped. Across the inlet at Hippie Hollow, the red and blue lights were flashing. My instinct for a story overrode the couple of dozen margaritas. I was instantly sober. I hopped in my V.W. and drove down. The scene was crawling with Nazis. And you know Rawlins, authority figures make Black folks like me itchy."

"That's your van outside?"

T. Rex nodded. "That was before I turned it into an art car." Rosa came for our orders. Two chile relleno platters, a Dos Equis for T. Rex and an iced tea for me. I wanted a beer but needed to finish my report which I had left half typed in the Selectric. Rosa left a big bowl of tortilla chips and salsa.

"Thanks Rosa."

"De nada, Señor T. Rex."

As we dug in, our conversation bounced from the Hippie Hollow murders to the upcoming Cowboy season, to UT football, to Austin, a great but out of control city, to the music scene, to real estate prices, to what new high-tech company was moving in this week, to Texas politics and alighting once again on murder. Rosa brought our food.

"I have clippings on the story from newspapers, magazines and transcripts from TV and radio shows, I'll share them with you if..." He paused, his chip loaded with salsa, in mid air.

"If?"

"If it helps you realize I'm not such a bad guy. You know Richard Hollers hates my guts?"

"Yeah, he told me not to waste my time on you. But dang it all, T. Rex, you know as much about that night as anyone I would be able to converse with. You were there. Did anybody ever talk to you about it? APD, FBI?"

"Sure. Since I arrived on the scene minutes after the first cruisers, one Gestapo type convinced himself I must have been there *before* they were. Put a mini-hassle on the T. Rex. Fortunately, there was a cop there who saw me arrive. Lots of folks at the party saw me and attested to my presence. I was indeed at the party the whole time. I'm a memorable character, wouldn't you say?"

I nodded as I shoveled a tortilla chip with salsa into my mouth. A little of the red stuff hit my white shirt.

"Shit!"

T. Rex grabbed my iced tea glass, fished out an ice cube, popped it into his mouth (I watched it gyrate around in there) and handed it to me.

"Here, rub this on it. I read about it in *Heloise*." I took the cube and wondered where T. Rex's hand, and mouth, had been lately. I rubbed the red stain until it turned pink.

"Lucinda Tanner came down the hill a few minutes later. When she saw the old Mercedes with its doors open and bodies covered with sheets, she went bananas."

T. Rex munched on his chile relleno and I worked on the stain.

"It's coming out!" Half the restaurant turned to see what was coming out.

"You know, Rawlins—In my opinion, APD did a piss poor job on Hippie Hollow. Horrible police work. For some reason I felt they didn't want to know who murdered Moses Harper, Kristie Bentley and Travis Tanner. So I don't think you'll get anywhere with the APD You got your work cut out for you, son. Got any help?"

"One old fellow in an advisory capacity." Helping me to put the right moon signs on the case, I thought. "But I hear what you're saying. I've been working on it a week and I've already dug up some things they missed." Damn, I'm a natural at this, I thought.

"That's very interesting," said T. Rex taking a healthy swig of his Dos Equis. He dabbed salsa from his chin with his tie. Tweety turned a shade of orange. "You just mentioned something, ran a red flag up in my brain. Did you or did you not say, you dug up something APD missed?"

"I don't think I said that."

"Oh, yes you did, Rawlins. Is there a story here?"

"Maybe so, maybe not."

"He didn't say no, ladies and gentlemen," T. Rex announced to the room. People looked at us and smiled. At least they didn't clap.

I needed to take some sort of control of the interview. "Let me ask you a question, Mr. T. Rex. Do you remember anything unusual happening at the party? Why were you there anyway? How well do you know Lucinda Tanner?"

"That's three questions. One, the whole *night* was weird. There are men who would *die* to be the Prince of Pink. Right up there with an Honorary Doctorate from Texas A&M or being hired as Austin's City Manager. Young Tanner at 20 years old was honored as the Prince of Pink. But he didn't seem very happy about the honor."

"Really?"

"Something was bothering the boy. Slammin' down the margaritas. I guess he was pink one moment and a streak of red the next."

"Oof."

"To answer question two, I was there to do a piece on the party, the history, the tradition. Some big names have been Prince, like Reverend Arvin Tanner—Travis' father, Cactus Pryor, of course Willie, Neal Spelce, Lloyd Doggett, Kinky Friedman, Red McCombs. But what got me out to the lake instead of just phoning or faxing my interviews from my bar stool at *Maggie Mae's*, was the surprise guest."

"I wish I could have been there for that one."

"Willie Nelson and his band were playing that night and he told me it would be incredibly, impossibly, bizarre. And you know, Rawlins, Bizarre is my middle name."

I looked the man over. Yellow yogi pants, Guatemalan shirt, Tweety Bird tie. Thought about the hippie-mobile parked out front with the Tyrannosaurus Rex head sticking out of the front. Bizarre?

"You know, Willie wouldn't tell me a damn thing about *who* the surprise guest was; only that I owed it to the literary muse to be there."

"This *is* good." I bit into the pepper stuffed with cheese.

T. Rex seemed comfortable just talking. "I was in the kitchen grabbing yet another margarita, when I saw Travis on the phone.

The Rev was leaning against a wall, glaring holes through the boy. Travis must have felt it. I hadn't seen that much hate since Nam, man. I went back outside and didn't think much about it."

"You were in Viet Nam?"

"No, saw the whole thing on TV." He smiled. "I went out on the patio firing up a square. The Rev, the Tanner kids, Moses and Kristie passed by me, heading toward the limo, which was parked on the circular driveway."

"Arvin Tanner was with them?"

"He led the way but, as you know, didn't leave with them. There was some jostling about whowould drive and Moses won out. As the others were getting in, someone came from inside to tell the Rev he had a phone call. He went in and a few minutes later the guy comes out a second time, tells the kids the Rev would be tied up for awhile. Go on without him. He'd catch a ride later. I was right there, saw and heard the whole thing."

"It would be interesting to know who called and who told the Rev about the call," I said, my mouth full of chile.

"The Rev didn't share who it was, but the guy who took the call worked for Lucinda. He told the cops it was a male voice was all. APD never identified the caller. That's the kind of thing I'm talking about. That's a crucial piece of evidence, don't you think? T. Rex downed the rest of his cerveza.

"How long after the limo left did you hear the sirens?"

"Half hour. The man who reported the crime was leaving the party and called it in on his cell phone."

"Someone I should talk to as well. You remember his name?"

"It's in my notes. He and I talked some time later. He was leaving the party and jockeying his car back and forth trying to get out, when he saw the 1954 Mercedes limo pass by. According to him, it took 15 minutes to work his car free. As he drove past Hippie Hollow, he saw the limo, lights on, doors open. Bodies scattered on the parking lot. Told me he thought he saw a cop car but couldn't be sure. Too scared to stop. Tried 911 on his cellular but was out of range. Got service ten minutes later. The dispatcher told him to return to the scene of the accident.

He thought it might be an accident at first. He drove back to Hippie Hollow and found Merrylee on the ground but still alive. No other vehicles were there. No mysterious cop car. He applied pressure on her head wound to stop the bleeding. Saved her life.

Travis was missing. Moses and Kristie were dead on the front seat. A few minutes later the cops showed up."

"So, there was or was not a cop car already there?"

"Not. Interesting thing though, the guy *thought* he saw a cop car but he told me he was pretty juiced and could very well have hallucinated it." T. Rex shrugged. "I did some checking and every cop car within a hundred miles was accounted for that night. Maybe it was a figment of his imagination."

"Did you see Arvin Tanner after the kids left?"

"In a word, no."

"Lucinda?"

"Yes. I moseyed over to the ledge to look out at the lake, looking for a joint, although my best chance to get high had just left in the limo. But I was tired of smoking squares, man. Thinking about hitting up one of Willie's roadies. Lucinda was there. As we talked, we heard the sirens. Heard them turn onto Comanche Trail. And like I told you, I looked across the inlet to Hippie Hollow and saw the flashing lights. Lucinda said the kids were stopping at Hippie Hollow for skinny dippin'. I said I'd drive my van down and check it out."

"What was it like when you got there?"

"In a word, it was a mad house."

"That's five words."

"Touché, mon ami. What we had heard coming across Mansfield Dam were the Bee Caves units."

"Dam site police."

"Right." He chuckled. "Andy and Barney. They were pretty accessible, willing to answer my questions but when the real cops showed I got bumped out of there pretty quick. Travis County Sheriff's Department, State Troopers, APD, even some Texas Rangers. There seemed to be a heated discussion about jurisdiction. APD won out.

"They cordoned off Comanche Trail. Cops interviewed partygoers coming down the hill. Cops went up to the party. It took hours of interviews. Before it was over, everyone who had attended the party, all the workers, and everyone with a boat on the lake was questioned.

"Every TV and radio crime reporter from Dallas to El Paso showed up to get in on the action. They were all tromping around. No wonder forensics couldn't find anything. It went on for days, man. The story was as big as the Branch Davidians getting burnt outta Wacko. The nationals were there. NBC, CBS, ABC, FOX, PBS, CNN. Wham bam, thank you ma'am. Every so often *60 Minutes* or some news show would do a piece on it, but the story she faded away. I kept writing it though." T. Rex ordered another cerveza, and we finished off our platters, plus another bowl of chips and salsa.

"Something I need to ask you. How'd you get that interview with Arvin Tanner? He won't return my phone calls."

"The Rev? Kind of a long story."

"I got time." I was having a better time with T. Rex than I had expected.

"He once made a fool of himself on *Politically Incorrect*. That was several years ago. He has learned his lesson and now he only talks to *National Review* and sometimes guests on *McLaughlin*.

"I'm sorry I missed that."

"Best thing about it, showed him for the asshole he is."

"Hate it when that happens to me."

"So, no more liberal media for the Rev. He agreed to talk to me for one reason. Big sister ordered him to. That's the way you're going to get to him, I'm afraid."

I shrugged.

"When Lucinda came down the hill she was on a collision course with the cops. I headed her off. As you know her niece was alive and her nephew was missing. They found traces of his blood along the trail down to the lake."

"Yeah."

"Goebbels and Himmler, these were my pet names for Captain William Warlick of the APD and our county sheriff, wouldn't let Lucinda in. Didn't even have the decency to tell her what was going on, man. The guy who stopped Merrylee's bleeding, told Lucinda she was still alive. We sat in my van, which wasn't so eccentric back then, and waited until the Star Flight helicopter landed. While everybody was watching it land, Auntie Loo hopped the barricade. Then about an hour later the Rev shows his ugly face. But since he was Merrylee's father and Lucinda was an aunt, he got to ride in the chopper. I convinced the fuzz after they conducted a thorough search of my van, to let me take Lucinda to the hospital to be with her niece. So, I dropped her and I went to the paper to file my story. So, to make a long story shorter, she appreciated the favor and got me in to see the Rev."

"What do you think about him?"

"A real asshole."

"Not one of those fake assholes?"

"There's an air about the man."

"An air?"

"You know, like a fart sprayed with *Lysol?* But the smell's still there? Hidden under the pine fresh scent? He said all the right shit, like offering a reward of a mil. for anyone who could I.D. the killer."

"I was in college and I remember thinking maybe I'd drop out and find the killer. Become a millionaire."

"And that's what you're doing."

"Yeah, it's just taken me five years to get here. I don't suppose the reward is still out there?"

"Don't know. There's something about the Rev makes the hair stand up on the back of my neck. And I'm not talking about his singing voice."

Rosa put the check in front of me. T. Rex did not so much as glance at it but stared off at the far wall as if in deep thought. I picked it up.

"Say, you want to take a walk down on the hike and bike trail?," said T. Rex after I dropped my Visa card. "I'll pick up the van later." There were so many things embedded and hanging off the vehicle, it was hard to take it all in.

"Sure. I'd like to walk off this re lay no." I slapped my belly.

"I got a righteous Thai stick," a loud whisper. "I've been saving it for an auspicious moment. You get high?" About half the restaurant looked our way.

"You go ahead." I signed leaving Rosa a 20% tip and we merged into Congress Avenue foot traffic, walking to the hike and bike trail that circumnavigates Town Lake.

"I'm *sure* the Rev had something to do with those murders," said T. Rex. "He couldn't stomach pulling the trigger himself but I *know* he hired a hit man. No proof. I just know it."

"What kind of a man would do that?"

T. Rex adeptly rolled a slim joint, lit up and took a big drag as we walked the path to an isolated point on the lake.

"Real asshole could do it."

"Something else, I'd like to talk to the Tanner's attorney and/ or financial man." I took out my pad and penciled in the item. "My dad was a cop in Austin for over 30 years. He used to say 99% of killings were either about love or money."

"Or the love of money," said T. Rex Rodriquez.

T. Rex and I sat on a wooden bench overlooking Town Lake, directly across the lake from the bigger than life statue of Stevie Ray Vaughn, legendary Austin guitar picker. Every time I walk by that spot someone has placed a bouquet of fresh wildflowers in the statue's hand. Sweet.

Town Lake is in actuality, the Colorado River widened and controlled by a dam on the east end of town. The Thai stick smelled damn good. Smoking it would not be a wise thing though. I needed to type the report, needed to be normal. But I nonetheless gave in to temptation and took the smallest of hits on the Thai stick joint. It tasted fine. Before much time passed, we were lying stoned next to a sign that read,

DO NOT WALK ON THE GRASS

Nothing about lying down in it.

"I think I met your father. Henry Rivers, right?"

"Harry. Name's Harry."

"Harry Rivers, that's right. Conjures up an image of this huge hairy river." We both laughed. "I liked him. Direct. Honest. Not afraid to tell you what he was thinking."

"Say this tastes real good," I took another hit.

"Be careful of that."

"Why's that?"

"If you're not used to it, it might get you stoned."

"You know what?"

"What?"

"I do believe I *am* stoned." We laughed. "And I've got an important meeting with my boss this afternoon."

"Richard Hollers?"

"Ricky," I coughed.

"Ricky?"

"That would be da man."

"Oh, oh. I should have told you this earlier, he doesn't much care for stoners."

"I don't think I'll tell him."

"Good move. Hey you're bogarting. Pass it over, por favor."

"Sí."

"Your Spanish is excellent, Rawlins."

"Gar-ci-ass."

"You know Rawlins, smoking this shit does not as it has been purported, give you any of the answers."

"Oh yeah?"

"But it does allow you to forget the fucking questions." We laughed hysterically. In retrospect it was not that funny. "Your dad was on the Task Force." Stoned or sober, T. Rex did not let up.

"Yeah, but I don't remember him talking about it. He came down with Alzheimer's and doesn't even know who I am. Back then I was so wrapped up in school and football and girls I let the last few years of his life get away."

"Hate it when that happens. Hey, you want to get a cerveza? I got a real serious case of cottonmouth."

"Sure, why the hell not."

"You know Rawlins, the reason I went to the fucking party was to catch the Dalai Lama's performance."

"The Dalai Lama playing Stevie Ray Vaughn, that must have been somethin'." I glanced over at the statue across the lake. Stevie's back was turned. I wondered, maybe the Dalai Lama was the one putting bouquets in Austin's legendary guitar player's hand. Naw. We got up and walked back down the trail.

"Oh, it was, it was." Said T. Rex. I had forgot what we had just been talking about, so I listened for a few. "The whole world's perception of the man changed in an instant. Everybody had this vision of this impossibly holy man, the reincarnation of Buddha for Christ's sakes, locked in his room spinning a prayer wheel for world peace at 4 o'clock in the fuckin' morning. But no! He's in there jamming to *Texas Flood*."

"Yeah."

"They called it *Hello Dalai, Goodbye Stevie.*

"My girlfriend and I have his CD *The Dalai Lama Unleashed*. A present from my Mom and we didn't think we'd like it, but it's good. Especially the acoustical takeoff on Jimi."

We stopped in at the first bar on Congress and I chugged two Shiners and convinced him I had to get back, so he downed his and by the time I left T. Rex at the Congress Avenue Bridge, I was feeling no pain, except the mental pain of knowing I'd be typing that report with an intense buzz on. Why did I stop for *a* beer? There is no such thing as *a* beer. How many times do I need to relearn that?

As I walked back toward Bergstrom, I realized I could not handle Bergstrom Investigations at that particular moment in time. Donna would bust me but quick. So I hiked over to the Austin Police Department. Excellent place to hang out when you're buzzing from beer and high on illicit drugs. I put on my sunglasses and sprayed a quart of Binaca in my mouth.

Barney Smith had been APD's ballistics man for 30 years. He was the best in Texas. Just ask him. He and my dad were good friends and worked together on the Task Force.

"Hey B. B., how's your old man?"

"He seems to be happy."

"That's all that counts. I got to get out and see him. We go way back you know."

"Yeah I knew that."

"So, what brings you here? You snockerooed?"

"Why do you ask?"

"Let's see, why do I think you're stoned? For starters, there's the strong scent of marijuana," he grabbed my hand and sniffed, "Afgani? No, something Southeast Asian. And there're the sunglasses, for two. And three, if I remember those days, when you were a kid you were *always* stoned. You were stoned when you got on that Brahma bull, right? I remember you were laughing your head off when you got on and crying your eyes out when you got thrown. That kick in the testicles musta hurt..."

"Okay. Okay. I am."

"Just curious. Not that I care. So what brings you to this fine establishment?" Barney dispensed himself a cup of slow moving coffee. His cup was one of those lime green opalescent garage sale jobs they pay you five cents to take away.

"I'm working with Bergstrom now. Looking at Hippie Hollow."

"Say B. B., you know I'm sorry 'bout the Asswipe dispute. You got a raw deal on that one. You had the makings of being a fine cop. (Barney was an *in spite of* friend)."

"I'm over it."

"So, Hippie Holler, huh? Let me pull it." When Barney went to the back room, it hit me. Damn. I was ripped. I needed to maintain. I was laughing for no apparent reason as Barney came back in. He looked at me, frowned slightly and shook his head.

"We recovered the slugs. Lead based. Very soft. Hand gun had to be a custom job, hand-made. Look at these markings."

Barney flashed me a photo. "Not stock ammo by any means. Low velocity."

"Low?"

"Very. I mean the guy could throw the bullets and they'd deliver as quick. Silencer for sure. Only time I've heard of anything like it was Castro's hit squads in Cuba."

"Really?"

"I turned my findings over to the Feds. But you know them. We must by law provide them but they don't have to reciprocate. If they ever made a match I sure as hell never heard about it. Last I heard, the Task Force was digging into sales of lead but found it way common. It follows that a guy making his own weapons would make his own ammo. Last I heard the Task Force was checking out shooting ranges. You want some coffee, B. B.? It's this week's." On Monday morning I might have taken him up on it but Friday afternoon. No way.

A pit stop at the closest Starbuck's for a latte, helped bring me back to earth. Down in the cave, I finished my report, sprayed the rest of my Binaca which must have had some alcohol because I felt even more stoned, and rode the elevator to Captain Hollers' office. The stairs were too daunting in my condition.

Exactly a week ago, I was there, knocking. I knocked again, waited and opened the door a crack. The lights were out and the captain's desk was clear of paperwork. All the boxes were absent, because they were in *my* office.

Relieved, I went over to his water cooler, drank three quick cups, noticed there was nothing in his trash can, I wadded up the cup and put it in my pocket. I then stuffed the report into an envelope and slipped it in a few inches down in the in-basket.

I was pulled in two directions. In one, I wished I could share my accomplishments with my new boss but conversely I was happy as shit my first week as an investigator was over. All I needed now was to fire up the Bubbamobile, ramp up on I.H. 35 South, get home, kick off the boots, assume the position on the couch, drink a cerveza or two and tune into ESPN. Being a detective was an awful lot like work.

Chapter Fifteen

*"Now entering the Edwards Aquifer
environmentally sensitive recharge zone."*

Sign at Austin City Limits

"Travis, you gotta try this salmon," said Merrylee. Auntie Loo's 10th annual fiesta, the Pink Flamingo Party, was full tilt boogie—another roaring success. Willie brought on a few of his best friends – Jimmy Dale Gilmore, Kris Kristopherson, Butch Hancock, Johnny Gimble. Each jammed with Willie and each played a handful of his own latest creations.

Travis held a margarita in each hand, yet somehow managing to wrap an arm around his date, Kristie Bentley. Merrylee, thinking she was a very smart cookie, had poured pink margarita into a pink lemonade glass, even though because of her tender age, was asked to refrain from alcoholic beverages.

Merrylee tossed a hunk of salmon toward her big brother's open mouth. It was a little off target, ricocheting off his chin, disappearing down Kristie Brinkley's ample cleavage.

"Oh, that's just great!" Kristie jerked away from Travis, receiving a frozen margarita down her back. She arched against the cold while at the same time trying to recover the errant piece of salmon.

"Hey, I'm sorry Kris," said Merrylee snapping a picture of the scene while suppressing a smile for the fish in the bra, ice-down-the-back, dance, "my fault, here, let me wipe it up."

"Fuck you! And fuck you too, Travis. Fuck the whole lot of you. I'll be outside when you grow up and are ready to take me home!" Kristie stormed out.

"I suppose this means I'm not getting laid again tonight."

"I'm sorry Bro, but fuck her too if she can't take a joke." She downed the bogus lemonade.

"This has not been my best day and where the fuck are you picking up that language?" Asked Travis smiling at the misery of the whole thing. "How old *are* you anyway?"

Moses came into the kitchen. He had been playing *Duke Nukem 3-D* in the game room upstairs. He caught the tail end of the scene and headed after Kristie. "I'll see if I can help," he said in his deep voice.

"And good luck to you too, sir." Travis toasted his friend. Turning to his sister. "Merrylee, there's something we need to talk about."

"Hey, I know I'm not supposed to be drinking this stuff."

"No, that's cool, well you shouldn't be drinking, but this is really important and I got to tell somebody. Let's go to the ledge and sit." Or jump the fuck off, he thought. Out the patio door, winding their way through the crowd of pink revelers, past the dancers, past the pool, they sat on the ledge overlooking the lake. *Blue Eyes Crying in the Rain* came through the speakers.

"I love Willie," said Travis.

"I hate Willie," said Merrylee.

"You don't hate Willie Nelson. Nobody hates Willie Nelson."

"You're right. I don't hate *him,* it's just the sound of his voice, and what he sings about, you know his lyrics and there's the music itself, and the way he dresses and looks. I'm sure he's a fine guy. So, what's up, Bro?"

"Me and Reverend A just had a big blowout."

"You all were in the library way long. But you know, Trav, you all will get past it, you always do. Dad, in his own strange way, loves you big brother."

"No. This one's different. Serious. I told him about Angel."

"Oh-oh. Why would you do that? You know he hates rappers and she's the rapper's daughter. And she's black. And you know how he feels… Why on earth would you tell him about her?"

"I don't know. I guess I wanted to get to him." Travis clenched his fist and turned it. "It's strange I know. I just got back from New Orleans. I went over there to see her."

"How was she?" Merrylee had never met Angel. Travis had once asked Angel to come to Austin to meet the fam, but she declined.

"They wouldn't let me see her. When I told this guard guy how she and I were at TCU together, it didn't impress him. I got passed around and this one dude sort of listened to me. Guess he wanted to know my intentions, since Angel's father was murdered and all. I almost told the guy how Reverend A was involved, but I wanted to tell Angel first."

"What are you talking about?"

"He didn't say if she was there or not. But I know she was."

"What was Dad involved in?"

"I told Reverend A I wasn't going to work for the Ark this summer, that I had volunteered to work for the Iced Chai Foundation instead."

"Ho. Ho. Ho. Bet he took that well."

"He got in that righteous mode. You know, with that nasally Ross Perot voice.

Travis Tanner, need I remind you that you have accepted Jesus Christ as your personal savior? How could it be possible then to trade in Our Lord for a common idolater, fornicator and general shiftless skunk? We keep tabs on those so-called foundations. They are run by Africans and Muslims and are fronts for prostitution and drug dealing. I can show you tapes and photographs. Thoroughly disgusting, non-Christian behavior."

"I didn't want to argue with him Merrylee, but the shit hit the fan when I told him I was planning to donate the bulk of my money from Grandpa and Grandma Tanner's estate to the *afro's* foundation. I hadn't planned on doing that but Reverend A got me so pissed..."

"You didn't give away your inheritance, Travis!"

"I told him, I'm 20. Next May, I'll be 21. Told him I went to the Iced Chai Foundation and I'd give them a big donation, hoping and praying it would make up for what Reverend A did to Angel's family. Guess I wanted to see him squirm."

"I'm sure you pushed all the right buttons, Travis. So, you told Dad you were giving your money away and he didn't like the idea?" Her words conveyed mock horror. "I can't believe that. Are we talking about the same Reverend Arvin Tanner we know and love?"

"After I got back from New Orleans, I saw Mr. Furman, our accountant. He set it up so the Foundation would get a chunk of money when I turned 21. I figured a million in there, maybe two. But it's huge, Merrylee. Seems Grandpa cashed in his oil wells at the exact right time and was an early investor in Xerox, Microsoft and Intel. I'm not going to tell Dad or the Iced Chai people how much there is, but between you and me, we are going to be a couple of *very* rich kids."

"I was wondering what was in the trust."

"Maybe if I show up in New Orleans with 10 or 15 mil, they'll let me see Angel." Travis downed his drink and threw the glass over the ledge. He imagined what it would be like to jump. There was a distant tinkle of glass breaking.

"You know Travis, no girl is worth that much money. I should know, I am one. Well, I'd like to think *I'd* be worth it but... And what did Dad supposedly do to Angel's family, would you answer *that* question?"

Travis wished he hadn't brought it up; Merrylee would never quit on it.

"He told me he'd tie up my inheritance in court if I tried to give it away."

"Wow. Travis, that's some heavy shit."

"Unfortunately, it gets heavier. I got mad, real mad. I got hotter and he got colder. I raked some books off the shelves. I'll have to apologize to Auntie Loo for messing up her library. Anyway, he couldn't take it—spun me around and pinned me to the wall, his hand on my throat. I thought he was going to kill me. He commenced to slap the holy shit out of me. Asshole's stronger than he looks. But I'm bigger. I broke loose, pushed him back and he fell down on the floor. I took off for the door, told him it was *my* money and not his."

"Good point."

"I told him if he tried to stop me, I'd tell everyone about his evil little project." Travis told his mother and the family financial advisor Larry Furman about Reverend Arvin Tanner's transgressions but had stopped short of going to the authorities. "I told Reverend A I was going to tell Angel all about it."

"What *are* you talking about?"

"Remember when Iced Chai was shot?" Merrylee looked in her brother's eyes. He could see the realization forming, and nodded.

"No, Travis! You're not saying Dad was involved in the killing somehow?"

"Up to his slimy little eyeballs."

"I don't believe you, Travis! Dad is a little conservative but..."

"Conservative?" Travis' laugh had a sarcastic edge to it.

Willie Nelson finished crying in the rain and as the applause began to ebb, Lucinda Tanner's husky voice came across the speakers.

"And now, the moment we have all been awaiting. Time to announce our Princess and our Prince of Pink. So gather 'round mi señores, señoras and señoritas."

"I guess we'd better," said Merrylee. "We can talk after. It'll work out Trav." She yanked him up by the arm. "But I still think you're wrong about Dad."

"The envelope please." Auntie Loo took a pink envelope from her other hand and tore it open. "This year's Princess of Pink – is a dear friend, a great writer, the funniest lady I know." Pause. Pause. Pause. A drum roll. "Molly Ivins! Molly, come up here and get your crown." Lucinda had toys, trinkets and a pink sequined crown for Princess Molly. Campy. Tacky. Prized.

"I'm at a loss for words," said Molly.

"That's a first," said someone from the crowd. Laughter. A short but funny acceptance speech. Congratulations all around.

"And now if that wasn't enough for you all." Lucinda tore open a second envelope. "This year's Prince. A man I've known for longer than I've known Molly. And believe me, that's a *long* time. I've known this gentle person for 20 years. I was nine when we met." Laughter. "I used to change his diapers. A short time later I taught him life's most valuable lesson." She paused.

"The blowing one's nose, lesson. Learning to tie one's shoes is a big one too. Shoelaces dragging behind you, caked with mud, flopping this way and that can be dangerous. But, if one cannot effectively and efficiently blow one's nose, one will never be attractive to the opposite sex. One will never get a date, never procreate. Sad but true. The curriculum was simple but, and if you don't know this maybe you should take notes, blow one side at a time, not both at once. To this day he is still doing it correctly. Of course, he still hasn't learned to tie his shoes. That's why he only wears shit-kicker boots or loafers." Pause. Pause. Pause. A drum roll.

"Presenting this year's Prince of Pink, my favorite nephew, Travis Tanner!"

"Oh, good God!" Said Travis under his breath.

Chapter Sixteen

"I don't care if it rains or freezes, 'long as I have my plastic Jesus, riding on the dashboard of my car."

Old Tent Revival Spiritual

My knock at the screen door of Moses and Etta Harper's duplex on East 11th Street brought an elderly woman and an equally elderly dog. The dog, of the species *grandmaw*, could barely bark and being a wide body, wasn't doing so well in the walking department either.

"Yip, yip, yip." The dog and Mrs. Harper trudged through the living room, around a couch, past a chair and end table. As they approached with excruciating slowness, I looked in to see open living room windows and a box window fan, at eight in the morning, already running. The television was on, tuned to a sports channel.

"I'm a comin'. I'm a comin'.'"

"Yip, yip, yip."

"Mrs. Harper? Hi, I'm B. B. Rivers with Bergstrom Investigations. I hope I'm not too early."

"Not at all young man, you come in now." She unlatched the screen door lock and pushed against the door. "We've been up for hours. It's just about lunch time for us." She chuckled. The dog sniffed the cuff of my jeans. I wore my old ranch wranglers since I'd be driving all day. There would be a faint scent of horse, cows, chickens, ranch dog and maybe the armadillo I had been staking out for the past couple of years that the Tide didn't get out. The mutt gave a wag of approval, let me pass and waddled along side.

"Come in and cool off a spell. Already gettin' hot out there on the porch." Mrs. Harper was a big, dark woman, as wide as tall, wearing a flower print dress, scarf and a white apron. She looked familiar. The lady on the brown glass syrup bottle. Her home was modest and clean.

"Moses, you get up now. We have a guest." Moses Harper Senior filled a black leather recliner. He had the Sports Page of the Statesman open on his lap, with a cup of coffee in one hand and a cigar in the other. My kind of guy.

"Would you care for some coffee? Fresh perked?" Asked Mrs. Harper.

"Sure. That would be great."

"I'm Moses Harper." After a couple of false starts, Mr. Harper rose from the recliner. His voice was low and deep. "You here to talk about Moses Junior?" He put the smoking cigar across a notch of a heavy glass Dallas Cowboy ashtray and delivered a bone crunching squeeze to my hand.

"I didn't realize folks were still working on the killin's."

"Seems I'm the only one working on it at the moment."

"Well bless you for that. What can we do for you?" Asked Mrs. Harper. "Here, let's go sit at the dining room table. You want some cream and sugar for your coffee?" We sat and I took out a sharpened pencil and placed it on a fresh page of my yellow pad.

"I've been going over the APD files. The police admitted they have no idea who killed your son and those other kids or even why it happened. Seems like a terrible waste."

"Oh, it was," said Mrs. Harper.

"Makes no sense," said Mr. Harper. "Our boy was just 18. Star football player for the Rollingwood Armadillos. His coach? He saw Moses Junior play middle school ball. Recruited him right then and there. Moses was over six feet tall and 200 pounds in the 8th grade. When Moses Junior got high school age, the coach set him up with an apartment over by Zilker Park so's he'd have a west side address. That way he'd be eligible to play for Rollingwood."

"Really?"

"Do it all the time around Austin. The money's over on the west side. You play football?"

"I played for Blanco High out in the Hill Country. I grew up on a ranch. Got a scholarship to Southwest."

"What position?" Asked Mr. Harper.

"Linebacker."

"Moses Junior was a defensive end."

"All District. All State. High School All American." I did my homework. Moses Junior would have gone far.

"In his junior *and* senior year," said Mr. Harper. "College recruiters came to see him from USC, Florida, Ohio State and even Notre Dame and we're not even Catholic, but he wanted to stay in Austin. So he committed to UT"

"Why was that?" A strange thought dripped through my mind. What if a rival university had Moses Harper killed? Was it a stretch that an irate Catholic Bishop was so disappointed in Moses not signing with the Fighting Irish he contracted a hit?

"He was a good boy," said Mrs. Harper. "Moses Junior didn't come along until we were in our forties. We're a little older than his friends' parents. Since he was our youngest, he felt like he ought to stay close to home, take care of his folks."

"What about the other kids that were killed? Did you know them?" Max said think outside the box. Who else could the killer have been after besides the Rev? Moses? Kristie? Merrylee? Travis? It didn't make any sense.

"Travis and Merrylee would come to the house. Merrylee was only fifteen but very smart. Travis was smart too. Helped us file our income tax. Remember that, Moses?" He nodded, his attention was back on the paper. "Moses Senior, when he was drivin'," she patted her husband on the shoulder, "would drop them off at the mall to play video games."

"That's right. I'd bring 'em to Highland Mall in the morning and pick 'em up in the evening."

"What about their father?"

"The Reverend?" Mrs. Harper's face turned darker, worried. "I met him once. He was mean spirited for a man of God. I don't think he liked black folks. But Travis and Merrylee pretty much did whatever they wanted. According to Merrylee, Reverend Tanner traveled a lot and was never at home. We never met their mother."

And what about the Rev's ex-wife? Maybe she hired somebody to bump him off. Wives have murdered their husbands before. Maybe I ought to head on over to Colorado and check it out.

"Moses Junior mowed lawns so's he'd have the quarters to play on the weekend. He got so good he could keep a game going..." Mrs. Harper teared up. "The Tanner family was well off. Junior always paid his own way though."

"The Tanner kids were both nice," said Mr. Harper. "Very polite. Always asked how we was doin'. Said *yes ma'am* and *yes sir.*"

"When was the last time you saw them?"

"It was that day."

"Really?"

"They came rolling up in that old black car," said Mr. Harper. "They honked and Moses Junior ran out to them. I saw her open the rear door for him and he jumped in. They rolled the window down and waved. That's the last we saw..."

"What time of day was that?" I tried to be understanding, concerned and found it was easy because I was concerned. I didn't like the idea some asshole got paid to end the life of those teenagers.

"Four thirty, maybe five," said Mr. Harper.

"You want a touch up on your coffee, young man?" Asked Mrs. Harper.

"No, thank you. My girlfriend and I are traveling out to West Texas this afternoon. She's waiting in the truck. Got to be hitting the trail. But I did want to meet you all and tell you I'm going to find out who killed your son." It *was* getting personal.

"We've been praying on it for five years." Mrs. Harper took her husband's huge hand in hers.

"Bless you, boy," said Mr. Harper looking up from his paper.

"You come back any time," said Mrs. Harper "day or night. We always got a fresh pot of coffee on."

I bet they do, I thought as I stepped off the cement porch. The dog was at the screen door barking as soon as I left. And I thought he liked me. Go figure.

"What a nice couple." I steered through the East Austin street scene down 11th to I.H. 35. Force of habit from APD days, I eyeballed everyone we passed. Two suspected crack deals, three prostitutes, four, if you count the midget.

"They seemed down-home," I said, getting on the freeway. "Maybe like Mom and Dad would be, if Dad didn't take a trip to where the wild things are."

I took the all too familiar U.S. Highway 290 west out of Austin, through Oak Hill and Dripping Springs. Five miles west of Dripping Springs was the turnoff to Blanco, which followed the Blanco River to the family ranch.

"Willie Nelson's from Dripping Springs."

"That's good info."

"Local folks just call it Drippin'. It's the first hill of the Hill Country."

"I'm getting hungry."

"Already? We just left forty-five minutes ago. There's not much here unless you like Dairy Queen. Or how about Taco Hut?" I named the eateries as we drove by. She shook her head at each.

Her curls bounced and then settled. "Hamburger Hill? That sounds about my speed. Was my speed. What are you hungry for?"

"I feel like a quiche."

"Oooh. You *do* feel like a quiche." I pinched her tummy.

"Watch the Road, Billy. 290 is a very dangerous highway."

"Okay. There's the Sidesaddle Café. Seems like they'd offer quiche, don't you think?"

"Sounds like a gay bar to me."

"Dry county. Baptists are big here, so no bars. Baptists are scared of alcohol, you know. Afraid it might lead to dancin'."

"Funny."

"I thought so. Looks like we done run out of restaurants. What'd you think Patricia? Do *you* want me to turn around." I had on my game show host voice. "*Or* should we go on to the next metropolis, Johnson City? Boyhood home of Lyndon Baines ..."

"Hey, there's a farm stand sign. *Goat cheese.* That sounds good!"

"I can't stand goat cheese."

"Why?"

"It reminds me of tofu and I already ate tofu this year. You know, I've had dreams about tofu. I was on this big boat, like the Titanic and was leaning out over the bridge like the Leonardo kid and I saw this mammoth block of frozen tofu. We were on a collision course with the thing and..."

"You're silly. Goat cheese is nothing at all like tofu. Except they're both good for you. You know, healthy. Let's check it out."

"Cowboys don't care about healthy. You never see a cowboy go into a bar..."

"Especially not in Drippin'," she said laughing. I pointed at her acknowledging her humor as we bottomed out on a cattle guard, smashing my hat on the roof of the pickup.

"When was the last time you saw a cowboy order a tofu sandwich at a bar? It'd be like—Hey bartender, gimme one o' dem sasparillas?"

"Tofu and goat cheese are not at all alike."

"Never see 'em bellying up eating a goat cheese sandwich either. Hippie food. Like hummus. Or was it humus? Hippies eat tofu and goat cheese and you know how I feel about hippies."

Silence. I guess that was about how far that conversation was going. During those times when you say something stupid and your main squeeze lets it hang out there and sort of consider your stupidity, I flashed on T. Rex and the Thai stick joint and his weird-mobile wondering if T. Rex would be classified as a hippie.

The desire to please the woman I loved was greater than my disgust for tofu or goat cheese, plus I hated reflective moments.

I maneuvered the big truck down a Hays County back road, across a low slung cattle guard that would have dented my hat if I hadn't removed it. I still banged my head on the roof of the cab as we lurched out the other side, and drove on to a pretty little white farmhouse with turquoise trim and walk-in cooler on the side.

The farmer's sign read:

Self Serve
Checks Okay
Cheese Inside

We parked in the caliche driveway and got out. There was nobody around. Some goats were lying in the shade of some huge oak trees. A big white dog lifted up his massive head and plopped it back down in the dust. We swung open a big metal door and went inside the cooler. A blackboard listed prices. Blue Ribbons hung on the walls between photos of goats. The goats looked to be smiling.

"It's a little cheese-tasting room. Isn't this nice, Billy? Wow, it's cold in here." She spread some cheese on a cracker and ate it in one bite. "This is good. Here, Billy, try this."

"I drove you back here but damned if I'll be eatin' no goat cheese." I was firm about it and grabbed her arm to fend her off but dang it all, she switched hands and shoved a big hunk of cheese and cracker into my mouth. Sneaky little...

But...

"Hey you're right. This *is* good. Spicy. What was that?"

"That was," Patricia, read the label. "*Chévre with New Mexico Chile Pepper.*"

"Let's get some of that. And one of these *Garlic and Parsleys,* and a *Pesto* and a *Chipotle.* I love chipotle." I tried the cheese which was laced with smoked jalapeno. It was tasty. We picked out four containers, a couple pounds of tomatoes, box of crackers, added it up on a calculator the farmers left and stuffed our money in the cash box.

As we returned to Highway 290, Patricia constructed miniature cheese and tomato sandwiches on crackers. She popped them one by one in my mouth as I drove.

"Real trusting folks, there must have been a couple hundred dollars in that cigar box."

"Billy, we're in the country now. Folks still trust each other out here."

"I know. My mom does a self-serve over in Blanco. Sells eggs and chickens, emu oil and turkeys for Thanksgiving."

"When am I going to meet your parents? Your mother sounds darling."

"Oh, she's darling alright, but she's mad at me right now because I haven't come to visit her."

"How long's it been, Billy?" I wondered how Mom was doing pretty much all alone on the family cattle ranch except for Dad, the singing ex-cop. Sounds like a re-run from *The Lawrence Welk Show. And now, from Blanco, Tex-ass, the singing ex-a-cop.*

We used to have some marathon late night chats after I blew in from a night of honky tonkin' and bootscootin'. I'd find Mom sitting in the kitchen drinking black coffee and smoking cigarettes, and we'd get down and dirty on every subject. It was as close as we ever got. Mom felt she was forced into independence, hawking chicken eggs to supplement the retirement check from APD. It wasn't how she thought it would be. First brother John left, then me and then Dad's brain left but his body stayed on at the ranch.

"I thought maybe we might could stop on this trip, but I know she'd rustle up a project for me, like rebuilding the barn or tracking raccoons or staking out the damn armadillo that's been terrorizing her tomatoes." I wasn't much good at stakeouts. I couldn't get comfortable. Once I drug an old couch out by the chicken house. Of course, I left it there and it's rain soaked and coated with chicken shit. It's still there I suppose.

I did enjoy the ranch, spending time with Too Tall, my horse and Hank, my dog. And Harry, my dad. I'd need to visit Mom pretty soon. Why is there so much unfinished business with women?

"You know something Patricia, I was wrong about goat cheese, although I still have strong feelings about goat ropers in general. But, you're right, it doesn't taste anything like tofu. I bet Max would like that place." She popped another goat cheese and cracker in my mouth.

We approached the Blanco turnoff, but I kept going. We sped down the highway through Johnson City, childhood home of

Lyndon Johnson. The LBJ sign was peeling and fading away like the local Texas Democrats. It read,

Home of ___don B John__
Heartland of a Great American

Most everybody, except Mom and Dad and a few hardcores, are Republican in Blanco County now. We drove past President Johnson's ranch and presidential retreat on the Pedernales River, where Lady Bird still lives. We stopped for peaches at *Oma's Haus* in Stonewall and down the touristy main drag of the German town of Fredericksberg. Shop after shop lined Main Street, offering everything from handmade furniture to food and wine to knickknacks to clothes.

"I can't stand it. You've got to pull over now."

"What's the matter?" I thought I'd run over a dog or something.

"There's the cutest little dress shop back there. We have to go check it out. I haven't got a stitch that fits me anymore and if I eat any more of this goat cheese I'll have nothing whatsoever to wear..." We had both put on weight since college. I suspected we had put on weight since we left the townhouse this morning.

As I pulled the Bubbamobile into the next available parking place, I realized, if I had detoured through Blanco to visit Mom at the ranch, we would have made a wide arc around Fred (what these locals called their little money-appropriating town), thus avoiding the darling, and very likely expensive, little shop.

"Okay, but let's be quick," theory was, the more rushed the female of the species, the less she would buy, "or we'll be driving all night."

Three hundred dollars to the plastic god later and we were on the road again, through Fred with one more necessary stop for gourmet coffee. This was the frontier, the border, we would soon be entering the land of bad coffee. Like my namesake Bilbo Baggins descending into the Caves of Moria, the coffee out past here would be weak and watery and served in a white Styrofoam cup. Cream would not be organic half and half but a chemical powder served in little paper packets. And it would be thus all the way to Santa Fe.

Scary.

On out 290 going west, we sped through a bump in the road called Harper, Texas. I thought of Mr. and Mrs. Harper and their duplex in East Austin and their dead son Moses. What a waste. What could posses a man, a religious man like Reverend Arvin Asshole Tanner to hire a hit man to kill Moses Junior. That is, if he did do that. T. Rex believed Reverend A capable of the deed. Max seemed to think the stars did not exactly point to him as the killer. I would tend to lean toward Max but my gut feeling was giving me a double message, saying not only that I had eaten too much cheese, but Tanner must have had something to do with it. Not with me eating too much, but with the death of Moses Harper.

But then again, Captain Hollers told me to be wary of gut feelings. I'm confused. Time for a cerveza break?

Highway 290 merged with Interstate 10 and since the speed limit was now 80, I bumped it to 85, hoping the cops still gave the average tax paying citizen the 5 m.p.h. buffer. We crossed the Llano River at the town of Junction.

"It's been a long time," Patricia's cute little feet were on the dashboard applying a coat of red nail polish to her toes, "since we've been on a road trip. Not since Graceland back in college. So much drier here than Austin. I wonder what the temp is?"

"About 105," I said looking at the dashboard thermometer. "I'm glad the Bubbamobile's got a high powered a/c."

"What time do you think we'll get to Balmoreah?"

"If we don't find any more cute shops or farm stands, we ought to be there by midnight. That's figuring in an hour for dinner. We can stop for gas and eat at the same time."

"Okie dokie. I'm going to take a napi-poo. Wake me if you see a prairie dog or something." Sonora flew by like a desert mirage. I bumped it to 90 and then to 100. 110 m.p.h. brought up thoughts of that tire recall last year and rods and pistons flying through the engine. Do diesels contain rods and pistons, I wondered? I backed off to 85 in self-preservation. While Patricia napped, I enjoyed a spectacular desert sunset. Would love some of that Thai stick right at that moment.

I pulled off the freeway at Ozona, getting gas for the pickup. We ate dinner there, some real greasy Tex-Mex, thus gassing up ourselves as well. The chile relleno at Mexican Madre's was not in the same league as Las Manitas in Austin. And the iced tea tasted like liquid metal. No way was I going to try the coffee.

"How's the case going, Sherlock? You haven't talked much about it."

"Reading through those boxes of files makes me appreciate how much paperwork the cops churned up. The killer was a bad ass motherfucker though," I whispered.

"Billy, your language."

"That's why I'm whispering. You know what he did? He killed Moses Harper and Kristie Bentley and then cut off their little fingers."

"Oooh. That's sick. I wonder what he did with them?"

I shrugged. I hadn't thought about where all those pinky fingers ended up.

"Maybe he ate them ala Hannibal the Cannibal. Maybe he's a collector and they're in a refrigerator somewhere?"

"Oooh. Maybe he sells them to Tex-Mex restaurants," said Patricia.

I took a sip of tea. "I am enjoying this case though. Meeting the people involved, like Max and Auntie Loo, the artist and socialite. And I'm pretty proud of myself for discovering something." I let it hang there for a minute until Patricia came back with, "What?"

I paused and looked to the right, to the left, under the booth.

"What?"

I whispered. "It's, ah, just that, well..."

"What is it, Billy?" She put down her fork of cheese enchilada.

"One of the kids in the murder case, the boy, young man now, Travis Tanner, whose body was never found? As it turns out, he's still alive."

"Everybody thought he was dead?"

"Been hiding out in Mexico. It's a secret. No one knows except his ex-roommate in Fort Worth, Travis's girlfriend because the roommate told her, and of course Max Culpepper, the florist, from his intuitive or psychic readings and stuff." I was counting on my fingers.

"And Auntie Loo, the aunt, she knows because she's the one who's been hiding him. Let's see. And the retired police officer, Captain Warlick, the man we're here to see. Me and now you. And the killer must know Travis is still alive, since he didn't kill him. Travis himself knows.

"Sounds like quite a few people know this little secret," she picked up her fork and headed to the mouth with it.

"Well, yeah, I guess it's not *that* big a secret," I was looking at nine fingers. "But I don't think anyone in APD, except for Warlick knows. It's not in any of the files. I'm not sure if the FBI knows or not. They're so sneaky. I trust them about as far as I can throw this chile relleno." I hefted it upon my fork. It was pretty heavy. I ate a little, chewed on some tea, dumped three packages of sugar in to cover up the hard water taste.

"Max, he's a real trip, seems to know what I'm thinking before I think it. A little spooky."

"That's how psychics are, silly. I'd like to meet him."

"Oh, I predict you will. You don't believe in that stuff, do you?"

"I knew you were going to say that," said Patricia, scooping some frijoles, salsa and Spanish rice onto a corn tortilla. "You know what I feel your problem is?"

"What's my problem?" I didn't want to know but I'm a polite guy.

"You're too serious."

"Murder is a serious business."

"That sounds like an excellent title for a book. *Murder Is A Serious Business,* by Bilbo Baggins Rivers."

"Hey, ix-nay on the il-bo-bay, somebody might hear you."

"Right, as if the murderer followed us out here. Where *are* we, by the way?"

"Ozona, Texas."

"Like he, or she, followed us out here to Ozona, Texas, and now he or she knows your real name is..."

"Don't say it." I put my hand over her mouth and she bit my pinkie. "Ow, Hannibal!"

"Okay Billy, your secret's safe with me. I wonder what's for dessert out here in the desert?"

"Cactus pie."

"You're funny. You are, and it's one of the two things women want from a man."

"Oh yeah, what's the *other* thing?"

"The other thing is to..." She scooted close to me in the booth (we always sit on the same side of the booth) and whispered the *other* thing in my ear.

I turned red. I didn't blush, my freckles expanded and melded together.

After the *flan,* as we walked toward the door to pay our bill, I glanced into the large mirror covering one whole wall of the restaurant. Wanted to make sure my Stetson was on straight. A beefy man in a dark blue suit, incongruous with the cowboys (I mean, I fit right in) in the place, sat in the back of the restaurant his eyes on us. He looked like a Fed or maybe a mafia hit man. I didn't tell Patricia, because I figured I was just being paranoid. But he could as easily have been a businessman exiting the freeway for a beer and some Tex-Mex. But an educated guess from a cop for five years? Nobody except the undertaker would be wearing a dark blue suit in Ozona, Texas on a Saturday night.

I hung back in the parking lot and when no one came out of Mexican Madre's to follow us, I drove back to the freeway. We took I.H. 10 past Fort Stockton and got off at the Balmoreah exit, drove three more miles to the State Park where Patricia reserved an efficiency cabin, compliments of *Texas Highways* agazine.

"I'm going to call Captain Warlick," I said as I unlocked the cabin door.

"It's almost midnight, Billy. You'll wake the poor man."

"He said to call when we got in. Stays up and watches the *Late, Late Show* every night. Said he was an insomniac."

"Like somebody else we know?"

"I'm not an insomniac. I'm just afraid I'll miss something."

I dialed the number. "Busy. Who could he be talking to this time of night?" We unpacked and strolled through the park. The cool desert night air was great after the evening humidity of Austin, where sometimes it would still be in the 80s at midnight. After we came back in, I tried Warlick again.

"Still busy."

"The man's got the phone off the hook. Probably decided to go to bed and didn't want to be bothered. Why don't you call him in the morning."

"You're right."

"And if you don't hop in this bed this very minute, you will miss one of the greatest fucks of..."

I was in bed next to her before she finished her sentence.

"...your life. But first the teeth." She sprung back out of bed, grabbing her toothbrush and floss, and paraded naked to the bathroom. God she was beautiful.

"Billy, you gotta wake up."

"What time is it?"

"I don't know, maybe seven. You gotta see this."

"What is it? You found a Starbucks?"

"Better."

"What could be better than a grande latte so early in the morning, with the possible exception of a venti latte?" I yawned, stretched and rolled back over. "Come on, have a heart, I drove all day yesterday and didn't get to sleep until two A.M."

"You were the one who had to watch the late, late movie."

"Somehow I don't think it was Christian Slater and one of those Arquette sisters being chased by bad guys across America that did me in," I thought back to the marathon love making. She was a woman who took forever to come. But when she did, I'm talking about waking the neighbors. Dogs howling. Gophers poking toothsome heads from holes saying, "What in the fuck was that? Did you hear that? Yeah, what was that?"

"You gotta see this." She pulled me out of bed. I was always surprised at how strong she was.

"This better be good." I was whipped.

She took off her shorts, halter-top and panties, turned around and did a *Penthouse* pose obviously for my benefit. I went from at easy to attention in about five seconds. But she slipped into her swimsuit, threw mine at me and taking me by the hand, pulled me through the door. I was hopping on one foot, struggling to put on my flip-flops and let go of Patricia to pull up my trunks.

"Pat!" She gave me that *call me Patricia* look and grabbed my arm.

"Come on. Nobody cares how white your butt is. It is pretty white though." We walked hand in hand down the well-worn dirt path to the pool.

"Wow." We stepped back in time as we passed through a rock entryway into a vintage 1940's bath house. The pool lay beyond, surrounded by trees and lawn.

"Nice."

"It's the biggest natural swimming pool in the world."

"Everything's bigger in Texas."

"Three times bigger than Barton Springs." We walked along the wide sidewalk shaded by sycamore trees. The bottom of the pool looked maybe six feet deep but painted on the sidewalk at the edge was *28 feet*. Scuba divers were already below in wetsuits.

"I wonder if it's cold." I looked over the edge through the crystal clear water to the bottom putting my big toe in to test the temp. Big mistake.

"Let's find out." She pushed me in.

"Whoa." For the second time in a week I was reduced to monosyllables as cold water took my breath away. She dove in and swam over to me as I flailed comically to the far side of the pool.

"This is great. So refreshing. Too bad it's so far. If we drove straight through from Austin, how long would it take us?"

"No stops for goat cheese or sun dresses? Maybe seven to eight hours."

We splashed. We frolicked in a school of minnows. We dunked each other. We played grab-ass. We kissed. I put my hand playfully down the front of her suit and got kicked playfully in the balls for my efforts. After I recovered, we kissed again.

I fearlessly (on the outside) climbed a rickety ladder and dove off the high dive, plunging deep into the clear blue water. I figured I would touch bottom but it remained beyond reach. A little deeper. Deeper. I had to give up and came up sputtering.

"You okay?"

After I caught my breath. "This pool is *deep*. Too much pressure on the ear drums. Yeouch."

I climbed out and sat next to Patricia, our feet dangling in the water. The minnows swam between our toes. I shook my head like a dog and water flew from my hair. She laughed. "This reminds me of when we first met Billy, do you remember?"

"The first time ever I saw your face? On the San Marcos River. You floated by in an inner tube. I remember you were such an *intensely* cute chick. I whistled at you and asked your name."

"And I said, who wants to know? And you said..."

"I'm B. B. Rivers, ma'am. Do you go to Southwest? And you asked me, "What's the B. B. stand for" and I followed you along the bank until I tripped and fell into a patch of elephant ears."

"I didn't stop laughing for a week. It made my week. Made my semester."

"Remember, as you were rounding the bend, I shouted, 'meet me at Pepper's at seven!'"

"What a brazen thing to do."

"But you showed up," I shrugged my shoulders, palms up.

"You were too cute, too, back then, all the red hair, falling off the bank like that, the huge leaf hanging from your head, shaking your head like a dog."

"You mean I'm not so cute now?" I reached down and scooped some iced cold pool water onto her exposed stomach.

"Cuter." She splashed me back. "At least there's more of you, and don't say there's more of me, too. Not if you want an enjoyable day, Mr. Rivers!"

"Why did it take so long for us to reconnect?"

"You had to go through the entire female student body at Southwest and then all those girls in all those offices in downtown Austin."

She had me there. "I love you, Pat…Patricia." I leaned over and laid a kiss on her wet belly.

"I love you too, Bilbo."

"Hey!"

"What?"

I sang, just loud enough for her to hear but not for everyone in the pool to enjoy—

"Well you can call me B. B.,
… or you can call me Bill,
… or you can call me Billy,
… or you can call me Will.
But ya doesn't have to call me Bilbo."

"Funny guy."

"It works for Dad. You know, I ought to give Captain Warlick a call." We got up nearly already dry from the early morning West Texas sun and walked, my arm around her shoulders, her arm around my waist, back to the cabin.

"Still busy. I wonder what's really going on here?"

"What time did you plan to meet?"

"Not 'til two o'clock. In the meantime we could see the sights."

"There's only one sight I want to see."

"Really? You want to see the large telescope at McDonald Observatory?"

"You're getting warm." She pulled the cotton string holding up my swimming trunks.

Chapter Seventeen

"It is a benefit to cross the great water."

Reading from the *I Ching*

"Hello, Maximus. It's Lucinda."

"Hi there. I knew it was you."

"Using your psychic talent?"

"Caller I.D. actually. Where are you?"

"I'm in the limo, on MoPac." Lucinda wore a Liz Sport white top, matching pleated tennis skirt and Adidas sneakers. As she talked, she twirled her tennis racket on the tip of her finger.

"All during my tennis match I couldn't take my mind, and a few other organs, off you. Are you free for lunch?"

"Saturday is our busiest day. Two weddings today and it's our best retail day—walk-ins and all. People will be picking up flowers for parties and church on Sunday."

"Are you turning me down? I don't know if I'm ready for that."

"I couldn't say no to you, love. Do you know how to find the shop?"

"Give us something for James to aim at."

"Take Windsor to Niles Road and look for the stand of bamboo."

Max and Lucinda enjoyed a healthy lunch of stir- fried veggies on the patio of Mother's Café in Hyde Park.

"I like you, Maximus."

"I like you too, Lucinda."

"I'm going to visit my niece tomorrow at the sanitarium. Do you want to come?"

"It's what the doctor ordered. I completed the astrological chart on Merrylee, and I believe I can help her."

"Help her in what way, Maximus?"

"There is something you should know about me, Lucinda. I am a student of the occult."

"Whatever do you mean? Witchcraft?" She reached for her cigar case and lighter and put them away remembering Mother's was a non-smoking environment.

"Nothing but ritual that...another bloody religion. What I study voyages beyond ritual and delves into the substance of the Universe."

"You're saying being a witch and being a Baptist are the same?" Lucinda laughed.

"More like being a Methodist." They both laughed. "No, I'm pulling your leg." And a beautiful leg it is, he thought. "If we wish to experience God, we should do as Jesus and the prophets advised." He paused and sipped his tea. "We must go into our closets, finding God within our own being. I've been privileged to study with living masters in their individual quests to find God."

"You ready?" She asked. Max picked up the check. "I knew you studied with the Tibetan Buddhists."

"I trekked to the Himalayas of Tibet and studied with the Lamas. I lived with a swami in India who could be in two places at the same instant and could operate in multiple levels of consciousness. I smoked ganja with the Rastafarians in Jamaica. I surfed with a Kahuna in Hawaii. I spent a summer with a Shaman and we hiked to the four sacred mountains of the Hopi. I even went to the Pacific Northwest for ice cream with Jerry Garcia."

She smiled. "You know, the Dalai Lama came to my house."

"Wonderful man. Unfortunately, I have yet to meet him. I have studied with some of his students, and teachers."

As they waited for the check, they talked more about spirituality, books, art and travel. And thought they would take a trip when this crisis was over. Max paid for the meal and they walked hand in hand to the limo.

"So, you are coming with me to visit Merrylee tomorrow?"

"I wouldn't miss it."

"Maybe you can come by my home in Westlake Hills and pick me up?" How would ten A.M. work for you? You don't work on Sundays?"

"I don't work on Sunday and I would love to pick you up, however, there is a dilemma."

"What sort of dilemma?" They got into the limo and Lucinda, fired up a cigar. She cracked her window so the smoke would not waft toward Max.

"The last car I drove was a 1961 Chevy. And it was new. Puts a damper on picking up chicks. But how about this, I shall have one of our drivers charge the battery on a delivery van and we'll both come by. As long as we don't drive on I.H. 35 we'll be fine."

"I don't know, Maximus. The Sanitarium is way up north. Let us just pick you up in the limo. Where do you live?"

Back at the shop, Max used the remains of the day to study the various relationships the astrological chart presented. He calmed his mind and again summoned Oracle. For his *I Ching* reading he received *The Creative*, a very powerful dispensation indeed. An upright and true reading. He now knew for certain what he was about to do was appropriate. He brewed a concoction of two very rare herbs and the root of a flower that blooms for three days a year brought back from a high mountain pass on the Chinese-Tibetan border. These would be mixed with other herbs, barks and roots obtained from a dusty shelf in Dr. Ling's back room.

After he closed the shop, he biked down Windsor and followed the trail across the Town Lake footbridge into Zilker Park. Every morning and evening, as he biked to and from the shop, he stopped for a contemplative moment at the midpoint of the bridge. That evening, two swans, one white and one black, flew under the bridge as he stared down into the water. A wonderful sight! The two landed gracefully on the water upstream. "If I were a betting man," said Max aloud, "I would bet there was significance to that."

He continued on to his travel trailer in the r.v. park across from the South entrance to Barton Springs pool. There was plenty of living space in the converted mansion where he ran his shop but Max needed a place to get away. A retreat. Here he would prepare for his most righteous adventure.

The following morning, Max biked the four-mile loop from his trailer, back across the MoPac footbridge down the North side of Town Lake, back across the First Street Bridge and up Barton Springs on the south side. He took his morning swim and sat in on the Texas 42 game with the philosophers.

"This almost seems normal." Max flipped over the dominoes, mixing them up.

"What's that?" Asked one of the philosophers.

Max shook his head. From his vantage point at the picnic table on Yogi Hill, he could see his trailer parked under an ancient live oak in the r.v. park across the soccer field. He considered the tree, *quercus virginiana*. A beautiful specimen, he thought. As he waited for a philosopher to play a tile, a white limo pulled up to the curb of the trailer park.

"Got to run, gentlemen."

Lucinda slid out of the limo, stretched, bent over to touch her toes. This simple act of stretching put smiles on the faces of the old philosophers. Those who could see that far.

"I have a date with destiny," said Max

"Looks like Destiny is a tall black-haired beauty with long legs," said one of the men. Lucinda fired up a slim cigar and walked toward the trailer.

"Indeed," answered Max.

"Is that Cher?" Asked one.

"Better." Max slid his dominos into the bone pile and got up from the picnic table.

"I always thought he was gay," said one of the philosophers as Max rode his bike across the field and out the exit waving to Lucinda. She was knocking on the metal front door of the trailer. "You know, being a florist and all."

"Guess not," said another.

"Hi, Maximus."

"Lucinda, you look ravishing this morning. Come on in. Shall I put on some tea?"

"That would be nice. Well, look at this. Here's one of my paintings. I haven't seen it for years."

"I've always admired your work. I could accommodate but a small piece in this tiny space. I've owned it for twenty years."

"I was nine when I painted it. Should I put this out?" She held up the cigar.

"Doesn't bother me."

"Speaking of long, slim, hot things, how's Minimus?"

"I thought we were on a schedule."

"There will always be time for the two of you." She called James, the limo driver, on her cell phone and asked him to run to Mozart's for cappuccinos and come back in thirty minutes.

A half hour later the two emerged from the trailer as the limo returned. The philosophers who could see that far whooped and hollered across the soccer field.

As they pulled away, Lucinda pushed a button and the skylight opened. Max arose, the top half of his body emerged through it and he waved.

"Who are you waving at?"

"Socrates and Plato."

The limo passed through Zilker Park, across Riverside Drive and up the interstate to Round Rock and then five miles out Sprinkle Road to the Oak Meadow Sanitarium.

"Ms. Lucinda Tanner is here to see Ms. Merrylee Tanner," said James to the guard at the gate. The large ornate gate opened. They drove through.

"Hello, Ms. Tanner. It's been awhile." Dr. Adams, a short, pudgy, balding man with a pencil thin mustache, was wearing a gray three piece suit.

"It has been. How is Merrylee?"

"Not much change I'm afraid. Vital signs remain quite good. She's in fine health." Dr. Adams made a flourish with his hand as he led Lucinda and Max up the stairs and down a hallway to Merrylee's room. "You know, Ms. Tanner, it's the oddest case. We continue physical therapy. She swims and walks, with help of course. Has all the bodily functions, eats, chews her food, but continues to remain below what we would call the conscious state, beta brain waves. She fluctuates between theta and alpha."

"It's like she's asleep," said Lucinda.

"Exactly. Twice this month she spoke aloud. I thought she might be coming out of her catatonic state. But alas, no." They were in front of Merrylee's room.

"Dr. Adams, this is my friend Maximus Culpepper. Mr. Culpepper, Dr. Adams."

"Pleased to meet you, I'm sure," said the doctor.

"We have met. It was some years back when I did the floral arrangements for the AMA convention."

The doctor nodded at the possibility. "I'll leave you two alone," he whispered, starting to walk back to the elevator.

"Doctor, has my brother Arvin been visiting Merrylee?"

"He's pretty diligent. Visits almost every Sunday after his church service. We play the televised program every Sunday in

Merrylee's room, following Reverend Tanner's wishes. If I can be of any further assistance, I'll be in my office. Now if you will excuse me." He left.

As they entered the room, Reverend Arvin Tanner was indeed being broadcast on the room's television.

It is true the end times are imminent. Reverend Arvin Tanner strode across the platform, microphone in hand. *The return of Jesus Christ is imminent. From scripture, we know this. However, truth is we don't know when an imminent event will take place. Do we? The Righteous should then be prepared for the end times to begin at any moment. Are you ready?* The diminutive preacher bounded down the steps and into the congregation, a portable mike in his hand. He walked five rows back and stood in front of a woman with large blond hair. She looked terrified. Why is Reverend Tanner looking at me?

Are you ready for the end? He put the mike in her face, looking like a undersized Jerry Springer. She shook her head. He walked on, asked the same question to a few more members of the congregation. One man was ready. "*Amen, brother.*"

"*We cannot say today is the day Jesus Christ will return to earth, or on this day the world will end. Nor can we say this is the day the rapture will begin. Nor can we say this is not the day. As soon as we say this, that is, set a date for an imminent event, we demolish the concept of imminence. Truth is we don't know when this will happen.*" He threw up his hands and returned to the stage. "*Setting a specific date for any of these events is incompatible with the idea it could happen at any moment. By imminence, it can be said it will occur at some time but we are uncertain of the exact date when Jesus Christ will return. It could very well be today. Do I hear an Amen?*"

"Amen," from the congregation. "*The signs are present, the proliferation of demon music like hip hop, rap and,*" his voice went deeper, "*heavy metal, and the fact the anti-christ is walking the earth. So come quickly Jesus, Thy will be done on Earth as it is in Heaven...*"

"Do you mind if I turn this off," asked Max.

"Be my guest." Lucinda crossed the room to the bed. She pulled up a chair and stroked Merrylee's hair. "You know Maximus, I used to tell her she was my favorite niece and she'd say *I'm your only niece, Auntie Loo!* I miss her being in my life." A single tear rolled down Lucinda's cheek.

"She is such a nice looking girl. Lucinda, do you trust me?"

"Of course, Maximus. Why do you ask?"

"What I intend to do may appear on the surface somewhat frightening."

"I know you wouldn't put Merrylee in danger."

"The danger would be to me, although danger may be too strong a word. But the upshot is this: Would it not benefit Merrylee most if she could extract herself from her coma?"

"I agree with that."

"Her existence in this state can be described as unfulfilling."

"Yes."

"I shall take this herbal medicine." Max removed the vial from his shirt pocket and showed it to Lucinda. "What I aspire to do is gain access to the adjacent dimension of consciousness where Merrylee is residing. The frightening effect, which is an outer effect mind you, is my body will move into a state resembling death." He put his glasses in his shirt pocket.

"Oooh. I don't like the sound of that. What is it? Did you say herbs?"

"I got the recipe from Colonel Sanders, the same ingredients they put on Kentucky Fried Chicken—highly secret, hush-hush and all that. A small dose and one falls asleep on the couch. Stronger doses..."

Max didn't finish his sentence. "It allows me to connect with Merrylee in the inner world the Tibetan Lamas know as the *Bardo*. Similar to the Limbo of Roman Catholics."

"How is that possible?"

"The Lamas have visited alternative dimensions for centuries. Tibetan Buddhists understand our essence, our soul, moves in and out of dozens of dimensions, many, many levels of consciousness. In the mansion there are many rooms, so to speak. We are present in this room operating within a level of consciousness. When we sleep and when we dream, we are on a level. Our body may be seen by others as in bed; however, our consciousness is in the realm of the dream world.

"The *Bardo* is a portal, or gatehouse, through which one may pass to other levels. One must be free of the body and its functions to enter the portal."

"And you believe Merrylee is in this *Bardo*?"

"I know she is. For some inexplicable reason, she is stranded there. It could very well be the traumatic experience of being shot that holds her. My belief is the closeness of her relationship with her brother and his apparent death holds her there. Once I get to her, I can uncover the reason she is there and help her out."

"She was very close to her brother but Travis isn't dead."

"Merrylee does not know that. We could tell her the truth right now, but she is shut off from our world. I have to go in there."

Lucinda thought that over for a long moment and then nodded.

"You be careful, Maximus."

Max tapped a portion of herbs from the vial into a quart of water he brought in his daypack, stirred and drank it down. "If Merrylee and I aren't back in an hour, hold my nose and pour this down my throat." He handed her a second vial of liquid.

"Would you call my name and Merrylee's as well? Every five to ten minutes? We will hear *you*, even though you won't be able to hear *us*. I'm getting a little sleepy. I shall go over here for a min..."

Max felt the separation, a slipping away as though he dropped his body on the floor. Total freedom ensued as the walls of Merrylee's room at the sanitarium dissolved and he began to float. Looking down he saw Lucinda, her hand on the forehead of an old man. How had I gotten so ancient? He had been to this place a half dozen times before when he lived with the Lamas in the mountains of Eastern Tibet. Each time he had forgotten how liberating it was without all the functions of a physical body.

The Lamas will enter the *Bardo* to aid those stranded there, to aid them in rising above confusion so they may continue their trek to higher realms. Or in some cases to reincarnate back to Earth. Even though, according to the Buddha, there is suffering to contend with on Earth, it is preferable to the *Bardo. Why stay in the airport when there are so many places we can fly to?* His Lama-teacher had told him.

When a Lama drops his body in death, his friends remain at the bedside for three days to help guide him onto his correct spiritual path. At times it is necessary to go to that level and take the friend by the hand. It is a secret Tibetan Buddhist practice. Max had been on a few of those hand-holding adventures, but he was younger and there were experienced Lamas with lifetimes of faith and courage to guide the process. This was the first time he would go it alone. He was concerned, as it was the most daring adventure he had ever taken, but was fortified by the powerful *I Ching* reading.

"Merrylee? Where are you, child?"

"Here I am." He and the girl were in a space without walls, floor or ceiling. It was misty blue and dreamlike. She was sitting in a lotus position and Max mirrored her. "Who are you?"

"My name is Max and I have come from the other side."

"The other side of what, Max?"

"Maximus? Merrylee? Maximus? Merrylee? Can you hear me?"

"Who is that?"

"That's your Auntie Loo. You remember Auntie Loo, don't you?"

"Auntie Loo?"

"Your favorite aunt?"

"My only aunt."

"There you go. I am here to ask you something."

"What do you want to ask me?"

"I want to know *why* you are here?"

"I don't know. I don't remember. Is this heaven?"

"No, it's called the *Bardo*. Heaven would be up through the bright light there." Max pointed to a bright swirling blue-white light overhead. As she looked up, the light grew brighter.

"Oh yeah, I started to go up there once but it was so bright and it tingled and then burned and I got scared. I wasn't ready for that."

"You were correct. It's not the right time for you to go there."

Someone walked by.

"Who is that, Merrylee?"

"That's Stevie Ray. He's looking for his First Wife. He told me if I ever get out of here tell Jimmy not to sell her."

"We'll both tell Jimmy. Look down there," said Max, "do you see that person in bed there?"

"Who is that?"

"That's you?"

"Me? That can't be me, I'm here."

"Listen, Merrylee. You are here, your essence, your consciousness is here. However, your body is down there."

"Oh, okay. And who's that?"

"That is Auntie Loo."

"Hey, that's you in the chair."

"You are correct. I am here and my body is there, just like you."

"Just like me."

"Maximus? Merrylee? Maximus? Merrylee?" Said Lucinda.

"Why is she calling us?"

"She wants us to return to our bodies."

"Oh."

"Do you want to go back?"

"I don't know."

"Maximus, it's been an hour. I'm giving you the second vial." Lucinda opened his mouth and poured the liquid down his throat. She waited. Five minutes. "Okay, I'll wait just a little longer, then I'm calling Dr. Adams. Maximus, come out, come out wherever you are."

"Merrylee, are you ready?" Asked Max.

"Ready for what?"

"Ready to leave this comfortable but somewhat boring place and rejoin Auntie Loo, your dad and Travis."

"Travis? I've been waiting for Travis. He always told me if I ever got lost, stay where I was and he would find me."

"I thought it might be the case." Max heard Lucinda and could not believe the time had passed so quickly. Time in the *Bardo* moved at a different rate. "Travis is not in here child. He's out there. I promise."

"Okay."

"You want to be with your brother, right?"

"Right."

"It's time to go back into your body. You see your body down there?"

"I see it."

"Let's both go back into our bodies now. Hold my hand until we get there." Max and Merrylee floated down from the *Bardo*.

"You will feel some sensations. Be ready for that. I want you to forget everything, except opening your eyes."

"Okay."

"Open your eyes Merrylee." Max stood over her. There was movement behind her eyelids. "Merrylee?" Max touched her eyelids with the tips of his fingers. "Open up Merrylee."

Merrylee Tanner opened her eyes for the first time in five years.

"Oh, my God! Merrylee!"

"Auntie Loo. I can hear you, but everything is so bright I can barely see you. I feel terrible. It hurts."

"It's okay, Merrylee, you'll get used to the light. You will have to re-learn to focus your eyes."

"It's a miracle," said Lucinda, "nothing short of a miracle." She gave Max a big kiss on the cheek.

"What is going on in here?" Said the short man in the white cowboy hat and tailored summer-weight, white western suit.

"Arvin?" Said Lucinda.

"Daddy? Is that you?"

"May the Lord's name be *exalted* from every mountain!" Shouted Reverend Arvin Tanner falling to his knees. "Merrylee?" Tears streamed down his face. He walked on his knees over to her bed and hugged his baby girl. "You don't know *how* I've prayed for this day."

Chapter Eighteen

*"There are only so many times I can say
I'm sorry and still mean it."*

Homer Simpson

Patricia and I took the McDonald's Observatory tour where we saw the real giant telescope, and then walked through the grounds of historic Fort Davis, learning how the west was won in that little corner of Texas. Afterwards strolled through town, got ice cream cones and munched on them as we drove back to Balmorhea. We stopped at the pool to rinse off the West Texas dust. It was Sunday afternoon and the solitary watering hole in a hundred miles was packed.

At the cabin we showered and checked out. We planned to stop by for the appointment at Warlick's ranch and head back to Austin.

"Warlick's place ought to be easy enough to find. He told me to look for Yucca Avenue and take it due south for three miles. And there's Yucca as we speak." It took ten minutes to drive through town. We found his red, white and blue mailbox and pulled into the ranch over a cattle guard, and a few minutes more we came upon a rock ranch house. We parked.

"Cute little place. I suppose you want me to stay in the truck?"

"Would you mind? He made it real clear I should come alone. I'll leave the motor running and the a/c on." Patricia gave me that *you're polluting the environment look.* I replied, "Diesel. Best to keep a diesel engine running." How the hell can you argue with that?

An immaculate, older model, two-tone Buick sat in the carport. "I'll ask him if he'd mind your coming in. It's hot, so maybe he'll be sympathetic."

"I'll be okay, I'll just read my book. You take your time." The book in her lap was *How To Talk So Children Will Listen And Listen So Children Will Talk*.

As I walked up the caliche path to the house, I thought, hey, we don't have any children. I shook it off and rang the doorbell. When no one came, I knocked softly at first and then with more force. I looked back at the pickup. Patricia was looking at me. I tried the door. Locked. I shrugged and held up my palms, "Now what?" I gave her my *I'm going around to the back of the house*, sign. At the rear of the house, I looked in the back window. The kitchen wall phone was off the hook, dangling by its cord. I tried the screen door. Unlocked. The kitchen door, also unlocked. I peeked my head in.

"Captain Warlick. Hello? It's Rivers. We have an appointment? Hello? Anybody home?" No answer.

I crossed the kitchen and hung up the phone. I took a quick check of the living room, bathroom and bedroom, looking in closets. Clothes on hangers. Very neat. A coffee table book on Big Bend sat diagonally across a coffee table. I wrote a note and left in on the Formica kitchen counter.

Captain Warlick. Sorry to have missed you.
Headed back to Austin. Will call you next week.
B. B. Rivers, Bergstrom Investigations. 2 P.M., Sunday.

I went out the back door, considered locking it but didn't. In case Warlick stepped out and left it unlocked on purpose. I walked over to a couple of ancient out-buildings and looked in. In a barn were a couple of fine looking thoroughbred horses. They had plenty of grain, hay and water. A field of sunflowers moved as one living entity in the slight southernly breeze, the huge heads following the course of the sun. I remembered reading that the flowers in this area were harvested for seed used in bird food.

"He wasn't there. And the phone was off the hook. I guess that's why it's been busy."

"I hope he's alright."

"Yeah, me too. I went in—looked around—no signs of a struggle, as they say."

"You went *in* his house?"

"Yeah."

"Billy Rivers. You don't up and go into a stranger's house."
An edge to her voice. What was that? Anger? Disappointment?

"I saw the phone off the hook, tried the door. Door was unlocked. Stuck my head in. I wanted to make sure he was okay, is all."

"And I just want *you* to be safe."

"Okay." I thought about that. Thought about opening the conversation up to the unresolved issues, getting married and having kids, but I'd wait. That talk was scheduled for tomorrow night after work. "You know Patricia, it's still early. We could take a swim and swing back here, see if we could catch him in a couple of hours?"

"I could take tomorrow off." She was warming to the idea. I was glad she wasn't mad at me. I'd have to remember not to discus the breaking and entry and supplementary unsavory aspects of the P.I. biz.

"Okay! To the pool." By the time we got there the crowds had cleared. We rented face masks, snorkels and flippers.

"Billy, I'm turning into a prune." She held up her wrinkled fingertips. "And I'm getting hungry. How 'bout we go to that cute little Mexican restaurant we saw in town?"

"And for you, señor?" Asked Lupe.

I closed the menu when I saw the chile relleno platter. After Lupe left, "I'm going to as many Mexican Restaurants as I can and order chile rellenos. I'm going for the Guinness Book record for most number of chile rellenos eaten in the most different restaurants."

"You're kidding?"

"A little. But I'm serious about chile rellenos. I just wish I found out about them twenty years ago."

"Oh, I get it, this is what happens when I suggest you give up hamburgers?"

"Suggest? It was more like a royal command, Your Highness. You made me promise, remember?" She couldn't argue about that one. "So, dang it all, I discovered a whole new food group. No beef or other visible chunks of flesh in the dish. Did I tell her I wanted chile rellenos with cheese?" I got up to see if I could catch Lupe. There sitting next to the kitchen door in the corner of the restaurant was a man who I swore was the same guy I had seen in Ozona. Dark Federale or Mafia suit. Head buried in the menu.

"Try the chile rellenos," I said. He ignored me.

After dinner, we cruised Main Street. I kept my eye open for a tail but never saw one. Patricia had me pull over so we could watch some children playing in the canal running through town. A tear came to Patricia's left eye. The one closest to me. She turned and looked as if she were about to say something.

"What's the matter Patricia?"

She didn't answer. We sat there several minutes watching the kids. They were splashing and dunking each other and seemed to be having a lot of fun. With nothing much else happening in the metropolis of Balmorhea, we drove back out to Warlick's ranch.

After a silent ride for several minutes, "At this point in my quest, I'd rate that chile relleno as the second best I've ever eaten?" I let loose a huge burp.

"How many have you had?" She was learning to ignore the various expulsions of air from her man.

"Solemente tres. First place vote goes to the one I ate with T. Rex Rodriquez in Austin and the third place goes to Ozona."

"The one floating in the red grease?" She smiled.

"Yeah, I'd drop that one solidly in third place. And a little *too* solidly, I might add," doing a bad Groucho Marx impression. "And likely to stay there for awhile." I wiggled a pencil like a cigar and raised my eyebrows a few times.

"Here we are," I pulled into the ranch, across the cattle guard and up to the house.

"Hey, the old car is gone."

"I see that." I got out of the pickup and knocked on the front door. When no one came, I retraced my earlier steps to the back. I did an abbreviated version of the, *I'm going 'round back* sign. The screen door was open as before but this time the kitchen door was locked. I peered through the window and the note I left on the counter was gone.

"He changed his mind about talking to you is all."

"Probably right. Must have been around somewhere. Just didn't want to talk to me, I guess. Ready to go home?"

"Let's get outta here."

Patricia napped most of the way back to Austin and feeling all rested up, decided she would go to work the next day after all.

Back home at the townhouse, I slept for a few hours and left early for Bergstrom. I wanted to get into Captain Hollers' office and slip my expense sheet for the West Texas trip into the *in*-basket so I would have plenty of dinero to cover my ruptured Visa card. Donna was already there on the phone, eating a donut. She held up the sack for me as I walked by. I grabbed one with multicolored sprinkles.

"Thank you," I mouthed. She nodded.

I dropped off my expense sheet and went down to the cave to get ready for the Monday A.M. meeting. I timed it so I wouldn't be early. A dozen detectives were sitting, standing, bullshitting, drinking coffee and eating donuts. I took a metal folding chair off a stack and set it in the back corner of the meeting room. A guy looking like Kramer from *Seinfeld* burst through the door at 7:59.

At 8 A.M., Captain Hollers boomed out, "Shut the door and flip the lock will you, Rivers." I had not gone unseen. "Oh, gentlemen, and I use the term loosely, hiding out in the back of the room is B. B. Rivers. He's joining our team. I'll need to see you in my office right after this meeting, Rivers." Half the investigators turned and waved, giving me a *hi* or *how ya doin.* The rest continued sucking on their coffees.

Moments after I locked the door, someone out in the hall tried it and said,

"Shit! Goddamn cocksuckin' mutherfucker," and stomped off.

The investigators in turn gave oral reports to the group. Insurance work. Investigations for local lawyers. Some assignments were finished and new assignments handed out. The way he said, "I need to see you in my office," bothered me. And what if Hollers wanted me to give a report? I wasn't ready to orate about my week and felt riding Brahma bulls or going to church was preferable to public speaking.

As the meeting wrapped up, I breathed a sigh of relief. I noticed I'd held my breath for a good part of the meeting. I followed Hollers back to his office. Boy, he's big, I thought as I watched him take up most of the space in the hall as he swayed side to side. Others flattened themselves in doorways and recesses in the hallway to avoid being squished as he passed.

"Shut the door, will you, Rivers?" I shut it and sat down in the chair across from the desk. "I read your report." Hollers spoke slowly and softly. What was the emotion here? "And there are some things we need to cover. One. You just turned this in?" He held up my amended report and travel expense sheet.

"Yes sir." I was about to explain that I wanted to get it in on last week's expenses because I figured since I worked Saturday and Sunday it was like the week didn't end for me on Friday and I had maxed out my Visa card and needed to keep in their good graces, but he didn't go there, so I didn't either.

"Now, correct me if I'm wrong here, but did I or did I not tell you to stay away from APD officers on this?"

"You said you didn't want me bothering any of the guys at the department in Austin because it might be a disruption." Hollers nodded in agreement. I had visited Barney at the APD Ballistics Department but had not included it in the report.

"Since Captain Warlick was no longer on active duty or living in Austin and since he knows more about what's going on than just about anybody, I thought it would be okay."

Hollers let that digest. It was cooler in the office than the last time I was in here. Dang it all, the Maintenance Department must have fixed the a/c.

"Okay. We'll let that one slide." He coughed and blew his nose with a white hankie. "But there aren't any details about your meetin'. *His phone was off the hook and his car was there but later it wasn't?* What's really happenin' here, Rivers?"

"Okay, I called him from the office Thursday. Asked him some routine questions. Figured we'd do a phone interview. But he wouldn't or couldn't talk about Hippie Hollow on the phone. If I wanted to come to his ranch he'd tell me the whole story."

"What whole story?"

"Don't know, I never saw him. We set an appointment for two o'clock Sunday but as I put in the report there, his line was busy when I tried to call him Saturday night, and he wasn't at the ranch for our appointment. I even stopped back by a couple of hours later and he still wasn't home. His car was there the first time but not the second.

"And so, you don't know what he was goin' to tell you?"

"That is correct, I don't."

"A wasted trip. That what you're sayin'?"

"Pretty much." I thought of the great sex with Patricia but now was not the time and Uncle Rick was not the person to share that with.

"We don't do wasted trips here." He let that sit and fester for a moment. "But I *can* understand why you might want to talk to Captain Warlick. But being a close personal friend of his, I ought to tell you, he had a pretty tough time of it. The media camping out on his lawn. The constant pressure to nail somebody. The feelin' he blew it. He left APD with a bad taste and it has taken him years to learn to relax again. I'll give him a call and let you know what I find out."

"Thanks."

"So, just so we understand each other, don't you bother the man. I'll talk to him. Okay, now item number two. I see you talked with Rodriquez? Forget that guy, he's a world class asshole, a liar, a troublemaker, a drug addict and you can't believe a fuckin' word he says." Hollers made a check mark on his paper.

"You should hear what he had to say about you," I said into my Stetson.

"What's that?"

"Nothing, sir."

"And three. You turned in a pretty hefty hotel bill for your stay in Dallas. What happened to moderately priced? I mean, the fuckin' *Four Seasons?* For Christ's sakes Rivers, what were you thinking?"

"Sorry. It was all I could find."

"Do a little checkin' first. Like Motel 6, okay? Super 8 is a stretch for this outfit. They have a fucking 800 number at Motel 6." I hate getting in discussions where everything you say becomes ammo for the other guy. This was becoming one of those conversations. Kinda makes you not want to say a damn thing.

"Will do."

"You didn't get a whole hell of a lot out of the Feds either, I see."

"No sir, as I mentioned in the report," I pointed to the line about my attempts to call in, "all the files except one were marked UNAVAILABLE FOR VIEWING. I tried to call you from Dallas several times but never could catch up with you."

"I got your messages and I called the FBI. Got those files and disks made *AVAILABLE*. Get with Donna downstairs. She'll book you a room and give you the fax from the FBI that will allow you access."

"Aye, aye sir." I resisted the urge to salute.

"All is taken care of." Hollers check marked the paper, put it in a folder and without getting up, spun around in his chair and filed it away in a hanging file in his desk drawer.

"A little background on those boxes of files in your office. They're from a friend of mine at APD. As a personal favor to me, this friend went through the APD Task Force files and grabbed as much as he could carry. He made copies and put the files back. He spent a whole weekend in front of a high speed copier." Hollers shifted in his chair from a righthand butt lean to a left. "We could be waiting 'til Elton John gets a girlfriend for APD to release anythin' to a private detective agency."

"I understand."

"Okay, the burr that's gotten in my boot is your comment about how our files are all fucked up. Reports from my investigators get signed off by me and then go on to Mr. B." Jimmy Bergstrom was old man Bergstrom's son, the company's CEO and the current Mr. B. "I don't want Mr. B to be reading this shit. I want nothing from this office," he stabbed at his desk with a big fat finger, "that is not top notch, A–1, numero fucking uno, every *i* dotted, every *t* crossed."

"I didn't say they were fucked up sir, I..."

"I *know* what you said and I'm not goin' to have it," his voice louder and then quieting down. I think I liked louder better. Quiet was scaring the shit out of me. "Now what I'd like you to do is to re-type this report." I gave him my best Hank-the-dog-spent-all-day-hunting-and-pecking-the-damn-thing-on-an-old-ass-typewriter look.

"I'll okay your expenses for the trip to Dallas-Ft Worth and let you off with a warnin' not to stay in Five Fuckin' Star *ho*-tels but I am *not* goin' to shell out for the trip to see Warlick. Pay for your own Tex-Mex."

"Yes sir."

"Good boy. Now, I'm givin' you 'til this comin' Friday to wrap this whole thing up. I must say I'm a little disappointed and I've got no qualms about cuttin' your ass loose from this assignment as of right now," he waited for a smart remark and when it didn't come, continued, "you'll be back handin' out toothpaste 'til your dick starts wrinklin'. But we still got money left to spend and goddamn it, we'll give our angel her money's worth."

"Yes sir."

"The bad news is I doubt our angel will want to fund another week of this kind of shit. The good news is we've got another opening here at Bergstrom. Maybe you'd like to apply? Cleanin' out the dog pens? You read me loud and clear?"

"Yes sir."

"And you know what's in those pens?"

"Dogs?"

"Dog shit. You take the dogs out first and what is left is dog shit. What I want is this report," Hollers threw it across to me, it fluttered and I caught it in the air, "back on my desk by two this afternoon. And, I want a detailed list of your appointments for the remainin' four days of this week."

"Yes sir."

"Anything else on your mind, Rivers?"

"Max Culpepper says *hello*." If it was Captain Hollers' intention to tear me a new asshole, I would say mission accomplished.

"That's good. Tell him hey from me if you see him. Now, get the hell outta here."

"Yes sir."

For the first time since I got the file boxes to the cave, I took the elevator instead of bounding down the stairs two or three at a time. I was bummed. I figured it had been a pretty good week but Captain Hollers saw it different. He was threatening to can my ass or transfer me to dog shit detail for Christ's sakes. This was not good. Maybe I should have leveled with him about Travis but I wasn't ready to let the cat out of the bag. Not yet. At least I still had a job. Until Friday.

"Shit. Shit. Shit. Shit. Shit." I considered slamming my forehead into the piece of shit door that was my piece of shit desk. I slammed my fist instead. That hurt bad enough. What the fuck would I tell Patricia? She never did understand how I could have gotten fired from APD. This was bad, very bad.

And on top of this, she and I had our appointment tonight. It was our heart-to-heart talk, about life, liberty (or the lack of it) and the pursuit of babies. Maybe I just wouldn't tell her I lost the job. I couldn't tell her. Not only would it break her heart, she might lose the horniness that bringing in good, steady money produced. This was very bad indeed.

I lost myself in the report. I re-typed it and the list of my whereabouts the rest of the week. As I pushed some files to the side, I noticed two *while you were out* messages —

URGENT
Please Call Me At Once, Max

Max left his shop number and another one I didn't recognize. I called the shop. Kelly said he hadn't come in yet. I called the other.

"Hi, this is Lucinda."

"Lucinda! Ms. Tanner. This is B. B. Is Max there? I'm returning his call."

"He's sitting right next to me. Here he is." I heard her tell Max it was Bilbo. I was so pissed about Hollers, taking my name in vain was no longer much of a problem. I mean, if Patricia cannot stand being called Pat (she thinks it sounds like a guy's name), why can't I stop people from calling me Bil...

"Hello?"

"Max, this is Rivers."

"Jolly good, I'm pleased you rang me, old boy. I have an item of some urgency to share with you."

"I got something for you, too."

"Jolly good. What say we meet for luncheon? How about El Arroyo on West 5th Street? 11:30, quarter to 12? Perhaps beating the rush a bit?"

"I know the place. I'll be there." I wondered if they served chile rellenos.

Chapter Nineteen

"Save The Ozone—Skip The Beans"

Sign at El Arroyo Restaurant

I was so sick of Bergstrom Investigations I went right over to the cultural center of the universe, a.k.a. the Ditch, El Arroyo. I was there early and nabbed a picnic table on the patio under a huge oak tree. An ancient ceiling fan hung from one of its massive limbs. I wondered how long the thing had been up there and when it was scheduled to fall. The fan attempted to cool the patio but merely moved the warm, June, Texas air around a bit. As I looked through the menu, I fended off a half dozen lunchers who wanted to share the table.

"I'm sorry it's saved."

"Expecting somebody."

"Yeah, there'll be a butt in every seat."

"Fuck off lady, oh sorry sir, yes every seat will be taken."

The waitress dropped off a second basket of tortilla chips with El Arroyo's homemade salsa and I was working on quatro equis de cerveza when Lucinda and Max showed up.

"Hi, Rivers."

"Hi, Max. Hi Lucinda. Have a seat."

"Dos Equis? What's the occasion?"

"I find there is a correlation," hammering my point with a tortilla chip, "between the toughness of the morning and the quantity of cerveza I drink for lunch. I was just about to order number six, six exes that is, three beers."

"Indeed," said Max, looking at the two empty brown bottles.

"Exactly," I answered. "What I wanted to tell you was Captain Hollers just fired me. At least I think that's what happened. Told me I should wrap the investigation by Friday." I replayed the sequence of events of the past week including the trips to

Dallas-Ft Worth and Balmorhea. "I'm a little pissed off right now. Sorry, Ms. Tanner."

"That's understandable, but please, Bilbo, call me Lucinda."

"Okay Lucinda, could you call me B. B. or Rivers or Bill even?"

"He doesn't like to be called Bilbo. I don't know why."

"I don't either. Bilbo is such a lovely and unusual name," said Lucinda. "It conjures up such images of adventure. Red dragons, magic swords that turn blue when orcs are nearby, gigantic spiders, drinking ale behind little round doors." She grabbed my hand that held a tortilla chip and bent it up to my throat. She gave me a one-eyed Long John Silver look. I took a bite out of the chip. We both laughed. It would be hard not to like Auntie Loo.

"Okay, okay, it's an adventurous name."

"Actually," said Max, "the correct usage would be adventuresome."

"You all ready to order?" I ignored the lesson in linguistics.

"Rivers, I know you've had a frightfully tough day. Such days occur when you're working for someone else. They even occur when you're working for yourself."

"They even happen," said Lucinda lighting up a cigar with her gold lighter. A few heads turned to see the striking black-haired beauty fire up her stogie. She blew a smoke ring toward one of the admirers. He reached to stick his finger through it but it dispersed before it got to him. "Bad days even happen when you are independently wealthy and don't have to work at all."

"You've got to be kidding? Tell me you're kidding," I said to Lucinda.

"A life of leisure when one possesses all the money one could want and can do virtually anything one cares to do, can be stressful and challenging."

"I don't believe you," I said

"Okay, you're right. It's not *that* bad." We all laughed. Either the beers were kicking in or I was enjoying the company of Max and Lucinda.

"But you know, Rivers," said Max, "it's all the tougher when Mercury is retrograde."

"When Mercury is what?" I scooped some salsa on a chip and guided it to my open mouth before I lost the load. I stuffed a napkin in my collar to protect my shirt. Dang it all, one must prepare oneself when one orders Tex-Mex.

"Retrograde. Astrologically, most of the solar year, the planet Mercury is a faster moving planet than Earth. In astronomy, Mercury, closer to the Sun and smaller than Earth, is faster." Max took the salt shaker and orbited it around the basket of chips. My bottle of Dos Equis was the Earth, Mercury the salt shaker.

"Mercury appears to be accelerating past us from our vantage point on Earth. From time to time throughout the year Mercury appears to back up in its orbit. It is an illusion due to the elliptical nature of the orbit. Mercury follows a different elliptic than Earth and at times during the annum Mercury appears from our vantage point to be progressing at a slower rate than we; thus it appears to be backing up. Astrologers call this retrograding. Your mother didn't tell you that?"

"That was the day I was kicked by the Brahma bull." I snapped my fingers and picked up the Earth and chugged it down.

"Astrologically, Mercury represents short trips, communications, that sort of thing. When Mercury retrogrades, the little things relating to short trips and communication go askew. Nothing serious. Flat tires. Missed appointments. Miscommunications. It is a minuscule globe, so it is the small things going wrong. Now when Jupiter goes retrograde... but that is another tale to be sure. With Mercury, one finds oneself doing everything twice. In your particular case, rewriting your report and missing your appointment with Captain Warlick in West Texas as well as the stalling of progress in Dallas."

"I guess that explains it."

"Mercury has been retrograde all week and it went direct at 11:43 this morning."

"So does that mean its back to normal again?" I asked.

"Whatever normal is. Mercury will not retrograde again until November."

"That's good news. I don't think I care for Mercury retro-whatevering. You didn't want to meet just to tell me about Mercury, did you?"

"What we have to tell you is somewhat more significant. Although, Uranus did move into my ninth house yesterday."

"Max, there's a woman present." I smiled. Max and Lucinda stared at me blankly. They didn't get it. Just as well.

"Lucinda, would you like to tell Mr. Rivers our news?"

"I would love to." She re-lit her cigar. "My niece Merrylee is no longer in a coma."

"Really?"

"She came back to us yesterday afternoon."

"That's great."

"I know Maximus would not want to advertise this, but it was he who brought my niece out of her coma. I don't pretend to understand how he did it, but she's awake now."

"Wow."

"My brother, Arvin, was there."

"Really?"

"He was so happy he cried his eyes out. He's convinced his prayers brought her out of it."

"Thank you, *Jesus.*" Max did a pretty decent Reverend A impression. "But the appeals did contribute. Prayer *does* work, but not in the manner most people believe."

"What's important is she's back with us," said Lucinda.

"Indeed."

"I need to ask her some questions." And then considering what I had just said, "I mean if y'all think she's ready."

Our waitress, Mae Mae, came to take our orders. Max ordered the guacamole salad, Lucinda the poblano burger, and of course I, the chile relleno platter, which included two chile rellenos, a veggie taco and a cheese enchilada. Max drank bottled water from his day pack, Lucinda drank a margarita and I decided, since Mercury wasn't jerking my chain anymore, I'd switch to iced tea.

In the chile relleno competition, I rated it dead even between the Ditch and Las Manitas, Balmorhea moved into third and Ozona still sank heavily into fourth place.

"May I suggest you wait a few days, Rivers, before stirring up those memories again," said Max. "There are some factors at work here. The bullet to the head had to be traumatic. But something else has affected her even more; she witnessed Travis being shot and believed her brother was dead. I think it is time we got her and Travis back together. Surely you did not mention the boy being alive in your report?"

"No, of course not!"

"Good!" Max and Lucinda together.

"B. B., you said this fellow, Travis' roommate...?" Asked Lucinda.

"Winslow Christian."

"You mentioned Winslow Christian told you he conversed on the phone with Travis?"

"That's right."

"This is all very interesting," said Max.

"Very. Like I was saying, I went to Warlick's ranch in West Texas. He was the first head of the Task Force. He wasn't there. His phone was off the hook. His car was there. The back door was unlocked. I went in and left him a note. He had a couple of high dollar horses in the barn. I came back later in the day and this time his car was gone, the place was locked and my note was gone. What do you all make of that?"

"Were the horses there when you returned the second time?"

"I didn't check, Max."

"I shall construct a chart on him. Will you be able to get me his date of birth?"

"Sure." B. B. Rivers, the skeptic was becoming the believer. I was ready to believe Max could shed some light on Warlick.

"Ricky Hollers and Warlick were chums, you say? Can you get Ricky's as well? I ran a chart on him twenty years ago, but my filing system is not at all extraordinary."

"You don't think Hollers has something to do with all this?"

"Only one way to find out. Well, more than one way but this is as good as any," said Max. "Let's see. How about Mistah Christian?" Max did a Charles Laughton impression.

"I should be able to access it from the Department of Motor Vehicles." I had just seen the 1930s vintage *Mutiny on the Bounty* on the Late, Late Movie and Max's Captain Bly was wretched. "I have a friend there who owes me one. If Winslow ever applied for a driver's license, his D.O.B. will be available and everybody has applied for a driver's license sometime."

"Not everyone, I never have."

"Why am I *not* surprised."

"My, my." Lucinda pointed to a man dressed in a multi-colored Guatemalan shirt, baby blue yogi pants, pink flip-flops and a Tasmanian Devil necktie. A Montreal Expos baseball cap fought to hold down a mop of dreadlocks.

"That's the fellow I was telling you about, Max. T. Rex Rodriquez," I said. "Should we ask him to join us?"

"Why not indeed?"

"Fine with me," said Lucinda, "he's a very nice man."

"T. Rex!" I shouted across the patio, waving him over. T. Rex Rodriquez excused himself from the name-taking girl and came over.

"Hi, Rivers, long time no see!" T. Rex in his too loud voice. "Oh, my god, Lucinda Tanner! I haven't seen you in, how long's it *been?*"

"Awhile. Care to join us?" I scooted over, and T. Rex unhinged his tall boney frame and worked his body into the picnic table.

"What brings you all to the Ditch? I guess the whole world's found this place now. Another chile relleno, Señor?"

"I'm hooked. T. Rex Rodriquez, do you know Maximus Culpepper?"

"By reputation. I work for the finest fish wrap in town but I'm one of the few who reads it cover to cover, headline to Circuit City ad. You just scored another award. Congratulations. Good to meet you." I got a whiff of patchouli as T. Rex reached across the table to shake hands with the florist.

"The pleasure is mine," Max smiled and looked over his glasses at the colorfully dressed reporter.

"Now isn't this a fine looking, and newsworthy, group of people. Anything you can tell me? Strictly on the record." He pulled a well-used steno pad from the back of his yogi pants and looked at each of us in turn.

I looked to Lucinda, then to Max. Max looked to Lucinda who looked to Max and then to me.

"Can't think of anything," I said looking to Max.

"Neither can I," said Max to Lucinda.

"Me either," said Lucinda to T. Rex, "except my niece Merrylee came out of her coma yesterday."

Chapter Twenty

"Poor Jesus never had a chance.
There's no one to save Him from those He has saved."

Kinky Friedman

I knocked on Captain Hollers' door feeling like a hungry dog knowing he was about to be whacked by master but hungry enough to endure the punishment.

"It's open!" After a deep breath, I passed through the door. He left a message with Donna he wanted to see me a.s.a.p. I sprayed my mouth with mass quantities of Binaca. The alcohol in the breath spray further enhanced the buzz from the cervezas at lunch. Switching to tea was a good move but too late to do much good.

Murine for the eyes to take the red out. My eyes were white but they still hurt. I carried my Stetson in one hand, the re-typed report and the list where I wanted Hollers to think I would go the rest of the week, in the other. My real plan was on my yellow pad in the cave.

Making a dummy list reminded me of my senior year at Southwest. During Christmas break I took a job as a salesman. My fellow salesmen didn't make sales calls, using their calling time instead calling out tap beer at the Broken Spoke Tavern, making up creative shit to put on their call reports.

"Have a seat, Rivers." Hollers smiled broadly, heaving himself out of his chair and coming around the desk to shake my hand. I dropped my hat at my feet and took his hand. I was confused, expecting at any moment for master to cuff my ears but instead he took the report from my hand and dropped it without looking at it into the in-basket.

"I believe I owe you an apology, young man. I just this minute got off a three-way call with Max Culpepper *and* Lucinda Tanner."

"Sir?"

"They sang your praises, son. Seems you've impressed at least two people in this town. And I understand you've found out Ms. Tanner is our benefactor?"

"Yes sir. Max Culpepper figured it out. Took about a minute."

"Sharp guy. Didn't I tell you? And Rivers, you're sharper than you look too."

"Thanks, I think." We both smiled, good buddies now.

"I'm going to be straight with you, Rivers. Ms. Tanner asked me, told me, you are to continue your investigation. She's impressed with the progress you've been making and will flat withdraw her monetary support if you are taken off it. Nothing gets my attention faster than..."

"I didn't mean to..."

Hollers held up his catcher's mitt of a hand.

"Enough said." He took my report from the in-basket and separated the sheets, laying them down in front of him on his desk.

"Here's what's going on. First off, Donna set you up for Dallas. You leave on Southwest this afternoon. She'll find someone to run you to the airport. The FBI will meet you at DFW. Agent Davidson, as you know, ran the Hippie Hollow investigation for the Bureau. He's flying in from D.C. Goin' to brief you tonight. Donna's got the details."

"I thought the Feds didn't like to pay overtime."

"What's that?" He had pulled something off his desk and was looking at it.

"Nothing, sir."

"Okay, another thing. Warlick's 1984 Buick was located. Nose down in a ditch by Big Bend National Park outside the town of Terlingua."

"What about Captain Warlick?"

"No sign of him. The car was trashed. Burrito wrappers. Beer cans. Here, take a look at this e-mail." Hollers slid the photos over. "Warlick would not, could not, treat his car like that. And he wouldn't have eaten a packaged burrito if his life depended on it, much less throw it on the floorboard. And he'd never drink canned beer. He was a scotch man and he loved that car. When he and his wife split up, she got the house, the furniture, the bank accounts. The one thing he wanted was that damn car."

"And the Crown Royal?"

"What? Oh yeah. So Rivers, I got egg on my face, a whole omelet even. Just a second." He punched some numbers on the phone.

"Donna. Any donuts left from the mornin'? Damn it." He hung up. "I admit I was a bit hasty when I said we couldn't cover all your expenses. On this comin' Friday's report, you put those expenses from the West Texas trip back on. We cut off expenses on Thursday and pay on Friday so we wouldn't be paying Sunday's expenses until next Friday anyway."

"So there's going to be a Friday?"

"Of course. Of course. So, don't you be quittin' on me now." He cocked his head and one-eyed me.

"No, sir."

"Good. Ms. Tanner will retain us until we tell her otherwise. Up to us. Up to *you*. So, don't worry, you have as long as it takes. Okay? And I'll see if we can get you some proper office space. Okay?"

I nodded. I took that dog out and dang it all, if I didn't hunt.

"Good. One more item." He checked off one and two. "The Tanner girl is out of her coma. And it happened right after a visit from Mr. Maximus Culpepper. I find it very interesting. What do you know about it, Rivers?"

"Not much. I was out west looking for Captain Warlick when it happened but I had lunch today with Max and Ms. Tanner, Lucinda Tanner that is. She credited Max with bringing Merrylee out of it. And I wouldn't put it past him, sir. He's pretty amazing." (I didn't mention T. Rex Rodriquez was there munching on a poblano burger).

"Yes, he is. That boy is a trip and a half."

I returned to the cave, this time bounding down the stairs. Man, what a roller coaster ride the last few hours were. I had a few spare minutes before the flight to Dallas, so I worked on getting the additional birth dates for Max. Hollers was easy. I just asked Donna. I got Warlick's from my friend at APD. I called my friend at DMV While I held, I stuffed my briefcase with files and reached for the light cord. I got Winslow's D.O.B., said thanks and hung up. The phone immediately rang.

"Rawlins?"

"T. Rex?"

"Yeah." His voice sounded even louder than usual. Had to yank the phone from my ear. I could hear him fine with the phone lying on the desk.

"We gotta talk, and soon. And I mean like, right now!"

"I'm going to the airport in ten minutes, getting some paperwork and my ticket and I'm outta here but I should be back..."

"No time. This is fucking important. I'll meet you at the airport. What time's your flight?"

"Southwest at 4:45 to Dallas."

"See you there." He rang off.

"Fuck." Patricia and I had our big meeting tonight. I buzzed Donna and asked her if she would call her since I might not get a chance and didn't have time for a long ass phone call.

"Oh, and Mr. Rivers, don't forget to stop by my desk on the way out. I have the confirmation numbers for your flight, your motel and the fax with the release numbers for the Feds." I again reached for the light cord and again the phone rang.

"Hi, Rivers, I'm glad I caught you."

"What's up Max?" I wasn't sure of the time, since I hadn't worn a watch since the Brahma bull kicked my Timex up into the stands. It took a licking and didn't work after that.

"Lucinda and I are flying to San Miguel de Allende tonight."

"Really? I'm going to Dallas." Whoop-dee-doo.

"We're going to be down there two or three days, should be back by Thursday."

"What airline you going on? Maybe I'll see you at the airport."

"She has her own plane."

"Oh, of course. I guess we're just a couple of jet-setters now." Somehow Big D did not seem as jet-setty or romantic as San Miguel de Allende, Meh-ee-co.

"Do you have those birth dates for me?"

"You got a pen?"

"I'm flying with you," said T. Rex, finding me at the urinals in the airport men's room. He stood about a foot back from the porcelain device and arced yellow liquid. I finished, washed up and got out of there. Didn't even put my hands under the blow drier. Let 'em air dry.

He caught up on the concourse and we walked together to the Southwest gates. He was wiping his hands on his vest. I wondered if he had washed up. Damn, I was getting domestic. What was *that* all about? I remember taking lunch breaks at the ranch in Blanco. Me and the hired hands would toss cow patties (organic Frisbees) for distance all the while eating tacos or barbeque sandwiches. Still, I didn't offer to shake his hand.

"I bought a round trip ticket, doing a quick turn-a-round."

"Why?"

"It's the peanuts. I go to H.E.B. or Albertsons and buy a brand name jar of peanuts and it sits in the pantry. But those Southwest Airlines peanuts in the pretty foil package? I don't know what it is. I just love 'em. Say, I got something to show you!"

Several heads turned to see us walking up toward the gates. A tall, well built, (so I've been told) redheaded cowboy, white summer weight Stetson, jeans creased sharp enough to cut a steak, tan wool jacket, spit shined reptilian hide boots, ironed western cut bright white shirt open at the collar carrying a hand-tooled leather briefcase. And a slightly taller, bone thin black dude, maroon yogi pants, ancient Birkenstocks with no socks, lime green Smokey Bear t-shirt, paisley vest, black and white dreads under a black and silver Oakland Raiders cap, carrying a *Gypsy Wings* oversized tapestry purse.

We sat together at the gate drinking Cokes, waiting for our boarding numbers to be called.

"I like your Smokey the Bear shirt." There was a hole in the shirt where Smokey's eye should be and I noticed there was a gold ring piercing his nipple.

"You know, Rawlins, Smokey is a pretty mellow bear. Two things piss him off." T. Rex sounded a little like Smokey. He pulled away his vest to show America's most famous government bear.

"What two things?"

"Forest fires."

"Of course, I mean, yeah. Should have thought of that one."

"And people who call him Smokey *the* Bear. His name is Smokey Bear." He showed me the name written under the picture.

"Sorry." I whispered. "So what's this all about, Smokey Bear? Why's it so important you...?"

"Honest mistake. I forgive you."

"Thanks."

"Couple of things. Here's the name of the man who called the police on his cell phone. Poodie Slack."

A good looking Asian lady at the gate announced it was time to board.

"Thanks. You're kidding about the name, right?" I looked at the piece of paper and the name, *Poodie Slack*. Shook my head and stuffed the paper into my jacket pocket as we walked out the ramp to the plane.

"Look at this." The plane was crowded, as most late afternoon flights to Dallas were. I grabbed a window seat, T. Rex scrunched up in the middle seat. A hefty lady was already in the aisle seat. We had to climb over her to get to our seats. I figured she didn't much care for the weird man who smelled like a damn patchouli forest.

"Nice purse."

"It's my version of a carry-on," he said, holding up the tapestry bag.

"You're not gay are you?" I asked trying to inch away a bit but I already filled the seat and there was nowhere to go. I thought of what Max told me about there being more gays in Austin than one might think.

"No, I'm not gay."

I relaxed.

"I'm bi." He tousled my shoulder effeminately. "Doubles my chances for a date on Saturday night." He laughed loudly slapping my leg and the leg of the lady on the aisle. She about jumped out of her skin, shouted something like, "Oh, my word," and left, I presumed looking for another seat. T. Rex moved over to her seat and put the bag between us. He reached in and pulled out a handful of paper.

"Cool move."

"Works ever' time. So here's what couldn't wait. When you told me you needed to talk to the Tanner's financial man, I went to see him. Name's Larry Furman, and he's the Rev's accountant. He handles not only the Rev, but the Ark, his church *and* Lucinda. The whole family estate actually. Quite the balancing act. I told him about Merrylee coming out of her coma. He said that variable would change a number of things."

"Really?"

"Larry and I go back to UT, to a time when I thought I wanted to be a C.P.A."

"I can't image you as an accountant."

"It's the tie, isn't it? I told my damn fashion co-coordinator this tie, the paisley vest and Smokey Bear shirt would not mix. Damn. I got a part-time job as a reporter for the *Daily Texan*, the University newspaper, and after threats, cajoling and an almost bloodless coop, I was named editor. From day one I had altercations with the powers that be. Inappropriate and controversial content vs. freedom of speech. They fired my ass. So I started my own rag, which became a clearinghouse for radical and alternative causes. Left-wing Pacifica-type stuff. *No Nukes. Save the Chocolate Mousse.* Larry came with but still pursued his degree. We didn't make a hell of a lot of green. Only places that'd advertise with us were head shops and pizza joints. But it was great fun. The first and only time I never got fired, 'cause I owned the joint."

"I thought you covered the music scene."

"That was later. Austin's a funny town. Almost overnight, people stopped giving a shit about which asshole to vote for, Nixon or whoever the hell the other guy was. Do you remember who Nixon beat?"

"Nah."

"See what I mean? The choices our two political parties offered, we Austinites found uninteresting. We became more concerned where the *Uranium Savages* or *Shiva's Headband* were playing on Saturday night. I gravitated to the interest— music.

"This is pretty detailed." I leafed through Reverend A's financial statement.

"I bailed Larry out of hundreds of scrapes in our youth. Guess he felt he owed me. Of course, I sort of stressed how *much* he owed me." T. Rex snapped his fingers so loudly several passengers turned in our direction.

"The Rev is dead broke," whispered T. Rex. "He owes everybody. There's a huge fucking tax liability."

"I thought churches were tax exempt."

"The church is going great guns. The board watches it like a bunch of hawks, which is literally true. They are a bunch of conservative, republican, fascist, hawk-nosed, son of a bitchin', right fuckin' wing, Christian coalescing cunts."

I nodded. I guessed T. Rex hated religiosos more than I did.

"Church's got money, it's the Rev's personal shit. Like his classic car collection. Like his three homes. High maintenance ex-wife. Daughter on around-the-clock care. Lucinda Tanner is paying half and he's paying half, but it's a huge ass monthly nut. Look at this figure." T. Rex leafed through the papers in my lap (he sort of brushed against my dick as he did it, which I did not care for) and showed me the entry for Oak Meadow.

"Remind me never to go into a coma."

"That's just *half* of the bill. The guy makes a nice looking salary as a televangelist but made some horrible investments. All three homes hold I.R.S. tax liens. The interest is accumulating at a sickening rate. Larry told me the Rev's gone through his daughter's inheritance. Since she was comatose, he became executor of her estate. Big mistake."

"He spent all her money?"

"In a word—thank God, no. Larry was able to shield the vast majority of it. He redirected it somehow, hiding it from the Rev. Figured if the Rev sniffed it out, it would be gone."

"Fuck. Can an accountant do that?"

"He's a creative accountant."

I nodded. "What about Travis' money?"

"Fortunately, he hasn't been able to get his self-righteous little right-wing mutherfu..." I stopped him in mid-sentence not wanting to be kicked off the plane by the flight attendants, who were looking at us and whispering. He got the hint.

"...hands on it. Larry told me Travis came to see him a couple of days before he was killed. Told Larry he wanted a part of his inheritance to go to the Iced Chai Foundation. You know, the rap star who was assassinated several years ago?"

"Really?"

"No shit Sherlock. After the Rev *invested* Merrylee's money, Larry was prepared for an assault on Travis'. Larry managed to fend it off by convincing the Rev to not make a motion to declare Travis dead and wait until the statute of limitations ran out, which is seven years. If the Rev would hold off, Larry would not disperse funds on the Iced Chai deal."

"Why would he do that?"

"When Travis came in with the request, he also left a mysterious envelope with Larry, with directions that if anything should happen to him, Larry was to hand it over to the policia."

"Whoa."

"Within a week, Travis disappeared, so Larry opened the envelope. Whatever was in it was powerful enough to keep the Rev in check." I figured I, B. B. Rivers, Ace Detective, knew what was in the envelope but I was not going to share with T. Rex. Not right yet. "Larry told me he put it in a *very* safe place. And if anything should happen to Larry, the letter would surface."

"Heavy stuff."

"Yeah, isn't it? It's been five years now, and if Travis doesn't arise from the dead in the next two years, Larry'll be obligated by law to return the inheritance to the estate of Tex Tanner, Travis and Merrylee's grandparents. Which means Lucinda and Arvin as the only living heirs would split it. *But...*"

"But?"

"That was before Merrylee came back from her little trip on the S. S. Minnow. Now with Merrylee alive and coming into her majority, Arvin and Lucinda would split half and the other half would go to their children, namely Merrylee."

My brain had reached its storage capacity limit. I knew Travis was alive but as far as I knew, T. Rex didn't. I wanted to add my two cents but could show restraint. Dang it all.

"So, Merrylee may come out of this alright?"

"No shit. There are millions, maybe even billions involved."

"Reason enough for murder?" I asked.

"No shit."

"How about Lucinda? She seems stable financially."

"She's in good shape. She could pay the Rev's debts and still have several million left. But she hasn't offered to do that."

"I don't think she cares for her brother very much."

"I think she cares even less than that." We laughed.

"So, Rivers, tell me, *why* are we going to Dallas?"

"Meeting with the FBI, they're picking me up at the airport."

"You want a hit off this?" T. Rex showed me a tightly rolled joint which I assumed was from the Thai stick. He cupped it in his hand. "We could go back in the little room back there, disable the fire alarm, I do it all the time. Catch a little buzz on before you meet with the Feebs."

I shook my head. Didn't sound like fun at all.

"Of course, I will be staying on the airplane," said T. Rex. "Me and the Feebs, we just never got along."

Chapter Twenty-one

"Every large problem has a simple answer
—that is wrong."

H. L. Mencken

Lucinda's white limo with James at the wheel stopped at the lake house. Lucinda needed to pick up a few essentials for the trip to Mexico. Then back across Mansfield Dam to the Lakeway airstrip where her Moonie was hangered.

"Good afternoon, Ms. Tanner," said the pilot, "she is all ready for you. It will be a three and one half-hour flight to Queretaro. As you requested, I've arranged for Señor Cruz to meet you there. He will drive you and Mr. Culpepper on to San Miguel de Allende." Lucinda stored her suitcase. Max his backpack. They climbed aboard and buckled up. Max carried on two large books and a notepad.

"Thanks John, you've thought of everything." The plane taxied out to the runway and took off.

"Lucinda, do you mind if I do a little calculating?"

"What sort of calculating did you have in mind?" She stroked Max's cheek with the tips of her long fingers.

"Not that kind. Rivers gave me some additional data and I wanted to plot it on the chart."

"Well, I'm disappointed," she said with a fake pout. "If you'll excuse me, I think I'll read a book." She was reading *Spanking Watson,* by Kinky Friedman.

Señor Samuel Cruz was waiting in the Land Rover at the airstrip outside Queretaro. After the Moonie touched down, Samuel loaded the luggage and after a brief stop at Mexican customs, they were into the next leg of their journey, speeding down the two-lane highway toward San Miguel de Allende.

"Hungry?" Asked Lucinda.

"Getting there. I'm running on a glass of orange juice and a spelt bagel."

"We'll be in San Miguel soon, if you can just hold out a little bit longer. Samuel, could you pull over right up ahead?"

"Sí, Doña Lucinda."

"This is one of my favorite views, Maximus." The Land Rover eased off the pavement and pulled up to the railing. They got out. A beautiful valley spread out below. The sun was a sliver, radiating multi hues on the horizon. Brightly colored houses were stacked up and down the sides of the mountains which surrounded the *colonia*. Max and Lucinda stood, arms linked, a long time. Max broke the silence.

"This is nice. I haven't been here for thirty years. I had forgotten the magic of this place."

"I attended school here as a child. San Miguel was one of my homes growing up. The burros have been replaced by the Hummers but I still love it. It's as much my home as Austin or Taos."

As the sky darkened, she continued. "See that highest light there on that mountain? Es mi casa. I think you're going to like it."

"There is not much about you I don't like."

"You're sweet."

Lucinda rolled to the middle of the king-sized bed, put out her hand for Max. He wasn't there. Opening her eyes, she saw the big ceiling fan turning overhead.

Max was outside sitting on a towel in his lotus position. He looked out over the valley watching the sun come up. A rooster crowed. A church bell rang. Another rooster followed by another church bell. The town was waking up.

Lucinda turned toward the window and saw him. She tiptoed outside naked and hugged him from behind. He felt her soft breasts on the back of his neck and turned and kissed one and then the other.

After an hour of slow, delicious lovemaking, they showered and dressed. Lucinda juiced two dozen oranges. They drank up and went through the front door. They strolled hand in hand, down through the cobblestone streets and alleys of San Miguel de Allende, Guanajuato, Mexico, the picturesque *colonia* nestled in the mountains a couple hundred kilos north of Mexico City.

Roman Catholic girls in uniforms, plaid skirts and white blouses, got in some play time before school. Commuters hung from overloaded buses smelling of diesel. Shopkeepers swept and washed the sidewalks in front of their shops, *preparano por las touristas* who would be emptying from hotels and condos, looking for pottery, silver, artwork, jewelry, trinkets, fresh produce and breakfast. They cut through a neighborhood park. Grass refused to grow in the park because of the constant tramping of playful feet. They connected with a wider street, winding down to El Jardin, the town square. They ordered breakfast in a little café overlooking El Jardin located at the heart of the *colonia*. Because of the influence from the U.S., El Jardin became *the hardeen*. Where is that cute little restaurant? Oh, it's up there across from the hardeen.

In the morning the population consisted of peddlers, beggars, policia and tourists.

At night, the hardeen metamorphosed into a street scene for chicos and chicas, too young or too poor to gain access to the discos. This morning, Max and Lucinda ate breakfast across from the park and waited for the illusive Travis Tanner.

"I'm so glad we're here together, Maximus. My favorite town and my favorite man." She squeezed his hand.

"This is splendid." Max was enjoying the clear, cool Mexican mountain air. "And it's wonderful having a cup of coffee. You know, I set aside coffee for special occasions."

"Like now?"

"Like now. And I forgot about the cream here. *La crema*. It's not white. Look at this. It's tan, dark and rich." He admired the cream as he splashed a bit more in his coffee.

"Auntie Loo!" A tall, slim young man emerged from the park, crossed the cobblestone street weaving through buses, cars, trucks and taxis. His blond hair was in a ponytail. Neatly trimmed beard, blue eyes, small round John Lennon-type glasses.

"Hi, Auntie Loo." Travis topped the steps of the café.

"Hello, Travis. You're looking well." They hugged. "Maximus Culpepper, may I present my nephew, Travis Tanner."

"Pleased to meet you, sir."

"And it's good to meet you as well, Travis." They sat down, exchanged pleasantries. The weather here, the weather there. News of Merrylee. Had Lucinda heard from Angel? Travis was happy to hear the private detective she hired in Austin was going to try and find her.

"So, Travis, as I mentioned on the phone, Maximus has insight into the murders and he wanted to ask you some questions."

"Sure, Auntie Loo. I figured it must be important or you wouldn't have come back down here so quickly. I just wanted to say, I'm glad Merrylee is okay. I understand you had something to do with bringing her out of her coma, Mr. Culpepper. I'm very grateful and can't wait to see my sister and talk to her again."

"Delighted I was able to be of assistance." Max reached under the table and retrieved the astrological chart, unrolling and spreading it out. I cannot discern your responsiveness to astrology. If you are like most, you are either a believer or you are not."

"I have an open mind."

"Good. I will get to it then. What I have is a chart, or map, of the moment the murders took place at Hippie Hollow. Anyone with *any* connection to the event, whether present on the scene or at the Pink Flamingo Party or connected in any way later is on this map. Here you are. Here's your sister. Your father. Here's Lucinda. Everyone at the party or at Hippie Hollow that night is in red. Others who were not connected at that moment but are connected now, such as myself, B. B. Rivers, the private investigator your aunt mentioned, and others such as the police captain, are in blue."

"Is that a skull and crossbones?"

"That is my representation of the killer. We know what, when, how and where it happened but we don't know *why* it happened, nor do we know who performed the deed, nor who was behind it. The thing I'm absolutely sure of, it is not your Auntie Loo." Lucinda wiped an invisible bead of perspiration from her brow. She pulled out her gold lighter and lit up one of her cigars as Max talked.

"Conventional wisdom says someone hired this person." Max tapped a knuckle on the skull and crossbones. "I do not suppose you can shed any light? Do you know who might have hired a hit man?"

"Haven't any idea whatsoever. Never made any sense to me."

Max held the young man's eyes in his for a long uncomfortable moment until Travis looked away.

"So, what happened that night?"

"After we left Auntie Loo's?" First looking at Lucinda, then Max.

"Exactly." Max and Lucinda leaned toward the young man in rapt attention.

"We left the party and were headed for Hippie Hollow. It happened so damn fast. A cop pulled us over. I remember I wasn't feeling too good, but I saw him after he flagged us down and we pulled into the parking lot. He walked over to Moses and put the gun up to his head. He just shot him. Then Kristie. Everything I had consumed all night was coming up and I remember opening my door. I know this is crazy, but I wasn't thinking about getting away. I was thinking, don't upchuck on Reverend A's precious Mercedes. The reason we were allowed to take the damn thing out of the garage was because he was going to be there and needed a ride home. His limo *must* be available to important people. We were never allowed to take it out on our own or drive any of his cars."

Max and Lucinda nodded.

"The shots weren't loud, like he had a silencer or something. The one that hit me was like I'd been kicked by a mule. I was leaning out the door and it knocked me the rest of the way out. I heard more shots and remember lying, my face in the gravel of the parking lot, upchucking and it oozing all over my face."

"Oooh," said Lucinda.

"Sorry. In desperation, I rolled under the back end of the limo and came up on the other side. I remember fighting to get the god-damned pink cloak off. It was then I saw Merrylee with blood all over her head. I was positive she was dead even though she wasn't."

"She thought you were dead as well."

"When I got up, my side was bloody. A chunk was missing. Here, look at this." Travis lifted his shirt revealing a large puckered scar above his right hip. "I was surprised to be alive I guess. The adrenaline kicked in and I took off running down the hill. I could see pretty well because of the full moon. But I knew I'd be easy to spot, too. I grew up coming to Hippie Hollow. I knew where the rocks were and the closest trail down to the water. I got there and dove in. Up the hill, I saw the flashlight shining here and there."

"You poor dear."

"Did you get a good look at the chap?"

"I was about as close as I care to be. I was convinced he was a cop. I mean he *looked* like a cop. Although I don't suppose he was, do you?"

Max shook his head and continued to look Travis in the eye.

"About six feet tall. Maybe one-eighty, one-ninety. Pretty good shape. Hard to tell how old. Not young though."

"Guess."

"I don't know, 45, 50? Big mustache, handlebar. You know, old fashioned. Bushy. I was in the water looking up at him. He took off his cap and wiped the sweat off his forehead. He was bald."

"He didn't see you?"

"No. It was a full moon but there were trees overhead, so it was dark where I was. He'd sweep the rocks and the lake with his light but I was behind a boulder. He didn't see me. After he left, I got out. I heard sirens and the only thing I could think was, get out of there. I mean, I thought the police were after *me*. Trying to kill me. You got to remember I was pretty polluted, scared, and I thought he was a cop.

"I took off my shirt and wadded it up, put it on my wound and tied the legs of my jeans around my waist to stop the bleeding. It looked probably worse than it was, but a lot of that night was a blur. Somehow I swam across the cove to Auntie Loo's. I waited I don't know how many hours until I didn't hear or see anyone above and climbed the cliff to Auntie Loo's. I guess I must have passed out for awhile. The cops interviewed everybody still at the party and sent them home, so the house was empty.

"I found out later you had gone to the hospital to be with Merrylee," he said to Lucinda. "Of course at the time I thought my sister was dead."

"I got quite a shock when I got back home. Finding Travis lying bleeding on the couch. One of my neighbors is a retired physician. Very discrete. He patched him up and I smuggled Travis down into Mexico. It's easy to smuggle into Mexico. I knew some folks here in San Miguel who could provide him a place to stay and a job."

After breakfast Travis went on to work and Max and Lucinda walked to the edge of town and picked up a trail through the dry desert landscape until they connected with the highway out of town. They hailed a passing cab for a ten minute ride to the local swimming hole, *Taboada,* a beautiful oasis of ancient palm trees, manicured landscape and cool, refreshing water. Since it was monsoon season in Mexico, thunderstorms were building. At four o'clock chances were good it would rain.

After swimming, Max and Lucinda climbed the hill where Travis worked at a greenhouse, specializing in growing many unusual varieties of orchids. Max knew the culture of all but a few of the more esoteric blooms and ordered a sampling to be shipped to Austin. There would be the inevitable red tape that accompanies shipments from Mexico, but Travis said he would see to it personally. The two men seemed to enjoy their floral connection.

Lucinda spent some time with her nephew while Max worked on the astrological chart. Then they caught a ride to the hardeen with some American jewelry makers who worked and partied in San Miguel all summer making rings and necklaces, returning to the States for the Christmas selling season.

For Max and Lucinda it was back up the hill to Lucinda's studio. They packed and Samuel returned with the Land Rover to take them to the airstrip where they boarded the Moonie.

"Now, Maximus," they were settled in now, "maybe you can tell me why we were in such a hurry to return to Austin?"

"I uncovered something in the chart which leads me to conclude Merrylee may be in danger."

"You're not serious? Why would she be in danger now?"

"Merrylee is transiting through a critical period in the next few days. Would it be possible to make a call on your mobile phone?"

"Of course, Maximus." She flipped it open and handed it over.

"I'll contact Rivers."

Chapter Twenty-two

"It's just a job. Grass grows, birds fly,
waves pound the sand. I beat people up."

Muhammad Ali

The person who hired him said Reverend Arvin Tanner would be flying into Austin from Washington for the evening and would be flying back to Washington the following morning. His chauffeur/bodyguard would remain in D.C. For once, Reverend Arvin Tanner would be without protection on the night of Lucinda Tanner's fiesta, Auntie Loo's World Famous Pink Flamingo Party.

He had infiltrated the rental company crew who set up the stage, sound and lighting for the party. As always, there was no record of his being there. He blended in; one more day laborer.

To disguise himself he could have shaved off his magnificent handlebar mustache. For sentimental reasons he chose instead to add a beard and shaggy wig and sport a red bandana around his forehead.

"I look like a goddamned hippie," he said as he took in his reflection in the rearview mirror of the crew truck.

To set up the hit, he had ripped off a cruiser-clone, same color and model used by the local police and stashed it in a cedar break near Lucinda's lake house entry gate. He had appropriated the light rack off a cop car in a dusty corner of the Round Rock P.D. vehicle lot and fashioned a door emblem that looked enough like the real thing. Stealing a real cop car would have put the cops on alert. They hate it when a perp fucks with their property or person. And there was always the possibility of a homing device. It would do no good for the cops to know what he was up to.

Not just yet. Soon, he would put theory to test. The theory? That he was god damned invincible. When he was good and ready, the whole world would know all about it.

While the real party pulsed on patio and in pool, the working stiffs conducted their own bash in the cedars behind the stage. As the guests drank pink margaritas and ate salmon; the crew opted for Natty Lites and Doritos. He didn't join in but instead monitored the action over at the real fiesta.

As Reverend Arvin Tanner was saying his goodbyes and opening the door to the old Mercedes limo, he took it as his cue to exit the party, sprinting down the driveway, through the open gate and past the guard who was too busy with a *Penthouse* magazine to notice. He noted earlier the guard looked up when a departing guest drove in or out.

Miss July saved the poor asshole's life, he thought. He estimated nine minutes to get to the hidden car, clear away the brush, shuck the roadie outfit and get into a realistic looking uniform he picked up at the Salvation Army Thrift Store complete with cap and police insignia. Job one was to speed down Comanche Trail to the first turnoff, the parking lot to the Hippie Hollow nude beach and ambush the limo. If for some reason the limo did not stop, he would have to run Reverend Asshole's limo off the road and over a cliff, which would be trickier and not as much fun as a cap up the sphincter of the world famous televangelist.

By his calculations, he was in place with five minutes to spare. Maybe more, depending on the thickness of the goodbye-see-you-later-bullshit Tanner would spread. He knew the Reverend Asshole personally and boy would the little preacher-man shit a brick when he saw El Jaguar! He rubbed his hands together in anticipation. He could not wait to add that self righteous little finger to his collection.

Standard operating procedure once a hit was made was to hole up in the mountains or some backwoods jungle village somewhere for six months to a year, until the initial heat had cooled. Law enforcement tended to push real hard initially and lose interest the longer a crime was on the books. This one being high profile, Austin's cops would put on an early show but he was sure the investigation would in due course degenerate as it always did, into the going through the motions mode. As usual, he'd left no tracks; however, plans to return to Texas to tie up loose ends were short circuited when he had gotten his ass thrown in the slammer on the assault charge.

Before the Austin job, he'd been living in Costa Rica, licking his wounds from a previous contract offing black rap star and cultural icon Iced Chai. Assassinating black leaders had become an enjoyable specialty but the Austin hit on televangelist Reverend Arvin Tanner would be a kick. The deal came in at twice his usual fee and killing a man of God posed no problem.

On the surface the contract was straightforward, but every time he got close, Tanner's chauffeur-bodyguard had been there. He was patient and in no particular hurry. He was thorough. He was good. He had waited until this moment. This was the right moment and his patience had paid off, as it always had in the past. After all, he was El Jaguar.

For the record, his birth name was Jackson Hamm, a.k.a. Colonel James Spivey. No connection had ever been made between Hamm, who until a few days ago had been serving time in a Montana state facility, and the infamous hero or butcher of Bolivia, James Spivey (depending on which side you were on); nothing about Hamm being a Colonel in Ché Guevara's army, no links between Hamm and the hired assassin, killer for hire Spivey, nothing about his special projects from 1968 to the present.

The U. S. Army trained him as a sniper, although the Army did not have an official M.O.S. for what Hamm performed. He found he not only enjoyed killing, he was good at it. When the Army no longer could rein him in, they locked him up. Only the highest echelons knew what Cpl. Jackson Hamm did. All others had him pegged a fuck-up, a deserter who served a bit of time in Leavenworth, had received a dishonorable discharge and had dropped off the grid until he reappeared after bashing in the head of a patron at the Crazy Horse Saloon in Missoula, Montana.

After his discharge from the Army, he killed a man named James Spivey because of their uncanny similar looks. He perfected identity theft long before it became popular. The reconstructed Spivey set off for Cuba (the closest conflict) to volunteer in fighting for freedom with the rebel, Fidel Castro. He wasn't as much interested in the freedom part as he was in the fighting part. Spivey was assigned to General Guevara, Castro's brilliant protégé; he further honed his skills fighting alongside Ché.

Ché's hand picked team had done well, had taken a great deal of Batista territory but one day they blundered and were surrounded by enemy troops.

"So, what do we do now?" Asked Spivey.

"Kill as many of them as we can before they kill us." Answered Ché.

"We're going to die then, aren't we?"

"No no necesariamente, señor. I have an idea. Let's you and I dig an hoyo and cover it with brush so no one will know there is a hole there. We'll send our amigos to attack and when they are

overrun and flee, the pigs will follow. We will slip down the hole,
the pigs will pass over us and we'll be behind them."

"Sounds like a plan to me."

After Cuba, Spivey followed Ché to Bolivia to fight by his side. After a vicious attack Spivey inflicted on Bolivian soldiers early in the campaign, Ché named him—El Jaguar. He possessed many gifts not the least of which was the extraction of information from the enemy. The Bolivian soldiers called him the Butcher of Bolivia, but Spivey preferred El Jaguar.

Outnumbered, Ché and his band evaded the Bolivia Army for months but were eventually captured and tortured and Ché was put to death. El Jaguar and the remainder of the unit were trucked across the mountains to a prison camp. Before the truck arrived he escaped.

One of his guards had fastened the handcuffs a fraction too loosely. Taking off the outer layer of skin like removing a bloody glove, El Jaguar worked his hand free. He disposed of the guards and then the prisoners. Although he liked and respected those he fought with, there would be no witnesses to the life or the death of El Jaguar.

He backed off the road at the Hippie Hollow turnoff, the nose of the cruiser on the pavement; he cut the engine, waiting and listening until he heard the distinctive sound of the Mercedes lumbering down Comanche Trail. He felt kinship with those great warriors the Comanche who he imagined had used the trail lying in wait to ambush a passing wagon train. In actuality, the road was named by a local real estate developer.

As the Mercedes came into view, El Jaguar pulled out, tires squealing, gravel flying under spinning wheels. The cruiser blocked the road. Hopping out, with his flashlight, he directed the limo off Comanche Trail and into the Hippie Hollow parking lot. The limo didn't stop immediately but pulled all the way through the lot. El Jaguar got back in the cruiser, backed off Comanche Trail, spun around and pulled up beside the limo.

"What the fuck?"

After culminating the big black dude who was driving, as well as the big-busted blonde chick riding shotgun, he was shocked when he looked into the back seat of the limo to see his contract was not in the vehicle. How god damned disappointing!

Chapter Twenty-three

*"The Universe is not exactly the sharpest pencil in the box.
Just as it takes everything you say quite literally, the flip side
of that is quite true as well. The Universe is quite naïve, like
the slow cousin you used to have fun with at Christmastime.
The Universe has no sense of irony."*

Ben Stiller

T. Rex returned from the lavatory with a serious case of the
munchies. As he blitzed through a dozen packages of peanuts
and downed three Cokes to my one, he told me how he had rear-
ranged the paper towels and cleaned the sink and toilet. Then
he placed his tray table in the upright and locked position and
leaned his seat back as far as it would go. He was all but lying on
the lap of the fellow behind him.

Our flight attendant put on the ABC World News Tonight.
We watched but did not listen as Charles Gibson's top story was
an interview with a banty rooster in a cowboy hat.

"Speak of the devil. That's the Rev," said T. Rex. We grabbed
our headphones.

"Well Charles," said the whiney voice, "now, I'm not taking
credit for my daughter coming out of her coma, now. In Jesus
name we are able to do things we simply cannot do alone. It was
a miracle, plain and simple."

"Well, Reverend Tanner, I would certainly have to agree that
something miraculous has happened. Can you tell us how this
came about? From what I understand, very few people who have
been in a comatose state for five years have ever recovered."

"True. I've heard that too. But I've never given up praying for
a miracle. God works His power in mysterious ways. As you know,
five years ago next month, my daughter Merrylee was the victim
of a senseless shooting. She was shot in the head. The crime

happened just west of Austin. My son Travis was gunned down as well as two of their friends but God in His infinite mercy spared my daughter. Surgeons from our hospital here in Austin worked non-stop for hours. God guided those surgeons and they saved her life. However, she has been in a coma as you mentioned for these past five years. Every so often it was as if she were about to say something. Like someone talking in her sleep but she never woke up. Until yesterday. The Lord's Name Be Praised!"

"So, you were present when she came out of it?"

"I had just walked into her room, like I've been doing every Sunday after church. I'm pastor of The Church of the Ark. Our congregation meets in North Austin. She said 'Daddy, is that you?' Just about broke my heart. I started bawling."

"How is Merrylee today, Reverend Tanner?"

"She's good. We're taking it real easy. One day at a time. I'm just so thankful that my child has been returned to me."

"I'm sure all the listeners are thankful as well, Reverend Tanner. Appreciate your talking with us this evening."

"Nice talking with you, too."

"The Middle East Peace talks, in a stalemate for the past several weeks, took a more positive note today. For more on this on again off again peace process, we join Sarah El Deeb on the Gaza Strip."

"The shitty little worm's taking credit for the whole thing." T. Rex yanked off his headphones and threw them in the aisle.

"Sarah El Deeb?" I thought it was funny. It was one of those situations where I think I am being funny and nobody else does. T. Rex smirked."

"You all didn't tell the Rev it was Maximus Culpepper who brought Merrylee Tanner out of her coma, did you?"

"He made us promise not to tell anyone. But like he said at lunch, what purpose would it serve to tell that story."

"Listen Rawlins, I've heard some pretty weird rumors about Maximus Culpepper over the years."

"You want a story, I know that. But you got to promise me you'll sit on it a while longer."

"Why the fuck should I?" He was angry.

"Because if you don't, I ain't a-talkin' to y'all no more." I crossed my arms, put a scowl on my face and looked out the airplane window at a cloud. It always worked for Patricia. There was an uneasy silence for several moments.

"I think the world has a right to know more about the man." His tone was softer now.

"Well, maybe. I've only known the man for a week and I've heard the stories too. Amazing stories, but if you run it now, you're going to ruin it."

"Okay. Okay. Let's just say I *am* writing this story... I'm just not printing it."

"Thanks."

"Yet."

As I deplaned, I looked back to see T. Rex explaining to the porters cleaning up, he was not going to get off the airplane. A youngish looking FBI agent met me as I came through the gate.

"Special Agent Davidson will pick you up, sir."

"Good."

"Not so good. He's not here yet. He's coming in from Washington D.C. and his flight has been delayed. If you will go to gate 36, I'm sure he'll be right along." The teen agent turned and left.

So I cooled my heels. Rush, rush, rush and then wait. I bought the latest issue of *Field & Stream,* a mug with *Dallas* on it for Patricia and a crossword puzzle book. I found the easy puzzles too easy and the hard ones too hard. The experts—forget about it.

Davidson came right along. Three hours later.

He looked like Jack Lord from *Hawaii Five-0.* The same lock of hair falling into his eyes. Unsmiling, cold blue eyes. I wanted to hear him say, "Book 'em Dano." Maybe I'd ask him later, after we got to know each other better.

"Hello, Mr. Rivers. I'm Mark Davidson. How was your flight?"

"Gosh, I don't remember it was so long ago. The peanuts were cold. Fish are biting on spinners in Northern Montana though," I held up the *Field and Stream.*" And I discovered I'm not very good with crossword puzzles."

Davidson allowed a quick smile on his hard chiseled face and it was gone again.

"I understand you went to Balmorhea to see Warlick?" He said, slinging his carry-on over his shoulder. I followed him out of the airport to the curb. He indicated I get into the back seat of a black Ford Expedition with extra dark window tinting. I slid in. An agent was already sitting in the vehicle and another followed after me, so there was one on either side. They both were big and burley. The one already in the van looked familiar. Where'd I seen him before?

"Do I know you?" I asked. He didn't respond. I figured hired goon. Muscle. But why? How could I, an ex-rodeo cowboy, newest P.I. in Austin be a threat to these people?

Davidson sat in front on the passenger side. The teen agent drove. Quickly, smoothly we flowed from the curb and merged into traffic and up onto the interstate. I glanced first to the agent on the right and then to the one on the left, trying to get a feel. Which one could I go through on the way out of there? It was a tossup and not real promising at 80 mph.

"I went to see Warlick, yeah. But he wasn't home. Say, what's going on? I thought you were to brief *me* and give *me* a chance to look at those files. What's Warlick got to do with it?"

"So, you didn't speak with him?"

"No, like I said, he wasn't there. Drove eight hours to see him. Stood me up."

"His car was found..."

"In Terlingua."

"Exactly."

"Why is the FBI so interested in a retired APD officer?" I asked.

"Why are you?"

"I asked you first."

"Okay Mr. Rivers." Davidson unbuckled his seatbelt and turned to face me. "What we have here is a..."

"...failure to communicate?" Why do I jump on everybody's lines? I have got to stop doing that. Patricia says I should join Line Jumpers Anonymous. Davidson laughed. Thank God he laughed. But like his smile, it was quick to come quick to leave. "No, what I was going to say is this," he waited for me to jump in and when I bit my lip to keep quiet, he continued, "we have a lengthy, on-going, parallel investigation. One that involves Warlick."

"Really?"

"Yes indeed. Hippie Hollow does come into play. I can't tell you how but I can tell you this, William Warlick, your Captain Richard Hollers, Reverend Arvin Tanner and some others have been under investigation since before the Hippie Hollow murders. I'm going to be in Austin in a couple of days but since you have clearance to look at our files, I thought I would stop here in Dallas first. Let me ask you something."

"Sure."

"Who the hell names stuff down there in A-Hole City? There's nothing about your little town I like. Do you know how tough it's been for me to write the words "Hippie Hollow" on all those reports?"

"I know man. It's tough. So what is the, ah, parallel investigation you're working on?"

"Can't tell you that."

"What's Captain Hollers have to do with it?"

"Can't tell you that."

"Tanner?"

He shook his head.

"National security?" I asked.

"You got it, chum."

"What can you tell me?"

"It goes back to when J. Edgar Hoover was running the FBI I can tell you that, cowboy. But let's get one thing straight," he glanced at the fellow on my right and then back to me, "any questions being asked will be asked by me. You, on the other hand, will be on the answering end of those questions."

"I don't know if I can handle the..." The agent on my right elbowed me hard in the ribs. I should have figured on it, but it caught me off guard and unprotected and took my breath away. It also hurt like hell.

"Okay, now that we have your attention. What is your relationship with these individuals?" Davidson flipped open a palmtop computer and stuck it in my face.

1. Reverend Arvin Tanner?
2. Lucinda Tanner?
3. T. Rex Rodriquez?
4. Richard Hollers?
5. Maximus Culpepper?
6. James Spivey?

After the one sided conversation with Davidson, I was dropped at Motel 6. Tom Bodett left the light on, but I still needed to ring the bell for the night clerk to unlock the door. My ribs hurt from the unexpected jab, but I managed to fill out the paperwork one-handed and get to my room. I threw off the lime green bedspread and beige blanket from the bed, took a cold shower and lay down wet on the top sheet in an attempt at coolness until the a/c kicked in. It did not smell as nice as the Four Seasons and there was no chocolate on the pillow. I felt fortunate there was nothing at all on the pillow.

Dallas was hotter than Austin in the summer and colder in the winter. It was a hot and humid night in Big D and I had seen way too much of the Feds and nothing of J. R.

I lay there wondering what all men with wives and/or S.O.s must wonder when they're out late and realize the time. Should I call Patricia at home now or hear about it in the morning? If I *didn't* call, she'd worry and I'd hear about it when we next talked. If I *did* call, I'd surer than shit wake her up and she wouldn't be able to go back to sleep. I'd hear about that, too. Of course, I might get the answering machine. B. B. Rivers, man of action, not one for delayed gratification or delayed ass chewing, dialed.

"Hello?" The voice that had very recently been sleeping.

"Hi Patricia, it's me."

"What time is it Billy?"

"I don't know. Let's see, it's..."

"No. Don't tell me. I don't want to know. Why didn't you call me earlier? Now I won't be able to get back to sleep." Her voice has a whinny tone.

"I've been tied up with the FBI for the last four hours."

"The FBI? What are you doing with them?" She was wide awake now.

"It's a matter of national security. If I told you I'd have to kill you."

"That's not funny."

"I'm sorry. I just wanted you to know I'm alright and to tell you my room number and stuff."

"Like what kind of stuff?"

"Stuff like I love you and wish you were here in Dallas with me instead of all these damn Dallas Cowboy Cheerleaders." Sometimes a man has to stretch the truth so the woman in his life won't realize the real truth when she hears it.

"At least they're being quiet. When are you coming home? I miss you. We had fun this weekend didn't we?"

"Yes, we did. And I'm sorry I woke you up. I figured you'd worry and I wasn't sure if Donna got a hold of you."

"She called and left a message on the machine. What's she like?"

"What's Donna like?"

"That is the question."

"Donna is nice. Very efficient. Blond hair. Buxom. Can type about a hundred words a minute."

"Yeah?"

"Weighs in at about 275. And that's before the morning donut run. She's tough but honest. I like her."

"Good! So, when are you coming home?"

"Probably tomorrow night. Or I guess later on tonight since its 1:15 A.M. Tuesday already."

"Billy, I asked you not to tell me what time it was."

"Sorry. My truck's still at the office. I'm going to take cabs to get around up here."

"Billy?"

"Yes, Patricia."

"We missed our meeting."

"I know. I didn't mean to, but Bergstrom set me up to meet with this pretty high level FBI dude. They bought my plane ticket and everything."

"It's okay. We'll talk when you get back. Thanks for calling. I think I can go back to sleep now."

"Okay good, I'll call you later. I love you."

"You too."

"Thanks for seeing me, Reverend Tanner." The diminutive minister popped up out his chair and shook my hand. His hand was tiny compared to mine but full of concentrated power. Our meeting was at the Oak Meadow Sanitarium cafeteria. I was up at six (missed my morning jog again). After a quick Egg McMuffin at my favorite Scottish restaurant, I checked in with Donna. I found out Lucinda set up a meeting for me at noon with Reverend A. It was the only time in the next week that would work, so I had to be there. Lucinda left the message, *do not be late!*

That gave me four hours to get to the FBI office, go over the files and disks and catch a cab to the airport for the 45 minute flight to Austin. Once in A-hole City, I'd cab it to Bergstrom, pick up my pickup and hightail it out to Oak Meadow by noon. It was a plan. Not a very realistic plan. I hated plans. Ditto appointments.

I did not make it on time. The preacher was waiting, drinking black coffee from a paper cup, the kind with playing cards printed on the side. I noticed the Rev had a possible straight flush showing and wondered if the little man checked the hole card on the bottom of the cup. Probably not.

"Sorry I'm late. I've had an incredibly busy morning."

"You know, to be honest with you," said Reverend A in a high nasally voice, "if you were even five minutes late last week, you would not have found me here, waiting. Tardiness is something I have never been able to cotton to." He sighed. "But that was last week. This week the sunshine returned to my life. The Lord's Name Be Praised. My precious daughter has been restored to me. Even this miserable excuse for a cup of coffee somehow tastes acceptable." He laughed, a charmer when he wanted to be.

"Lucinda implied it was vital we talk. So, what's this all about?"

"I heard your interview with Charles Gibson last night."

"What do you want, sir?" Reverend A looked at me with a no nonsense, intense stare. So much for chit chat.

"I'll get right to the point."

"Thank you." He re-fixed his gaze away from me and out the window into the landscaped grounds of the sanitarium.

"I guess it's no secret your sister hired me to look into the Hippie Hollow murders." If Reverend A hadn't heard this, I'd give him a nice juicy scrap of information. Always worked for Jim Rockford. Rockford always got a vital piece of information in return.

"And since you were at the party and one of the last people to see those kids alive..."

"I see. You want to know what happened, etcetera, etcetera, etcetera. I've told this story a couple of million times to every policing authority you can imagine."

"Yes sir. If you don't mind once more?"

He nodded.

"Can you tell me what happened?"

"Auntie Loo's World Famous Pink Flamingo Party. A sinful event."

"Why did you go?"

"Ah ha! Excellent question. You're asking why would a pompous, pontificating, preacher of the gospel, attend such a bacchanalian bash? Is that your question?" He didn't wait for an answer. "I did not go to save souls. I did not go to witness for our Savior. I did not go to spread the Holy Word. I went for the most base of reasons."

He paused. I waited him out.

"Money. Not what you expected? I didn't feel good about my motives but I was broke. Made some investments that were not guided by the Holy Spirit. I am human after all. Praise the Lord.

So, I attended the festivities, descended into the belly of the whale to borrow money from my sister, Lucinda."

"Were you able to do that?"

"No, I was *not* able to do that. It is Lucinda's policy to flatly deny me any money whatsoever. Goes back to our childhood. I didn't feel she would be receptive, and she wasn't, so I also planned to discuss my needs with my late son, Travis. He and his sister Merrylee were, are, heirs to my mother and father's estate. So, after Lucinda turned me down, Travis and I had a father and son chat. It started as a chat and escalated into a disagreement of biblical proportions."

"What happened?"

"Travis informed me he planned to go live with a cult." He was still staring out the window. "And not only was he going to live with them, he planned to give his inheritance to the scumbags." Reverend A downed the last few drops of coffee turned the cup over and looked at his hole card.

"I was against his move and I advised him of the foolishness of it. He was not yet 21, so legally he didn't possess the right to give it away. I made it clear to the boy that I, his father, would not sign an approval for him. I was disappointed in the choices he was making, of course. The police thought I might have been angry enough to murder my own son, and they went about harassing me for over two years."

I wondered if my dad had been one of the harassers. Maybe Captain Warlick.

"Before he dropped the bomb about joining the cult, I was planning to ask him to sign a letter of intent to turn over a portion of his inheritance to myself. and if that didn't work, to the Church of the Ark, our church, perhaps you've heard of it?" He looked toward me and away again.

"Of course."

"I figured I would write it up in such a way as to allow me to borrow against his pledge. He didn't like my idea. Told me he'd sign a letter of intent alright, but to give his money to the cult instead of me or the church. I didn't like that idea. As it stands right now, the money is sitting in trust, invested in the stock market, which is good since up until lately the stock market has been so strong. And now my son is dead, God rest his soul. I've made a lot of mistakes with my children, Mr..."

"Rivers. B. B. Rivers."

"Mr. Rivers, do you have children?"

"No. Not yet." Oh, shit, I just heard another door slam.

"As a father, I've made mistakes. Big mistakes. I can only hope Jesus will forgive me." I knew from my conversation with T. Rex, Reverend A drained off a good deal of Merrylee's money to cover various unwise investments.

"I know what you mean. So, what else can you tell me?"

"I planned to—say, is this going to take much longer? I have a very busy day."

"No, shouldn't be but a few more minutes."

"I planned to travel to the party in our limo, a classic 1954 Mercedes 300 stretch limo, as I had done in past years but was called away to Washington to meet with the President. He wanted my advice on winning over the conservative Christian voter. He was not of my political party so at first I was reluctant to help. But, he is, or was, the President of the United States. Even if I did not respect the man, I have always respected the office.

"We had our preliminary meeting. I flew back to Austin, planning to return to Washington the following day. I came to Lucinda's by cab from the airport. I figured I'd ride back home in the stationwagon. I call it that, even though in actuality it once belonged to the Austrian billionaire, Andre Kriss. He built it with a section added in the middle, making it the world's first stretch limo. I still own it. After the police kept it in their garage for over a year, it is now in my garage, one of a dozen classic automobiles."

"I understand you got a phone call as you were leaving the party and sent the four teenagers on."

"This is true." Much to my amazement, Tanner got up and walked toward the door. "I need to go to my next appointment."

"I'll walk you to your car." I caught up with him in the hall. "Who was the call from?"

"Now," he clasped his chin thoughtfully as he walked quickly out the front door, "I don't rightly recall. It has been five years."

"Don't recall, huh?"

"No sir, I don't." I felt like Morley Safer of *60 Minutes* as he got in a Jaguar XKE and shut the door on me.

"One more question. Are you still offering the reward for the apprehension of your son's killer?" But he had already left the parking lot. I thought about chasing him down in the Bubbamobile but instead went back to the cafeteria to gather up my stuff. I turned over his paper cup. Pair of jacks.

Chapter Twenty-four

"My father was the creature from the Black Lagoon.
My mother was a black widow spider."

Pushmonkey lyric

June was a lean month for those hardcore sports fans. NBA playoffs ended a couple of weeks earlier. The NFL preseason was still a long ass couple of months away. No college action this time of year. Not much left.

Baseball? Boring.

Golf? Boring.

Tennis? Maybe if Venus and/or Serena or one of those Russian chicks were playing. Otherwise, boring as shit, man.

Women's pro basketball? Could be acceptable to these fans who whooped and hollered as the ladies bounced balls, butts and breasts up and down the court.

"Hey, look at the motherfuckin' jugs on that babe!"

"Oh yeah, I'd like to sink my body between *them*."

The TV corner of the rec room was hot, sweaty, raucous, and the game was coming down to a close finish. Here, the passage of time was slower than shit, so six o'clock approached much the same as any other hour, virtually without notice. One man knew the time, though. The majority of the fans were black. A few Latino. One bald Caucasian sat in the back, eyes on the clock. Everyone was dressed in orange and/or gray.

5:58 P.M.

As they watched, a well-built black woman stole the rock and took it to the hole. And she was fouled. If she makes the foul shot it would tie the game and put it into overtime.

5:59 P.M.

Overtime!

The bald man rose without hurry, folded his grey metal chair with cell number stenciled on the backrest and carried it to the front.

"Get your sorry white ass out the way, motherfucker."

"Hey, asshole, down in front!"

El Jaguar, the Butcher of Bolivia, was not bothered by the rejoinders and walked to the TV set and changed the channel from the WNBA game to the ABC World News Tonight.

"Change it back mothah fuckah!" From an inmate, massive arms hanging like sides of beef from an institutional gray sweatshirt, the sleeves ripped out. Bulked up from two hours a day at the weight pile, figured he'd had just about enough of this shit and got up quickly for a big man. He reached for the channel changer.

El Jaguar grabbed the wrist belonging to the side of beef and clamped down hard. The inmate, who's inside name was Big Boy, tried to wrest his arm free. Big Boy looked to make sure it was a hand that held him and not a pair of vice grips. The man's hand did not look or feel real. What was that, scar tissue?

"Sit down. And quietly please," said El Jaguar. "Wouldn't want the C.O. to throw any of our sorry asses in isolation, would we?"

"Hey, let go my arm, man." Big Boy was puzzled and could not comprehend why he was unable to wrest his arm free. He had seen this bald-headed white bread before. In the yard. At the weight pile. In the library. A loner. Didn't hang with the Nazis or other white groups.

"Sit down." The look was cold as death. "Six o'clock, TV channel gets put on the news." The bald man leaned his chair still unopened against his leg and with his free hand, pointed to the wall chart where there was a listing of mandatory programming. There it was. Six o'clock P.M. ABC World News Tonight with Charles Gibson.

"Game's going into overtime, man," said another inmate, not knowing what to make of the scene. Here was an old bald white guy making Big Boy sit down. And Big Boy possessed a mean ass rep.

When Big Boy sat, the bald man let go, flipped open his chair and sat, focusing on the TV.

"Go down the hall, watch the other TV. Now if you'll excuse me, I'm watching the news." The crowd filed out. A handful stayed for the news or to see what would happen next. Charles Gibson talked. The bald man listened with half an ear. The other half tuned to a possible retaliatory strike, stupid as that would be in the rec room. Unfortunately, these assholes were not known for their smarts, he thought.

Charles Gibson asked a question. Another man answered. The bald man leafed through *Time* magazine as he waited for updates on wars and conflicts around the world.

"Well, Charles, now I'm not taking credit for my daughter coming out of her coma, now. In Jesus name we are able to do things we simply cannot do alone. It's a miracle, plain and simple."

"Well, Reverend Tanner, I'd certainly have to agree that something miraculous has happened. Can you tell us exactly how this came about? From what I understand very few people who have been in a comatose state for five years have ever recovered."

Tanner? The bald man thought.

"True. I've heard that, too. But I've never given up praying for a miracle."

He put down the magazine and looked at the TV screen.

"Shit."

"Every so often," said Reverend Arvin Tanner, "it was as if she were about to say something. Like someone talking in her sleep but she never woke up." The TV held his undivided attention.

"So, you were present when she came out of it?"

"I had just walked into her room..."

He stared at the TV long after Charles and Reverend Asshole, as he used to call him, gave way to other stories. He considered the implications of the girl coming out of her coma. Time to move out, he thought. He never worried about getting out of prison, been in lots of jails and prisons, tougher cages than this one. Here, life was too easy. He was getting soft.

Prisons were good for a free meal. Didn't have to think. The Confinement Officers did do that for you. Prisons were for laying low and surviving. Now that the girl was awake, the Feds would come for him. Prison was not the place to hide out when those assholes were looking for you.

It was a dumb ass thing to do to Big Boy but if he hadn't pushed it, he wouldn't have watched the news and he wouldn't have known about the girl. The urge for elbow room had been getting stronger and he was making enemies. Time to get shut of the niggers and the drug addicts. He missed his guns. He missed women. There was only six months left but he would leave when he felt like it. And he felt like it.

El Jaguar kept his large drooping mustache. It was a bother. He had to pull the hair out of the way with one hand to eat with the other. But he liked the look. Muy suave.

Inside, the other inmates called him Baldy. In other places, he was known as the Colonel. It was Ché who had named him El Jaguar.

He folded his chair, swiped his I.D. card in the coke machine as he walked by. Five bucks left on the card but he wouldn't be there to cash it out. As he walked across the yard, the guys from the WNBA game, plus a few were waiting for him. He finished the coke and tossed it aside.

"Hey, mofo, we been talking it over and what we came up with—you need a lesson. Don't see no Confinement Officer around ta save your lily white ass this time, boy."

El Jaguar made a quick appraisal of the situation. Five big men in shades from dark yellow to very black. A couple more hanging back. A foot to the groin and now there were four. As part of the same continuing motion, the metal chair he was carrying came up catching one in the nose. Blood spurted, adding a dash of color to the drab scene. The looky-loos took off. Now three. That evened it up.

"Stick 'em time, asshole." The smallest of the remaining three held a shank alongside his thigh. He came up with it, slicing through the air, arcing for the white man's gut. It was a fine move. Strong. Direct. Except the goddamned mofo asshole son of a bitch bald-headed white bread was no longer there. The knifer, off balance, shuffled half a step attempting to recover. Recovery never happened. The metal folding chair came up behind the man, nearly removing the top of his head. The shank fell to the pavement. The bald man put a black steel enforced prison issue boot across the throat of the second to last man, who crumbled into a pile of orange and gray.

One man standing.

"Hello Big Boy," El Jaguar said sweetly. "How's the arm?" He almost sounded concerned. Big Boy rubbed the arm. He had been in gang fights all his life but had never seen anything like this man. He turned and ran as fast as his big body would take him.

"Hey isn't that lard ass Big Boy jogging out there on the track," said a C. O.

"I didn't know he could move that fast," said another.

"I'm impressed."

El Jaguar slipped through a hole in the chain link fence he had made a few days before. He disguised the cuts with solder, so the dickhead guards couldn't tell that, with a stiff kick, a hole would appear. Outside the prison, he scored some clothes at a laundrymat, popped the lock on a Jeep Cherokee, pulled into a parking garage and switched plates with another vehicle. Quick as that he was on the road. He'd be hours gone before they noticed the hole or took head count. He counted on the cons whose asses he had just kicked not to rat him out. It would not be good for their cred if word got around they had been whipped up on by a sixty year-old white dude.

He'd stop for gas, pay at the pump with a credit card pick-pocketed from a fellow on the street. He felt good he could still pull a wallet, extract a card and put the wallet back without the man knowing it.

Traveling, he drank a lot of liquids but would not stop. Piss in a Big Gulp cup, slow down, pull over to the shoulder, dump it out the window. Rate of speed was essential. Too fast and the piss will come back at you. Take your time, he thought. He made good time that way. Never so fast to draw unwanted attention, but average speed at 60 to stay in the flow of traffic.

First stop, the bar in Missoula. One quick, immediate score to settle. It feels good to be back in action again, he thought. Can't believe I didn't whack those assholes down in Austin when I was there. I *never* have this many loose ends. Maybe I'm losing it.

"Naw," he said laughing out loud. He was in excellent shape for almost sixty. Mentally *and* physically. Inside, he worked out at the weight pile seven days a week, alternating arms and upper body one day with legs and lower body the next. He ate as well as possible on the revolting high-carb prison diet and ate no fast food except for cokes. No smokes, no drugs, no alcohol, no sex. Sex. That was a hard one. Even at fifty-nine he still wanted it. He had to have it at twenty and thirty. By forty he had taken control.

His belly was rock-hard. He had the arms, legs and stamina of a thirty-year old. "Better," he said aloud. "There are very few

thirty-year olds or even twenties I can't beat to a bloody pulp."
He flexed his biceps, admired the look of it and kissed it with
affection.

He found Crazy Horse Saloon and went in, tire iron alongside his thigh. The bartender, the one who testified against him
was still there! He walked over, looked at the guy until the recognition came into his eyes and bashed his head in. No one stopped
him. No one ever stopped him, except this one particular asshole
lying in his own blood behind the bar.

Two stolen Cherokees later—he wouldn't keep one for
long—and he caught the ferry at Anacortes, Washington, to Friday Harbor in the San Juan Islands. First things first. Before
heading south, he'd need some essentials he'd left in storage.
And he wanted a look at the Pacific Ocean, which he loved, but
would not tarry there. He had some cleaning up to take care of.

At Friday Harbor, an island town off the coast of Washington
state, El Jaguar sat in an Isuzu Trooper. A Jeep Cherokee was not
available when he was ready to change vehicles. He was in line
for the ferry that would return him to the mainland. At first he
felt anxious. He was exposed. An escaped convict in a stolen car.
But then he considered the facts and figured he was where he
needed to be. The line of vehicles would move when the ferry
docked. The horn would sound when it came in. The wait would
allow him much needed shut-eye.

Even a well fit fellow like me needs sleep, he thought.

Later, when the horn blared, the traffic tightened even
though it would be another half hour before the cars would be
allowed to board. First the ferry needed to discharge the vehicles
arriving from the mainland.

Off to the side of the line of traffic was a young hippie couple.
The boy's head rested on his backpack. The girl squatted, holding a sign that read *New York City*. In her other hand snuggled
against her breast, she held a tabby cat.

"Hop in," said El Jaguar as the Trooper came alongside. "I'm
not going to New York but I'll get you a few clicks in that direction." El Jaguar wouldn't tell them how far east he was going
until he could work the deal he wanted.

"All right!" The boy got up and stretched.

"Nice pussy," said El Jaguar as they got in. The couple looked
at him suspiciously.

"I meant the cat."

All three laughed.

"Kevin, wake him up will ya, we're coming to the mainland," said Heather.

"Huh, what?" Said Kevin.

"I'm awake," said El Jaguar.

"Anacortes, Washington, dead ahead."

"Good! I'd like you to do as we discussed. Kevin my man, if you'll take your backpack and wait over by the side of the boat. Heather, you'll ride with me. I'll give you the other half of the $100 bill when we get through this."

"Well, alright," said Kevin, "are you sure this is not illegal?"

"Not even immoral."

"I know it's against Wyoming littering law," said El Jaguar, flinging the remaining backpack off the side of the mountain, "but I doubt anyone will find any of this shit in this century." He talked to the cat which was sleeping on Heather's red plaid shirt. He dumped Kevin's body in Washington, Heather's in Idaho, sleeping bags and packs were scattered here and there along the way. IDs and papers he burned at roadside parks. The young couple's pinky fingers he stored in a Ziploc bag in the bottom of a Styrofoam ice chest. The pistol used to dispatch the couple, tossed in the Snake River. He carried three more handguns stashed in a false bottom of his suitcase.

"Can't trace them to a gun shop if you don't buy them from a gun shop." He packed his own loads using shells he picked up at shooting ranges. At the ranges, he always rented. He'll be visiting his favorite range south of Denver on the way to Austin.

"They call me the *Colonel* at Wild Bill's." He stroked the cat. She purred. "Those assholes don't know I never made corporal before the Army locked me up." He pulled a Ziploc bag away from the cat and put it back in the ice chest.

"Now, now, Puss, you don't mess with that. Just a little souvenir to remember them by."

He pulled his latest Jeep Cherokee into Wild Bill's Shooting Range a couple of clicks south of Denver. Wild Bill was opening up.

"Hey Colonel, long time no see."

"Hey back at ya."

Wild Bill set up the El Jaguar with pistols, ammo and targets. He could handle himself very well with 22 and 45 and the calibers between and passed the morning ironing out the kinks of prison. By 1030 hours he was squeezing them off as good as ever. Wild Bill often told the Colonel he could ace any competition.

"You're as good as I've seen, Colonel. We got a regional match in two weeks and if you need a sponsor you can count on Wild Bill's backing. What'd ya say, Colonel?" He was tempted, but there were places yet to go, many miles yet to drive, many people yet to kill. He laughed aloud at his own sick humor.

Wild Bill laughed along with him, not knowing what for.

El Jaguar estimated one hard day's ride left to Austin. If he drove all night, he'd be there at noon tomorrow. Should he need sleep, he'd pick up a hitchhiker. They're a dime a dozen. Not even that much. He laughed.

"How the fuck did I let this happen?" He talked to the sleeping cat stretching in the driver's seat. He moved the cat over as he got in the Jeep Cherokee. He daydreamed about prison and how he had gotten caught. Bar fight in Missoula, Montana. He'd beaten the holy shit out of a guy and was looking at the poor bastard lying in his own blood on the barroom floor, when the bartender blindsided him. The tire iron evened the score.

He entered Texas but was a long way from Austin. He drove day and night on sheer will power, as he did in Bolivia thirty years earlier. He looked at his scarred wrist and thought of Ché. After South America, he returned to the United States, hooked up with a right-wing hate group and was contracted as an assassin. After a high level hit, with lots of Federal heat, he left the country. He hired on as a merc in wars of liberation and unification around the world. Political leanings never meant much. He would work for leftists. He would work for the right. Communists or Nazis. Didn't matter to him. He would not work for Black Africans. "Never for monkeys," he said to the cat.

Chapter Twenty-five

"I am not afraid. I was born to do this."

Joan of Arc

"Hi, Merrylee, I'm B. B. Rivers, with Bergstrom Investigations? Working for your aunt, Lucinda Tanner?" I had the double blessing of Lucinda and Reverend A for my visit with Merrylee. Lucinda told her brother it needed to happen if they were ever going to find out who killed those kids, so he gave me the okay. Lucinda told me her brother did want to get to the bottom of it. If he were involved, he was one slick dude, that's for sure.

"Hello there yourself, Mr. B. B. Rivers. What does B. B. stand for?" Merrylee moved with high energy around the room, jogged in place for a few minutes and then plopped on the bed.

"Bilbo Baggins." I was happy to be with a real person and not a comatose body. After sharing my name with her, I waited for the inevitable laughter.

"That's so *cute!* You're awful big for a Hobbit, though, aren't you?"

"Pretty sure I was littler when Mom laid it on me. But anyway, your aunt...."

"Auntie Loo!"

"Auntie Loo hired me to follow up on the incident you were involved in five years ago. She didn't like how the investigation was handled."

Merrylee popped back off the bed, walked to the window and looked out. "It's strange knowing I'm twenty now. I mean the last thing I remember I was in 10th grade. My biggest problem was a zit on my cheek. Now look at me. I'm an old hag!"

"I wouldn't say you were an old hag, Merrylee."

"Thank you but I've chunked on thirty pounds lying here in bed. Say, you want to go for a walk?"

"Sure." We left her room, talking as we walked to the elevator.

"My skin's as white as that sheet in the Tide commercial. Badly in need of some rays. I wonder what Mo would think about..."

She remembered Moses Harper was murdered in front of her. "Fucking asshole!"

"Who?"

"The fucking asshole who shot Mo. He was my best friend. We played video games together, watched TV, went to movies. Nothing romantic. He was too much of a gentleman to take advantage of a kid like me. *All* the bitches at Rollingwood High wanted a piece of Moses Harper. I know I fantasized about his huge..." She turned red. "His poor parents."

"Mr. and Mrs. Harper."

"You know them?"

I nodded. We were silent for a moment as we rode down the very slow elevator.

"If it's okay, I'd like to ask you about that night? You don't have to talk about it if you don't want to."

"Is the memory too traumatic, that what you're asking? I don't think so. She leaned against the back wall of the elevator, finger tips over her closed eyes. "The party was great. The most fun I ever had. I even enjoyed Willie Nelson, believe it or not. Of course I wouldn't admit that to anyone, especially Trav. He's alive right?" She looked at me.

I nodded. I liked Willie.

"The Dalai Lama was great. Such a talented guy."

"Tell me about it. What happened after you left your aunt's?"

"I was sitting in the back seat of our old Mercedes. With Trav. He'd been drinking, and I do mean putting them away! He drank so many pink margaritas he was turning pink. Of course, it might have been the cloak. That was pink. You know about the Prince of Pink?"

"Oh, sure." The elevator doors parted and we walked down the hall.

"Is Auntie Loo still putting on her parties? I forgot to ask her."

"No, that was the last one."

"I've been to all of them then. She must figure it wouldn't be the same without me."

"I'm sure it wouldn't."

We reached the door to the grounds and were hit by a blast of hot Texas summer air.

"Wow, it's hot." She grabbed me by the arm. "I don't remember it being this hot."

"Trust me. It's Texas. It's June. It's hot."

She looked at me, smiled and continued. "So anyway. I was sitting in the back seat with Trav. I pulled out this joint. They can't still bust me for it can they?"

"No, I wouldn't worry about it. Our last President smoked marijuana, didn't inhale though."

"I remember. I haven't been gone that long." She ran her fingers through her hair. She gave me the *look*. You know the one. Like here is a good-looking man, older but he still has his teeth? She held my forearm with both hands.

"What was I saying?" She was chewing bubble gum and popping loudly. "Oh yeah, I took a drag off the joint. You ever smoke?"

"I've been known to take a drag every now and then."

"Alright! Anyway, Travis had alcohol poisoning or something and wanted nothing to do with it, so I passed it up to Kristie in the front chauffeur's bench with Mo. Mo was driving. Kristie had about had it with my bro and was making her move on the big guy. So, Kristie takes a hit, passes it to Mo and he flips it out the window! I was *pissed*. It was some pretty righteous stuff. You wouldn't happen to have any..?"

I shook my head.

"Too bad. Then Mo says, 'Cop car ahead!' But I guess he wasn't a cop, 'cause he was the asshole who fucking shot everybody."

"Really?" I thought about the guy on the cell phone who reported he thought he saw a police cruiser on the scene when he drove by.

"Yeah, really. You know, even though it happened five years ago out here," she spread her arms to encompass the whole world, "in here," she tapped a finger on her temple, "it happened last week. Does that make any sense?" We strolled down a winding, well-landscaped pathway as we talked.

"Yeah, I think so."

"He blew Mo's brains out, then shot Kristie, leaned in and shot a bunch of times at Travis. Self-preservation was kicking in. I remember thinking I got to get outta here. I had been taking pictures with one of those disposable cameras. Just as he was about to shoot, I clicked off a picture, the flash went off and I ducked."

"Good thinking."

"Yeah. But I thought everybody was dead, including Travis. I mean, the guy was real close. And he *looked* like he'd be a good shot. I opened my door, figuring I'd duck out before he got around to me. Where we stopped, my door opened at the trail to the lake. I hoped if I could just get down the trail before he could get to me, I had a chance. But he aimed his gun at me and I froze like a goddamned deer in the headlights. The last thing I remember was a big flash of light. Then the long ass dream."

"Really."

"And what's this all about?" Merrylee held up her hand showing a missing pinky finger.

"Some sort of sick trademark I suppose. Moses and Kristie both had missing pinky fingers. As far as I know since Travis got away, he still has all his digits. Did you get a look at the man? I mean could you identify him?"

"He looked like a cop. Cop hat. Big bushy mustache. You know I took a picture of him."

"Really? I never heard anything about a camera."

"Here." She handed me a sketch of a man with a big bushy mustache. "I've been working on it for the last couple of days. Figured somebody would want it."

"Good, Merrylee. The APD and maybe even the FBI will want to talk to you."

"I figured I'd have to talk to somebody. Auntie Loo, before she left for Mex with Max," she smiled and shrugged at the alliteration, "told the doc here, nobody was to see me, no police, no press, nobody except family, until they got back, and I guess you're okay, 'cause here you are."

Merrylee jumped up and planted a rather sweet departing kiss on my lips. Her lips were soft and there was some fire there. We both turned red. She turned red, my freckles melded together. I figured, what the hell, as far as I knew, it was her first kiss in five years.

After I drove through the gates of the sanitarium, I pulled over, turned the truck off and just sat there staring off into space.

I pulled out my *to do* list and realized that I had just knocked off a couple of my most distasteful entries. It was at that moment I got a wild hair to visit my parents. It had been such a wild and crazy few days I needed to come back to earth. And there was no place more grounding (with the possible exception of sitting on a mountain in New Mexico, my appaloosa munching on alpine plant life) than the family ranch in Blanco, Texas.

Instead of calling first I just drove out. It took me an hour and a half to work my way to my hometown via the north side of Lake Travis, across the dam on Lake L.B.J. at Marble Falls and straight south to Blanco.

"Hi Mom," I stood at the screen door looking in.

"Hi Mom," said Paco, the family parrot. Paco was the sole survivor of one of Dad's animal raising schemes.

"Do I know you?" Mom had a scowl on her face. It was hard to believe she was the same person who used to get stoned and dance on her V.W. Bug. Living out in the sticks working her fingers to the bone for no recognition was taking its toll.

"Come on Mom, it's me, B. B."

"Come on Mom."

Mom didn't invite me in so I pulled open the screen door and entered anyway.

"Who's out there a-knocking, knocking on my door?" Sang my dad.

I introduced myself to Dad and sat down on a metal kitchen chair between the kitchen and the den. Mom was cooking or canning or something. Dad was staring at the TV. It wasn't on.

"You still working at that titty bar?" Asked Mom.

"Titty bar. Titty bar," said Paco.

"It's not a titty bar, it's a saloon, and no, I'm not working there anymore. I got a job at a detective agency. I'm on an investigation. Been up in Dallas and out to West Texas." I flipped the chair around and re-sat.

"How you doin' Hank?" I pushed my Stetson to the back of my head and scratched my dog under his chin. He wagged his tail, but did not get up. I considered bringing Hank to Austin to live at the townhouse, but such a confined space was no place for a dog like Hank. On the ranch he could roam free on a couple hundred acres. Go in and out of the screen door, eat dead armadillos, crap freely, piss on anything he wanted. I had to admit

I missed taking a leak off the porch and firing my 45 at the stars, both behaviors frowned upon in civilized society.

"You hungry?"

"I don't know."

She stared into me. Hard. Unsmiling.

I got it, trying not to laugh out loud. "Yeah, now that you mention it, Mom, I *am* hungry. Would you be so kind...?"

"Don't overdo it now," she smiled. "Can I fix you a hamburger?"

"Ah," I thought about my Patricia-imposed boycott on red meat. "You wouldn't know how to fix a chile relleno?" I bet if she could cook them, they would be blue ribbon material.

"Chile relleno," said Paco.

"I could do that. Take about a week. Got to find the right kind of peppers, anaheims or poblanos, probably won't carry 'em at Poor Boy Market, so I'd havta go down to San Antone. Then I'd need to char the skin on 'em..."

"You know what; I'll just take a peek in the fridge." I opened the ancient Frigidaire. "Mind if I take one of these beers?"

"Don't mind at all. *You* left 'em here 'bout a year ago." She went out the back door. The screen door slammed.

"So, Dad, how you been doin'?"

"Take me out to the ball game. Take me out to the park. Buy me some peanuts..."

"Paco wants a peanut."

You know when you're talking on the phone and in the middle of your sentence, the other party hangs up? You immediately stop talking, right? My conversations with Dad were like that. I had to stay with the emptiness to carry on with it. I told him about the Rangers and Dodgers game in Arlington. Dad continued to watch the blank TV. I wanted to fill him in on the case, but there was no recognition in his eyes; talking to a disconnect.

I filled him in on meeting Captain Hollers and how portly he was and that he said, *hey*. I told him about Max and then switched gears to Patricia and how he would like her and how we planned to have a creek or two someday. A tear ran down his cheek.

"What the hell. Dad, I know you worked on the Hippie Hollow Task Force and I had a question for you."

I looked at Dad and he looked at the blank screen.

"I was hoping if there's anything left in there you might could tell me somehow where I can find Iced Chai's daughter Angel?"

Nothing.

I got up and gave him a kiss on top of his head. As I turned to leave, he did something that flabbergasted me. He started singing. That wasn't so unusual. It was *what* he sang that gasted my flabber.

"I'm walking to New Orleans..." And not a bad Fats Domino impression.

Before I left, I gave my horse, Too Tall, a kiss on the nose, telling him I'd come out soon and we'd ride. Mom was in the chicken coop gathering eggs into her white apron.

"I need to do this several times a day, Bilbo. Stay one step ahead of the raccoons. Did you find something to eat?"

I chugged the beer and was about to set the empty on a hen cage when I remembered how much Mom hated picking up after my brother and me and jammed it into the back pocket of my Levi's "I gotta go."

"You just got here."

"I know. And I'm sure as hell sorry I haven't come out, but I'm coming back real soon and I'm bringing Patricia. You remember we went out in college? We got back together and you know what? She's the one, Mom."

Mom reached up and pulled my head down, took off my Stetson and laid a kiss on my forehead.

I got to the airport in record time, bought a ticket and waited an hour before the flight. I hunkered down at the Starbuck's, nursing multiple venti lattes, my notes spread out on a corner table. I flipped open my *to do* list. I'd already crossed off most of the items and re-written the list a number of times.

- ~~Visit Max @ flower shop~~
- ~~Visit Max @ Barton Springs Pool~~
- ~~FBI Dallas, call first~~
- ~~Visit Arvin Tanner~~
- ~~Visit Lucinda Tanner~~
- ~~Go to scene @ Hippie Hollow~~
- ~~Go to lakehouse~~
- ~~Visit Merrylee @ Oak Meadow~~

- Visit Travis and Merrylee's mother, Lily Morganthal in Aspen—would need to clear it with Hollers
- ~~Visit Moses' parents~~
- ~~Visit Kristie's parents~~
- ~~Interview reporter, T Rex from newspaper~~
- Compile a list of APD detectives who worked on case
- Interview Captain Hollers
- ~~Phone John in Houston~~
- ~~Contact Mark Davidson, FBI agent in Washington, D.C.~~
- ~~Max's list attached~~
- ~~Warlick, retired, where? Balmorhea = Visit~~
- Guy who reported the murders on cell phone
- ~~Ballistics man~~
- ~~Was Angel in New Orleans? The Iced Chai Foundation was there~~ – yes!!
- Get a cell phone
- ~~Tanner financial guy = T. Rex talked to~~
- Go to N.O. and talk to Angel

I wrote *yes!!* Angel was in New Orleans, crossed it off and added a trip there to see her. I hoped that's what Dad was trying to tell me. I was either makin' progress or was so deluded I couldn't see shit. I took an initial sip of latte #3. Angel would either be in New Orleans and I'd either find her, or she wouldn't be there and I would not find her. Either way it was my opportunity to toss down mass quantities of Dixie Beer and a hurricane or two. Or three.

Maybe I could corner Captain Hollers tomorrow. Find out why the FBI had him on that list. For some unknown reason, Hollers didn't want me talking to the Task Force guys. He seemed upset when I contacted Warlick. And then made sure I didn't talk to him a second time. Wonder what's *really* going on here?

And there was the guy who reported the murders by cell phone that night. He *had* seen a cop car. Now, what did I do with his name and number? I guess I couldn't cross that one off yet.

I swiped my Visa card, hoping I still had enough room for a phone call, freed the phone from the airplane seat in front of me and dialed *Texas Highways* magazine, Accounting Department. The boarding announcement for my flight came over the loud speakers while I was talking with Max and I figured there wouldn't be enough time for my normal long ass conversation with Patricia. I hung up when her voice mail came on. I dialed Bergstrom. Donna told me Captain Hollers left the office sick.

"Well shit."

"Let me give you the Captain's number at home. You also received three calls from a Mr. Culpepper and two from Patricia Pearsall."

"Hey, thanks." I called Patricia again. Still unavailable. I called Hollers at home.

"Yeah?" A barely audible voice.

"Captain Hollers? This is Rivers."

"Rivers?" Silence and then, "Glad you called. Caught a bad case of summer flu or somethin'. Got it comin' out both ends." It was more than I wanted to know.

"Sorry you're feeling poorly. I've been trying to reach you, give you an update and ask you some..."

"Yeah, Rivers, I know. I got some things for you too. I heard from, cough, cough, from Captain Warlick."

"Really?"

"He's okay. Told me he was sorry he stood you up. Didn't feel like he was ready to talk about Hippie Hollow after all. Cough, cough."

"What about his car?"

"It *was* stolen. Either teenagers joy ridin' or wets trying to get back to Mexico. His insurance will cover the damages."

"That's good."

"I posted a 24-hour guard on young Miss Tanner's room at the sanitarium. Going with Max's instincts. Anyway, I'm not feeling worth a shit. I've got a couple of years of sick time comin', so I'm takin' today, maybe tomorrow off."

"Oh, really? I was going to ask you if I could take a..."

Whatever you need, go ahead. I'm sure Lucinda Tanner will spring for it. Just drop your report and expense sheet in my in basket on Friday. I told Donna..." Hollers had a coughing fit, sounded like he was gagging, maybe upchucking on the phone, "told Donna to pay your expense sheet from last week. Check in with her."

"Captain...?"

"Gotta go."

"But Captain Hollers."

"No, I mean I really gotta go!"

The 737 touched down in The "Big Sleazy" and I took a cab to the French Quarter. The good news? It was only 89 degrees compared to 99 in Austin. The bad news? 89 percent humidity. Sweat popped out of my pores and flowed freely as soon as I stepped from the cab. Felt not unlike Captain Hollers' office. I hadn't been to the city that care forgot since college when the Bobcats played a bowl game here. My first impression was the weather was nicer in December than June. My second impression was it was dirty in the Quarter, a detail not noticed when one is shit-faced drunk, stoned and partying one's ass off.

I don't remember a whole lot about the game either (too many drinks with cute little umbrellas) but I do remember it was *party on dude* the whole weekend. We Bobcats thought San Marcos was fun, but New Orleans really had it down.

The Iced Chai Foundation offices were located behind a tall, black, wicked-looking wrought-iron gate in the middle of a block of ancient connected buildings. Through the iron bars I could see a sign that read, *Iced Chai Foundation.* I rang the bell. No one came. I tried again.

"Mercury is not retrograde, goddamn it, what's going on here?" I walked to the corner to a wall-mounted phone and contacted Information. I got the phone number and dialed.

"Iced Chai Foundation. Please leave a message."

"Well, fuck." I hung up and went back to the gate and rang the bell again. Passersby gave me a wide berth as I rattled the gate and then ran a two by four I picked up in the alley, across the bars. No response. The sweat poured now. And I thought Austin was humid.

I walked around the block looking for a back entrance but the layout was confusing. Which back door belonged to which front? Again to the front. This time I counted steps heel to toe as I stepped off first to one corner of the street to the front door. To the back again, I stepped off from the corner to the place where a back door should be.

Sure enough, my quest put me in front of an ancient door. I mashed on an old-fashioned thumb latch and pushed against the door. It opened.

The room behind the old door looked like it had been abandoned a couple of centuries back. Ancient dust stirred as I walked through the first room straight back to another door. I turned the knob and pushed. It gave a little. It didn't seem to be locked. Probably stuck. I put my shoulder into it and gave the old linebacker shove. As the door lurched open, a bookshelf which was placed on the other side, fell over sending books, papers, office supplies and myself onto the desks of a half dozen workers.

"What the?" From a middle aged woman who did a pretty decent Whoopi Goldberg impression. I had knocked her off her chair, a fax machine landing in her lap.

"Sorry. Here let me help you up." I reached under her arms, attempting to lift her to her feet.

"Who the fuck are you?" She shouted, pulling away. She wanted nothing to do with me or my assistance. Within moments of my surprise entrance, three large men looking like the rap singers from Run-DMC were on me.

"That's the whitey was ringin' our doorbell, makin' all that racket," said the first one.

"What the fuck you doin' man?" From #2. "You are trespassing." They surrounded me. They were shorter but broader.

"I'm here to see Angel."

It looked like my question, instead of adding some sanity to the situation, had further incensed them. Two of them grabbed me and pulled me to my feet, holding me while the other wailed on my face and torso.

"I heard you were looking for me. I'm Angel." A beautiful, long-legged woman with cat eyes moved in close and pushed the three aside. She bent over me. After they dropped me, I landed hard on my back. I knew it was coming and took a deep in breath as I fell, but still lost most of it on impact.

Her skin was pure bittersweet dark chocolate. At least 75%, maybe more. She wore an elderly Malcolm X t-shirt hacked off at the bottom. The neck was cut wider too, taking off a chunk of Malcolm's afro and as she leaned over me, I could see down between two nice looking breasts, all the way to her navel. A slight outie. I mean it was an *outstanding* view.

Okay, this was like I imagined being a P. I. would be. Lying on my back, my nose broken and bleeding, looking up at a beautiful young woman who seemed concerned with my well being. Pain and pleasure. I pressed my knuckles against both sides of my nose to stop the bleeding.

"Here, you look terrible." She handed me a box of tampons. "It's all we could come up with," she shrugged. I sat up on an elbow and jammed two of the cotton cylinders up my nasal passages.

"Now don't you look fine," she said laughing. I bet I looked a hell of a lot more ridiculous than fine. My ribs hurt as I laughed along with her. One of the DMC dudes caught me on the exact same rib as the FBI agent nailed in Dallas.

"What are you doing here?" She asked. "Your ID says you're from Austin. Why you asking about me?" She didn't seem angry, merely curious.

"Do da name Travis Tanner ring a bell?" I smiled. In unison, the DMC took a step toward me. Not the optimum time or place for my Kingfish impression. Angel stopped them with a look.

"Let's take a walk, get some java." She gave me a hand up. She was talking my language.

Angel and I strolled to the wharf on the Mississippi River and on to Jefferson Square and the Café du Monde coffee shop. The recent storms had not really altered the French Quarter all that much. But then again I am not much of a noticer. Probably better if I were in my line of work. But hey, even Rockford had off days.

"I don't get what y'all see in these things." I removed the tampons from my nose and tossed them in a trashcan. She laughed. According to Patricia, humor was the second most important thing a woman was looking for in a man.

We ordered two cafés au lait, dark and thick New Orleans coffee with chicory and hot milk, with a dish of sugary beignets, New Orleans donuts.

"Wow. These are good!" I felt her eyes on me as I took a tentative sip of the hot coffee.

"Have you seen Travis?" Her question seemed genuine enough. "His roommate got a message to me that he was still alive."

"Yeah," I said. "I haven't actually seen him, but I have it on good authority that he's okay and living in Mexico. Fellow I'm working with went down there with Travis's aunt. You know Auntie Loo?"

She nodded looking down through her coffee. Her eyelashes were extra long and very black. "Never met the lady but sure enough gets a lot of press."

"I hear Travis has been asking about you."

She shook her head and looked up. "Surprise, surprise," she said in a pretty good Gomer Pyle, U.S.M.C. impression. If I wasn't hooked by her looks, her humor (the second most important thing to a man) had gotten me. "He showed up here in New Orleans to see me just before that thing happened. I did want to see him actually, but figured it wouldn't be such a good idea. We never..."

"Got it on?" I completed her sentence for her even though I'd been trying like hell not to do that. Seems I can't help myself.

"What I was going to say... But, yes, you're right. That *is* true; we never did get it on. To be honest, I went to TCU to find Travis Tanner and exterminate his ass."

"Whoa," I managed to hold onto my beignet.

"Here's the deal, his father killed my father. To be accurate, his father had my father assassinated." She waited for that to sink in.

"I, the passionate and dutiful daughter, was after retribution. A little quirk in our family tree. I think there's some Sicilian blood flowing through us. A whack for a whack, just something we do in our family. Registered at TCU, worked myself into Travis' life, had to pretend to like accounting," she rolled her beautiful black eyes, "and found much to my dismay, I liked the guy. Not as a lover, as a friend. He was sweet. So, I changed my mind. A woman's entitled to that, right?"

I nodded. Yeah, I knew that one.

"He wasn't anything like his father. He hated the Right Reverend Arvin Tanner worse than I did. You okay?" She pointed to a drop of blood that splattered on my white shirt.

"I think it might be broken. Damn it. Not on the shirt," I whined. Boy, I was going through shirts on this job. I dabbed my nose with a Café du Monde napkin. It hurt like hell. Not the napkin, the nose. I had broken it numerous times footballing, rodeoing, once in a pick up rugby game, and once policing and a couple of times tossing drunks, and it always felt like someone backed over it with their truck and then parked it there. My ribs hurt about as bad.

Angel offered me a couple of tampons she had brought along, but I refused. I'd make the napkins work. Dang it all.

"I might have broken a rib, too," I was holding on to my side. "Why the reception committee?" I could barely breathe much less flirt with the lovely lady.

"Sorry about my boys. We get a death threat a day from one of your various hate groups or another. When they saw your white ass crash through the wall... My father, Iced Chai, was assassinated and since I took over, there have been attempts on my life. Boys are protective."

"That's an interesting way to put it," I managed to get the bucket-sized coffee cup up to my lips without embarrassing myself.

"Why are you here, Mr. Rivers?" She looked me straight in the eyes and moved to within kissing distance.

"B. B. Just call me B. B."

She didn't ask me what it stood for and she didn't call me B. B. She didn't call me Bilbo. She didn't call me Bill. She didn't call me anything. She didn't look away either. Her eyes were black and enigmatic. Her breath was as sweet as a French Quarter donut.

"Hippie Hollow."

"Where Travis was supposed to have been killed?" I was looking at her mouth. When she smiled, her teeth were bright white. Her lips were pretty and full and about two inches from mine. I didn't back off either.

"Are you prejudiced, Mr. Rivers? Are you uncomfortable in the presence of a person of color?"

"Not the least little bit." If I ever was before, I sure wasn't at that moment.

She closed the gap between us. She moved to the top of my fantasy list.

I continued.

"Here is what we know," I said to my reflection in her eyes. "Someone hired a hit man to take out the Rev, and two innocent teenagers were killed instead. Tanner should have been in that limo. And I'm here to ask you a question."

"What question is that?" She broke our connection and sipped her coffee.

"I want to know if you, or your foundation, put out a contract on Arvin Tanner?"

"That's crazy."

Chapter Twenty-six

"Multi-tasking pisses me off."

Bumper Sticker

I bought the next available ticket back to Austin the same day. Fortunately, I didn't fly Southwest, so I wasn't required to eat my weight in peanuts. Max and Lucinda said they would meet me at Chuy's Restaurant where we would talk over our latest adventures. Lots of Elvis memorabilia at Chuy's, the tail end of a Cadillac Eldorado sticking through a wall, thousands of wooden fish hanging from the ceiling. Loud, high energy place.

"Hi, Lucinda. Hi, Max."

"What happened to you?"

"Got into it with some of Iced Chai's thugs. Don't think they much cared for my Amos and Andy impression. I did find Angel. But I no longer feel she was involved with the murders."

"I might have advised you of that. I believe I did counsel you of that very..." He knew by the glare I was giving him through puffy, blacked eyes he was pushing it and stopped.

I nodded. Max was right but I was glad I went to New Orleans even though I came back with a broken nose, bruised ribs and a one pound can of dark roast coffee with chicory.

"That's quite a shiner," said Lucinda. "Actually, two shiners."

"You ought to put a fresh beet on it," said Max.

"Not a steak?" Asked Lucinda.

"Old vegetarian recipe from Tibet. Or you could try yak butter. The Lamas swear by it."

"Sure, Max. I bet they carry yak butter at Central Market."

"When was the last time you saw a Lama with a black eye?" The man was in rare form. Getting laid will do that for a guy. What happened to the cranky old asshole I had grown to love?

"We've just come from visiting Merrylee," said Lucinda. "She's doing very well. Maximus is worried though, because of the chart."

"Would you care to see it?" Max reached under the table.

"No, not really," I held up a hand." I wouldn't know what I was looking at anyway." I stared through the picture window at the passing cars on Barton Springs, Road but my thoughts were on New Orleans. I let the DMC get a jump on me. Don't mind a good fight, after all I've been a bouncer in a cowboy bar, but I didn't remember that fight. I also thought about Angel. Man, she was good lookin'. And those legs, and eyes, and...

"You okay?" Asked Lucinda.

"It's been an up-and-down day. Although I did call Patricia and she's going to meet us here. So, I guess it must be on the up swing. There she is."

"Great," said Lucinda. "A double date! I've been wanting to meet your girl."

"Oh my God, Billy Rivers. What happened to you?"

"He got beat up by a glass of tea," said Max.

Patricia looked at Max and then at me, confused by the answer.

"Iced Chai bodyguards. There were three of them," I said feebly.

"Three glasses of tea. Well, well." Sometimes Max could be flat irritating. He thought he was so funny.

"Lucinda Tanner, this is Patricia Pearsall. Patricia, Lucinda Tanner. And Max Culpepper."

"Hi, Lucinda. Hi, Max. I've talked with you on the phone." Patricia sat next to me.

"Nice to meet you," said Lucinda.

"Indeed." I could tell Max was considering kissing her hand but I sent a frown at him and he shook her hand instead.

"Billy, you need to be a little more careful." Patricia lifted my top lip and checked my mouth. "Your teeth are still where they should be. Your nose looks a little off center and why is it purplish?"

"Ow!"

"Broken?" I shook my head even though I figured it was. "Did you remember to increase our coverage on the life insurance?" She passed from concerned to hilarious. Max and Lucinda laughed along with her. I laughed as I am wont to do but a shooting pain ripped through my rib cage toning it down to a weak smile.

"So, how was your meeting with Travis?" I asked Max and Lucinda, hoping to move the conversation away from my face.

"Nice young fellow. He seemed genuinely pleased to hear Merrylee emerged from her coma. You've been busy yourself since we last spoke. I would like to hear your thoughts on Angel, Merrylee, Arvin, and what about the FBI fellow?"

"Liked her, really liked her, hated him, really hated him." That drew a laugh, which didn't help my ribs situation.

Julie, our waitress, appeared. "Y'all want some tortilla chips 'n salsa?" We agreed that would be in order. "And can I get y'all's drink order? We have a special on iced chai this evening."

I spit a mouthful of water across the table. Everyone jumped back. Max had that "can't take the boy anywhere" look on his face. The girls laughed. Danny Thomas rolled over in his grave.

"What?" asked Julie, looking at each of us seated at the table. No one said anything and Julie pulled out a cloth napkin and wiped up the mess. "Drinks?" She didn't mention the chai this time but looked at me warily.

Max had his own bottled water. Lucinda opted for the iced chai as did Patricia. I went for the fortification of dual equis.

After Julie left, I told the group about the FBI interrogation in Big D, my quick trip back to Austin to meet with Reverend A and my equally quick expedition to see Mom and Dad, and then on to New Orleans and back. It took me as long to tell about it as it did to do it.

"I don't know if I'm coming or going."

"I'm proud of you for seeing your parents," said Patricia.

I nodded at Patricia and squeezed her arm. "I told Mom I'd bring you out to the ranch." Patricia seemed to like that and grabbed me under the table. I did not know why a trip to Blanco would make a woman horny but I never professed to understanding women anyway. I looked over to Lucinda. Patricia did not let go. Girl's got a grip.

"Speaking of trips, Lucinda..." My voice went up a couple of octaves. I not only looked like Opie Taylor, I sounded like him. "Captain Hollers said I ought to ask you if a trip to Colorado to see Lily Morganthal was in the budget?" Please, please, let me go to Colorado. I'll be good. The Mountain State is on the opposite end of the spectrum from Louisiana.

"Won't be necessary. Lily is coming here. As a matter of fact, we're picking her up at the airport tonight."

"How serendipitous. Didn't I tell you things would fall into line for you?" said Max.

"You did, you did," I was thinking it would be even more beneficial for my personal healing process to be at a higher and thus cooler elevation (the old Plan A) as July descended upon Central Texas. The weather in New Orleans all but put me over the edge. On the flight back, I fantasized taking the Bubbamobile to the ranch, loading Too Tall into the horse trailer, with Hank on the front seat with me, and two days later we'd be riding past alpine lakes and streams, marmots scampering out of our way, our sights set on the Maroon Bells of Aspen. I could see myself on the mountain, shooting my 45 in the cold night air and howling at the moon.

But no! Seemed like *everybody* was getting quality mountain time except me. And Too Tall.

"We're going to Oak Meadow tomorrow," said Lucinda. "Lily too. She doesn't know Travis is alive but Maximus thought it would be high time to tell her. Isn't that right, Maximus?"

"I advised Travis when we visited with him in San Miguel that it would be safe to come back to Texas now. He told us he would think it over. And yet there is something going on there I don't understand."

"Something *you* don't understand? That's a little hard to fathom."

"Now, Bilbo, let us be pleasant. Travis may possess long-term trauma; however, I feel there is something beyond this he is still not sharing with us."

At seven A.M., I arrived for my second weekly Bergstrom Monday morning meeting. I was so early I walked in with Donna and her donuts. She offered me one.

"What happened to your nose?" Asked Donna. "You and the little woman get into it?"

"Funny. But naw." I gave her a capsulated version of my weekend as I bit into a strawberry jelly-filled donut.

"No meeting today. Captain's still out sick."

"Really? It doesn't seem like I can carry on a decent conversation with the man."

"Say, Rivers." Donna stopped me as I headed for the stairs leading the lower bowels of Bergstrom and my cave.

"Yeah?"

"I want to be straight with you." I walked back up to her.

"Straight about what?" I was finishing up the donut and sipping on a venti latte. She was eating a glazed and drinking from a styrofoam cup. She offered me another donut.

"You know when you were up with the FBI in Dallas that first time?"

"I remember it very well. The nightmares have stopped now, which is good."

"And you called in for the Captain?"

I nodded.

"He told me to tell you he stepped out. But he was here all the time. I don't like that flavor of doo doo and I told him so. And as a matter of fact, I told him I would tell you what was going on around here. I think it made him sick."

"Really?"

"I don't think he figured you'd accomplish much with this case. I think he hired you because he thought you were a screw-up and no way would you come up with anything, so the whole thing would sort of go away. Our department would get a much needed infusion of funds from Ms. Tanner. That's what he was interested in. He could care less about solving this case. He's lost his edge over the years. Used to be…"

She took a sip of coffee. "He thought he had it under control, but then something he hadn't figured on happened—you started closing in on something and he got scared. I don't really know why."

"Thanks, Donna." I bopped down to the cave and pulled out my "to do" list. People have underestimated me before. It did not hurt my feelings. What hurt was my nose and ribs. Sticks and stones sort of thing.

I sat there for a moment between bites and sips and daydreamed about paying my respects on the *DMC* dudes. A fist in the gut to each doubling them over in pain seemed appropriate. And while they were sucking for air, I'd follow with a good kick in the butt with my pointy-toed, reptilian-skin cowboy boots. It momentarily made me feel better.

I put my feet up on the desk, put my hands behind my head and tilted the chair back into thinking position. I stared at the hanging light bulb.

Why does the FBI have Captain Hollers on their list? What was that fat bastard up to? Was Hollers the one who wanted me off the case? Hey, somebody sure as hell wanted me off the case.

Hey, why was Lucinda on the list? Was Max on it? God, I don't remember. And T. Rex was on it. Was my name on it now?

Warlick was under investigation by the FBI. Something not quite right here. What did he know? And if Hollers isn't being honest then maybe he isn't telling me everything about the Warlick deal. Hmm.

Still needed to talk to the fellow who made the cell phone call. He was the first guy on the scene, for Christ's sakes. Always gotta talk to the first guy on the scene. What did I do with the phone number? It would be embarrassing to ask T. Rex for it again. And what if he offered me more of the Thai stick?

T. Rex had given me a handful of articles dating all the way back to the beginning on up to current stuff. I grabbed one at random.

POLICE BAFFLED
Two years into the Hippie Hollow murders and the Austin Police Department still has no idea who killed Rollingwood High School football star Moses Harper. This reporter asked Task Force Leader, Captain William Warlick, about the prog-ress of the investigation. "We have made very little progress. I know that is not what everyone wants to hear, but it's true. The only leads we've had to follow up on have been provided by crank calls."
Honest but inept, is Captain Warlick suited for...

That's it. No more. I already knew that during the entire five years of the investigation, the Task Force never got it out of granny gear.

I considered Max's prediction the killer would cross paths with Merrylee. It seemed logical if I stayed close to Merrylee, the killer would cross my path. I called Max.

"Flower Shop."

"Hi, Max. I wasn't sure you'd be at work this early. I was going to leave you a message."

"Short swim today. My designers were getting restless with-out me, and our bamboo is attacking the neighborhood. As you know, Lucinda, Lily and I are going to Oak Meadow later on this morning. You'll be meeting us for luncheon, correct?"

"That is correct. You know, Max, you said something yester-day while we were eating chile rellenos at Chuy's."

"That's chiles relleno, actually."

"Okay, whatever. You said when you were talking with Travis Tanner down in Mexico, he mentioned his father, Arvin Tanner was supposed to go back to Austin with the others in the limo, but at the last minute he didn't go."

"That's right. He received a phone call."

"I asked Reverend Tanner about that. He told me he didn't remember who called him. Do you believe that? I mean you're a reader of human nature. Does it seem to you he would forget who called him? If he wasn't the person who hired the killer but was instead the person who was supposed to be killed, then wouldn't that phone call have saved his life? I know *I'd* remember who saved my life and my memory is for shit."

"Where are you right now?"

"At Bergstrom. Why?"

"What say we meet at some beverage establishment between your office and mine?"

"Sure. Any ideas?"

"How about Sweetish Hill on West 6th in fifteen minutes?"

It took me seventeen minutes to get to the coffee shop and bakery. Max was there, drinking a glass of fresh squeezed orange juice. I waved, dumped some half and half into a cup of dark roast coffee and sat down across from him at the picnic table under the painting of ex-Texas Governor Ann Richards.

"Good to see you Max. Whatcha got?"

"When we were in Mexico, Travis mentioned his father, Arvin Tanner had been involved in something, quote, "very bad," end quote." Max did the quote thing. Everybody was doing it.

"Really?" I asked, blowing and sipping my coffee. "You ought to try this, Max. I'm sure it's better than what you're drinking."

"Nothing is better than fresh squeezed orange juice, Bilbo."

"Hey, quit calling me Bilbo."

"I'm sorry. Lucinda and I call you Bilbo when we speak of you; however, I know I agreed to call you Rivers."

"That's quite alright," I did my Maximus Culpepper impression. "Did he mention what Reverend Tanner was involved in?

"No, he did not say; however, we do know he told his mother, Lily Morganthal, about it. Maybe we can ask her tomorrow."

Chapter Twenty-seven

"Fire on the mountain, run girl, run."

Charlie Daniels

El Jaguar figured he'd whack Merrylee Tanner first, a sitting duck at the sanitarium and the most likely to identify him. Before her blood cooled, he'd pop a cap in Reverend Asshole, who had kept quiet so far. Bless him. Cops would come out of the donut shops for this one.

He would use his powers of persuasion to find out where young Travis Tanner was hiding. Reverend Asshole or Auntie Loo or maybe even sweet Merrylee would happily supply that piece of information. If he was good at anything, it was extracting information from those unwilling to give it up. They didn't call him the Butcher of Bolivia because of his skill with pork chops.

He was at a critical crossroads. This could very well be the time to test his theory of invincibility. He could choose Austin. Do Charles Whitman's room with a view. The cops would *not* kill him. He knew that. Whatever he did, it was his choice. With this choice he would no longer be an unknown.

The alternative was to tidy up the loose ends here in Austin, do the extravaganza, and then chill out, maybe go find a war. Lots of action in the Middle East right now. For the first time, he was wanted by his own name and his actual fingerprints were on file. That could be a sign, the time is right to do this. The FBI had been after him for a long, long, time but up until now they did not know who he was. Maybe he ought to show them who they were dealing with.

Or he could go back to Costa Rica. He liked it there. He would not go to Bolivia. It would not be a good idea to go back to the Pacific Northwest either. He thought about his stash. When they found it, which they would, they would be in for an unpleasant surprise. A smile crept from under his mustache.

Only I know I'm smiling, he thought.

Sprinkle Road exit. Down the two-lane road, anxious to get the ball rolling, or maybe a head rolling, he thought laughing. He pulled through the gate of the sanitarium. A long white limo pulled out as he pulled in. Fancy place, he thought. He had called ahead and talked to Dr. Adams about placing his dear mother (he never knew her) in the sanitarium. The Doc seemed to be receptive to the notion, especially when El Jaguar mentioned money was no object.

"Colonel Charles Whitman here to see Dr. Adams," he said to the guard at the gate. He was let right in. He walked in the front door and past the reception desk, taking the elevator to the next floor. He walked down the hall to physical therapy.

This will do, he thought.

"Hi. I think I'm lost. I'm looking for Merrylee Tanner's room."

"307." The man pointed to the ceiling without taking his eyes off his massage. "One floor up." He visualized taking the guy's finger off.

However, first things first, back on the elevator. The doors to the elevator parted and he peeked out. No guards. Good. He walked down the hall to her room. When a white clad orderly pushed a very old looking woman by, he pretended to be looking for a room number. Glancing down at a piece of paper and then up to the room number on the door. The orderly and the woman ignored him.

He waited a moment and took a homemade handgun with silencer from his jacket pocket. Holding it against his thigh, he opened the door to Merrylee's room carefully, quietly, slipping the handgun back into his jacket pocket. Two candy stripers were taking sheets off the bed, piling them on the floor and putting on new ones.

"I'm sorry, I was looking for Merrylee Tanner's room. Must have gotten the room number wrong." He turned and walked out.

"Sir," one of the girls caught him in the hall, "this is her room, *was* her room. You just missed her. Her family just checked her out."

The limo.

"I was supposed to ride with them," he said laying on a Texas accent, "but I guess I missed that bus. And to top it all off, I plum forgot where they was a-goin'." Damn, that was bad. "Y'all wouldn't happen to know...?"

"I did hear someone say they were going for lunch at Fonda Restaurant."

After getting directions to the Mexican restaurant, "Thank y'all ever so much." He rolled his eyes as he turned and left.

Chapter Twenty-eight

*"This program has performed an illegal operation
and will be shut down."*

Microsoft Windows

"Lily Morganthal," said Lucinda, "I would like to present Bilbo—whoops, B. B. Rivers. B. B., Lily."

"Hello Mr. Rivers, pleased to meet you. I met your father when he was working on the investigation." Lily was tall, slim, elegant, subdued. Lucinda and Lily, a lot of class there. I planned to ask at the earliest opportunity what she knew about her ex-husband's improprieties. Max and I worked up a list of questions.

"Wow, these are the best chile rellenos, chiles relleno, I've ever tasted." I put them at the top of my list.

"It appears you are gathering some valuable data on the chile relleno," said Max.

"That is correct, sir." I said. The conversation up until this point was centered around the weather in Aspen (nice and cool), the weather in Austin (fair and hot), how long it has been since Merrylee, Lucinda and Lily had been together. "Say, we're all friends here, right?"

Max and Lucinda nodded. Merrylee said, "Sure." Lily, to whom the question was intended, made no indication of agreement or disagreement.

"I guess what I'm getting at is this, Lily." She turned toward me as if in slow motion. "It's no secret your, ah, sister-in-law Lucinda hired me to look into the unfortunate events involving your children, Travis and Merrylee." When she didn't reply, I went on. "Time to share a little secret everyone here already knows."

"What sort of secret, Mr. Rivers?" She looked to each of the others and back to me.

"Your son Travis is alive and has been living in Mexico for the past five years."

"Oh, my..!" Her margarita glass slipped from her grasp. Max, who was sitting next to her, caught it in mid air. Way to go, old chap. He put it back on the table well out of reach of the trembling Lily.

"But, I don't understand. Why didn't anyone tell me? Lucinda, did you...why did *you* keep this from me?"

"Since that night at Hippie Hollow," said Lucinda, "Travis feared for his life. He thought it safest to disappear, thinking if there were no contact with you or his father, he could somehow spare you from danger. I don't believe he thought it would take quite this long."

"Well, I can understand why he wouldn't want any contact with Arvin Tanner but I'm his mother."

"He wanted me to tell you he missed you terribly," said Lucinda, "and can't wait to see you."

"Here's a picture of him." Merrylee came around the table to her mother, putting an arm around her shoulder."

"He looks good."

"Yeah, he does, doesn't he?"

"I can't believe this. I'm going to book the next flight to Mexico..."

"Whoa," I said, "just a second now. There's a couple of things. Travis is coming here, right Max?" Max nodded. "But there is something else you need to know. There still might be some danger."

"Danger?"

"Yes." Max stepped into the conversation. "I believe whoever killed Moses Harper and Kristie Bentley is, or soon will be, in Austin."

"That's terrible! What are we doing about that?" Lily looked to each of us in turn.

"That is a good question, isn't it, Maximus?" Said Lucinda.

"A very good question indeed."

"Okay, now this is where you can help, Lily," I said.

"What can I do?"

"May I?" Max took over.

I nodded, sipping my iced tea.

"When I last conversed with Travis in Mexico, he related a story about the summer at the church when he worked on the financials. As you recall, he uncovered some rather damaging data on his father, Reverend Arvin Tanner. He stopped short of revealing the exact extent of it; however, we were lead to believe you have some knowledge of this."

"I didn't know Arvin before he found Jesus. I understand he was quite a hell raiser. A drinker and who knows what else. When first we met, he seemed so sincere. I've never been able to understand how a man of the cloth like Reverend Arvin Tanner could do such a vile and contemptible thing." She stared at her plate of enchiladas molé, moving a piece around with her fork but not attempting to eat it.

"What did he do, Lily?" I asked.

"Travis found it and brought it to me."

"What did he bring, Lily?" Asked Lucinda also not eating.

"Yeah, what?" Merrylee was having no problem with her fajitas. Lily looked at her daughter and then to Lucinda.

"That summer Travis and I worked together at the Church of the Ark. It was a wonderful time. I felt so blessed to be working with my son. Travis had just graduated from Rollingwood. He's a very intelligent young man. My ex-husband, Reverend Arvin Tanner," she paused, looked back down at her food and said in a barely audible voice, "hired a man to kill another man."

"Travis tried to tell me that night, but I refused to believe it," said Merrylee. We all waited for more.

"Travis' job was to work on the chart of accounts that had been set up for the Church of the Ark. He was a real whiz with numbers and said he could help streamline our accounting system. I thought, why not? It would be a natural. Our CPA, his name slips my mind at present..."

"Larry Furman," Lucinda and I together.

"That's right." She looked at us curiously and then continued. "Mr. Furman advised it would be alright but he would need to approve any changes. He didn't want Travis to delete the software system, for example, or to lose vital information. Travis dug into the files. On one dreadful day, just before he was to begin his freshman year at Texas Christian, he came rushing into my office. Reverend Tanner and the church elders were off traveling, and it was just the two of us in the office.

"He was tracking a paper trail for a rather huge disbursement of funds, several thousand dollars. According to Travis, the accounts were basically okay, we just weren't using them correctly. I remember he was upset with our practice of posting so many transactions to the miscellaneous account. He was working on identifying and reposting those misfiles. He latched onto it. He was that kind of boy. *Is* that kind of boy." Her hand was to her mouth. I figured she wouldn't be able to believe her son was alive until she saw him in the flesh.

"Anyway, one by one he identified each transaction and reposted to the appropriate file until he came to the big one for several thousand dollars. He dug in and tracked it down. It was paid to Colonel James Spivey and sent to a post office box in Washington State. I'll never forget *that* name. He found it in a password protected account and found the money was paid for the purpose of *eliminating* the black rap singer, Iced Chai."

"Angel's father?" A crucial piece of the puzzle clicked into place. Angel did tell me Reverend A hired a killer to assassinate her father, Iced Chai. So, this Spivey character was the one who did the job. Spivey's name was on Davidson's list. I had jotted it on my wrist the night Davidson mentioned it in Dallas. The FBI already knew about the guy.

The FBI was looking at him in their parallel investigation which also somehow included Warlick and Hollers and the Tanners and who knows who else. The important question had to be, what did the FBI know about Spivey that they weren't sharing? No wonder the rest of law enforcement didn't trust the Feds.

Lily continued. "Arvin was blatantly foolish by keeping a computer file on it." She seemed outraged. "Names, places, times of meetings, sums of money paid. And it was on the church's computer!" Like killing somebody was not as bad as leaving the evidence for all to see.

We all shook our heads in disbelief. What a dumb ass.

"Travis printed it out and brought it to me. Asked me if I knew anything about it, which of course I did not."

"So, what did you all do about it?" I asked.

"I didn't do anything. It scared me out of my skin. I quit the church that day and arranged to ship my things to our family place in Aspen. Arvin and I divorced two years prior but I was still vested in the Church of the Ark. Travis' revelation allowed me to become rapidly unvested. I moved to Aspen, Colorado and haven't been back to Austin until today. I never returned to visit you, Merrylee. I'm ashamed of myself for that."

"How terrible for you, Mother." Merrylee put a hand on her mother's arm. "From what I understand, you didn't miss much."

"Travis was not scared," Lily continued. "His emotion was not fear but anger, and he told me he would deal with it in his own way and in his own time."

"Do you know what he meant by that?" I asked.

"Travis," she almost said was, "*is*, a patient young man. When he finds something he wants, he is very methodical in its pursuit. That car for instance. He started working on me in the ninth grade. He knew the make and model he would want as a graduation gift. He had cut-outs from magazines of the car on his walls at home."

"He had a pic of the Beamer in his locker at school," said Merrylee. "Most of the boys had pics of those bimbos from *Baywatch* but not Trav."

"During his senior year he talked about it daily until I got it for his graduation. He was patient. I got the feeling he would apply the same kind of pressure to Arvin."

"Blackmail?" I asked.

"That's what I thought when he told me he would deal with it in his own way. I moved to Aspen and Travis went on to Texas Christian, and that day was the first, last and only time we discussed it."

"Do you remember anything in particular about Colonel Spivey?" I asked.

"According to the file, Arvin and the elders of the church met Spivey in Costa Rica on a church mission. They were ostensibly in Central American to help the natives find God. Seems they made a pact with the devil instead. There were photos in the file of the victim, Iced Chai, the one they murdered. He was a big man with long curly hair. There was one of Arvin and Iced Chai when they debated each other on *Politically Incorrect*. Arvin came off as small and insignificant. If you know Arvin, you know he would have a difficult time with that."

"I thought Iced Chai came off sounding rational and Arvin sounded like an ignorant racist," said Lucinda.

"But is humiliation motive enough for murder?" I asked.

"I still can't believe Dad hired this Spivey character to kill Iced Chai."

"But it is true," said Lily.

No one said anything for a long time.

"What about Mo and Kristie? Did Dad hire Spivey to kill them too?" Asked Merrylee.

"I don't know anything about that. I left Austin a year before that happened. But I cannot think of one reason why he would do such a thing."

"My chart does not show your father had a role in their deaths."

"Maybe Spivey and Arvin had a falling out," I said. "And Spivey thought Arvin was in the limo." I was trying to force that last piece into place.

"That is a possibility," said Max.

"You mean there is something you don't know?" I was being borderline sarcastic. "Were there photos of Spivey in the file?"

"Yes, there was one of his face. He was bald with a big, bushy mustache."

"That's the assho..., the guy, who killed Mo and Kristie." Merrylee pointed a fork full of fajita at me.

"You wouldn't have saved a copy of that file?" Asked Max.

She shook her head. I knew who had the file.

Max and Lucinda chipped in on the check and left me with a wad of cash. I used the restaurant pay phone next to the quietest parrot I had ever been around. Our ranch parrot, Paco, was loud and raucous and had the irritating habit of repeating everything you said. One by one, children came up to Fonda's parrot hollering "Polly want a cracker?" and "I'm a pretty bird," but the bird ignored them. Good bird.

Everyone except moi was traveling by limo to the lake house. I would love to party with the gang but I was feeling the weight of responsibility. It was time to follow through with the biggest lead since I found out Travis was alive. We had a face. We had a name, maybe even a motivation. We knew, and it had been confirmed, Reverend A hired Spivey to kill Angel's father, Iced Chai. And I was pretty damn sure, Larry Furman, CPA, had the physical evidence locked away somewhere safe.

Was it possible Reverend A hired Spivey an additional time? And if so, who was the target? Travis? According to Merrylee, Travis and Reverend A had a knock down drag out fight that same evening. But hiring a hit had to have been set up way ahead, and Reverend A needed Travis to direct some money from his inheritance into his personal coffers. Why would he kill the golden goose? Merrylee? Same thing. He thought he already had gotten her money, and he obviously loved her. Why kill her? Kristie? No evidence he even knew her. Moses? He was black, and Reverend A hated blacks. If he thought his precious Merrylee and the big black dude were a number, that might put him over the edge.

He paid some coin to knock off Iced Chai, but Moses Harper? There was a pretty good chance he didn't even know Moses was coming to the party. I should check it out.

How about Travis? Travis could have been blackmailing his father. That's reason enough for murder. Reverend A could have staged his withdrawal from the homeward-bound limo. Maybe he never intended taking that trip.

How about Spivey? Why would Spivey want to kill Reverend A? Maybe Spivey didn't like televangelists. Maybe preacher man didn't pay Colonel Spivey for the last job. But that had been a while ago, and Lily said there had been monies paid.

According to Basil Rathbone, if none of the possible clues panned out, it had to be one of the impossible ones.

Before my trip to New Orleans, I thought Angel hired a hit man of her own, but one, she'd enjoy pulling the trigger on Reverend A herself and two, no way would she have hired the man who killed her father. So, if Spivey was our killer, that ruled her out. And her breasts were too firm (a bit subjective I realize).

I called a friend of mine at APD, giving him all the facts on Colonel James Spivey, and asked him to run a check.

"Tell Lieutenant Ashby this guy is the contractor who did the hit on Iced Chai and the murders at Hippie Hollow. The Feds already know him so if y'all don't have anything on him, they will." I thought about calling Captain Hollers, but figured he'd be out sick or still avoiding me, so I hung up and went out to the Bubbamobile. Figured I'd swing by the Starbuck's drive through and get a tall latte and head for the cave and write all this up. See if I could figure out what was really happening here.

Summer had returned to Austin with a vengeance. Through the radiated heat of the parking lot, I saw the limo disappearing from the far exit. I snugged on my Stetson and as I stepped off the curb, a black Jeep Cherokee zipped past. I stepped back to avoid being run over.

"Hey, watch it, asshole!"

Something about the driver. Did I know him? A bald headed man with a big, bushy mustache? I shook my head. Some people.

I sat in the pickup and looked at my notes from the past few days. Merrylee had sketched the face of her bald-headed man. Around fifty years old. Big bushy mustache. I had shown the sketch to Lily and she agreed it was Spivey.

"Fuck!" What if the guy in the Jeep Cherokee was Spivey? He fit the description. "I have to catch up with him." I pulled out of Fonda's parking lot without customary engine warming up period (does one even warm up a diesel?) and caught up with the Jeep Cherokee a couple of blocks later, parked at a convenience store. I saw the limo up ahead at the traffic light, blinker on, for a turn onto MoPac.

Traffic lights in Austin are long. Some friends procreated a baby while waiting for a green light at Burnet and 183. I had plenty of time to pull over to a pay phone and dial Lucinda's cell phone number.

"When am I going to get my own cell phone? (Number 734 on my *to do* list). This is ri-goddamned-diculous." I said to myself as I got her voice mail.

"Hi, Sweetie. You have reached the mobile phone of Lucinda Tanner. Looks like I'm doing something else. And wouldn't you like to know what it is? So be a sweetheart and leave me a message, with your phone number so I can call you right back. Bye, now."

"Hi Lucinda, this is B. B. Rivers. I'm at a pay phone a couple of blocks behind you all. You're turning onto MoPac, heading out to your lake house. I don't want to alarm you, but I think you're being followed and the guy looks an awful lot like our Colonel Spivey. I don't know if it's him or not, but I'll make sure and get his license number. This all could be just a coincidence, but he is bald with a big mustache and..."

"Beep."

I re-dialed. Busy.

"Shit."

Lucinda's limo turned onto MoPac and the Jeep Cherokee pulled out, following five cars behind. Damn. It did seem the alleged Spivey was following the limo. Surely Lucinda would get a beep and she'd realize she had voice mail. The limo exited MoPac onto F.M. 2222 and headed west toward the lake.

The Cherokee made an exit.

So did I.

At the big hill a couple of miles before the 3M plant, I stomped into passing gear. The gas gauge dropped toward empty as I flew around the cars. The Bubbamobile could move when needed. Just like me. As I passed the Jeep Cherokee, the good news—I took off my Stetson and looked away so the man wouldn't see my face. The bad news—the maneuver didn't allow me to get a good look at his face.

As I passed the limo, I scribbled a makeshift sign on the back of my makeshift *B. B. Rivers Private Investigator* cardboard shingle and held it up to the back window of the pickup, right over the Southwest Texas State Bobcats sticker. This was a difficult move since I was going about ninety and had an extended cab to reach through.

Cell phone!!!

Call police!!!

I pulled over at the next pay phone I saw and called Lucinda again. "I'm sorry the number you dialed is out of range. Now connecting to voice mail box for..."

"...Lucinda Tanner."

"Shit." I waited while Lucinda repeated those same cute things and left her another message. "Hi, Lucinda, it's me, B.B. I'm now at the pay phones on the corner of 2222 and 620. Damn, there you are. You just went by. I suppose if you get this message you will have already heard my previous message." I waited for the Jeep Cherokee to pass. Five cars, ten, fifteen, twenty. No Jeep Cherokee. "Okay, there was this guy I thought was following you but now I don't see him so maybe I'm just being paranoid."

I talked fast so I could get it all in. "He was a bald guy with a big, bushy mustache driving a Jeep Cherokee, older model. Jeep that is. The guy was an older model too. I got his license number so I'm going to call a friend at the Department of Motor Vehicles. Get him to run it for me. Then I'll know for sure what the hell is..."

"Beep."

"Shit." I dialed D.M.V. and gave my friend the license plate number.

"It'll take a minute." I held on for what seemed like the length of *Hey Jude*.

"Rivers?"

"Yeah, where'd you go?" I had continued to watch for the Jeep Cherokee but I never saw it pass.

He ignored my impatience. "I got it for you. Registered to Malcolm Madrid in Dalhart, Texas."

"Dalhart? Isn't that up in the panhandle?"

"Indeed it is."

"What kind of a vehicle? Jeep Cherokee?"

"1995 Dodge Ram."

"Shit."

"Something wrong?"

"I'd say probably yes. Call APD, Lieutenant Asswipe..., Ashby and tell him there is a good chance the Hippie Hollow killer is making an encore engagement at Lucinda Tanner's lakehouse."

Chapter Twenty-nine

"Lots of people confuse bad management
with destiny."

Kin Hubbard

I figured after my long-ass phone calls, I was a good ten maybe fifteen minutes behind the others. If it was Spivey behind the wheel, and he was able to slip by me, it would not be too much of a stretch to believe him capable of switching plates in Dalhart. But why Dalhart?

I was happy with myself for calling in backup. Too many times, Rockford or Magnum or Mike Hammer would go in alone without the cops. What were they thinking? The TV viewers at home on their couches were shouting,

Don't do it Jim! Don't open that door, Mike! But what would they do? Open the damn door anyway.

My dad used to say, "This is the last show for Mannix. He'll never make it this time. There's a guy with a shotgun on the other side of the door. Didn't I tell you somebody wanted him off the case?" But Rockford lived to come back another week but what the hell, it was his show.

It took me but a few gas-guzzling, pedal-to-the-metal minutes to pollute the road from the intersection of 2222 and 620 to the Comanche Trail turnoff. The oversized tires of the Bubba-mobile squealed as I wound up the road past Hippie Hollow to Lucinda's front gate. I punched in the last known code numbers. The gate sat there, looking at me, unmoving. I tried the phone at the gate which connected to the house. No dial tone. Sort of like talking to my Dad. I pulled the truck up against the fence over to the side (so reinforcements could get through if they chose to believe me) and hopped up on my hood.

Ten-foot-tall fences were not meant to be scaled in cowboy boots, but with the extra height of the Bubbamobile, it wasn't quite so daunting. I slipped a couple of times in my attempt, skinning my shins and ruining the crease in my jeans, but eventually I negotiated the damn thing. On the other side, I crept up the driveway to the house.

Besides a cell phone, I wished I carried one of my guns instead of the Bobcat umbrella in the gun rack. Like most folks in Texas, I felt better armed. I had considered tossing my 45 in the glove compartment but figured if I got pulled over and searched, I would be in deep shit with no permit thus ending a brief but explosive P.I. career. I didn't need to lose another profession.

I would try to remember to put, "file for a concealed weapon permit" on my *to do* list, if I ever saw the list again that is. I looked around for a makeshift weapon, a log, a stick, a good-sized rock but Lucinda kept the place immaculate. I found one old plastic pink flamingo that had been over looked hidden under an agarita bush. I picked it up.

"This'll work." It had some heft to it. It was made from hard plastic and there was sand or something substantial inside.

My cautious approach seemed painfully slow. I started to jog, also not real easy in boots (but good exercise), up the driveway and around a corner. I crossed to the garage and looked in the window. The limo was inside.

"At least they're here."

I walked across the lawn to the patio and saw Lucinda, Max, Lily and Merrylee laughing and talking. Everybody was having a good time. Elena was serving drinks. Merrylee's high-pitched laughter was great to hear. The gang looked happy. I was just being paranoid.

"Bilbo!" Lucinda noticed me standing at the edge of the patio. "What in heaven's name are you doing here, and what was on the piece of paper? What's with that flamingo?"

"Hi, everybody. I called you on your cell phone, but I guess you didn't get my messages."

"No, I'm sorry. We all saw you holding up the sign, but none of us could read it. And I turned the cell phone off when we went into the restaurant. I hate to hear 'em going off in public. And everybody I want to talk to was right there with me."

I stuck out my lower lip in a fake pout and hung my head. "But didn't you want to talk to *me?*" I was pitiful. Okay, everything was alright. I was imagining all sorts of negative things but I had been wrong.

"Of course I want to talk to you!" She came over and gave me a big hug. Her body was soft in all the right places. It felt good. She smelled good. And dang it all, I needed a hug. I dropped the plastic bird.

"So, is everything all hunky dory after all?" Max's bright blue eyes twinkled over the top of his granny glasses.

"It's probably nothing but..." I launched into my supposed sighting of the bald-headed man with the bushy mustache in the Jeep Cherokee I supposed was Colonel Spivey only to be interrupted by Merrylee's ear-piercing scream.

Lily put the back of her hand to her mouth, her eyes on full bright. She dropped her margarita glass to the patio. Max did not catch it this time, but along with Merrylee, Lucinda and Lily were looking at something behind me.

I felt like the dolt in the horror flick. You know the guy with the creature wielding the wicked looking cutting instrument breathing down the back of his neck. I turned and at the same time moved deftly to the side. I did not turn quickly enough. I did not move deftly enough to the side and felt something very hard against my head. I dropped but it didn't put me under.

"Now, if everyone will be calm, sit down, and shut the fuck up." He laughed. "That's it. Sit down. You too, Pops." El Jaguar gave Max a little shove. He was a tank—six-feet tall; close-cropped gray hair, big bushy black mustache, black t-shirt and jeans, heavy boots, dark sunglasses. G. Gordon Liddy on the juice.

"Señora?" He waved his pistol at Elena who came down the steps from the kitchen carrying a tray of food and drinks. The tray crashed to the stone patio.

"Now Auntie Loo is going to be very pissed about that." The guy was having way too much fun. "Sit. Sentarse, por favor. Bueno."

Merrylee had been screaming nonstop for about a minute.

"Miss, if you don't stop that fuckin' racket I'm going to finish the job I started on you five years ago." He had clobbered me with an aluminum watering wand, which he held in his left hand, threatening to backhand Merrylee with it. In his right hand he held a pistol.

Growing up in Blanco, a.k.a. the sticks, everybody had a gun. Rifles, shotguns, handguns, we all got b.b. guns for our seventh birthdays and pellet guns for our tenth, but I had never seen one like Spivey held.

Merrylee stopped screaming.

"Thank you."

"What do you want, sir?" Asked Max, who instead of doing as he was told and sitting down, came over to where I was sprawled semi-conscious on the stone patio. Fortunately, my habit of always wearing my Stetson no matter what, had a somewhat neutralizing effect on the blow. Considering all those years of being kicked in the head by horses, bulls and miscellaneous ranch and rodeo animals, punched by drunks in bars and slapped by women I had offended, getting hit on the head by an aluminum watering wand wasn't all that big a deal.

"You alright, Bilbo?"

"'Bilbo'? What the fuck kind of name is Bilbo?"

"Sir, I have had just about enough of your lascivious mouth. There are ladies present. I should like to request you please curb your language." Max was on a roll. "And for your information, young Mr. Rivers was named after the great adventurer Bilbo Baggins of Middle Earth fame."

"Never fuckin' heard of the motha fuckin' asshole. How's that for dirty language? And, I've never liked fuckin' white bread limeys, so please lay face down, hands behind your backs. *Now!*"

I feigned a struggle to a sitting position, attempting to get up and then collapsing to my knees. Like I just did not have the energy. I was faking it. Come just a little closer, Spivey. He did, putting the gun in my face. I grabbed the barrel with one hand, pulling it aside as a round went off, *thunk!* One of Lucinda's hanging bougainvillea pots shattered. With my free hand, my other still holding the gun barrel, I grabbed his wrist, which was so scarred it felt like leather to the touch. I rose, spinning, putting my entire 250 pounds into his elbow. Old linebacker trick (when the ref wasn't looking).

He dropped the gun. That was good. Makin' progress. But my move did not break his arm as I hoped. He danced backward with the move. I was driving him across the patio, first one way and then another. I had forty or fifty pounds on him, and he was easy to move but continued to dance along backwards able to counter move. I did feel like a linebacker who had gotten the upper hand on a running back and would keep pushing until I fell on him or the whistle blew. (Maybe even after the whistle).

He kept his footing up to the steps of the lakehouse, where he tripped. I slammed him hard into the limestone rock.

He expelled an "oof," as he hit. I landed the full force of my weight on top of him and put his wrist in an arm lock behind his back. With my other hand, I banged his head three or four times against the edge of the stone step. That should have done him in right there, except his neck strength was so great I couldn't slam with total abandon.

What I was not expecting, was his picking up the hard plastic pink flamingo and swinging it around his back with his free hand, hitting me in the temple with it. Cool move. Sure got my attention. I had loosened my grip just enough.

The guy was fast. He was up as if I had never touched him and after me with the flamingo. I scooted across the patio backwards on my butt, he swinging the bird, me scooting backward, missing me each time by inches. In self-defense, I slipped into the pool. He came in after me. I wanted to get him away from the others and kill some time until reinforcements arrived. I swam for deep water and dove under figuring he wouldn't be able to swing quite as hard under water but the guy was strong and hit me several times on the legs and arms before I could grab the damn thing.

It was a fight in slow-mo. I'd hit him. He'd hit me. He popped my nose once and that sent shooting pains up into my brain. At about the same time we both ran out of air and swam for the surface. The fucker somehow wrested away the somewhat mangled bird and hit me over the head with it. I sank. My Stetson floated off.

Unfortunately, none of the others took the opportunity to leave. I guess they wanted to see how it would turn out.

"Okay," he said to the group as he got out of the pool, "I want you to lay face down on the ground. And where the fuck is my gun?"

"Sir," said Max getting up, "You said *lay* face down. The correct form of the verb is to *lie* face down..." El Jaguar kicked Max in the ribs, not interested in a grammar lesson.

"Why are you doing this?" I asked getting up out of the pool. Blood was running down my face.

"Oh, comments from the Bilbo?" He took a step toward me and I kicked out into the deep end. He was looking around for something to throw at me. The flamingo had sunk. His gun was missing. I figured one of the gang hid it. As he picked up a bag of charcoal briquettes and held it overhead, we heard sirens in the distance and getting closer.

"I asked you, why are you doing this?"

"I have my reasons which I don't have time to go into right now." Heaving the briquettes at me he came close but missed. He picked up a two pronged barbeque fork and put it to Merrylee's neck. I slipped out of the pool when his back was turned; figuring two good sized steps and I'd be on the guy.

Step one. Step two. Jump. I landed short.

Bam. Bam. Shots? As I lay there on the patio catching my breath, I was aware that limestone was quite a bit harder than turf. Merrylee screamed and as I tried to get up, Spivey's body fell across me. The killer's sunglasses, which he somehow kept on throughout our fight (maybe because I didn't get any good licks in), clattered across the stone patio. I saw the face, gray eyes open and vacant.

There was a warmness on my chest and I thought, although it didn't hurt, maybe I had been shot. Maybe, like they say, you don't feel it. I was afraid to look down but looked anyway. It was Spivey's blood, and he was bleeding on me. I pushed him off.

"Travis!" Everyone turned around to see who Lucinda was looking at. Travis Tanner was standing at the ledge with a shotgun. He lowered it and let it clank on the stone patio. Blood had splattered on Merrylee's face and blouse. A quick check by Lucinda determined it wasn't Merrylee's. Merrylee, Lucinda and Lily ran over to their long lost relative.

"Orchid delivery for Maximus Culpepper." He smiled. "I thought I'd bring it myself."

"Oooh." Max got up, holding his ribs. "What an asshole, excuse my French," whispering so the ladies wouldn't hear his swearing. Ever the gentleman. We sat on the stone patio watching the family reunion.

"I do have some bad news," said Travis. "Spivey killed both Felipe the gardener and your driver. Their bodies are in the garage. I'm so sorry Auntie Loo. I was here waiting for you all and I saw Spivey dragging a body across the patio. I snuck around to the front of the house and took Papaw Tex's old shotgun off the mantle, and by the time I remembered where you kept the shells you all were pulling in."

We could hear the police at the gate. They must have made short work of the lock because they roared up the driveway. FBI agents in black jackets with *FBI* in big white block letters on the back, followed by APD officers in black jackets with *APD* on their backs stormed the patio.

"You're a few seconds late," I said to my old pal, Special Agent in Charge Davidson. My other old pal, APD Lieutenant Ashby was on the agent's heels. A reunion of assholes. Hey, that's a good title. I'd have to tell Patricia about that one. They passed me by without so much as a *how ya doing fuckhead?* An agent kicked the shotgun off the patio toward another agent who retrieved it.

Lucinda dug up Spivey's handgun, which she had hidden in a potted plant, and offered it to Davidson. He took it by inserting his Cross pen in the barrel handing it off to another agent who was ready with a Ziploc bag. He nodded as if it was a significant find, but no thank you to Lucinda. He brushed past all of us and went over to Travis.

"Travis Tanner, I presume?" Davidson put out his hand. Travis returned the gesture. Davidson clasped a pair of handcuffs on his outstretched hand.

"Hey," I rushed over. A shooting pain flashed behind my eyes. I staggered but recovered. "What's going on here? This man saved our lives." A couple of agents grabbed my arms. The bookends from Dallas. It dawned on me where I had seen the Fed on my right. The Mexican restaurant in Ozona. He *was* following us.

"There's your killer," I turned to where Spivey was lying.

Something my Daddy, Harry Rivers, always told Gandalf and me when we were growing up. *When killing a snake, don't turn your back 'til you're sure it's kilt.* Spivey wasn't there! The killer of Moses Harper, Kristie Bentley, Iced Chai and who knows how many others was now crouched behind Max who was still doubled over from the kick in the ribs. Spivey had the barbeque fork to the older man's throat.

"Oh my God, Maximus!" cried Lucinda. The agents restraining me let go, re-drew their weapons and took a couple of steps toward Spivey and Max.

"Hold it right there, mother fuckers. If you value this old fart, you'll lower those weapons." The agents looked toward their fearless leader, Agent in Charge Davidson, for further instruction.

"Okay, stand down. Let's everybody take it slow and easy." Davidson held out his hands palms out.

"I'll see what I can do," said El Jaguar.

"Let's keep our heads here," said Davidson. "Everyone, this is *Colonel* James Spivey, also known as El Jaguar, also known as the Butcher of Bolivia.

"He never was a colonel, at least not in our army. Served under the Communist rebel, Ché Guevara, in Bolivia. Paid assass-in, murderer for hire. We have been looking for him for a long time. He killed Iced Chai. And he killed Moses Harper and Kristie Bentley, and is wanted for questioning in the assassination of Martin Luther King." That raised the eyebrows of everyone including Lt. Ashby.

"Good, so you know all about me. You know for instance I would not hesitate to punch this, whatever this is..."

"It's a barbeque fork, you asshole," I said. "You're not from around here, are you?" I heard Merrylee giggle behind me. I had grown attached to Maximus Culpepper and was going to be highly pissed if anything should happen to the bloke.

"Sure, a fork, I knew that, and you ought to know I will without a second's hesitation, punch this fuckin' fork into this artery." Max's neck was exposed. The fork looked to be on the artery alright.

"What do you want?" Asked Davidson.

"That is the appropriate response. I've been to that seminar. Of course it was in español. What'd I want, is for all of you to drop your fuckin' weapons."

"No can do," said Davidson.

"Well then. I guess the old guy gets it."

"Hold up here. I know you may think this is a hard line and you'd be right but this is as far as you go. There are ten FBI agents and twice that many Austin policemen taking dead aim at your head. I give the order and you're history."

"I've always liked history. When I was in the joint, the cons were studying law so they could file appeals. I studied history. Strangely enough, part of the reason I'm here in Austin is to fulfill my personal history. My destiny."

I looked at Davidson and I could see he wanted Spivey so much Max was expendable. I could see Spivey knew he had to make a move.

"You will *not* shoot, because you know I will kill him. Gentlemen and ladies, I'm leaving. You shoot and his death's on you." He jerked Max to his feet with one arm, the fork denting his throat with the other and backed over the ledge, disappearing down the cliff trail.

"Okay," said Davidson, as the agents and officers began milling around looking for direction. They weren't going anywhere, but boy they sure looked busy. "I imagine that is the path that leads down to the lake?"

Lucinda nodded and went over to the ledge to look, but was muscled away by the agents and officers. Merrylee and Lily went to the handcuffed Travis.

"We need to deploy," said Davidson. "If he gets to a boat, there must be a hundred places he could get to."

"Maybe now that you know who the real killer is, you can take off these handcuffs." Lucinda confronted Davidson.

"Yeah, let Travis go," I said. "Spivey or El Jaguar or whatever you call him is your killer, not Travis."

"One little problem with that, Rivers," said Lieutenant Ashby walking up to the group.

"What's that Asswi, Ashby?" He shot me a look of disgust. I smiled.

"Travis Tanner is under arrest for contracting with Spivey to kill Reverend Arvin Tanner. That's as significant as pulling the trigger and you know it, Rivers."

"You've got to be kidding." She turned to her nephew. "There is some mistake, right, Travis?"

"Auntie Loo, Mother, Merrylee. It is true. I discovered Reverend A and the church elders had hired Spivey to kill Iced Chai. Iced Chai was Angel's father." I wondered if I should interrupt Travis and tell him Angel had enrolled in TCU with the sole intent of killing him? Naw.

"They left all their transactions in the computer files, which I do have a copy of in a safe place, by the way. Of course there was security on the computer but through a combination of video game skills and vacation bible school, I figured out the password. Took all of twenty minutes to crack. I had to think like Reverend A." Travis talked and we all listened, mouths agape.

"I tried all the easy ones first. *John 3/16. Jesus Is Lord,* and so on. Then, wouldn't you know it, *Vengeance is mine* worked. I saw what they were up to. I hired him," said Travis looking into his mother's eyes.

"No, Travis. Don't say anything more," said Lily, "let us get you a lawyer, its best not to..."

"That's okay, Mother. I need to say this. I hired him to kill Reverend Arvin Tanner. The night I saw Spivey dressed as a roadie at Auntie Loo's Flamingo Party, I knew why he was there.

"I saw Spivey at the party and told him not to do it, I cancelled the contract. He didn't say a word, just punched me in the stomach. Hard. Blood came up into my mouth."

"You poor dear," said Lily, patting him on the arm.

"He told me he couldn't cancel, an arrangement had been made, a deadly arrangement. So, I got shit faced. Drank a bunch of margaritas, popped some pills. Smoked some pot. Tried to figure out what to do. I didn't want Reverend A to get whacked, but there didn't seem any way to stop it. I was going to tell Father what was going to happen, but we ended up talking about my inheritance and Angel, and started shoving each other.

"Miraculously at the last moment, Father didn't go with us. I thought we were in the clear then. But Spivey didn't know Reverend A wasn't in the limo. He was waiting at Hippie Hollow dressed as a cop. When it was just us kids in the limo, he must have thought I warned Reverend A. I figure he killed Mo and Kristie just to teach me a lesson. Show me how big a bad ass he was.

"He put a bullet in me and glanced one off your head," Travis said to Merrylee. "Somehow I got out of the limo and he chased me down the trail to the lake. He couldn't see me because I hid out in the water behind a boulder. Killing Mo and Kristie. What a waste. And Reverend A was still alive. Another waste. I've had to live with it for five years now. So, I don't care what happens to me."

Chapter Thirty

"A man who carries a cat by the tail learns something he can learn in no other way."

Mark Twain

One of the agents stepped in front of me as I looked over the edge. I pushed him aside and saw El Jaguar holding Max by the nape of the neck like a bully in a playground, and hauling him down the trail to the lake. At the bottom, he swam with Max in tow out to a motor boat moored offshore. FBI and APD were bounding down the trail behind them. There were enough twists and turns on the trail as to not offer the agents and officers a clear shot. Using Max as a shield, El Jaguar got into the boat. He seemed to make short work of the ignition and the boat hauled ass out of the inlet.

The FBI and APD ran off the patio, got into their vehicles and sped off. The driveway up to the lake house was narrow and allowed for the passage of one vehicle, so there was a lot of scrambling to get back out and onto Comanche Trail. Also there was no way to tell which way Spivey would go and where he would land. Lucinda came up to me and whispered.

"There's a very fast jet ski docked next door," she said. "Take the path over behind that Mountain Laurel there. They hide the key under the pilot's seat cushion." I was honored she hadn't told the Feds about the boat but told me instead.

I fished my hat from the pool, knocked off the excess water and bounded down the trail. At the neighbor's, I lifted the cushion, grabbed the key, started the jet ski and took off after El Jaguar and Max. In the rush of adrenaline, my nose and ribs stopped hurting. Funny how that works. I figured I'd pay for it with pain later. If I survived. I hugged the shoreline, watching the much less powerful outboard making a direct line across the lake toward the dam.

My craft was faster so I would hug the shoreline and cut back to the dam shortly after the outboard landed. There were plenty of sailboats and motor boats on the lake so I went unnoticed. I could see Max was still alive and sitting just ahead of Spivey who was in the back, hand on the tiller. He still had that damn barbeque fork aimed at Max's neck and I didn't want to rush in and cause the killer to prematurely poke my pal.

I figured sooner or later someone up at the lakehouse would realize Spivey was heading for the dam. It was a shorter distance across the lake than around it but a police cruiser could make up the time.

As the outboard hit the beach to the west of the dam, I could see Spivey reach out and pull on the older man who had fallen over into the bottom of the boat. I gunned the jet ski and cut the engine and could hear the killer talking as I coasted right at him.

"I guess your bum ticker saved you from a slit throat, or a poked throat," he laughed, tucking the barbeque fork into his belt. I came up on his blind side so he didn't see me. He ran up the embankment to the old two lane road that runs along the top of the dam. The road over Mansfield Dam which separates Lake Travis above from Lake Austin below was no longer in use by the public and was replaced by a new four lane bridge on the Lake Austin side below.

I looked in the outboard.

"Oh fuck no! Not Max." I felt for a pulse—nothing. I performed CPR. Lucinda and Davidson came running down the embankment. They had made good time.

"Something's wrong with Max," I shouted. "Maybe a heart attack or something. I checked him over and don't see any wounds except a superficial cut on his arm. But no pulse and he's not breathing."

"Hey," said Davidson into the walkie-talkie, "get a stretcher down here. Now!"

Lucinda was crying. Davidson was barking orders into the walkie-talkie and trying to get his cell phone to work. An EMS attendant with *JETHRO* stitched on his shirt eased me aside. I watched for a few seconds and my feet took off up the embankment. FBI and APD swarmed the road at the top of the dam. Most were looking over the edge.

I ran over as fast as my cowboy boots would take me to the overlook. Down below, we all saw Spivey crawling up on a boat. It looked to be a couple of hundred foot drop.

"He dove over the side hit the spillway and now he's getting on a tour boat," said an agent into his walkie-talkie.

"I'm going down!" I shouted, taking off my boots and making a running jump over the guardrail. Unfortunately, nobody tried to stop me. I sailed out into space. The bottom of the dam slanted out and was wider than the top and I wasn't sure I had jumped far enough out. It was an impetuous thing to do. Like smoking the Thai stick. Like getting on the *Sterilizer* back in high school. Like lassoing a bunch of bikers. Like kissing Angel's ample sugar-coated lips. I could go on. Max would say it was my bull-dogged Taurus influence. The good news was there was a stream of water coming through the spillway and I had jumped out far enough to hit the stream and was sent flying out into the lake below. I thanked the Lower Colorado River Authority for maintaining the lake level. But there was some bad news.

"Oh my god, I'm going to hit the fuuucckkkin' boat!!!"

My ankle made a strange popping sound as I hit the water feet first. The force generated by the distance of the drop drove me far under. Flashback to Balmorhea, but the water here was murky. Flailing arms and legs attempting to retard my descent into the abyss, I got it under control before I hit bottom. But I perd-near lost my breath on impact and the rest went south on the way back up. At the surface, I whooped in a deep breath. Something hit the back of my head—hard. Bonk. It was the same spot Baldy hit me with the pink flamingo wand at Lucinda's.

"You are one stupid, dumb fuck, but you don't give up, do you cowboy?" Came a voice from the boat. El Jaguar had climbed aboard the Duck Tour boat, which was making a turn around at the top of Lake Austin below Mansfield Dam. I imagine he got quite a kick out of my jumping off the dam, arms flailing and landing next to the boat (he dove, probably a perfect swan dive).

"Lost his cowboy hat on the way down. Did you see that?" He seemed proud he had hit me with the wooden life preserver. "Let's get the fuck outta here, driver." The tour boat captain gunned the engine and took off at a moderate pace down the lake in the direction of Austin, leaving me floating in the lake. My hard head kept me from losing consciousness. I reached for the life preserver and grabbed my hat as it floated down, landing in the water next to me. I put it on.

"Ouch!" My head was hard but sore from the banging around. As I swam to the edge where a bass boat was moored, I realized my nose hurt from my New Orleans trip, my ribs from my trip to Dallas and my head and ankle from today. I reached the bass boat and pulled out the choke button, flipped an ignition switch and yanked the cord. It started and I took off after the tour boat.

By the time the descending authorities got to the lower lake, El Jaguar was long gone. Cruisers drove the winding circuitous route from the top of Mansfield Dam, down to the next bridge at Lake Austin. Also too late.

The bass boat was pretty quick and I was able to keep the Duck in sight. Making a sharp turn just past a bend in the lake, it climbed the bank, went up through a backyard, destroying a carport and bouncing out into the street.

I ran my boat up on the bank. The sudden halt as the momentum of the boat met the inertia of the land threw me over the front and into a yard. I rolled and landed on my sore ankle. I hopped up and dodged thru the carport rubble in time to see the Duck disappear onto a golf course.

I sprinted, working through the pain in my ankle as I flew over a berm and tumbled head first into the bunker at the 13th green. My ankle hurt like hell. It wasn't broken but when I stopped there would be hell to pay. My head ached. My chest heaved. My nose felt like someone parked their truck on it. But I recovered and ran across the green. B. B. Rivers, the Relentless Bulldog.

Thoughts of bulldogs brought up thoughts of bulls and riding the *Sterilizer*. When you're on the bull, you might as well hang on for the full eight seconds, 'cause the bull's goin' to kick your ass whether you get off early or stay late.

A foursome of knickers-clad golfers, recovering from the passage of the Duck, re-spotted their golf balls.

"What the fuck was that all about?" Asked the first golfer.

"Shit, I've been playing this game for forty years and this is the first time a damned boat ran over my ball!," said the second, looking at his Titlist buried in the green. "How in the hell am I supposed to putt this thing? It was brand new."

"You've never owned an old ball," said the third golfer.

"That's the biggest god damn golf cart I've ever seen!" said the fourth.

I had accidentally kicked the fourth guy's ball off the green. "Sorry." I ran over to it and picked it up. "Which way?"

They pointed east. I picked up the ball and tossed it toward the pin. It went in. I could still hear the discussion as I sprinted down the fairway.

"I'm putting it down as a birdie," said the fourth guy.

"Oh no you don't. You wouldn't want it to count if he pitched it in the sand trap," said the first golfer.

"What's good for the goose is good for the Duck," said the second. The others nodded. They could live with that.

At the 18th hole, I could see the Duck plowing through a white wedding tent scattering champagne glasses, wedding cake and flowers. Tables were dumped over and smashed. The bride, groom and guests scrambled out of the way. The Duck bounced across a parking lot and through a ten-foot-tall ligustrum hedge and out into traffic.

"Nice zinnias," I said as I dashed by. The bride clutched what was left of her bouquet. I picked up a champagne glass off the one table that hadn't been upturned, toasting the couple who sat in the grass. She was crying. He was laughing. I drank it down in one gulp and tossed it onto the lush lawn. I caught up with the Duck as it crashed through the shrubbery. I jumped, clinging to the spare tire affixed to the stern. We were on the street now, weaving through traffic, running red lights, horns honking.

Once I caught my breath, I peeked over the railing. Spivey was up front directing the driver. The fork was laying, or was it lying, on the driver's neck, his other arm was wrapped around the neck of a teenaged girl.

He was talking to the driver. "Okay, now that we are on a street, we need to pour it on a little bit, por favor. That means faster." Dragging his hostage to the front, he stomped on the guy's accelerator foot with his steel-toed boot. The boat surged ahead, its wheels whining on the pavement. "Keep it there. I don't want to see this piece of shit going any slower than this." He slapped the scruff of the driver's neck almost playfully.

"Anybody packing?" He asked. "Come on now. I know one of you must have a gun. This is Texas, people. A knife? Empty your pockets. Now!"

"Do not touch this button," he said to the driver and turned to an attractive female passenger. "If you would be so kind and take off this shirt and vest." She unbuttoned his shirt, her hands trembling. She pulled it off one arm at a time. He winced but smiled as well.

"I kinda like this," he said as she unstrapped the bloody kevlar vest. It was peppered with shotgun pellets. Most were stopped by the vest but it looked like some hit flesh.

The Duck was aimed at downtown Austin. A West Lake Hills cop car squealed tires as it pulled in behind us. Lights were flashing, sirens wailing. I tried to wave the guy off but instead the asshole leaned on his horn. His gun was drawn and he held it out the window, motioning me to get out of the way.

"What are you going to do, shoot?" I mouthed. Up ahead at the low water crossing below Red Bud Dam—this one separates Lake Austin from Town Lake—I figured Davidson and his gang would set up a roadblock and situate themselves behind their vehicles, guns drawn.

A few minutes later, Spivey saw the road block and made the driver turn on the dirt road running down the center of Red Bud Isle. The hefty Duck pushed aside the cruisers there to deny access. The men at the roadblock got in their vehicles and sped after the Duck. First in line behind the Duck were the West Lake Hills cop and then Davidson, then Ashby, followed by the others. We were all headed down a dead-end road.

The Duck, however, did not stop at the dead end as was expected. Spivey did not jump out with his hands in the air, saying, "Okay coppers, ya got me." Instead the Duck took to the water like a duck.

Of course the coppers stopped. Davidson and the agents and officers piled out of their cruisers and aimed their weapons at the Duck. At me. It was not a pleasant feeling. I hoped no one was too trigger happy. I was giving them the international sign for please don't shoot!

"Shit!" I could hear Davidson clearly across the water. Davidson slammed something hard to the ground. He was pissed. I waved.

"Bilbo Baggins?" I heard him shout. Whatever it was that he smashed, his assistant, a regular Dano type, picked it up, dusted it off, and handed it back to him.

The cruisers and vans took turns backing up and turning around in the tight quarters of the slender island. One after another burnt rubber as tires grabbed pavement. I could see them traveling at high speed down Lake Austin Boulevard on the north side of the lake, trying to make up for lost time and thus gain a superior position ahead of the Duck.

From my vantage point on the back end of the Duck I could see another pack of cruisers roaring down Barton Springs Road through Zilker Park on the south side of the lake. The Park Police had one of the West Lake Hills cop cars off to the side writing him a ticket. Nobody speeds through Zilker Park, I thought.

A green helicopter, with the U. S. Army white star printed on the side, was hovering overhead as we coursed down the middle of the lake which at this point was not as wide as some rivers. The Colorado River flowed through the middle of it. A stream of cop cars lights flashing, sirens wailing, on the right; ditto on the left, looking like the Sugarland Express with a mean ugly bald-headed guy playing the part of Goldie Hawn.

I peeked around the corner of the Duck ahead toward the MoPac bridge. The bridge would be the ideal choice for a SWAT unit to belay down onto the Duck but we passed the spot too quickly. As we went under I looked up and saw the not quite deployed team on the bridge. Realizing they were too late, they piled back into their SWAT vans and sped off to the next bridge, upon which this time they should be set up in plenty of time. I stole a look into the boat and saw Spivey had positioned himself in the center, gathering passengers around him.

"I know I'm invincible," he shouted, "but why take the chance before I'm good and ready. When those assholes see what I got planned, they're going to shit."

Crouching, he peered through the crowd laughing and lobbing snipers the bird.

"Of course, digging an *hoyo* is not going to work in this situation. We're in the middle of a fucking lake." He chuckled. The passengers looked at him as if he were crazy, which of course he was.

When Spivey turned to watch the SWAT team pulling onto the next bridge, I hopped over the stern rail, flashed my official looking Bergstrom badge and put a finger to lips to quiet the surprised passengers. I eased closer, keeping a somewhat broader than normal lady between me and the killer. He still had the barbeque fork to the neck of the teenaged girl. I could tell she was scared shitless and started shaking her head when she saw me. We both could see I wouldn't get to the fork before he poked her in the jugular. I would wait.

Spivey, I could tell, was considering the situation at the upcoming Lamar Street bridge. "Here's what we're going to do, driver. And say, what is your name anyway?"

"Felix."

"Never liked that name. How 'bout I just call you Dip Shit?"

Felix did not reply. What an asshole this El Jaguar was.

"So, Dip Shit. Here's the plan. When I give you the word, I want you to turn this bucket sharply to port. That's to the left. You know which way is left?" Felix pointed.

"Excellent. And leave this alone." He pointed to the dashboard throttle.

Felix opened his mouth to say something like about how it wasn't such a good idea to make a ninety degree turn with the throttle on full in a top heavy boat in the middle of the lake, but thought the better of it.

El Jaguar looked at the shore on the north side of Town Lake. He looked for the right place to land. He saw it.

"Okay, okay, *now!*" The Duck turned north. Passengers were sent flying to the right as the Duck leaned like a sailboat catching the wind. A few passengers slid right over the rail and into the lake. We hit the shore with a bump and crossed the hike and bike trail at the Austin High School baseball field (a couple on a tandem bike bailed just in time but lost the bike), cut through a parking lot and continued through the underpass at Caesar Chavez Boulevard, the thoroughfare that runs along the north side of Town Lake. Some cruisers were passing overhead. Climbing the hill by the dog pound, mowing down a forest of sapling trees, crossing the railroad tracks, the Duck headed away from the lake. I watched the cruisers turning in unison, creating a bottleneck as they jockeyed to get through the underpass at the same time.

Chapter Thirty-one

"Some low down son of a bum stole my sleeping bag.
Down on the Drag."

Butch Hancock

The Duck crossed the tracks at 4th Street in front of an oncoming Amtrak and tore through a vacant lot on the north side of Sixth Street, cutting through the Clarksville neighborhood with its many parks and greenbelts. Attempts to follow or cut off the Duck failed, as the big canvas-topped truck/boat plowed over, around or through fences and like a tank, made its own path.

Between 9th and 10th streets, the Duck bottomed out on a huge tree root. The passengers were flung forward. El Jaguar was knocked off his feet as well and let go of the girl. He grabbed the driver by the shirt and hurled him aside.

"Excuse me, Captain Dip Shit, I'll drive now."

I saw my chance, eased the girl behind me (she had a scratch from the fork on her neck and was hysterical but alive). I hauled off and hit Spivey square on the back of the head with a wooden life preserver.

"That felt good." The blow caught him unawares and propelled him over the top of the steering wheel, across the dashboard and out onto the hood. I mean, I Barry Bonded him. I hit him a lick! But damned if he didn't scramble off the hood and look back at me.

"Cowboy?" A look of disbelief, reaching to the back of his bald head. There was blood on his hand. "Shit. That hurts." Sirens wailed from several directions at once.

"That's the second time we've had to cut our meeting short." He hopped a fence and took off running through back yards. I hopped off the Duck and landed wrong on my bum ankle. It gave out and I toppled like a big red cedar in a heap.

Davidson and a fellow I took to be the Dano-type pulled up as I muscled my way to my feet.

"Hop in."

I didn't exactly *hop* in, more like crawled into the back seat. The cruiser burned rubber as we weaved up and down the residential streets of west Austin. Davidson and Dano took in my dirty white socks and my general wet and disheveled appearance, and once we got past that, began a quadrant scan on each house as we passed.

"The god damned guy is indestructible. I saw him hit at close range with a shotgun, dive several hundred feet off Mansfield Dam and I hit him with this." I was still holding half a life preserver. "I hit him as hard as I've ever hit anybody. Hard enough to knock him outta the Duck. So he gets up, wipes the blood off the back of his head, smiles and takes off running."

"We'll get him. We got a couple dozen cars already in this neighborhood."

Davidson's cruiser was tuned to a jazz station. It was surreal listening to the mellow vibes of Miles while chasing America's number one fugitive.

"We interrupt our regularly scheduled broadcast to go to Keith Nickes on the scene of this bizarre story—an Austin Police Officer has just high-jacked an unknown quantity of blood from the downtown blood bank," came the voice over the radio.

"That sounds like our boy," said Davidson. "Where's the blood bank?"

"Across the street from the library on 10th. We can be there in 2-3 minutes."

By the time we got to the blood bank, El Jaguar was gone. In his place were reporters from the various radio and TV stations. T. Rex Rodriquez was there, reporting for the Statesman. I saw his van parked off to the side, the engine was on, white smoke was pouring out the exhaust pipes with the solar system turning at a much quicker pace than I would have thought normal. Weird.

The stolen cruiser was parked half way up the front steps. The shotgun was missing from the rack, the bloody barbeque fork lay on the front seat. Dano reached in with rubber gloves on and picked up the fork and put it in a Ziploc.

"Sir," said T. Rex, "what can you tell us about the APD officer who broke into the blood bank?"

"This is the work of a criminal impersonating a law enforcement officer. The officer who belongs to this vehicle is missing. The man who robbed the blood bank is an armed and extremely dangerous criminal. This is a very perilous situation and we are advising all citizens to stay off the streets, to be on the lookout for the man but please stay indoors. Let us do our job."

"Hey, Rawlins. Whacha doin' with the Feebs?" Asked T. Rex.

"Is your van alright," I said pointing to the weird-mobile. T. Rex scrunched up his nose and shrugged his shoulders.

"You know this guy?" Asked Davidson as we walked back to the cruiser. T. Rex was his usual outrageous self, dressed in olive green cut-offs, his skinny black legs sticking out, shower clogs on long boney feet. He wore a bright orange athletic shirt sporting a big picture of Mickey Mouse. His wild black and grey dreadlocks made him look like an old lion or someone who had just walked 40 days and 40 nights through the desert and was looking to baptize Jesus.

"He's okay," I said to Davidson. I turned back to T. Rex. "The Hippie Hollow killer was here." He held out his hands as if to ask, "Okay, what else?" But we were out of there before I could answer him. His V.W. van coughed, let out a big bang from the exhaust pipe and the solar system fell off.

"Did you see that?" Said Dano. Davidson wasn't paying attention. We both watched Jupiter rolling down 10th Street.

"His Mercury just retrograded," I said thinking it was funny but it must not have been to FBI types because they didn't laugh.

"Sir?" The driver got Davidson's attention. "You're getting a message."

"Identification made on James Spivey. His name is Jackson Hamm," said the voice. "Age 59. 6 feet. 190 to 200 pounds. Bald. Large grey/black mustache, wanted for prison escape earlier this week from the Flathead Lake State Correctional Facility, Central Montana. Serving six years for manslaughter in the bludgeoning death of a man in Missoula, Montana."

"Does it show Hamm was ever in the U.S. Army?"

"Yes," from the radio operator, "he was dishonorably discharged for desertion. Not much after that until the manslaughter conviction five years ago."

"So, Jackson Hamm is his name." Davidson looked around as if El Jaguar might be walking across the street at that moment. "But where in the hell is he?"

The radio cracked to life again. "This is Max Culpepper calling FBI Agent Davidson."

"Mr. Culpepper, good to hear your voice. You're okay?"

"Yes indeed. Have you seen B. B. Rivers, perchance?"

"He's here with me. Just a moment. "Hey," said Davidson to me. We were cruising up and down the streets between Sixth and Enfield. "It's your pal Max. I guess he's alright after all. Wants to talk to you."

"Max, is that you?"

"Rivers, I suppose we are both alive, what?"

"Max, I was sure you had bought it. I mean I felt your pulse and everything."

"I assure you Maximus is just fine," said Lucinda's sweet husky voice.

"Lucinda? Where are you all?"

"Rivers, listen to me. It is imperative we disconnect from this radio and, furthermore, you call Lucinda's cell phone. Find a pay phone. I hope you remember the number. Right you are then." Before I could answer he was off.

"Say, Davidson. Can you drop me at that 7/11 up ahead?"

"Whatever you say. Stay out of trouble."

"Can I borrow a quarter? I lost everything jumping off the dam."

Davidson rolled his eyes and indicated to Dano to flip some spare change my way.

"Hi, Max. Hi, Lucinda."

"This is Homer, and..."

"Jethro."

"Hi, Homer. Hi, Jethro." Max introduced me to the two guys in the ambulance. "What is up, Max? I'm glad you're alright." I gave him an unexpected hug. I couldn't help it.

"You look a fright and you are wet, and you smell like fish."

"Took a dip in the lake."

"And you're bleeding," said Lucinda.

"You should see the other guy."

"Fix this fellow up with a dressing," said Homer to Jethro.

"What's going on, Max? I mean, I really did think you were dead."

"I had a little of my Tibetan formula left that I used for my previous excursion to the Bardo to meet with Merrylee. It simulates fatality. My breathing slows, my pulse slows to the point there is the appearance of death."

"Spivey thought you had a heart attack and left you for dead."

Max nodded.

"Where to?" Said Homer.

"The University of Texas, Main Entrance."

"How do you know where he's going, Maximus?" asked Lucinda.

"Something he was babbling about when we were crossing the lake gave me pause to think. He said a name, Charles Whitman."

"I know the name but I can't place it," I said.

"A man very famous, or shall I say infamous, in Austin's history. I've done an astrological chart on him."

"Special Agent Davidson?"

"Davidson here."

"This is Max Culpepper. I should have contacted you earlier with my suspicions but I..."

"What is it, Mr. Culpepper? I'm very busy at the moment."

"I have no reservations now."

"Reservations about what?" Davidson's voice had an edge to it. Was he losing patience?

"Not only do I know where Spivey is, I am looking at him at this very moment."

"Where are you, sir?"

"At the UT Student Union and he is traversing the parking lot on foot."

"Wonderful. Get over to the University! Now!" He said into the radio. He obviously put his hand over the radio but did not fully cover it.

"Culpepper, we're on our way. Be there in five. Under no circumstances are you to approach this guy. And that goes double for your pal Bilbo Baggins. Just watch where he's going," said Davidson.

"Oh, I know where he is going."

"You do?"

"Yes, indeed, to the University of Texas Clock Tower to fulfill his fantasy."

After Max filled me in on what Spivey was up to, I had him drop me on the opposite side of the tower. I hobbled into the building a minute before Spivey. Damn, if I only had my Colt, I could end this thing right now. First, I asked the lady at the front desk if I could borrow her weapon and when she declined, I told her to alert whoever needed alerting and get the fuck out of there because a bad dude was a-coming.

"Get down. Now. This guy is very dangerous!" Would she believe a wet and bleeding cowboy? It appeared not. I slipped into the stairwell door despite her protests and fighting the pain, ran (maybe too strong a word) up the stairs. I wanted to be there when Spivey got off the elevator. I had been on a field trip to the University of Texas Tower when I was a kid and remembered some of it. I knew when the Longhorns won a game, the top of the tower was lit orange. If I could get to him, I'd light it myself.

I heard the elevator pass my position going up. It had been a bad idea taking the stairs. Taking too damn long. Two shots came from above me. After pausing at the door to catch my breath, I heard another shot, the sound of a ricocheting bullet and the sound of a chain hitting the floor. I eased open the door, looking in. A pair of blue-uniformed, black-booted legs stuck out from the open elevator. Every few seconds the door attempted to close, touched the legs and sprung back open. The second elevator door was also open and a wooden desk was keeping the door from closing.

The telephone was torn from the wall. I eased over to the elevator. A UT security guard and the receptionist from downstairs lay in commingling pools of blood in the elevator.

"Damn it." I looked away. I checked the room. The chain securing the upper stairway leading to the observation deck was lying on the floor.

I put my head in the stairwell and jerked it back. The stairs circled up and around winding to the top. I could see only as far as the next turn. It was Jimmy Stewart in *Vertigo*.

Inner chemicals were kicking in because my various aches and pains were still not aching or paining. I took a deep breath and checked the dead guard for weapons. Spivey had removed pinky fingers from both victims, had shot the man in the top of the head and had slit the woman's throat.

I tried to tell her.

The guard carried a decent sized Buck pocket knife in his boot, which I pocketed. I unpinned the note on the lady's underwear and read it.

El control más la atención iguala energía.

I thought back to Spanish 101. Attention plus energy equals power. Well, Spivey was certainly getting plenty of attention. I pulled the lady's dress down and pushed the legs of the guard back into the elevator, which allowed the door to close. The elevator did not descend. I looked back in and saw Spivey had yanked the wiring from the elevator control box. He had done the same in the other elevator. I went around the room checking the drawers and cabinets for weapons and communication devices. Nothing.

"Double damn. I don't want to be doing this," I noticed skid marks on the floor leading to the stairwell. It looked like a combination of boot wax and blood. I grabbed some breath, slipped into the stairwell, inching up a little at a time, looking ahead not knowing how many steps to the top. I was pretty sure Spivey was lying in wait up there.

Climbing slowly, my senses were alive. Adrenaline was pumping. It reminded me of turkey hunting. Listening, walking softly. Trying like hell to be quiet. I could hear my own heartbeat, feeling it beating in my temples. It was hunting, except this time the fucking turkey had the gun. I wondered if that's what Max meant by Karma. As I neared the top, I felt something touching my ankle. I froze.

Trip wire rigged to grenade.

I tried to back down the steps. The wire went slack. A grenade pin-handle clanked down the stairs.

"Oh shit!" Not a good sign, I thought. I figured 4 to 5 seconds to get the hell away from there. Down? I knew how long it took to get this far. I'd never make it back down to a safe place. That thinking process took about a quarter of a second; another half second congratulating myself on how fast I was thinking; another half second to get my ass off dead center and start moving.

Up! Up as fast as my legs would carry me. Coach B. B. beating the team up the bleachers. The pain in my ankle overridden by the fear in my gut, the fear I was not going to make it through the door at the top of the stairs. Seemed like I had been on these stairs for more than four or five seconds. Maybe it was a dud, maybe...

"Ka-bam!" The impact lifted me off my feet and carried me up the rest of the stairs, banking me off a wall like a pool ball. Probably the eight ball. It was a tooth-cracking explosion. I could feel it in the roots of my hair.

"Oh Shit!" It picked me up the rest of the way and through the door, which was closed but not latched, dropping me onto the observation deck.

"Hey, cowboy. Glad you could drop by." El Jaguar was no longer surprised when I showed up. He stood over me and I tried to get up, but my body wasn't working and I couldn't move. The observation deck at the top of the UT Tower seemed quite a bit smaller than my fourth grade memories. Spivey had his weapons leaning against a wall. A blue-clad security guard was handcuffed in a corner. I could see the asshole had taken his pinky. What does he do with those fingers?

He was on me before I could catch my breath. Putting a steel-shanked boot on my head, he handcuffed me. He grabbed my Stetson, which had blown off in the explosion and sailed it out over the UT campus.

Spivey took a look through the door as a hundred year-old cloud of dust and particulate debris floated up. He waved at the dust and coughed.

"Ought to slow 'em down a little. Hey, look at this view!" He jerked me up and dragged me over to the edge as effortlessly as a little girl dragging her Raggedy Andy. He lifted and dropped me over one of the orange light fixtures so the only thing holding me to the building was the handcuffs. The guy was strong. "You're a big one, Cowboy."

"Oooof." Being dropped like that and stopping with a quick jerk, caused sharp pain in my wrists and arms. The phrase "hung out to dry" came to mind. I'm a pretty optimistic guy but I must say, I was concerned. How in the fuck was I going to get out of this one?

Hanging there I thought of how I might be able to make the best of the situation, maximize the moment as Max might have put it.

My wrists burned from the pain. I got a toe hold in a crack in the limestone (I had been in sock feet since Lake Travis), which took a little pressure off my wrists. It didn't do my toe much good though. My boots, I assumed, were still sitting on top of Mansfield Dam. I hoped nobody had impounded them. They were very expensive. I bought them several years ago when I was at the top of my rodeo game and the money was flowing, when the buckle bunnies thought my shit didn't stink.

Down below, I saw cruisers and SWAT vans plus TV crews below the tower. It was reminiscent of an Arnold Schwarzenegger movie. As the officers and agents got out of their vehicles, El Jaguar popped a half dozen of them before they could move to cover. I pulled up and from my vantage point I could see him squatting along the outer wall hooking up a transfusion.

"Hey Cowboy, you still out there?" He rapped my knuckles with the barrel of his 30-06.

"Hey! Yeah, I thought I'd hang out for a while longer, asshole." I would have broken out laughing but it hurt too much.

"Be nice now. When the federales storm our position and they *will* storm our position, I'll have to set you free. Sorry about that."

"Fuck you."

"Maybe I ought to pop this right now." Spivey fired a round into the handcuffs and I could see there wasn't much left holding me to the tower. "It's only 300 feet down. Unfortunately this time, there ain't any water to break your fall. Sorry."

I grunted.

"I usually like to take a little memento of each person I pop but I seem to have misplaced my knife. You wouldn't happen to…"

"Fuck you." I had the guard's buck knife in my pocket but didn't feel like sharing.

"Did anybody tell you not to interrupt your elders?"

"Fuck you." It was the only thing I could think of and I guess I was never going to stop interrupting people. Then again, maybe this was the last time.

The U.S. Army helicopter swooped into range and El Jaguar fired off a few rounds from the 30-06, wounding the sharpshooter inside. After another round zipped through the chopper's shell close to the pilot, it veered off.

Spivey moved around to the other side of the tower to get out of a sudden hail of bullets. I hoped everybody saw me hanging there. The agents and officers positioned themselves close into the tower and I could no longer see them, but neither could Spivey. With no cops to shoot at, he took it to another level and began firing on the vendors and street personnel 500 feet away on the Drag.

"This is too much fun. No wonder Charlie liked it so much. I don't remember how many hits Charlie made. If I could stay up here for awhile, I bet I could beat him." He ran over to the stairwell. He could hear rubble being cleared from down below. He bounced a grenade down the steps.

Ka-bam! The concussion knocked him off his feet and smashed his last bottle of plasma.

"Whoa," he got up and dusted off his pants and shirt. "Looks like time for our big Woody Woodpeckerwood to be free now." He fired into the handcuffs and they broke loose. "See ya later, cowboy." I clung to the tower by my fingernails and toenails for a long ass second.

Then something miraculous happened. It rated right up there with re-connecting with Patricia, surviving the bull, Dad's Fats Domino impression, intercepting a pass from the Heisman Trophy winner and running it back for a t.d. in the Sugar Bowl, jumping off the Mansfield Dam and not hitting the dam or the damn boat. The helicopter swung around the tower to my side and dropped a rope ladder. I saw it, jumped out and caught it on my way down. Eat your heart out, Arnold.

The helicopter put me down on the parking lot out of the line of fire. Lt. Asswipe of the APD came up and unlocked what was left of the cuffs. It was the nicest thing he'd ever done for me. My wrists were bloody and sprained, and the hurt was back. Within seconds, all too familiar pain sprang back into the various molested areas of my body.

"Anybody got any ibuprofen?" I asked.

"Man, you are one lucky dude," said one of the officers.

"Not my time to go. Right, Max?"

I sat at the back door of the ambulance, listening to the tac commander's radio who was next to Davidson and Dano.

"I'm on the observation deck," radioed agent #1. "The missing security guard is in the southwest corner. Looks to be handcuffed. Doesn't look good."

"What about the shooter?" Asked the tac commander.

"The shooter is lying face down. His body is up against an inside wall. He's holding a shotgun."

"Use extreme caution. This guy has killed a dozen law enforcement officers," said Davidson coming in over the radio.

"10-4. Check the guard," said agent #1 to #2.

"There is a pulse but he's lost a lot of blood." Damn, I thought the guard was dead. Something not right with that.

"We're bringing down the guard, and we have the shooter covered."

"Be careful for booby traps," said the radio. I imagined them running their hands under the shooter's stomach, legs, shoulders and chest.

"No pulse," said #3. "No sign of booby traps. Let's flip him."

"Careful," said #5.

"What?" Said #4 to #3.

"What's the matter?" Said # 5. "What's going on?"

"This is *not* the shooter."

"Damn it," said #3, "the guard is the shooter." "What's going on?" radioed Davidson.

"I'm reasonably sure the shooter is coming down dressed as a UT security guard," said #3.

Jethro, the EMS attendant, was dressing my wounds with bandages while I was giving him a full accounting of the day's events. A coed caught my Stetson, which had floated all the way to the Cactus Café at the student center, and she brought it back to me with a flirty little smile. I put it on.

"How'd you know it was mine?" I asked.

"We've all been watching you on TV." She pointed up to the Channel 7 chopper circling overhead.

My ankle, from all the running and jumping on it (when I should have been soaking it in Epsom salts while watching American Movie Classics from the safety of my couch, all the while drinking mass quantities of fermented brown liquids), was swollen twice its normal size. Jethro cut off my sock. There wasn't much left of it anyway. The bottoms were tattered. I took off the other one.

We all heard more shots and then silence. Davidson was screaming into the radio. Max and Lucinda were holding hands when the tower door opened. An FBI tactical agent in full assault uniform emerged.

"We got him, sir," he said to Davidson. "The guys are bringing the shooter's body down now."

Cheers came from the agents, officers and bystanders.

"That's him," said Max.

"I heard. They got the asshole."

"No, I mean he *is* the asshole, that man there, with the mask
and assault rifle, regaled as an FBI agent. That man is Spivey.

"How do you know?"

"I never forget an aura."

"You sure about this?"

"Most assuredly."

"Final answer?"

"Absolutely. I am 100% positive," said Max. As the crowd
relaxed, climbing the steps to the main building and the tower,
the agent with the assault rifle eased off to the side. FBI, APD,
reporters, UT students, faculty and bystanders mingled.

"Hey! Stop that man," I shouted. No one was paying any
attention. Agent in Charge Davidson was standing closest to the
man talking to my co-ed.

"You look like the guy from..."

"Hawaii Five-O?"

"Yeah. Five-O. I love that show."

"I know."

Lieutenant Ashby was leaning over a cruiser, his back turned
to me, talking on his cell phone. "Yeah, we're about to wrap it
up here. So, you want a bottle of cab, baguettes, goat cheese and
what else was that?" He scrunched up his face and put a finger
in his ear so he could hear better. The sound of the helicopters
overhead plus the buzz of the crowd, which had grown quite
large, was making it hard to hear.

The bulge of a handgun was visible under Ashby's flack
jacket.

"Need to borrow this." I reached under his jacket and
extracted his weapon. It was a Glock. That's not police issue, I
thought. I knew the weapon. It had a faint odor of gun oil, but I
was pretty sure it had not been fired lately. I hoped there was a
clip in the damn thing. No time to check.

"Hey!" Ashby reached for me. An elbow in the gut doubled
him over and he dropped his phone. That was the second time I
had decked this particular police lieutenant and it was becoming
a habit. I smiled but was hurting in too many places to laugh.

"John, what's going on? John?" Little voice from the cell phone.

As the agent shoved home a clip in the assault rifle, I shouted, "Hit the deck," as loud as I could and fired the 9 mm into the air. Everyone except me and the man I hoped was Spivey dropped to the pavement. As he raised the rifle, I fired two quick rounds, hitting the man dead center in the forehead. Ashby kept his weapon well calibrated. I'd have to remember to compliment him on that.

If Max was right, I had just finished off the murderer of Moses Harper, Kristie Bentley, Iced Chai and maybe even Martin Luther King. (Was M.L.K. missing a pinky finger? How would one check that out?) On the other hand, if Max was wrong, and this was an FBI agent, I was on the way to death row. Max sold flowers to the Governor's mother, so maybe I could get my sentence commuted to life without parole. But this was Texas where the juice flowed freely. And I don't mean orange juice.

As the man fell, rounds from his assault rifle kicked up chips of asphalt across the parking lot. We all sucked our auras into our sphincter muscles and dove for cover. When the shootout ended, all the cops pulled weapons and aimed them at me.

Max put his body in front of mine and held up his hands. It was the least he could do.

"Wait. Wait. That's your killer there," he pointed. Deja vu all over again.

The line of bullets in the asphalt had stopped about an inch from Agent in Charge Davison's head. "Stand down!" He shouted at the armed mob of law enforcement types. He walked over to the body, pulled off the helmet revealing a bald man with a big bushy mustache and two holes side by side in the center of his forehead. He whistled.

"It's him alright. And this time I do believe he's dead." He gave me a thumbs up, cocked his index finger and fired it twice at El Jaguar, and after it air-kicked the second time, blew away the virtual smoke. It's a guy thing. A little embarrassing for Davidson since Channel 7 caught in on tape for the 10 o'clock News.

The agents and officers lowered their weapons. No cheering this time but a collective easing of tensions was evident. The roller coaster rush of adrenalin that had been surging and ebbing since the patio at Lucinda's lake house, shut down and everyone felt very tired.

Chapter Thirty-two

"Keep honking—I'm reloading."

Bumper sticker seen on I.H. 35

"I like your hair. It reminds me of someone else we know," said Max. Lucinda had dyed her hair the exact shade of red as mine. Auntie Loo was famous for just that sort of thing. She put her cheek next to mine and our hair appeared as one. We smiled as Merrylee snapped a photo. Auntie Loo had worked hard and fast to plan and execute the 11th Pink Flamingo Party before July blew on by.

Willie was invited. As a guest this time. "I feel like I'm coming up in the world." Jimmy Vaughn, lead guitar for the *Fabulous Thunderbirds* and brother to Stevie Ray Vaughn, was the entertainment. He brought the *First Wife*, Stevie Ray's most famous guitar, the one with *SRV* tattooed on her body. Jimmy promised Max he'd never ever sell her.

Max told him he had talked with Stevie and he would reincarnate soon.

"Be on the watch for a three-year-old who can play the blues like nobody's business."

The surprise guest this year would not only blow everybody's socks off, but, "Y'all ought to make sure your undies are good and tight for this one," said Lucinda. As usual, no one, including Max, Merrylee or Travis, had any idea who it would be.

Lucinda retrieved the flamingos from wherever she had them stashed (except for one bent and dented one she now displayed on her mantle crossed with Papaw Tex's vintage shotgun) and ordered some very special hand-made tofu shipped in from Kyoto, Japan. Been hanging with Max too long, I thought. She too was now a vegetarian. Beef from Australia or salmon from Alaska was no longer going to cut it. And she was down to one cigar a day.

"One rarely hears of a case of mad bean curd disease," said Max. When they told me about the tofu, I could only say, "Oh, come on now! What is really going on here?"

Larry Furman, CPA, made sure everyone got their fair share of the Tex Tanner estate, except for Reverend A who was absent at the distribution meeting. Merrylee and Travis were very rich indeed and Lucinda was richer than ever.

I collected a nice looking check from Bergstrom Investigations, a bonus the size of which would choke my horse from Lucinda, and the promise of a double reward from the Iced Chai Foundation for finding the killer of Iced Chai and the man who hired him. The only requirement? I needed to go to New Orleans and collect the check from Angel Chai in person.

Reverend Arvin Tanner's reward disappeared along with Reverend Arvin Tanner as did all the elders of the Church of the Ark. The church building was forfeited to the IRS. and would be open for bids next year. My old boss, Jimmy Don, was considering bidding on the building. "Great place for a gay cowboy bar." The first thing I did with my money was to go to a kiosk in the mall and buy a cell phone with internet capability, modem hookup for the laptop I would soon buy, voice recognition dialing, digital and analog roaming and free nationwide long distance, plus a couple of zillion night and weekend minutes, and one hundred anytime minutes. I also bought a chile relleno cookbook at the bookstore and had a real wooden shingle made up instead of the cardboard one, inscribed:

B. B. RIVERS INVESTIGATIONS

And a diamond ring for Patricia.

I was still hurting the day of the party. My ribs, nose and ankle pained me but I could walk with a cane. Many folks at the party thought the cane made me look distinguished. It made Patricia horny.

Captain Hollers never returned to Bergstrom and retired citing health reasons. His doctors recommended a less humid climate, so he moved to Balmorhea to room with his old pal Warlick at his ranch. Mr. B. sold off the Investigations Division of Bergstrom to Pinkerton and was glad to be shut of it. Of course, I was out of a job. I did get two weeks severance pay.

Donna was cut loose, too, and I hired her as my secretary. To be honest, I had my sights set on liberating a stripper from the Yellow Rose, but Donna could type 90 words per minute (85 wpm faster than the stripper and with no typos). And Patricia approved of Donna. And dang it all, that's good enough for me.

Captain Warlick confessed to being an undercover FBI agent the entire time he ran the Task Force. Warlick had gotten wind of the hit on Reverend A, and it was he who called Tanner the night of the party to warn him about Spivey. Warlick figured when Spivey saw Reverend A was not in the car, he would put off the hit for another day. This would give the FBI another chance at him. The Feds had been after him since the Martin Luther King assassination. Warlick misjudged the viciousness of El Jaguar, the Butcher of Bolivia, not thinking he would kill those innocent teenagers. The murders rattled Warlick and after five years he was still dealing with it.

Special Agent Davidson and his team located Spivey's storage room in Friday Harbor, Washington. They found a cache of weapons, Merrylee's disposable camera which had not been disposed of and which included some very interesting photos of the last Pink Flamingo Party, and a freezer locker full of pinky fingers. Davidson told me the sight of the fingers nestled neatly in Ziploc bags made him upchuck.

Travis Tanner, out on bond as five-year Prince of Pink, drove to the party in his five-year-old Beamer, now considered a classic. He was more than happy to relinquish his pink cloak to this year's prince.

Lucinda hired the top law firm in Austin to defend her nephew. Their defense? Travis could not be guilty of murder or attempted murder. He could not be guilty of shooting Spivey with the shotgun since he was defending his family. He could only be guilty of hiring Spivey to kill Arvin Tanner and since Spivey did not kill Arvin Tanner or even attempt to do so, he could not be guilty of any crime since no crime was committed.

Additionally, Travis Tanner did not hire Spivey to kill Moses Harper or Kristie Bentley and could not be responsible for those murders. Only Spivey himself would be guilty of that.

Colonel James Spivey, a.k.a. El Jaguar, was not invincible after all. And he did not go down in history as the World's Greatest Killer and didn't even come close to wiping out as many people from the UT Tower as Charlie Whitman.

El Jaguar wasn't going to come up out of Lucinda's swimming pool and stab the girls in pink polka dot bikinis with a barbeque fork. He wasn't going to show up at my wedding and dump over the zinnias. What he was going to do was stay very, and most assuredly, dead.

Lily came to the party. Shortly after Reverend A disappeared (he was spotted in Costa Rica), Lily moved into the Westlake mansion. She liquidated Reverend A's classic car collection. I bought one cheap, the 1956 Ford Thunderbird. I am considering converting it to a pickup. I drove Patricia to the party in our new old car. Mom drove Dad in the Bubbamobile.

Mr. and Mrs. Harper came to the party.

"Beautiful place, Ms. Tanner," said Mrs. Harper. "You all just call me Lucinda." "And you call us Moses and Matilda."

Elena had recovered from her encounter with El Jaguar and was twirling around the patio handing out pink margaritas to the guests. Winslow Christian took a break from his dissertation and came down from Fort Worth to see his old roommate. Angel Chai did not come to the party but sent her regards.

Merrylee found and adopted El Jaguar's cat, which had been wandering around the lakehouse grounds, and named her Jag. She was crowned Princess of Pink. Not the cat, Merrylee.

To no one's surprise, Maximus Culpepper was named Prince. Travis placed the pink cloak (bullet holes from the last party patched up nicely) around Max's shoulders. "I've owned this thing long enough."

Patricia (who ate pickles and strawberry ice cream at the party) and I were getting along very well. We talked it out. I was too incapacitated to run away anyway. And where would I go? To Blanco to live with the folks? She and I would pull the trigger on our wedding plans and make our announcement during the party. I would ask Maximus Culpepper to be my best man.

Patricia, T. Rex and I hung out together. I promised T. Rex I would tell him the whole story and Patricia also wanted to hear it, so we sat on the ledge overlooking the lake and I told all. Except the part about kissing Angel in New Orleans. I kept that to myself. I had learned one thing living with a woman—you say one wrong word, and you have a four-hour conversation on your hands.

Mom and Lucinda hit it off. They laughed and smoked cigars and drank pink margaritas all night long. It was good to see her loosen up. Max and my Dad sang World War Two songs, like

"Sentimental Journey" and "I'll Be Seeing You." Max told Dad he could get his speaking voice back, but it would necessitate a trip to the Bardo.

Later, the Dalai Lama showed up, and he and Max got to visit. Max told me the Incarnation of the Buddha made so much money from his *The Dalai Lama Unleashed* CD that he was negotiating with China to purchase Tibet. All the hippies now have *BUY BACK TIBET* bumper stickers on their VW buses. "If you can't beat 'em, buy 'em out," His Holiness reportedly said. Even though I did not consider myself a hippie, I stuck them on both my vehicles next to my NRA stickers.

I heard the "Marine Hymn" going off in my jacket pocket and wondered what was really happening there until I reached in and pulled out my new cell phone. It was T. Rex on his cell phone sitting about ten feet away. He laughed loudly. The phone companies had erected a tower across Comanche Trail from Lucinda's lake house and the reception was a little too good. I jerked it away from my ear.

"Hang on a second," I read the note I felt when I reached in my pocket, the one T. Rex gave me with the name and number of the guy who called in the murders at Hippie Hollow. I wondered what I had done with that.

"T. Rex, my man, I'll get back to you," I pushed the red *end/power* button. I punched in the number. Max was right, I ended up with several dozen items on my *to do* list but I crossed everything off except for the man I was now calling and filing for my concealed weapons permit and my P.I. license.

"Poodie Slack here."

"Hi." I explained to Poodie who I was and why I was calling, and that the Hippie Hollow investigation was now over, the killer had been killed and some of the victims came back to life. As we talked, I crossed his name off the list. Poodie told me this was the first Pink Flamingo Party he had missed and the reason he wasn't there was he had been in Colorado visiting his brother Rudy who was serving time in a federal prison. Also his pink suit was in mothballs.

"And Poodie, you *did* see a cop car at Hippie Hollow that night after all."

"I didn't think I was crazy but nobody would believe me. You said you're a private investigator?"

"Damn tootin'," I was sipping a pink margarita doing my Gabby Hays impression. Poodie explained he was in a situation that needed some investigating. I got a new case! He told me his brother, Rudy Slack, was incarcerated at a federal prison and saw something inside that scared the shit out of him. Would I look into it?

When I got off the phone, T. Rex brought me a plate telling me I ought to try the chile rellenos. "Made with tofu but quite good," he said in his too loud voice. People in ski boats down below looked up when he said it.

I, Bilbo Baggins Rivers, ever the adventurer, took a bite. I savored the unique beany flavor. Thought about all other chiles relleno I had eaten these past few weeks and ranked it dead even with Ozona.

The Armadillo Whisperer
murder behind bars

"A fool and his money can throw one hell of a party."

Sign at El Arroyo Restaurant

My pointy toed reptilian hide cowboy boots were on my desk. My feet were in them. My stomach was working on digesting breakfast, a cheese omelet, whole wheat toast and what we born again vegetarians call fakin' bacon. My brain was engaged not with the pressing business of getting my fledgling private detective agency off the ground but rather on my honeymoon a couple of months earlier.

My daydream dealt with gunning the *Vespa* motor scooter until it whined and shuddered in pain. I could still feel Patricia's warm sensuous body clinging tightly to my back. Her perfect thighs clamped my sides as we attempted the hill one more time. I was reasonably certain we wouldn't make it since we attempted the cobble-stoned hill four times in as many days. Four times we got off and pushed that damned motor scooter the rest of the way up to *El Jardin*.

San Miguel de Allende, a quaint albeit touristy *colonia* in the Mexican State of Guanajuato, is perched on the side of a mountain a couple hundred kilos north of Mexico City. It's a haven for Americans, Euros, artists and film makers looking for authentic Mex. It's where Lucinda Tanner, a.k.a. Auntie Loo, a client and friend has her art studio. She allowed Patricia and I the use of her studio apartment for our honeymoon.

The timing of our post nuptial festivities could not have been better. Once in every generation in generally warm and sunny Austin, we catch a serious blast of winter sinking all the way down from the Arctic to Austin. During this past February, the month we Central Texans usually think of as pre-spring, we were first deluged non-stop with rains of biblical proportions; creeks, streams, rivers, lakes and stock tanks were overflowing.

Then came the cold snap—a month of rain morphed into a night of sleet; the following morning someone (we always blame it on Troy Kimmel, our local know it all weatherman) left the door to the freezer open. The bridges glazed over, ice heavy tree limbs ripped from their trunks, and came crashing to earth. Then we got a foot of snow. Nothing new in Upstate New York, just an everyday occurance in Fargo, North Dakota, but Austin's a town that only sees snow plows on Christmas vacation in Riodoso, New Mexico: we have never had a sale on tire chains. I guess what I'm saying is we don't know about Snow days 'round here.

The Blue Norther that hit Austin petered out before sinking south below the Tropic of Capricorn, lacking a couple of hundred clicks from reaching San Miguel; Patricia and I caught the whole thing on the TV in the back room at Casa Mex while eating fresh cooked tortilla chips with jalapeno salsa and tossing Negro Modelos. As we watched Troy trying to explain what a snow bank was and reassuring the viewers that our pick up trucks where indeed under all that white stuff; I wondered how Mom was handling chores at the ranch in Blanco—tossing hay to the cattle, slopping the chickens, cracking the ice in the water troughs, things I'd probably be doing if I weren't in San Miguel. Oh, the guilt.

While Central Texas was freezing its collective ass off, in La Colonia de San Miguel we enjoyed cool clear spring mornings and warm balmy afternoons. Evenings were typical of desert locales, as the sun slowly sang in the west, the temperature dropped.

Our wedding took place in August, but Patricia and I agreed to postpone our honeymoon until after I got the agency up and going. First things first. She was thinking we ought to earn the money to pay for the honeymoon (i.e. vacation) rather than start out our new marriage with a load of debt. She was leaning toward a cruise in the Caribbean later in the spring. I thought a pack trip to the mountains of New Mexico or Colorado to be the ticket. My idea was cheaper and something we could do without maxing out the Visa card. She thought my idea sounded more like camping out than the pampered luxury of a Princess Cruise to the Virgin Islands. And as always she was correctamundo.

When Lucinda Tanner, my first and only client, made us an offer we could not refuse—namely, the use of her studio apartment (she was doing an art show in Taos followed by a jaunt to

Paris, and wouldn't be using it for at least a month) – our plans crystallized. Patricia had a bunch of vacation time built up at the magazine where she worked, and since we slid on by the optimum window time-wise for my idea, missing Autumn in the mountains, I figured saving our get-out-of-the-state-of-Texas-before-we-all-go-up-in-flames-time for Summer when we really needed a reprieve from the inevitable 100 degree heat.

However, San Miguel did have mountains, was cheap, was a perfect climate, the apartment was free, it proved to be luxurious, and best of all wasn't anything like work.

"Now you know Babe, if we were riding Too Tall we wouldn't be sweating our balls and various parts of our anatomy off, pushing this damn thing up this damn hill," I gasped for air as I fought both the gravity of the hill and the altitude. I felt obligated to contribute the vast majority of the shove it up the hill effort, since Patricia was pregnant and I was six four, 240 to 250 pounds and she was five two, 105. The temperature was about seventy but sweat poured freely.

"I wonder what those burritos would think if they saw your horse? Probably think he was some sort of equine god." Patricia pushed the motor scooter from the rear as I wrestled the handlebars. A group of Mexicano fathers and sons herding a dozen mini-donkeys (she called them burritos which I suspected was a rare politico incorrecto statement for her) passed us on the way down the hill. All turned for a free peek at Patricia's fine ass as we went by. Someone whistled. I ignored it. See, I can control my temper.

Patricia was showing some tummy. I was showing some tummy as well but figured in my case it was the mucho botes de Cervezas Mexicanas and chiles relleno that were forcing me to keep relocating that metal thingy on the belt buckle to the next notch.

We flat had a ball down there. Up at the butt crack of ten o'clock. Cranking up La Vespa and careening down the first hill as fast as we dare go on the bumpy, uneven cobblestoned calle, my legs flared to the sides for balance, Patricia's legs clamped against my hips, flying out of control as we hit the bottom hard and careened up the second hill at the top of which lies *El Jardin* and our favorite outdoor restaurant.

After a breakfast of eggs, tortillas, home made salsa, fried potatos and onions, with coffee and raw Mexican cream and fresh papaya juice, our routine was to walk or scoot the town, shopping the farmer's markets for fresh-cut calla lilies, fruit and veggies for the evening meal. I insisted Patricia carry the flowers because with her suntanned good looks she was a walking Diego Rivera painting, which left me to muscle the produce. I figured if she looked like Frida without the unibrow, I had to come off as a cowboy version of Andy Warhol on steroids, but I didn't give a shit. I never really cared much if I were wealthy or broke, but I had to admit, the richness of our honeymoon threatened to make a Republican out of me.

After our morning shopping spree, it was up the hill to the studio apartment to make love. Later in the day we would search out gifts for friends and relatives from the mercados. Both Patricia and I were raised to believe in the American tradition of carrying home presents for each and every friend and relative each and every time we left town. What was that all about?

After our afternoon outing we climbed back up the hill to make love, after which it bacame our routine to cab it out to Toboada, (too far to walk, too dangerous traffic-wise to take the scooter) San Miguel's foremost swimming hole, a huge clear blue pool surrounded by massive palm trees and beautifully landscaped lawn. Later, it was back to the studio for more love making or as the locals call it, *siesta*. We took side trips to view the monarch butterflies which homed close by on their migration to Mexico, and church ruins and bull fights (which Patricia walked on) and to *El Institudo de Art*. Artists at work in an educational setting. Lucinda taught classes there. And there was a short bus ride away to the villiage of *Delores,* packed with potters, creating *talavera* plates and colorful Mexican tile.

It was Patricia's and my first and only vacation and even though we had known each other intimately, albeit off and on for years, making love half a dozen times a day seemed like a natural thing to do at the time.

Looking out my second story office window, feet as I mentioned, on my desk, I thought about the woman I adored, black curly hair, petite but stacked bod, and watched the typical Sixth Street A.M. crowd below. An assortment were office types looking for a mocha frappachino or maybe tofu migas; others were revelers still at it from the night before. In Austin it was not so easy telling the difference. But I knew the Street, having a year's worth of experience as a bouncer under my belt.

The Bubbamobile, my Ford F-350 diesel pickup with the oversized dually tires, looking like a beluga whale with a cellulite condition, was parked on the sidewalk directly below my window in front of Kickers Saloon, the bar where I had worked up until not quite a year ago when I became Austin's newest private eye.

Cops did not mess with Bubba since Jimmy Don told them it was there for color, décor for Kickers, something like a two-sided sandwich board advertisement, only bigger. The only downside to my free parking place (which if you have been anywhere near Sixth Street in Austin you know that "free" and "parking" are just not used in the same sentence) were afixing a Kickers metallic sign on each door and daily removing the beer cans that were inevitably tossed in the bed. But there was always the aluminum recycling money to be made.

Jimmy Don owned the whole block which included the bar, a rodeo arena out back and a once empty tiny two room storage facility upstairs which were now the offices of —

B. B. RIVERS INVESTIGATIONS

A skinny set of stairs led up, or down, depending if one were coming or going, to or from, my new office. It was Friday and with all the day dreaming and such, I really hadn't accomplished a damn thing all week. As a newly married man, things had changed. Patricia filled my once so *what shall I do today, will it be a movie, or perhaps a sporting event?* weekends with *Billy, would you please take out the trash and while you're at it take the old newspapers and empty Shiner bottles to the recycling center, and on the way back swing by Whole Foods Market and get us some organic lettuce and tomatos and...*

Even though the office was not bringing in greenbacks it did offer respite from honey-do-induced activity. We had been scouring the papers for a house, which for me was right up there on the boring meter with shopping for a new spring outfit. A new house also meant the chores would really become all the more meaningful. We'd be going to the *Natural Gardener* for trees to plant and *Home Depot* for decks to build. I knew for instance that whatever roof the structure came with, would not cut it, and thus *had* to go. If there were a St. Augustine lawn, we would need to install buffalo or zoysia. Patricia loved my friend

Max's restored mansion. Fortunately, we could not afford even a fixer-upper (i.e. – lots and lots of chores) in his neighborhood.

"I got us some donuts." Donna had come in unnoticed by the ace private detective, and if it had not been for the secure lid Starbucks puts on their lattes, I'd be looking for a roll of paper towels. Donna was my girl Friday. She was not the buxom blond I had envisioned fetching me donuts, not the stunning creature one associates with the truly hip private detective agency. Oh, she was buxom all right. Very much so. And yes, she was blond although with dark roots. Fact was she weighed in at about 275.

Donna had been the Investigations Department secretary when I worked a short but happily lucrative engagement at Bergstrom Investigations as a private investigator. When the powers-that-be at Bergstrom shut down the investigations department I picked her up. Not in the literal sense. I can jump from a horse and wrestle a steer to the ground in ten seconds but no way was I going to lift that girl off the ground; especially not since the energy zap of my honeymoon siesta. After two months of wedded bliss, I was just now sitting up and eating solid food, for Christ's sake.

Donna and I were getting along quite well. There wasn't a lot of work to interfere with our conversations. I wasn't temped to flirt with the lass so there wasn't the extraneous bullshit that ruins so many a workplace relationship. She made a good donut run, knew the investigations biz inside and out, and I was not the dude to try and change her.

Our ex-boss, Richard A. Hollers at Bergstrom tipped the scales at four hundred donut induced pounds. I tried to imagine what it might be like to have an additional 150 to 200 pounds on my six four frame. Not good.

She saw my concern. "Low cal?" She extracted a donut and plopped the bag on my desk. I selected a low calorie chocolate fudge studded with M&Ms.

After cracking the five year old *Hippie Hollow* murder case, I collected my pay from Bergstrom to which they added a decent bonus. The assignment involved finding out who murdered two teenagers at *Hippie Hollow,* a park on the East Shore of Lake Travis outside Austin, and bringing the killer James Spivey, a.k.a. El Jaguar, to justice (two 9 mm bullets side by side in the forehead spelled justice NRA style). On that same job, I brought the killer of the rap singer Iced Chai to justice (same dead killer, same two slugs in the forehead). I wondered how much that worked out per slug

On top of Bergstrom's money I got a wallet choking reward from the wealthy, socialite Lucinda Tanner who had hired Bergstrom and therefore had hired me. It was Lucinda's studio apartment Patricia and I had inhabited on our honeymoon in Mexico.

Additionally, the Iced Chai Foundation of New Orleans had offered a reward for information leading to the arrest of the person or persons who had hired the assassin and/or who had murdered their fearless leader, the rap star, Iced Chai. Since I had discovered the hirer, one Reverend Arvin Tanner, and had discovered and dispatched to hell, the hired gun, the same James Spivey-El Jaguar character, the Foundation had cut me a check for an amount considered obscene by everyone save pro athletes and movie stars.

The aforementioned check was supposedly made out, signed and was waiting for me to retrieve. Angel Chai, Iced Chai's daughter, insisted I come to New Orleans to pick it up in person.

I know, one should not expect to make as much as I had from one measly case, but it did seem like a decent private investigator, who happened to be in the right place at the right time with a loaded firearm could do well in Austin. Completing the collection part of the job required merely a quick hop, an hour and change, over to New Orleans. So, that's no big deal. I've never much cared for *the city that care forgot,* and figured I'd fly in, pick up the check and fly back out the same day. And if it was no big deal, why ain't I done it already?

Angel Chai.

ABOUT THE AUTHOR

Denniger Bolton lives in the Texas Hill Country west of Austin, Texas. He and his family operate an organic farm and goat ranch called Pure Luck Farm & Dairy. They produce award winning goat cheeses. Says Denniger, "I'm a country boy and success to me is doing what you want to be doing, with whomever you want to be doing it with, where you want to do it." He has been writing all his life but Hippie Hollow is his first published novel.

4 = Ⓐ LAS MANITAS CAFE (CONGRESS)
5 Ⓒ CHUY'S
    FONDA RESTAURANT
1 ———— OAK MEADOW
6 Ⓑ OZONA (MEXICAN MADRE'S)
       w/ TOFU

2 = EL ARROYO (THE DITCH)
3 BALMORHEA

Printed in the United States
113096LV00002B/118-144/P